THE
W*of*RLD
TOMORROW

THE
WORLD of RLD
TOMORROW

BRENDAN MATHEWS

L **B**

Little, Brown and Company
New York   Boston   London

Little, Brown and Company
Hachette Book Group
1290 Avenue of the Americas, New York, NY 10104
littlebrown.com

First Edition: September 2017

Little, Brown and Company is a division of Hachette Book Group, Inc. The Little, Brown name and logo are trademarks of Hachette Book Group, Inc.

The publisher is not responsible for websites (or their content) that are not owned by the publisher.

The Hachette Speakers Bureau provides a wide range of authors for speaking events. To find out more, go to hachettespeakersbureau.com or call (866) 376-6591.

ISBN 978-0-316-38219-9
LCCN 2017932052

10 9 8 7 6 5 4 3 2 1

LSC-C

Printed in the United States of America

To Margaret

THE WEEK BEFORE

AT SEA

FRANCIS NEVER EXPECTED THE silverware would be his undoing. Seated in the first-class dining room of the MV *Britannic,* halfway between the Old World and the New, he surveyed a landscape of crystal stemware and bone china, of crisp linen and centerpieces ripe with flowers he had never seen, in colors he had never dreamed. High above, the coffered ceiling glowed, its milk-glass panels outlined in brass. A frieze marched around the upper reaches of the room — an angular, art deco skirmish of horses, stags, and dogs. Every wall, even the air itself, was awash in hues of honey and amber, and at every table sat men and women gilded in good fortune and turned out in tuxedos, or gowns, or regimental dress. But what did all of this abundance matter when his own plate was blockaded by a medieval armory in miniature? He counted five forks, four spoons, and at least as many knives. He hadn't a clue where to begin.

Francis had hoped to take his lead from one of his tablemates: on one side, the Binghams, a mother and daughter returning to New York from their self-styled Grand Tour, and on the other, the Walters, a mismatched pair of marrieds from Philadelphia, accompanied by the wife's laconic, chain-smoking brother. Yet when the bowls of chilled broth—consommé, the menu called it—were placed in front of them, they all seemed to wait for Francis. Was that how it worked? The nobility dined first, and only then did the robber barons feast?

Easy enough. All he had to do was select the right spoon, and thereby prove his merit to the Americans, who were under the impression that he was a Scotsman, and a wealthy one at that, and perhaps even one with a castle overlooking a Highland loch. Before he was forced to choose, however, Mrs. Bingham resumed the conversation about the journeys that had led each of them to the *Britannic*.

"I'm curious to know, Sir Angus," she said, for Angus was the name Francis had given, though the *Sir* was entirely her own addition. "How did you find Ireland?"

"Oh, it was quite simple, really," he said. "I took the ferry from Liverpool. The boat knew just where to go."

Mrs. Bingham giggled, almost girlishly. Francis might have guessed that she was in her thirties, if not for her daughter, who looked to be about twenty. The missus insisted that he call her Delphine, and as for the miss, she was called Anisette. When Francis inquired about the Frenchness of their names, Mrs. Bing—strike that, Delphine—explained that she had been born and raised in Montreal, where the citizens spoke a purer form of the language than the pidgin bandied about in your average Paris café. As she told it, Quebec had acted as a safe haven where the French language endured without contamination by Continental dialects and the occasional trespass of Prussian troops. And hadn't the possible return of Prussians or Germans or whatever they were calling themselves these days been one motivation for their trip? It was only last year that Germany had anschlussed Austria, then chased it with a shot of the Sudetenland! Spurred by the fear that there would be no fall collections that year, they had ended four months of touring in a frenzy of Chanel and Schiaparelli.

"And if it all settles down?" Francis-as-Angus said.

"Can it ever be a mistake to visit Paris?" Mrs. B's eyes twinkled, and he saw how easily Mr. Bingham, whoever he was, must have fallen.

During Mrs. Bingham's recitation on family, fashion, and all things *français,* the Philadelphia trio had begun with their broth, and Francis tried to take note of which spoon they had chosen. He thought he was being clever, but as he caught the eye of the silk-sheathed Marion Walter, she stared back at him with feline hunger. His blood surged — a jolt from groin to gullet — and he looked away, only to meet a similar gaze from her brother, Alex, a small man neatly encased in a tuxedo. Horace Walter, much older and rounder than the others, was already clouded by his first two cocktails; he had eyes only for the next course. The Walters were returning from a trip through Italy and Germany, where they had taken part in a brisk tourist trade catering to Americans eager to see firsthand the proper way to run a modern nation. They had rendezvoused in Le Havre with Alex, whose itinerary had taken him through the seaside resorts of the Mediterranean. Apparently, there was a Mrs. Alex still on the Continent — something about friends in Biarritz who simply could not part with her until after some festival or other. He seemed unfazed by her whereabouts — his only mention of her was accompanied by a jet of cigarette smoke — but the Binghams tsk-tsked and fretted about how lonely he must be without her.

Conversation turned to Sir Angus, his reasons for traveling to New York, and oh-by-the-way, was he traveling alone? Francis explained that he was escorting his younger brother to New York for medical attention. That much was true, though he transformed Michael into Malcolm to keep his alias intact. Young Malcolm had been grievously injured while foxhunting, he told them, and there wasn't a doctor in Britain or Ireland who could help him. "His case has baffled the finest medical minds in London, but I have high hopes for what the American doctors can tell us," he said, taking a swipe at the old empire while goosing the national pride of his companions. He quickly saw that his story had elicited another reaction: Anisette, who had lips like a bow on a box of sweets, practically cooed in admiration. This Sir Angus was both landed aristocrat and benevolent protector — a Scottish Mr. Darcy, minus the unpleasantness of the first thirty-odd chapters.

"It's admirable," she said, "what you're willing to do for your brother."

"The question, Miss Bingham, is what wouldn't I be willing to do for my brother?"

Francis was growing more confident with the quality of his counterfeit Scotsmanship. As the entrées were presented, he asked the Binghams what news they had from home. "I must confess that I devote little time to ex-colonial affairs," he said, but the truth was that life in Dublin had offered only a moviegoer's knowledge of New York: newsreels, *The Thin Man*, *Forty-Second Street*, *A Night at the Opera*. He should have known more about the city. His older brother, Martin, had emigrated years before, but Francis knew little of his life; he was a musician, married, had a child or two, and lived in a place unmusically called the Bronx. Over the years, communication between the brothers had gone from strained to nonexistent. Martin knew nothing of Francis's escape, Michael's condition, or their father's recent death. Of course Francis would seek him out, but first he had to decide what to tell him. Martin was sure to have questions that Francis wasn't ready to answer.

But while Martin could be difficult, the Americans were easy. He had assumed that they would be a uniformly anti-royalist lot; what about their man George Washington, and Thomas Jefferson with his "all men are created equal" talk? Surely the Americans would have been bred with a distaste for crowned heads and any hint of duke- or earlishness. But no. Thanks to Francis's accent and the rumor of a peerage, the Americans aboard the *Britannic*—the women, especially— were drawn to him like crows to corn. And Francis, for his part, was playing the peacock. The suits he had purchased in Cork were not backbench grays and clubbish blues. He had paired glen plaids with boldly tartaned waistcoats; if he was in for a Glasgow penny, he was in for an Edinburgh pound. It should not have surprised him, once he saw the stir he caused, how easy it was for word to spread. He'd had one brief chat on the top deck with a woman whose hat he had rescued from the rapacious winds of the North Atlantic, and by the late dinner seating Angus MacFarquhar was the most eligible bachelor on the *Britannic*.

While the Binghams courted the favor of Sir Angus, Horace Walter engaged in vociferous, fact-free talk about Roosevelt and his latest plans for the ruination of the country. His greatest fear was the final takeover of America by communists, socialists, freeloaders, court-packers, and others bent on stripping the best members of society of all they owned and passing it willy-nilly to the drunks and the wastrels who still lined up for free soup and stale bread. Before he resumed drowning himself in gin and creamed herring, he opined that the Depression hadn't been all bad—that it had, in fact, helped to thin the ranks of a certain class of bounders who had gate-crashed high society in the '20s.

"A necessary winnowing of the wheat from the chaff," he said. As he spoke, his hand went, as if by its own volition, to the diamond-topped stickpin in his lapel. He touched it the way Francis had been taught to strike his breast when the priest intoned the Agnus Dei.

The others nodded, either in agreement or out of a desire to move on to another topic. Francis offered a "Quite, quite," though with little gusto, and fixed his gaze on the man's pouched sow eyes, then on the diamond, and finally on his wife.

"And what of the royal visit?" The question came from Alex. He and his sister had the same narrow build, the same shell of brillian-tined black hair. One of the only deviations between brother and sister was the pencil-line mustache that traced the ridge of his upper lip. Alex eyed him quizzically as wisps of smoke drifted from his cupped hand. "Will you be taking part in the festivities?"

Royal visit? Alex had mentioned it in such an offhand way that it must be common knowledge, but which royals? And visiting where? This was exactly why Francis had meant to stay out of society during the voyage—to avoid just this sort of stumble. He knew that as quickly as his notoriety had spread, so too could his unmasking. He dabbed at his mouth with his napkin, buying time. "My first responsibility must be to my brother," he finally said. "Any festivities will have to wait until after I have consulted with his doctors."

Alex arched an eyebrow: unconvinced or unimpressed. Francis folded his hands. He meant for the gesture to be nonchalant, but it looked like he was fidgeting.

"I don't see what all of the fuss is about." Marion's words came slowly, languor mixed with white burgundy. "The crowned heads of England, certainly that's exciting. But at the World's Fair? Wild horses couldn't drag me there."

"Yes, my lovely," her husband said, "but what about a wild horseman?"

"Do pipe down," she said. "No one—"

"Oh, I think the World's Fair sounds lovely!" Anisette positively beamed. "The crowds may be horrid, I know. But the pavilions look so bright and so full of light and so—oh, what's the word?"

"I think you struck the nail on the head when you said horrid," Marion said. "First thought, best thought—right, dear?"

Anisette persisted: "Modern. Everything looks new, but not just newly built. Newly imagined. As if the whole world has been remade, but better than before."

"Now, that does sound lovely," Francis said. He was happy to steer conversation away from this royal visit, and to find another topic on which Francis and Francis-as-Angus could agree: a better world—a world of fresh starts—sounded lovely indeed.

"I don't know that *lovely* is the word for it," Alex said. "The aesthetics have an aroma of the fascist about them. All those hard angles and empty-eyed statues. A bit too orderly by half, for my tastes."

"You've got it all wrong," Horace said. "A more fascist aesthetic is just what the World's Fair, and in fact the whole country, needs. The

Italians, if you can believe it, they've got it figured out. And of course the Germans. Exemplary. Government and business working together, hand in fist——"

"Oh, Horace, not this again," Marion said.

From the next table came a swell of oohs and aahs: dessert, a ziggurat of glazed fruit, had been set alight. Francis was nervously aware that it had been almost two hours since he'd left his brother, and seeing his chance, he rose from his seat, begging leave of the ladies of the table. "My brother," he offered by way of an excuse. "He needs minding, and I fear I have dallied too long in your charming company." He gave a curt nod, a winsome smile, and then he was striding out of the dining room. Only Horace failed to mark the moment that he disappeared from sight.

No one at the table knew that ten days earlier, Francis Xavier Dempsey had been an inmate in Mountjoy Prison, Dublin, where meals were strictly a one-spoon affair. Convicted of trafficking in books banned under the Censorship of Publications Act as well as in other luxuries proscribed by the tariff-hungry, priest-fearing politicians of the fledgling Republic of Ireland, he had been halfway through a three-year sentence. At the same time, his brother Michael, not yet eighteen, had been an inmate of a different sort, locked up in the seminary and preparing for life as a missionary in some steamy, godforsaken corner of the globe. And their father? Ten days ago he was still alive, no doubt muddling through another lesson instructing the sons and daughters of farmers on the proper conjugation of the Latin verb *amare*.

Now their father was in the ground and his death had made possible a new life for his sons. One moment, Francis and Michael were kneeling in prayer at his funeral, each expecting to return to his own place of confinement. The next, a map was pressed into their hands, they fled in a stolen car, a house was blown to bits, three men lay dead, money rained from the sky, and Michael was broken but still breathing. Somehow, through the workings of God or luck or the unrecognized genius of Francis himself, he rose from that cock-up of death and wreckage and seized the day. Wouldn't his father have told him to do exactly that? *Carpe diem*. Well, he had *carpe*'d the *diem* and squeezed it for all it was worth.

Pursued by the massed forces of the church and the state—not to mention the Irish Republican Army, whose safe house–cum–bomb factory Francis had played *some* role in demolishing—he devised a way to spirit Michael and himself out of Ireland. They would travel first class, dress first class, and act as first class as Francis could manage. It sounded mad, but the First-Class Plan, as he christened it, landed the Dempsey brothers in a stateroom on the *Britannic,* with the crew and passengers convinced they were a pair of young Scottish lords. Francis hoped that his peerish pretensions would keep lower-born passengers at bay, and that his affected Scottishness would scramble the senses of better-born Englishmen. He had no plans to socialize with the other passengers, and, before tonight, had relied on room service for his meals. He was, after all, a fugitive, and after ten days on the run, he needed to rest.

As for Michael, he needed more than rest; he needed restoration. The blast had left him badly damaged. He came in and out of consciousness, and when awake, he was prone to fits. Two days earlier, as they prepared to board the ship at Cobh, the sun had punched through the clouds for the first time in weeks. Francis took a moment to admire the way the harbor came alive under the sun's influence, gray flannel transformed into a field of diamonds. He had an arm around Michael, supporting his unsteady steps, and as Michael lifted his face and the warmth of the sun touched him, he seemed to smile. But then his lids fluttered open and it was as if someone had stabbed an ember in his eye. His hands went to his face, his legs buckled, and he emitted a gurgling cry. When he tumbled, two of the pursers double-timed it over to the brothers and between them lifted Michael off the quay and carried him up the gangplank. That had been the first test of the FC Plan, and the quick attention of the pursers, each of whom Francis rewarded with a pound note, was proof positive that the plan was working.

Now the FC Plan had passed another test. He had navigated a first-class dinner, steered conversation away from that pesky royal visit, and perhaps impressed an American or two with his—dare he say?—nobility. He had even chosen the proper spoon, a sure sign of good things to come.

MICHAEL — YES, THAT was his name. He knew that now, though he had been grasping at it for what seemed like weeks, so long that he had begun to wonder if he even had a name, or if his mind had become so porous that names could find no purchase. But now he knew. He was Michael. He was Michael and he was in a bed with a red and gold cover, in a small room with round windows on one wall. Next to the bed was a table with a glass of water and a lamp that cast a pale glow, beyond which lay another bed just like his. On the other side of his bed was a leather chair and in the chair sat an old man with a sharp, beakish nose and a spray of white hair above his lean face. The man wore spectacles—round, black, and heavy—and a creamy white suit and waistcoat. A black cravat, like some leafy night-blooming flower, ran riot from his shirt collar. Michael nodded to the old man and the old man nodded in reply. He'd never spoken to the old man but he knew the man had been there—in that chair, in this room—for...for...for as long as Michael could remember. Was that a day? A week? More? It could not be his whole life because out on the fringes of his memory, in that spot where his own name had hovered just out of reach, there were other, brighter moments, and he could only hope that they would return to him like the wreckage of a ship pushed, ebb after ebb, to the shore.

"I'm Michael," he said to the man, who raised his shaggy eyebrows as if appraising this bit of information. The man nodded again and crossed one knee over the other, letting his left foot bob above the carpet. He did not seem to be in any hurry to answer. He looked like a man who had resigned himself to waiting for a train that was still many hours from the station. Michael shrugged and reached for the glass of water on the nightstand, but his grip was feeble, and he watched as the glass hit the table, splashed water across the polished wood, and toppled to the floor. All of this transpired without a sound. Michael sat back against his pillow and clapped his hands: all was silence. He shouted, *Halloooooooooo*, felt the strain in his throat, but where was the sound?

"Why can't I hear—" he began to say to the old man, and startled at the sound of his voice. He lurched forward. "Why can I only hear myself when I'm talking to you?"

The old man looked at Michael over the rims of his spectacles as if he were noticing him—really taking note of him—for the first time. Then he tilted his chin up and peered at Michael through the lower half of his lenses. During his inspection of Michael he became distracted by something on his trousers, and with great care he plucked a tuft of dust from his knee and flicked it to the floor. Slowly his tongue wet the corners of his lips. All of this seemed preliminary to speaking, but he said nothing. Was this man a doctor? Michael wondered. Was that the reason for his excessively white wardrobe? He considered the possibilities: hospital, infirmary, sanatorium, insane asylum.

The man's chin dipped and Michael leaned closer, expecting some explanation—*My boy, you've been in a dreadful accident but all will be well.* When the man's mouth opened, however, a torrent of sound— the Noise!—came pouring out of him. If Michael had been pinned at the bottom of a waterfall, the sound could not have been any louder; it was the fury of sea waves assaulting the cliff face. He clapped his hands over his ears but it made no difference. The circular windows roared like the mouths of cannons. Michael writhed on the bed and drew himself into a ball. The Noise continued to pulverize him. Not until the old man shut his mouth did the sound wane, though it did not cease entirely, but merely seemed more distant, as if he were in a cottage above the sea rather than chained to the rocks below.

Not a doctor at all, Michael thought. A torturer, that's what he was. But he also had to admit a third possibility, that the old man was an angel of the avenging variety. That would explain the white clothes, the voice like a thousand brass cymbals. He had not seen it immediately because he had always thought of angels in flowing robes with brilliant halos and massive wings of white. Still, that cravat troubled him: it was black, as were those hard owlish spectacles. Could the man be a devil? Or a pooka, of the sort he'd heard in the stories told by the woman who did their washing back in Ballyrath?

Ballyrath. The word jarred something loose: that was his home. The woman—Mrs. Greavey, that was her name. The washing on the line, like white pennants strung between two posts. The cottage with its white walls and thatched roof, and the green hills in all directions. This and more came rushing back at him. Ballyrath. He had been a boy there, and he had left home for the seminary with its gray stone and gaudy stained glass, its black cassocks and narrow cots. The long tables, the gloopy eggs and gristly rashers of the morning meal. He could smell the sugared fumes rising from the censer during the consecration, could feel the pages of his Augustine and Aquinas; each leaf crackled when turned, as if the books had been waterlogged and poorly dried. All of this had bloomed suddenly in his head, but none of it explained how he had arrived here, or where here was.

He had his name, he had these moments in time, but there was an unfathomable gap between there and here. He thought about finding a mirror, hoping his appearance could offer some clue, but he couldn't make his body do its part. He wasn't paralyzed—he had figured out that much. But he felt so heavy, so tired, as if the effort of remember-ing had sapped him. He took a deep breath and let his head loll on the pillow. The old man—not a doctor, possibly an angel, likely a devil—remained in his chair. If this was a visitation by some divine or demonic presence, then Michael had to ask: What had he done to deserve this pain? He felt sleep coming on again, the exhaustion of his limbs overtaking him, and in that moment he stumbled on one last question: Am I dead?

FRANCIS EASED THE door open, just wide enough to slip through the gap. He didn't want to risk waking Michael if the mercy of sleep had been granted to him. And if Michael was awake, or in that half-aware state that had gripped him since the accident, then the light from the corridor would only increase his punishment. Sound didn't bother him—he seemed deaf as a post, to be honest—but Francis had seen the way sunlight or a bright room could send him into spasms. In the quiet of the cabin, Francis removed his tuxedo jacket and black trou-sers and hung them in the closet, next to the three suits he had bought for the trip. In the days before the *Britannic* set sail, he had stashed Michael in an upmarket quarter of Cork where he thought it least likely anyone would look for them. He had heard praises heaped on a local forger while he was in Mountjoy, and while he waited for his false papers from the man, he found a tailor who could provide him with clothes befitting his new station. He had paid a small fortune for the passports and a smaller but still substantial sum for his new ward-robe, but that investment was already paying dividends. More than looking the part, he *was* the part. For Michael, he had pulled two changes of clothes from the racks of a men's shop, guessing at the sizes. He would tell anyone who asked that his brother had lost so much weight that nothing fit him right. Michael had always been a stripling, but honestly, he was a skeleton now.

Just as Francis turned out the bedside lamp, there was a soft rapping at the door, barely audible but insistent enough to catch his attention. His heart skipped and he cast about for something, anything, he could wield in his defense—but no; if it was the visit he was dreading, it would not come with a genteel knock. That would be a foot-against-the-door sort of visit. He rose and pulled on his dressing gown, another new purchase, and cautiously turned the knob.

Anisette stood in the corridor, her fist poised for one more dainty knock. At the sight of Francis, she beamed; she had a bright, chipper, *Oh, there you are!* way about her.

"Sir Angus," she said, her expression shifting from smitten to solemn. "You must forgive me—well, forgive all of us. Here we were at the table, gabbing away about nonsense, while you carry this terrible burden. Not that your brother is a burden—far from it, I am sure—but you must think us the most insensitive, callous, heartless—"

"Really," Francis said, "it's—"

"Deplorable," she said, with a note of finality. "That's the word for it." Anisette lowered her voice to a whisper. "If I may ask, is everything...all right?"

"Yes, quite," he said. Since becoming Angus, he had come to rely on that word. "Or as well as can be expected, under the circumstances."

"Our sympathies are with you. We—well, I—I wanted you to know that."

This business of dining with heiresses was new to him. Should he be flattered by the attention or was this part of the routine? An after-dinner visit to a young man's bedroom seemed like a bold stroke, but perhaps in the world of the bejeweled and be-moneyed these late-night tête-à-têtes were as commonplace as Pimm's Cups and tea sandwiches. Anisette stood before him as if at a garden party; it was almost midnight and she looked as dewy as the morning. If she lowered her voice, it seemed not out of deference to the hour and the possibly scandalous nature of her intent, but rather out of a well-bred wish to respect Sir Angus's privacy regarding matters medical. The young Miss Bingham exuded calm and good grace, blithely unaware of—or, he had to consider, completely uninterested in—the disordered state of his robe and pajamas.

"Thank you for your concern," he said. "You're very kind."

She pressed one hand over her heart and canted her head to the side. Her lips puckered into something between a kiss and a pout. Tears were a distinct possibility. "No," she said. "*You* are very kind."

Before Francis could continue the volley of mutual admiration, her mood shifted: in a flash she was again all smiles and dry eyes, a vision of milk and apples. Her fingers plucked the sides of her gown and she bobbed, just slightly. Was that a curtsy?

"Well," she said. "Good night, then."

Francis closed the door and returned to bed. *"Equo ne credite, Teucri!"* he said aloud, into the darkness. *"Timeo Danaos et dona ferentes."* The words felt clumsy in his mouth. He hadn't used his Latin in ages. If Michael were awake—if he weren't stone-deaf, Francis reminded himself—he would have no trouble with that one. Aeneid. *Book Two. Give me something harder than that,* he would say. *I'm not a* complete *eejit, you know.* It was a game they had grown up playing, the only game their father had ever played with them. He would toss out lines—Homer and Virgil were a regular part of the rotation—and the boys would compete to be the first to identify the source and render an on-the-spot translation. That they considered it a game, rather than an endless final examination, said a lot about life in the cottage in Ballyrath. A schoolmaster father, his three sons, and no feckin' idea how to talk to one another like normal folk.

And now: another knock at the door, louder than the first. Had the young Miss Bingham screwed up her courage and returned for another round of compliments? Yes, he was very kind, but he was also exhausted and desperate for a night's sleep. Francis hauled himself out of bed and readied his smile, his *Quite, quite.* Only it wasn't Anisette. He opened the door to Marion Walter leaning against the jamb. She did not speak, but he was sure that he could hear the purr in her throat. She looked at him in a vague and unfocused way, then over his shoulder at the dark room behind him, and then she was inside and the door was shut. She leaned against the wall and drew him toward her, plucking loose the drawstring on his pajamas. She tasted of gin and tobacco, and the scent of her neck was sharp: dried flowers wrapped in leather. He had a fleeting thought of nights on the cheap along the Grand Canal in Dublin, but this was no dark alley. This was first class. She pulled him closer, and as he bunched the watery silk of her gown around her hips, she bit him hard on the shoulder. The rest was sudden, frenzied, and audible from the corridor.

ANISETTE SNUGGED THE duvet under her chin. What would Maman say if she knew? To go to his room? To knock on his door? To have him answer half dressed—which meant half undressed? After everything that had happened in New York, Maman would kill her, plain and simple. But what a gentleman he had been! And hadn't Maman been telling her for months that the purpose of the trip was to meet a better class of people? The best thing to do, Maman had said, was to let the dust settle and then return in triumph.

And hadn't tonight been a triumph? She had worried that the Walters—such awful people—might ruin everything with their bickering but they hadn't been anything more than a distraction: the drunken fat man stuffed full of roast beef and loud opinions and his fairy-tale witch of a wife. Mrs. Walter was the wicked queen in *Snow White*—the same pale skin, black hair, and nasty laugh—with just a dash of Anisette's older sister, Félicité, thrown into the mix. That woman had tried to draw Angus into her web all night—yes, she was a spider, too; that's just what she was—but he was too good for her, too quick on his feet, and maybe (fingers crossed!) a little too interested in Anisette to get tangled up in that woman's web.

But now New York was waiting for them and it was the same old New York they had left. Except that they had made the acquaintance of Angus MacFarquhar, and he was the most charming man Anisette had ever met. If that witchy Mrs. Walter was the evil queen, then surely Angus was the prince and Anisette herself was Snow White (she could hear Father's voice: *Foolish girl!*). Maman had already promised to invite Sir Angus to dinner and who knew where it would go from there? She did hope that Félicité would be in Newport or Greenwich or anywhere that wasn't New York, and while she was making wishes she added another that Father would be on his best behavior.

Father on his best behavior—that was the silliest thought she'd had all night. Hadn't Father made a joke of their entire holiday? The storm before the *Sturm*. He'd called them a two-woman economic-aid package for the jewelers and dressmakers of Europe and said it would be their last chance to use their French—that soon the whole continent would be speaking German. Anisette hadn't found this funny in New York and now, months later, she considered it cruel. Despite some sunny days, the mood in Europe was mostly one of gloom and doom. It was already infecting her fledgling memories of their travels. She wanted golden recollections of the Piazza San Marco and the Uffizi and the Louvre. In the months and years to come, she wanted to take solace in Botticelli's *Venus,* the sunrise over Santa Maria della Salute, the verdant angles of Versailles, and the view from the top of the Eiffel Tower. It was her dream vision of Europe, shadow boxes built from books and paintings and her hothouse imagination before she'd even left New York. All she'd needed was the actual stuff of experience to fill out the spaces she had already cleared for each perfect, crystalline moment of her Grand Tour.

The reality of Europe wrecked it for her. Yes, she saw Rome and Venice and Florence and Paris and plenty more and they were beautiful—so much like she had imagined them. But the delicate case she had made for each porcelain memory had been smashed to bits by sights too big and ungainly to fit neatly into any frame. In Munich, soldiers walked the train platforms with their machine guns and their dogs, eager to bark and to bite. Vienna was buffed to a gleaming carapace of red and black, like painted lips over savage teeth. And all of France seemed to be holding its breath, waiting for the punch to land. Just on the other side of the French border, gangs of workers were digging in the fields. When she asked a man on the train what they were planting, he gave a sad, tired laugh and said, "Cannons."

Lying in the dark, with the ocean moving beneath her, she thought of all the lovely people she had met and she wondered when the net would fall upon them. They would all be caught up in whatever came next. But here at least was Angus, and for a little while he would be in New York, not in Europe, and he would be safe.

THE FARM

CRONIN HAD LEFT ALICE in the kitchen, on her hands and knees giving the floor a good scrubbing. The mess was his fault, but it couldn't be helped. The people here called the time between winter and spring *mud season,* but this year the mud just wouldn't end. The snow had been late in melting, then came a month of rain, and then out of nowhere it was as hot as the middle of July, and here it was barely the first of June. Alice insisted on a clean house, and she wouldn't take any lip about clean enough. The plates were kept to a high polish, and the pans scoured with steel wool until they shone like they were newly bought from the store. Alice was house-proud, and Cronin might tease her about it but he wouldn't think of saying a word against her. She had saved his life. Simple as that. The house, the farm, the boy, and now the baby—all of it he owed to her. Without her he would be a broken-down man, a stranger in this land piling one day on top of another with no hope of it ever adding up.

Cronin was a man who still woke, stricken, in the middle of the night, wrestling ghosts he had thought he could outrun by putting an ocean between them and himself. The old stories said that fairy folk couldn't cross water, and he was a fool for thinking that ghosts were bound by the same rules. Now he knew better. Your ghosts were always with you. They rode you like a jockey rides his mount, and if you ever got half a mind to throw them, that's when they dug in their heels and went to the whip.

He should have known when Alice came to the barn that he was seeing the whip hand of the ghosts being raised. He had gotten too comfortable. He had begun to feel—what? Contentment, was it? Happiness, even? He knew that was asking too much—not after all he'd done in the years before Alice—but sometimes he wanted to believe that he deserved a little peace of mind. That he might even have earned it. There he was in the barn looking at the new calf, born just last month to one of the Holsteins. He had the boy with him, like his own little calf. Henry was five and wanted to know everything and God help the lad but he thought Cronin had all the answers. *Tom, how does the calf know where to find the milk? Tom, can I ride the calf like a pony? Tom, who's the calf's daddy?* The boy had first known him as Tom and that had stuck, but a part of Cronin hoped that once the baby started talking—once she started calling him Daddy—maybe Henry would pick up the habit, too.

At the sight of Alice in her heavy boots scuffing through the hay that lay loose on the concrete floor, the boy brightened and said, "Mommy, come and see the calf!"

Cronin gave Alice a look because it was hours until lunch and hadn't she just told him to stay out of the house and keep the boy with him—this for tracking in mud not an hour before?

She held up her hand, half a wave, and arched an eyebrow. "There's a man here to see you." She was trying to be calm for the boy's sake but Cronin could tell she was unsettled.

"Who is he?" Cronin said.

"I don't know."

"What's he want?"

"He won't say. Says he needs to speak with Tommy Cronin."

A ghost name. No one had called him Tommy in years, not in his waking life.

Alice told him the man was dressed like a banker or a mayor. It wasn't often that they had visitors to the farm, and Alice was a champion for sending mischief-makers packing. For her to haul on her boots and hurry down—right in the middle of scrubbing the kitchen floor, a task she attacked with the fury of a holy martyr—meant that she was spooked. Cronin was going to make a joke about winning the lottery or inheriting a castle from a rich uncle back in Ireland, but he saw in her eyes that she was deadly serious. He wiped his hands on his trousers and said, "Let's go see what he wants." He nodded in the direction of the boy. Henry was Cronin's shadow but the shadow needed to stay put.

While Alice asked Henry to show her the calf, Cronin left the barn, turning over in his head who it might be that had come to see him.

THE MAN IN the driveway stood with his back to the barn. With one hand he shaded his eyes, as if surveying the wooded hills that ringed the property. Mountains, some people called them, but they were too beaten down to be mountains. The man wore a dark suit and a large gray hat with a black band, and he was old: his hair was white, and he stooped over a cane. A little ways up the driveway a car idled, sleek and black. Cronin's feet crunched the gravel and before the old man turned Cronin knew it was Gavigan.

"What are you doing here?" Cronin had to keep himself from shouting. "How did you—"

"I came to see you about a job, Tommy. Everyone's looking for a little extra work these days, aren't they?"

Cronin could only glare at the man.

"I need you to find someone for me."

"Get one of your boys to do it."

"Come on, Tommy. There's none better than you. And he's a danger. Already killed three of our own outside Cork. Blew them to pieces and stole a pile of money—money that was meant to support the cause."

"Don't talk to me about *the cause*." The words were acid in his mouth.

"Don't you want to know his name?"

"What difference does—"

"Francis Dempsey."

Cronin flinched.

"I thought that might get your attention."

"It can't be the same—"

"It is and it isn't. It's his son. And if he's anything like his father...well, you can see why I need my best man on it."

"I'm not your man."

"Think of it as unfinished business, Tommy."

"I'm done with all of that."

"Well now, I'm sure there's plenty who don't see it that way—Francis Dempsey among them. And plenty more who'd pay dearly to find out where Tommy Cronin lives." With the tip of his cane, Gavigan worked a large white stone loose from the driveway. "Wouldn't they be surprised to find that he has such a nice, happy family by his side."

Cronin stared hard at the smaller man.

"I've protected you all these years. I've known where you are and I haven't told a soul."

Cronin's hands were gathered into fists. Had Alice and the boy stayed in the barn? Could they see him with this man? And the baby, was she still asleep in the house?

Gavigan let out a low, light chuckle. "Don't get any ideas. You could take me, sure, but Jamie behind the wheel is a deadeye shot, and even if he missed you...well, he'd be sure to hit something around here." He reached into his breast pocket and produced an envelope. "For expenses. I even put in a little something extra—think of it as a gift for the missus."

Cronin held his ground. He looked at the envelope. At Gavigan's wet rheumy eyes, his palsied sneer. At the man in the car—Jamie, was it?—sizing him up from a distance.

"Of course, if you'd prefer to think of it as volunteer work..."

Cronin snatched the envelope from his hand, crushed it in his fist. "You're the devil," he said.

"You didn't always think so, Tommy." Gavigan reached into his trouser pocket and withdrew a gold watch. His lips worked through a silent counting, like a child learning to read. "There's a train in two hours. And when you get to the city, the boys on West Fortieth'll fix you up with a car. Nothing fancy, but"—he scanned the property—"that should suit you fine."

"How do you know he's in New York?"

"I'm playing a hunch," Gavigan said. "Word is the oldest Dempsey boy lives in the city. What's his name, now?"

"Martin." The name jumped, unbidden. The boy's face from all those years ago flared in Cronin's mind like an apparition.

"Yes, Martin. A musician of some sort. Like his mother."

His mother. Bernadette. Just the thought of her name tightened the barbed wire that wrapped Cronin's heart. Of all the things he had done *for the cause*—Cronin cleared his throat. "When I find him," he said, and paused. "What am I to do with him?"

"You bring him to me. Simple as that."

"And then I'm done." It wasn't a question.

Gavigan nodded impatiently. "Isn't that what I told you?"

THE SMELL OF hay and manure had always been a comfort to Alice—these were home smells, childhood smells, the smell of her father when he came in from the first milking—but even this early in the day, the heat in the barn was almost more than she could take. She and Henry let the calf into the yard so he could nip at the grass and find his mother for another taste of her milk. Inside the house Alice poured a glass of milk for Henry from the metal pail they kept in the icebox, and while he drank she cut a slice of bread and slowly buttered it for him. She didn't even ask if he was hungry. Feeding him was a way to keep herself busy.

She gave the boy his plate and lingered by the table. She could just see through the dining-room window and into the driveway, where Tom loomed over the old man. She had never before heard anyone call him Tommy. It didn't suit him; it was a little boy's name. He had always been Tom, a name as stout as the man who wore it.

Farther up the driveway lurked a car, a black thing buffed to a high polish beneath its patina of road dirt. The old man turned and hobbled toward it. He appeared to be in no hurry. He placed his cane carefully amid the stones and soaked dirt and puddles as he went, and inched his way farther and farther from the house. Tom was already stalking down the driveway. His jaw bulged and his eyes were shut. One hand was wrapped into a fist, the other clutched something made of paper. Had he borrowed money and not told her? Had some debt suddenly come due, right here at the beginning of the summer season? He looked ready to tear the door off the hinges and she prepared herself for the sound of it, but when Tom came into the house he was calm, shuffling out of his boots and lining them up by the door. She was about to send Henry out into the yard so Tom could give her the details of their mystery guest, but he marched up the stairs without a word to her. From their bedroom came the squeal of drawers being opened, the sound of Tom's feet in the closet. She understood that men needed their privacy but if a bill collector was making house calls, then it was no longer a private matter; it was family business.

She left Henry at the kitchen table and went upstairs. On their bed lay Tom's battered leather valise, the only piece of luggage he'd carried when he had shown up years ago on her doorstep. Neatly piled next to it were two shirts, a necktie, two pairs of trousers, some boxer shorts. He was removing his church clothes—his one good suit— from the hanger when she came in.

"Where are you going?"

"To town," he said. "But just for a few days."

"Town? What town?"

"I won't be gone long," he said. He hadn't looked at her, not once, since he'd come in the house.

"What did that man want?" Alice said. She crossed the narrow room in a few short steps and took hold of his arm. "Do you owe money?"

He gave a grim laugh. "I wish it were money. Money I could pay off and be done with." Cronin kept his eyes on the stack of clothes, which he began loading into the bag.

"Tom Cronin! Didn't we promise—"

He looked her full in the face, and something in his eyes—heat, anger, sorrow—stopped her from speaking. This man was putting the squeeze on Tom and now she was squeezing him from the other side. Alice could see he was suffering, but they had promised from the start: *no secrets*. It was an easy promise to keep on any given day when they sat together at dinner as a family, more than she'd ever imagined she could have, with nothing more to talk about than cows and weather and Henry starting school in the fall. But right now was when it mattered most, when you thought that telling the truth would ruin what you had built. Hadn't she told him everything about herself, and about the husband who had left her and Henry? Hadn't she made plain her love for Tom even though she feared she might scare him off for good? Hadn't Tom figured it out? That secrets could destroy what they had faster than any truth could.

"Tom," she said again. "Tell me what he said."

"Unfinished business," Tom said. "There's a piece of unfinished business and it's on me to finish it."

"Tell him to go to hell," Alice said. "Tell him you're done with all that."

"It's not that simple. There's a job I have to do, and then I'm coming home. And once I get back, I'll never leave your side again."

"But Tom—"

"You'll get sick of me, you will." He forced a laugh but there was no spirit in it.

Alice folded her arms and watched him pack the rest of his clothes. He left the room and when he returned she was there, arms still folded, staring at the open mouth of his valise. He set down a small canvas bag—razor, toothbrush, soap, aftershave—and went to the wardrobe against the far wall. Standing on his tiptoes, he reached one hand to the top and pawed around behind the carved parapet that rose to a peak over the doors. He pulled a stiff ladder-back chair from the corner of the room to use as a step stool, and the moment his gaze reached the top of the wardrobe, he froze. He looked first at the ceiling, then at Alice.

"Where is it?"

"Where is what?" she said.

"The box. There was a small metal box up here—a toolbox."

"Only it didn't have any tools in it, did it?"

He stepped down from the chair, his momentum carrying him to within inches of her. He lowered his voice to a whisper. "Where's the box, Alice?"

"You're better than that. You know you are."

"Alice." His voice grew louder and more heated with each word. "The box."

She stared at him, right into those black eyes of his. This wasn't him. He didn't give orders—not to her. As much as she told him over and over again that the house and the farm and the family were theirs—that all of it belonged to him as much as to her—he still seemed more likely to ask permission than to give a command. As if it was hers to own, and he was only renting. This old man had a claim on Tom that she did not, or he was able to summon up some part of Tom that was off-limits to her. Whatever the old man had ordered him to do, Tom was spooked by it. If he wanted the box that badly, she would get it. But the box meant nothing; it was what was inside the box that mattered.

Alice edged toward the closet. Inside, she pulled the chain and in the burst of light she got her fingers around a hatbox and pulled it out from under a stack of cardboard cartons: hats and shoes she had not worn in years. Two of the boxes tumbled to the floor with a hollow thud. She handed the hatbox to Tom and he peeled open the round cover. Buttressed on all sides by wadded tissue paper was a small metal box secured with a latch. It could have held tools or tackle, but when Tom opened it the only contents were a holstered revolver wrapped in an oilcloth and a box of cartridges. Without looking up at Alice, he unwrapped the gun and felt its weight in his hand. Tom spun the cylinder and released a catch: the barrel hinged open, revealing six empty chambers. He drew back the hammer and pulled the trigger. Alice flinched at the sharp sound it made. With one hand, he worked six bullets out of the box and filled the cylinder, then snapped it back into place. The whole operation had taken less than half a minute.

"You don't need that." Alice's voice was more whisper than words.

"It's not for me," he said. "It's for you."

"Me?"

"I made my promise to you, that I'm coming back soon and that I'll never leave again. Now you've got to make a promise to me. If anyone you don't know comes to the door—anyone—you'll be ready to use this."

"Tom, you're scaring me. What's this all about?"

"I told you, it's unfinished business. And I'm sorry that you're caught up in this—I never wanted any of what I did and who I was to touch you, but there's people who won't let it be that way."

"That man," she said. "That's the man you worked for in New York."

"It is. And if there was some way that I could leave here and know that you and Henry and Gracie were safe as long as I stayed away for good, I'd do it, believe—"

Alice slapped him hard across the face. She felt the sting in her hand, throbbing, electric with pain and shock. "Don't you for one minute say that. You're not getting away from me, now or ever." She grabbed the revolver by the barrel, as if it were a hammer, and pulled it out of his hand. It was heavier than she had expected; Tom had handled it so easily. "You do what you have to do and then you get back here," she said. "But if you run away from me—from us—then I'm coming after you with this."

ALICE AND THE children rode in the truck with Cronin but he would not let them wait with him at the station—not that Alice wanted to. At first, Henry thought that they were off for a grand family adventure, but when he was told that only Tom would be getting on the train he started up with the tears, a signal to the baby to start crying. Soon both of them were in full clamor. Henry didn't want Tom to leave and it was no fair that he had to stay behind. Why couldn't he go with Tom, and Gracie would stay with Mommy? This wasn't the good-bye that Cronin wanted; my God, he didn't want any sort of good-bye, and certainly not this. Alice gave up trying to quiet the children and when Cronin looked at her amid the wailing he saw her own eyes shining with tears about to fall.

It was twenty minutes to the Rhinecliff station and when they arrived Cronin idled the truck and grabbed his valise from the back. He pulled the envelope that Gavigan had given him out of his pocket and fished out a few bills, which he stuffed into his wallet. The rest he gave to Alice.

"What's this?" she said.

"Buy them some ice cream," he said.

"But where did this—"

"Take it," he said, and she did. He looked straight at her and when he leaned into her she gave him a quick, fierce hug. He said nothing more, and he only once looked over his shoulder as Alice drove off, the baby in a basket at her side and Henry in the rear window calling, *Tom! Tom!*

JUST TELL ME *the truth.* That was one of the first things Alice had ever said to him, when he showed up at the farm with nothing but the bag in his hand. Gavigan had sent him upstate chasing a bad debt, but as the train lurched along the Hudson River, he had resolved that he would not go back. That he was done. It was early in the morning, the light was on the opposite bank, and the mist was so thick and the water so close to the mountains that the scene conjured for him the landscape outside Glengarriff, his boyhood home. He thought of the days before he had left for Cork and started heaping sin on top of sin. In Ireland during the war, it had been about making sure the Irish were in charge, and then it became about making sure the *right* Irish were in charge, but it was also about blood, and how much you could spill, and how the stain never left you. It might have been for a good cause, but he couldn't tell himself that any longer, not once he went to work for Gavigan.

That day, when he stepped off the train at this very platform, he wasn't thinking about starting fresh. He was thinking only of stopping. He shuffled as if in a daze into the station, where a hand-lettered note on a bulletin board read HELP WANTED. He might not have given it another look but the second line promised HONEST LABOR and Cronin thought maybe that could be a remedy for his years in the city. He wasn't seeking wages. He was a country boy who needed dirt on his hands and the sun on his face.

At the farm he found Alice, heavy with child, and Alice's father—an old man bent by a lifetime of work and then broken by a stroke. There was no sign of a husband and no mention of one either. Alice asked Cronin a few questions and when he hesitated she was blunt: *Just tell me the truth,* she said. If there were questions he did not want to answer, he was to say so. But every word from him had to be the truth. It seemed unwise—no, more than that, it was madness—for Alice to take him on, but there was work to be done and Cronin set about doing it. He tried in the years after Alice came into his life to atone for all that had transpired before. The priests had always said that you could never dig yourself in so deep that Jesus couldn't pull you out, but what if all you ever did was dig, even when you'd sworn your digging days were done?

And now, because of the Dempseys, he was back at it, digging himself deeper! Francis Dempsey—that was a name that came roaring out of his past, and yet was as close as last night's fitful sleep. Black Frank, they had called him. He was the one who'd set Cronin on the path that had poisoned every night for these past twenty years. He had turned a gardener into a killer, fashioning Cronin into a tool useful to *the cause,* urging him on whenever he felt Cronin's will faltering, chiding him when he came up short, cheering him when he did the job right. Frank Dempsey had governed Cronin's every step and even now what Cronin saw when he slept was born of Dempsey's guiding hand.

Enough! Cronin had been through all of this, over and over. Frank Dempsey wasn't the devil, no more than Gavigan was. They were all men, and when Cronin's time came, he knew his sins would not be assigned to Dempsey's account. He alone would be damned for what he had done. Alice had urged him to throw himself on God's boundless mercy, to beg forgiveness for the lives he had taken and the people he had hurt. But Cronin knew that there could be no mercy without contrition; he must, in the words of the prayer, be *heartily sorry* for all that he had done. And while he longed to avoid the fires of hell, he knew that it was terror alone that would push him into the confessional. As

Frank Dempsey had often told him and as Cronin still believed—in a part of his heart that remained off-limits even to Alice—those things had needed to be done. Even at the cost of nightmares. Even at the cost of hell.

Cronin also believed that the life he had now—with Alice and the boy and the baby, with their cows and their fields and their orchard—this was his heaven, and it was the only heaven he would ever know. If finding Black Frank's son was the price he had to pay to keep his family safe and to live out his days with them in this earthly paradise, then so be it. He could only hope that there was no God and no final accounting for his actions on this earth—or else put his faith in God being an Irishman who would understand why he did what he did.

MIDTOWN

THE ROCKEFELLERS' MIDTOWN KINGDOM soared above its earth-bound neighbors. While their battered faces were smeared with soot and pigeon shit, the RCA Building burst from the pages of a comic book: its faultless lines were inked with shimmering quick-silver; its ascending pin-striped setbacks formed a giant's staircase from street to sky. Here the promise of the modern world had been fixed in place by tons of granite and Indiana limestone. Murals hatched in fever dreams stretched across the lobby walls and every-where were muscle-bound statues with jagged beards and roaring mouths and thunderbolts leaping from their hands. It was as if the gods of the past had been put to work building a brighter tomorrow. Waiting to ascend to the observation deck, the crowds of the curious could be excused for thinking they were boarding a rocket ship bound for a shiny future—leaving behind a world of torpor and disappoint-ment and dull, grim streets lined with ruined buildings.

As she watched her reflection in the elevator's polished bronze doors, Lilly Bloch let herself get swept along in this tide of optimism. It was Friday morning and she was scheduled to meet with Mr. Mus-grove, her benefactor at the Foundation, which had brought her from Prague to America on an artist's fellowship. During her three months in New York, she had often visited Mr. Musgrove's office. He was fond of hosting freewheeling soirées with the other artists the Foun-dation had sponsored—a motley collection of aging Dadaists, surly constructivists, renegade expressionists, and a lonely surrealist who always asked for his cocktail to be served in a man's hat. *I'm beginning to wonder,* she had written to her beloved Josef, *if I'm the only one who has not pledged allegiance to an ism. Can you suggest the right one for me?*

Two weeks earlier, after Lilly had shared with Mr. Musgrove the latest dire news from home, he had promised to use the Foundation's considerable clout to keep her in New York and—what's more—to spirit Josef out of Prague, where life had become precarious since the Reich had invaded and taken up residence in Prague Castle. In their letters to each other, Josef would ask, *How is life in the Tower?* and Lilly would respond with a blow-by-blow of the most recent dustup from one of Mr. Musgrove's parties. She would always sign off by inquiring, with growing anxiety, *What is the news from the Castle?*— as if it were something from a fairy tale, unconnected to reality. The Tower and the Castle: it sounded like a game, but as the expiration date on her visa drew nearer and the reports from Josef became grimmer, the stakes had become impossibly high.

But today Mr. Musgrove's promises would become reality; today the Tower would outfox the Castle. She had an appointment at ten o'clock, where she expected Mr. Musgrove would first present her with a fresh bouquet of compliments—he was fond of calling her a Major Talent, a Daring Visionary, and even, once, a Genius. Then he would sit back in his chair—a work of art in itself—with nothing but the clouds and the blue sky behind him and he would present her with a new visa and inform her that a similar document would soon be in Josef's hands. She could already see the smile wrinkling the corners of his mouth, could almost hear him say, *Didn't I tell you I'd take care of everything?* But Lilly didn't need him to take care of everything. If he could make good on his biggest promise, to find some way to get Josef out of Prague, that would be more than enough.

As the elevator doors opened for her on the fifty-first floor, Lilly

Bloch believed this dream of escape and reunion was still possible. She did not yet know that all of Mr. Musgrove's promises had already come undone, and that the careless joy of two people in love had conspired against her.

ONE WEEK EARLIER, Alvin Musgrove—Mr. Mousegrove to the girls in the typing pool—had left his job and his wife and run off with his secretary to Reno to get himself a quickie divorce. At least that was the story circulating around the office. The detail about Reno was based largely on whispers and misapprehensions about Nevada's divorce laws. What was known was that Mr. Musgrove, director of the Foundation's arts and culture section, had abruptly announced his resignation on the previous Friday, citing reasons of a personal nature. On the following Monday, just as word of Mr. Musgrove's sudden departure was creating ripples through the hallways and offices of the Foundation, somebody wondered out loud why his secretary, Carole Turner, was also a no-show that morning. One of the girls called Carole's home, only to reach her distraught mother, who had spent the weekend grappling with the news that her daughter had run off with a married man. This latest wrinkle sent the Foundation into a tizzy. Carole had never breathed a word of the affair to any of the other girls, and now the story on Carole was quickly being revised from "quiet and sweet" to "stuck-up and scheming." Who did she think she was, running off with Mr. Musgrove? And how long had this been going on, right beneath everyone's nose? And of all the girls in the office to run off with, why Carole Turner? And of all the men, why Mr. Musgrove?

While most of the office debated the wheres and whens of the Musgrove-Turner tryst, Ruby Kadetsky was tasked with cleaning up the mess. Ruby was a trouper; everyone knew that. She was a roll-up-your-sleeves kind of gal, a quit-your-bellyaching-and-get-to-work kind of gal. But still, this was some pickle: losing a senior program officer and his secretary on the same day! And to make matters worse, Ruby couldn't make heads or tails of the files. They were like a crossword puzzle without any clues. One of Mr. Musgrove's pet projects was a scheme that brought European artists to the United States on the Foundation's dime, but there was no way of knowing who the latest batch of fellows were or whether or not they were still in the country. After three days of digging, Ruby could tell only one thing for certain: Carole Turner had not been prized for her secretarial skills.

It was typical, really. Girls like Carole got the man with the name on the door, and Ruby got to clean up after them. It was bad enough to get stuck with a thankless task, but what really got to Ruby were the bigger questions. Such as: What if happiness depended on making other people miserable—on robbing them of their happiness? That was what Carole had done. Her mother was a wreck, but mothers were like that: they turned on the waterworks whenever life (yours) didn't go according to plan (theirs). Ruby knew that story, cover to cover. But what about Mr. Musgrove's wife, who had to be honest-to-God miserable? Ruined, even, and all so Carole could be happy. But maybe Carole didn't care. Maybe she was just selfish. Or maybe she told herself—because Mr. Musgrove had told her first—that the Musgroves had a bad marriage and his wife was sick of him and there would be no hard feelings if he left. Ruby couldn't imagine anyone falling for a line like that, one that made it all so easy. The desperate business of wanting what you did not have was never easy.

WHEN LILLY ARRIVED for her appointment, she did not find Mr. Musgrove's quiet, moonfaced secretary, but instead a dark-haired girl in jeweled cat's-eye glasses surrounded on all sides by stacks of jacketed files.

"Pardon me," Lilly said. "I am looking for Mr. Musgrove."

"Join the club," Ruby said. She had spent the past hour trying to square receipts with Mr. Musgrove's comings and goings. "Mr. Musgrove isn't here anymore."

"But I have an appointment," Lilly said. A leather-bound calendar was on the edge of the desk, atop one of the piles. "The other girl should have written it down."

There was a lot that Carole Turner should have written down, but for the benefit of her visitor, Ruby flopped open the cover to the current week. Every box was blank, which should have been a tip-off, if anyone had been paying attention. The previous week wasn't much better: Carole's loopy scrawl indicated the odd meeting or lunch, and at the end of the column for Friday she had written *!!!!* in red ink. This had made her private-secretary material?

Ruby snapped the cover shut. "I'm sorry, ma'am, but there's no appointment, and no Mr. Musgrove."

"But where is he?"

"We've got a pool going on that. The smart money says Reno, but it could be Mexico, for all I know."

"Mexico?" Lilly tried to absorb what this meant. The girl might as well have said that Mr. Musgrove had gone to the moon.

"Yes, *Mex-ee-ko.* It's a country, just below America."

Lilly was losing patience with this girl and her join-the-club, her smart-money, her *Mex-ee-ko.* Two weeks ago, Mr. Musgrove had promised they would get things fixed. "You just have to know the right people," he had told her. But now everything was unraveling because she couldn't make this girl understand.

"I know where Mexico is," Lilly said, "but why is Mr. Musgrove there?" She took a deep breath, an effort to steady herself, but it came back out in a series of short, ragged bursts. "Mr. Musgrove," she said, trying to take it slow, "brought me to New York, for the Foundation. I am from Prague—you know Prague? You know Czechoslovakia?"

Ruby wrinkled her nose. Did she know Czechoslovakia? Wasn't her brother talking about it all the time, him and his City College friends? When they weren't ransacking the icebox at the Kadetskys' apartment in Astoria, they yammered on and on about the Czechs and Hitler and the Bund and Lindbergh. In the college's Great Hall, her brother and his friends had already started draping black sheets over the flags of nations that had fallen to fascism: first Germany, then Austria, Czechoslovakia...

A panic was blooming in Lilly's chest. When the girl didn't reply, her words came in gasps. *"Check-oh-slo-wa-key-ah,"* she said. "Yes? And soon my visa expires, and I must go back. But this is impossible. And he—Mr. Musgrove—he told me he was going to help me. If Mr. Musgrove is not here, then how is he going to help me?"

Lilly knew she was raving like some kind of lunatic. She balled her fist in front of her mouth like a stopper in a bottle, unsure of what would come out next: a word, a scream, a sob. How had she been so stupid, to place her faith in Mr. Musgrove? Here in the Tower with its polished floors and bronze doors, its bird's-eye views and cocktails in the clouds, everything seemed possible. But Lilly knew better—she knew that the world was not so easy. Though it defied logic and everything she had seen in Berlin, Munich, and Barcelona, she had let herself believe that she could escape the inevitable, and that she could rescue Josef as well. Only now did she see what a fool she had been.

Ruby looked away, trying to be polite, trying to offer a little privacy in this suddenly cramped room. She shifted the position of the stapler, moving it away from the box of paper clips. There was a kind of pleasure in bringing order to all this mess, and before this woman made her appearance, Ruby had experienced a mote of satisfaction, a light thrill, each time she ratcheted down the head of the stapler and bound together what had been a sheaf of loose, badly shuffled sheets of paper. But this woman had put a stop to that. She stood in front of Ruby's desk, hand over her mouth and her eyes burning a hole through the door that still bore Mr. Musgrove's name.

Ruby wasn't trying to be difficult—really, she wasn't—but she had been given a job that would take five girls to sort through, plus one of the other program officers to decode, and then that wiseacre from accounting would have to run the numbers to see if they all added up. Maybe this lady had been promised help and maybe she really did need it. But you know who else needed help? Ruby Kadetsky, that's who. And yet here was this woman, not three feet away, and Ruby wouldn't even look at her—wouldn't exercise the common decency of recognizing the pain of another human being. She was a regular Carole Turner. No, worse. She was a dime-store version who wasn't even getting love in return for satisfying her blind, selfish heart.

Ruby returned the stapler to its resting place and closed the jacket on the file.

"Ma'am," she said, and leaned over the desk, as if someone might be eavesdropping or she was about to share a secret. "Can you tell me your name?"

The sound of the girl's voice helped in some small way. Lilly nodded and cleared her throat. "Lilly Bloch," she said.

"I have to tell you, Miss Bloch, things around here are nutty today, all thanks to your Mr. Musgrove. Frankly I wouldn't know who to send you to—it's that bad."

Lilly opened her mouth, as if about to speak, but what was there to say?

"I'll tell you what," Ruby said. "You come back Monday morning and I'll have figured out a thing or two. Somewhere in all this mess is your file, and once I find it, I'll get it into the right hands. And then we'll just go from there. How does that sound?"

Lilly could only nod. She managed a whispered "Thank you," then a real one, louder than she had intended, which led to a round of nervous laughter—first from her, then echoed by the girl behind the desk. Lilly reached across the desk and touched the girl's wrist once, lightly. "You are very kind," she said.

Ruby smiled. Was that really all it took? She hadn't promised the woman anything more than a few questions around the office, along with whatever it took for her to dredge her file out of this clerical landfill. She wrote Lilly's name on a slip of paper and held it up for Lilly to inspect. "Did I get it right?" she asked.

Lilly had always considered her last name to be blunt and inelegant, but this girl's *B* was a swirl of liquid curls that formed a four-chambered heart, and the *L* on her first name was looped like a bow around a finger, a promise not to forget. Josef would laugh at her for being so superstitious, but she needed a sign, and this one would do. "It's lovely," Lilly said, her fate now in the hands of this girl who could take a stranger's name and make it into something beautiful.

SATURDAY
JUNE 3

FORDHAM HEIGHTS

MARTIN DEMPSEY HAD DONE it. He had really done it this time. And he had told the story a dozen times or more, in bars from Fifty-Second to 140th Street, to men who were drawn to his madman's glow—his flashing eyes! his jet-black hair!—and who stood him round after round of drinks to hear every detail. Martin had just walked out on Chester Kingsley. He had taken his spot in a big band that was heard weekly on the National Broadcasting Company and tossed it right back in Chester's jowly roast beef of a face.

The final straw was a new addition to the band's set list—Chester's own arrangement of Count Basie's "One O'Clock Jump," cleaned up and toned down for the geriatric crowd that filled the lounge at the Kensington Hotel, where the Chester Kingsley Orchestra was the reigning house band. Martin had heard the song from Basie himself last summer at the Famous Door, and he had immediately broken his promise to Rosemary—no more record albums until next month's payday—and snatched up a fresh pressing of the single. "One O'Clock Jump" was a shiny locomotive powered by piano, brass, and drums, but in Chester's hands it had all the glamour of an uptown bus. Martin stopped playing his clarinet before the band was even four bars into the number, and when Chester shot him a look, Martin took his instrument and walked off the bandstand. Not only mid-set, but midsong.

Now it was six o'clock in the morning and Martin's head buzzed

43

with gin and cigarettes and the hot jazz he had used to flush the last traces of sweet dance music out of his head. Sweet—that's what they called the music that Chester played, but there was no truth in that. The music was stale, lifeless; it had the sweetness of a rose that had wilted and begun to molder. He couldn't blame the twilight-years crowd, but what baffled him were the younger people who hadn't gotten the message that sweet had gone the way of the Charleston. They lived in the world capital of hot jazz, the kingdom of the Lindy Hop! It had been more than a year since Benny Goodman had brought jazz to Carnegie Hall. Chick Webb had been demolishing all comers at the Savoy Ballroom for almost five years; band to band with Goodman, Ellington, and Basie—and Webb had always come out on top.

This was the music everyone was screaming for; everyone, it seemed, except the fresh-faced squares and the gout-riddled couples who flocked to hear Chester Kingsley's band make good on its motto: The Sweetest Sounds You Ever Did Hear. Through every number, Chester smiled and waved his baton like a hypnotist, further somnambulizing a crowd that was already sleepwalking through the golden age of swing.

After Martin walked out on Chester, his remedy had been a wide-ranging search for a red-hot band playing "Jumpin' at the Woodside" or "King Porter Stomp." He had started in Midtown at the Roseland and the Hickory House, then gone to Harlem for the Savoy and Minton's and Monroe's Uptown House. He had hoped to see Webb behind his drum kit, but the word was that the Little Giant was still in the hospital, playing against the only bandleader he couldn't beat. In his place, Benny Carter held down the main bandstand, but by the time Martin climbed the stairs to the Savoy, the crowd was spilling out onto Lenox Avenue. Carter had called it a night.

Ten years earlier, Martin had come from Ireland with the dream of being a working musician in New York City, and the dream had come true and then some. Whatever Chester's faults—and those would take all night to tally—he led one of the city's most sought-after dance bands. All over Manhattan, well-connected brides-to-be organized their weddings around Chester's availability, and every August the band headlined a white-jacket tour through Connecticut, the Hamptons, and the finer spots on the Jersey Shore.

But the years had taught Martin that being a musician alone wasn't enough if you wanted to make it in music. You had to be a salesman, a politician even, to get where you wanted to go. Maybe that wasn't true for the best of the best, whose chops were so undeniable that one note could vault them to a spot on any bandstand in the city, but Martin knew he wasn't one of the anointed. Still, while he may not have been great—not Coleman Hawkins–great, or Gene Krupa–great, or Ella Fitzgerald–great—he wasn't a complete square. He was a hotshot on the piano, a surefire clarinet, and a half-decent alto sax. He had even penned a song, "That's More Like It," that had briefly broken through to the Hit Parade for 1937, and for a while it looked like the start of something. Only there hadn't been a follow-up. He wrote other tunes but no one put them into their sets at the ballrooms, or if they did, they never bothered to record them, or if they did, no one bought the record or played it on the radio or cued it up in a jukebox. One hit, and he had to wonder if there would ever be another.

Now as he stepped off the subway and approached the Grand Concourse, he was light-headed and ready for sleep. By some miracle, his clarinet case was still in his hand. He wouldn't need to retrace his steps in the morning through every bar and subway car in New York. As much as he loved the electric charge that came from moving in a sea of bodies surging from one place to another—crossing a street in the moment the traffic signal changed, a swell of suit-and-tied men and sway-hipped women, each of them racing to get somewhere that seemed so important—there were times when he wanted to call a stop to it, to slow it all down and not be carried along in anyone's tide. This was why the early-morning hours were his favorite. Walking a nearly vacant street, with only a couple slouched against each other in the distance, steam drifting lazily from a manhole, a splash of neon thrown into a puddle, an after-hours bar whose last diligent drinkers hunched over their highball glasses—this was the New York he had come seeking. The city in a country hour. A time of deserted lanes and privacy amid the millions.

Not that you were ever entirely alone, not even in the Bronx. At this hour, the subways rumbled and the delivery vans trundled along the side streets and the broad, trolley-tracked avenues. Milk. Eggs. Ice. Bread. Beer. Coal. Newspapers. But it was quieter than in the daytime, more desolate, and Martin felt as if he had slipped through the cracks in time itself. His walk was no more than five or six blocks—a straight shot from the station to the corner occupied by the Bluebird Diner, which in the wee hours shone like a fire in the middle of a dark wood. The Bluebird was a twenty-four-hour joint, its bulbs burning through the street-to-ceiling windows. From a block away he could see the waitress with her fanlike paper hat pouring coffee for the nighthawks at the counter. The counter was L-shaped, so that the backs of some of the men were visible, and the profiles of others. Through these nightly glimpses into the Bluebird, he had come to recognize some of the regulars, though he never knew if they were catching a plate of eggs and hash at the end of their shift or preparing themselves for the start of the day. Among the usual crowd were bus drivers, cabbies, men in the coveralls of utility workers, and always one or two dressed like him—Bronx Beau Brummells on a shoestring budget. They could have been drinkers, carousers, or cardsharps silently totaling the night's gains and losses, whether financial or physical.

But who was he to comment on the appetites of others, a man who was dragging himself back to his wife and children at six in the morning with a heart full of hot jazz and a head bursting with the news that he had just quit his job? Once he passed the Bluebird, he was three streetlights from his front door. As he did after every long night in the city, he would count them down, one by one, until he was home.

"MR. DEMPSEY! MR. Dempsey!" The landlady's voice rose in volume as Martin ascended the staircase. "Mr. Dempsey!"

Martin stopped halfway to the top. He had already loosened his tie and opened his collar. His suit jacket was secured over one shoulder by a hooked index finger. There was a window at the top of the stairs through which pink light cast soft shadows on the runner's faded florals. He cocked his head, offering no more than a profile, to let the landlady know he was listening.

"There was someone looking for you last night," she said.

"Thank you, Mrs. Fichetti."

"But don't you want to know who it was?"

Martin exhaled—not so much a sigh as an admission of defeat. "All right," he said. "Now, who was it?"

"I don't know," she said. "Not for the life of me. He came last night ringing the bell to beat the band, and Mrs. Dempsey not at home to answer it. Once he was on his way, I knocked on your door and still didn't hear a sound." Mrs. Fichetti throttled a handkerchief between her hands. "You and Mrs. Dempsey aren't having troubles, are you? Because that would be a terrible shame. You had best go to her and beg—"

"There aren't any problems," he said. "Rosemary and the girls spent the night with her parents."

"But don't you see? That's what worries me. When a woman returns to her parents' house—well, it's already too late."

"We're grand," Martin said, but he could tell that she was not convinced. The Dempseys on the rocks was a better story to share with her bridge partners than any truth Martin could tell her. "Now, about this man. Did he say what he wanted?"

"He wanted you, but he wouldn't say what for. And he was a rough-looking one. Hard eyes. A fighter's nose. Not so big, but beefy—oh, Mr. Dempsey, don't tell me that you owe money. Are you a horse player? Have you gotten yourself mixed up with bookmakers? I know men have their vices—"

"I'm sure it's nothing of the sort." Martin owed small sums across the city, but most of those were to tailors and haberdashers, not the types to seek out a bum debt in the last hours of a Friday night. And if it was a friend—well, anyone who knew him would know to ask around at one of his regular haunts.

"You know I've had my misgivings about renting to musicians. I've always rented to hardworking people. People who need a good night's sleep to prepare for an honest day's labor. It's only on account of your wife that I overlook your late hours. She's from a good family, and it's a privilege to have her here."

Martin resumed his ascent. "Rosemary is the better half," he said over his shoulder. "No question about it. But fear not for our marriage. I will seek out this mystery caller—but at a more reasonable hour. For now, I must prepare for another night of dishonest labor."

Mrs. Fichetti sputtered but Martin pursued his retreat with such purpose that by the time he opened the door to the apartment, he could hear Mrs. Fichetti's door shutting, followed immediately by the *thunk* of her dead bolt being thrown. Catching his breath, he added this latest run-in with Mrs. Fichetti to the long ledger of reasons why they had to get into a house of their own. When they had first moved in, they believed this apartment was nothing more than a way station, a place to get settled, where Rosemary could have the baby and they could figure out what it meant to be husband and wife—to be a family. He had never bargained on four years upstairs from Mrs. Fichetti, had never imagined that part of the cost of these rooms was required attendance at their landlady's spontaneous, rambling sermons on the evils of popular music, strong drink, horse racing, FDR, communism, the way women wear their hair these days, or any other topics of concern gleaned from Father Coughlin's radio program and the pages of the *New York Journal-American*.

Certainly Rosemary would have agreed; she was one who bore the brunt of Mrs. Fichetti's attentions and opinions. But for now Martin was alone in the apartment, and this was a rare event. Not being alone, but being alone here. He often felt that the apartment belonged to Rosemary and their two girls, Katherine and Evelyn. He was only a visitor, an interloper, whose greatest contribution to these five rooms — other than the rent that kept them here — was the wardrobe that sprawled across one side of the bedroom he shared with his wife. A double-tiered rack ran the length of one wall, bearing up the small fortune in shirts, suit coats, blazers, trousers, ties, and other items of apparel that Martin had accumulated during his first years in New York. The wall was a riot of gabardine, serge, and worsted wool; there were tweeds, plaids, pinstripes, herringbones, windowpanes. The run of shirts was more muted — white, blue — and all French-cuffed. The wall came to life again where Martin draped his neckties: polka dots, rep stripes, batiks, angular geometrics, undulant paisleys. Every color of the rainbow was represented, along with colors that nature had never imagined. Next to this was stationed a hat rack, where fedoras perched like plump, shadowy doves.

It would have been easy to dismiss Martin as a dandy, but there was more to it. When he had been newly arrived in New York, he was eager to claim the golden, Hollywood-bright destiny that all Americans seemed to believe was their due. He hoped that by attiring himself in the unmistakable regalia of the American man — the suit worn by Clark Gable in *It Happened One Night,* a hat pitched at the same angle as William Powell's in *The Thin Man* — this careful crafting of the outer shell would transform his inner being as well. In the right collar, foulard tie, and double-breasted, broad-shouldered gabardine jacket, he would not only look like an American but become one: a creature freed from the sordid history of the Old World and looking boldly to the future. This half of the room was more than a walk-in closet, more than Martin's attempt to create in miniature his own Macy's menswear department. It was an alchemist's workshop, in which he endeavored, through daily application of cotton, silk, leather, and pomade, to transform his base nature into something more noble.

But now the wardrobe was outmoded. He kept his clothes in impeccable condition, but the suits were no longer the latest styles, not since Evie had come along. Another mouth to feed, and even with a dresser full of her big sister's hand-me-downs, there were plenty of other expenses. Martin wasn't so coldhearted that a new suit came before Easter dresses for the girls—not that Rosemary would have allowed it anyway. Back when his song had been popular, when it seemed that it was all the start of something big, Martin thought they were moving beyond the need to make those sorts of choices. Now every day was full of the small deprivations and constant calculations that always seemed to work their way between him and Rosemary.

And there was a man looking for him—a hard-eyed, rough-hewn fellow who wanted to know his whereabouts—and what could that be about but money? Apparently the man hadn't said when he would return, or where he could be found, should Martin want to seek him out. Something about the whole episode struck Martin as queer. If it had happened downtown, he wouldn't have given it a second thought. The Manhattan night world where he spent his time was lousy with bounders and stay-outs, boozers and loudmouths and sloppy drunks who bellowed at all hours and in all places for another round, the loan of a five-spot, a fourth encore, or simply a firm handshake and a slap on the back from a bosom friend of three hours' acquaintance. He saw it every night, more often as the little hand on the clock ended its climb and began the greased descent through the small numbers leading up to dawn. But it wasn't a world that followed him back to the Bronx.

Up the echo chamber of the stairwell came Mrs. Fichetti's shriek, impossible to sort into words. It was a wavering melody punctuated by the percussion of feet thumping against the stairs. The melody faded and there was only the insistent rhythm of footsteps drawing nearer, a low bass rumble that erupted into the snare-drum crack of a fist against his door.

"Martin!" a voice called out. "Martin Dempsey! Open the feckin' door!"

Martin swung his feet over the edge of the bed and before he was fully awake he was out the bedroom door and into the living room. He scanned the room for something that could double as a weapon, and discounted his shoe (too small) and a secondhand saxophone (too valuable, even secondhand) before yanking an electric cord from the wall and taking up the Bakelite lamp that sat next to the sofa.

The knocking came again. "Martin! Open up!"

He stood in the middle of the living room, clad only in his billowy boxer shorts, his hand around the stem of a lamp whose shade was decorated with a tableau of two long-plumed birds of paradise preparing to mate or fight, depending on your attitude and the angle at which you viewed the image. Once again, his mind cycled through names, faces, debts, and other offenses that could have brought this fist, and the person in possession of it, to his door. He placed one hand on the knob, ready to yank it open and gain some element of surprise. But before he could turn the bolt, the voice spoke again, this time a sharp whisper pressing at the seam between the door and the jamb.

"Open the door, Martin! It's Francis! It's your brother!"

He hadn't seen Francis in ten years, not since they were teenagers, but the man who stood now in the doorway was without a doubt his brother. He was three years younger than Martin, but had always been stouter, more solidly built. His red hair, once a thicket that defied the ministrations of all combs and brushes, had been pomaded into a rakish wave. His nose was small and fierce like a fist, and his eyes were deep-set and black as peat. There was nothing suave and elegant about his face, but it was a handsome mix of toughness and deviltry nonetheless. It was James Cagney's face, that's what it was.

"Jaysus, but you're a hard man to find," Francis said. "I've been all across the Bronx looking for you." He said *Bronx* like it was two syllables—"Bron-ix." "Now would you let a man in before that woman has my head."

Mrs. Fichetti was laboring to the top of the stairs, her steps slow and her breathing heavy, desperate to be noticed for the effort expended despite her age, the hour, and the likelihood that she would be martyred in defense of her home. So here was his brother and there was Mrs. Fichetti to deal with, but all of this was coming at Martin in a headlong rush: Francis was supposed to be in Ireland. Martin was supposed to be asleep. Mrs. Fichetti did not factor into any sort of reunion between the Dempsey brothers, except here she was, huffing and panting her way along the dim hall, her face red as Christmas wrapping and her gray hair spidering out from her head.

Martin looked at her, looked at his brother, even took a moment to glance down at himself (bare chest, boxer shorts, birds-of-paradise lamp). He took hold of the lapel of Francis's jacket and yanked him into the room. "Not a word from you," he said to the back of his brother's head as he stepped into the hallway.

"An awful rumpus," Martin said to his landlady. "But let me assure you there's no funny business or foul play of any sort."

Mrs. Fichetti opened her mouth to answer, but in place of words she took a gasping breath.

"It's my brother, you see. Another Mr. Dempsey, and I'm as shocked as you to find him here." Mrs. Fichetti gulped again, and Martin could sense that words were about to pour forth—questions, threats, ultimatums—that he was in no condition to answer. "I will explain everything," he said. "You deserve nothing less. But"—and here he looked down at his spindle legs, the wrinkled cotton of his underwear—"I'm not at all presentable for that conversation, you'll have to admit that."

Her eyes bulged, whether from the shock to her propriety or from oxygen deprivation due to her hurried ascent, Martin could not say.

"Mister. Dempsey." Each word was propelled with a great puff of air.

Martin inched toward the door, one hand on the knob, the other on the door frame. "Absolutely, Mrs. Fichetti. We will have quite the chat about this—but not now. We're neither of us in any condition for that."

She inhaled, the next volley forming, but with a single glide step— Astaire himself would have been jealous—Martin bobbed behind the door and shut it with a resolute click. He stood frozen, listening to her breathing, waiting for the torrent to be unleashed. He turned once, locking eyes with Francis, a stern *Not a word out of you* glare. After half a minute and a sound not unlike a hen unkindly lifted from her nest, Mrs. Fichetti stuttered to the stairs in her slippered feet.

Martin sighed heavily and turned to face his brother. "Jesus, Mary, and Joseph," he said. "How in hell did you get here?"

"How's that for a warm welcome?" Francis said. "My own flesh and blood, and you're raining curses on me. Do you know what a trial it was to find you? If there's a better hidey-hole in all of New York then I'd sure like to see it."

"Look at your man, already an expert on New York."

Francis broke into a grin that set a shine in those black eyes. "Would you look at the two of us," he said. "Major Cat and General Dog, just like Mam used to say." He opened his arms wide and Martin stepped into his embrace. The two men pounded each other on the back, then held the clinch a moment longer, like boxers waiting to be separated by the referee.

"You're a sight," Martin said, "but what are you doing here? How did you get out?"

"Of Ireland?"

"No—of jail."

"Oh, they let me out," he said. "On account of good behavior."

"Why didn't you tell me? If it wasn't for Michael's letters I wouldn't know if you were alive or dead."

Michael's letters to Martin, sent to commemorate various Holy Days of Obligation, were full of spiritual uplift and fond wishes for those actions necessary to secure the salvation of his eldest brother's soul. (*I pray that you are partaking of the sacraments, that you are honoring your marital vows, and that you are living a life free from the demonic effects of vile liquors.*) It was all a bit difficult to take seriously from a boy who had been seven when Martin left home, and little in the way of news—a word that smacked of worldly concerns—could be gleaned from the lofty skywriting of Michael's epistles. It had been two months since he'd received Michael's Easter letter—the Ninth Letter of Michael to the Americans, he called it—and it hadn't breathed a word of Francis's impending release from prison.

"You got those, too?" Francis drew a sharp breath across his teeth. "All that talk of my immortal soul and the perils I'd put myself in. It was taxing, reading one of those—but the joke's on us, apparently. Michael says they were all written in code."

"Have you seen him?"

"Of course, at the—look, Martin, get yourself dressed. We've got places to go."

"I've had an hour's sleep, Francis. I'm knocked over seeing you here, but I'm not going anywhere."

"I've got a thing or two to tell you, and—"

"So tell me. The landlady won't be back to bother us, not for a while yet."

"What about the missus? Or did she find herself a better piano player?"

"She's at her parents' for the night."

"Trouble in—"

"You're as bad as the old woman. Now, what've you got to tell me?" Martin dropped down on the sofa and crossed his legs. He couldn't help but notice his brother's suit: pale gray and expensively made, it was distinctly Savile Row. Rather than flaring winglike before wasping back to his waist, the jacket was cut close to his frame. His tie was a deep crimson overlaid with a grid of white diamonds—a harlequin pattern.

"It's Da." Francis fidgeted with his hands before folding them in front of him, as if in prayer. "He's dead."

Martin heard himself say, "How?" but what he thought was, *This can't be real.* He'd had too much to drink and hadn't gotten into bed until dawn and now he was in a dream with Francis and Mrs. Fichetti and *Da is dead.* That had to be it. He was sitting in nothing but his boxer shorts, and Rosemary and the girls were nowhere to be found, and here was Francis, dressed like a gentleman instead of a prisoner, and he was telling Martin that he had just seen Michael, and now he was saying that their father was dead. Martin reached for the box of cigarettes on the coffee table and plucked one out. He lit it in one clean motion, hoping that this exercise of will would snap him awake.

"His heart. Doctor said he must've had a bad heart."

Martin took a drag of his cigarette. "Did he suffer?"

"Now, that's a big question, isn't it?"

"You know what I mean. Did he linger?"

"No one knows. One of the neighbors found him, facedown in the garden. Said it looked like he'd been struck by a bolt from the blue."

Martin tried to conjure an image of his father's face, but what he got was faded and ragged around the edges, like a photograph left in the rain. He foundered for something to say. "When did it happen?"

"It's been two weeks," Francis said.

"Two weeks! And you're only telling me now? You couldn't have sent a telegram—a letter, even?"

"I thought you should hear this in person, from someone who shares your blood."

"You came all this way to tell me that Da is dead?"

"Would you've rather gotten the news alone, with nothing but a torn envelope in front of you? We're family. That's what family does for family."

Francis offered a weak smile, a show of sincerity, but there was something odd in his manner. He had an edge in his voice and Martin couldn't tell if he was making a joke or saying it straight. They had shared a bedroom almost from the moment Francis was born, and Martin thought he knew his brother's every twitch and sigh, but Francis had changed. He had acquired expressions and ways of speaking that Martin could not decode. Or maybe nothing had changed, and Martin was simply out of practice.

"Look, it's more than just that," Francis said. He went to the front window, looked up the street and then down the other side. The sun was on the curtains, the heat of the day already coming into the apartment. "Come with me and I'll explain everything."

"I've been up all night —"

"Get yourself dressed. Something nice. Something sophisticated."

What was the point of arguing? Here was his brother, appearing as if by magic. If this was a dream, then going off with his brother was the logical next step. His head was still scrambled by the late night and the lack of sleep, the shock of seeing Francis and the news of his father's death. This last item was the hardest to account for. He did not know how or what to feel about it; it was curiously without shape or weight. He knew that there would come a time when the full force of his father's death would hit him — his absence not only from the world, but from Martin's life — but for now, the fact of his father's death didn't change anything, or so he thought in those earliest moments. It would matter later — or so he hoped, because if it didn't then Martin must be a cold, soulless son of a bitch. *I'm in shock*, he told himself, even as he knew that he was not.

WOODLAWN

EVERY TIME ROSEMARY CAME back to the house, she felt the old routines waiting for her, like a shawl that hung by the door. All that she had become—Martin's wife, a mother twice over—melted away in the face of those older identities: list maker, load bearer, peacekeeper, daughter. Married or not, she would always be their daughter, but she had hoped that a family of her own would alter how her parents thought of her. And it had—just not in the way she had imagined. Her father took it the hardest, which shouldn't have been a surprise. She was the oldest, and hadn't he always expected great things from her, or at least that she would lead a husband to great things? Her hasty marriage to Martin put a stop to all that. *A penniless immigrant musician,* he had called Martin. *Rosemary's dirty little tinker. What kind of a girl would—*

The baby helped. Kate was fat-faced and full of smiles and from her earliest days had reserved a special grin for her grandfather—as if she knew that he was the hardest to win over and the easiest to disappoint. Evie was only a baby but she was more standoffish; more like her grandfather than Kate was, and so more likely to vex him. He was still awaiting a grandson so that he could pour his ambitions directly into a more reliable vessel.

Where Rosemary had made a hash of her father's designs, her sister, Peggy, was sticking with the plan. In one week she would marry Timothy Halloran, a Fordham Law School graduate who had landed a job in the Manhattan DA's office. The wedding would be held at the best church, St. Barnabas, with a reception to follow at the best banquet hall, the Croke Park Club. The original guest list had topped five hundred, with its legions of cousins, aunts, and uncles reinforced by squads of favor seekers looking to score points with the father of the bride: Dennis Dwyer, the vice chairman of the Bronx Democratic Committee, was a man whose goodwill could deliver half the Bronx come election day, not to mention a fortune in contracts for all manner of city services.

The wedding gave her father a chance to do what he did best: turn any family milestone into a campaign rally. It was not only the public launch of his younger daughter's glorious future but also an opportunity for him to demonstrate to the voters and the power brokers that, despite rumors to the contrary, Dennis Dwyer was still a man who could not be ignored.

But a seismic shift had struck the Dwyer-Halloran nuptials when it was announced that Their Royal Majesties King George VI and Queen Elizabeth would be visiting the World's Fair on the same day as the wedding—a date that the Dwyers had chosen almost ten months earlier. The royal visit and the official functions attached to it immediately siphoned off the most prominent names on the guest list, including the mayor himself. And once La Guardia sent his regrets, lesser lights in the city's political firmament lined up to undo the *Pleased to attend* they had checked on the cream-colored response cards.

Rosemary's father had been chewing glass for months about another botched wedding, and how there must be a curse on the family, but if there were curses in this world, Rosemary knew that none of them had ever, or would ever, land on Peggy. She had always led a charmed life. All the royal visit did was peel away the bounders and the party hacks from the guest list—people that Peggy had never wanted to invite in the first place. She wouldn't be able to pick the deputy mayor out of a lineup, so why would she want him at her wedding? No,

Rosemary knew how this would all play out: Peggy and her perfect husband would recover from the not-quite-perfect wedding, and have a boy and then another and another, and with each one her father would busy himself with plans that would save the boys from ever having to think about where life would take them. *Do as Papa says and all will be right with the world.* One of them in the mayor's office, another in the governor's mansion, and the third in Washington. Peggy's job would be to shepherd them along, keep their faces clean and their hair combed straight, and make sure that her husband didn't interfere with the comet-force dreams of Dennis Dwyer.

ROSEMARY ARRIVED AT her parents' house on Friday evening for the final run-through before the wedding. She should have ignored her mother's backhanded compliment, delivered as the plainspoken truth— *Peggy is better at making choices; you're better at making decisions*— and come over early on Saturday when they could all start the day fresh. Despite what her mother had said on the telephone, she knew the details would not get sorted over dinner. Sure enough, her father was in no mood to ruin his meal with wedding talk and as soon as the plates were cleared he was into the Scotch and then it was time to put the girls to bed. When Rosemary came downstairs, her father was hazy around the eyes and her mother was brooding over her teacup. And Peggy? When she finally returned from the World's Fair, where she was performing as an Aquagal in a water-ballet revue with a cast of hundreds, she insisted that she had already made plans for one last night out with her best girlfriends—all of which led to another dustup with her mother about how Peggy wasn't taking the wedding seriously: Why was she splashing around in a pool when she should have been thinking about the seating chart?

Rosemary slept badly in her old bedroom, thanks to the narrow mattress and Kate kicking in her sleep and the baby up every two hours.

She came downstairs convinced that the day was going to be a wash, but wouldn't you know it, by midmorning they had settled on the hymns, double-checked the centerpieces with the florist, triple-checked the order with the liquor store, and compiled the checklist for the photographer (*wedding party, bride & groom, b&g w/ her parents, b&g w/ his,* etc.). Peggy had already been fitted for her wedding gown, and the dress now hung upstairs in the closet of Rosemary's old room. Even Martin had been brought into the fold. Rosemary had assumed that he would approach the wedding with equal parts complaint and dread, but when he was conscripted into fielding a band for the reception—his first stint as a bandleader—he took to the project with gusto.

It was the seating chart that bedeviled them. Every time it seemed settled, the next day's mail would scatter the artfully arranged tables like some mad game of fifty-two pickup. It was bad enough that the head count continued to drip-drip-drip as putative guests scored invitations to one of the official receptions for the royal visit, but the Dwyers also had to contend with less majestic upheavals: the Baltimore aunts had stopped speaking to the Boston aunts, the Teamsters' chief was feuding with the head of the pipefitters' union, a city councilman facing indictment had to be moved from the center of the room to a more distant orbit.

Rosemary scanned her parents' dining-room table, crowded with numbered paper circles and strips the size of fortune-cookie predictions bearing the name of each guest at the reception. It resembled a tabletop battlefield where generals maneuvered armored divisions with a croupier's rake. Peggy and her mother sat at one end, the latest guest list in front of them, while Rosemary and her father considered ways to group the unassigned second cousins, maiden aunts, party faithful, and midlevel cronies. They worked their way down the list, ticking through the names.

"What about the Hartigans?" Rosemary said.

"Oh, they canceled last week," her mother said.

This news snapped her father to attention. "Do you mean to tell me that given the choice between seeing our daughter get married and standing in a crowd with a million idiots hoping for a five-second looky-look at the crowned heads of Europe, they chose the goddamn king and queen? John Hartigan can go to hell for all I care." Her father stubbed out his cigarette in an ashtray that resembled a lead-crystal brick. What kind of message did it send if John Hartigan—who owed half of his wrecking firm's city contracts to the good graces of Dennis Dwyer—thought he could get away with skipping the nuptials? "This whole thing is looking like one big mistake."

"Daddy, please do not refer to my wedding as a mistake."

"Your wedding is not a mistake. The timing of your wedding is a mistake." He worked his jaw as if he were grinding a piece of hard candy between his molars, a habit he'd had as long as Rosemary could remember; another of those familiar signs of home, as timeless as the floral couch with its stiff plastic cover.

"I don't know why you're getting mad at me," Peggy said. "Tim and I wanted a *short* engagement. But for some reason, *you* insisted I had to be a June bride—"

"I never insisted on anything. I haven't made a single goddamn decision since this whole fiasco got started!"

"So first it's a mistake and now it's a fiasco?" Peggy flopped the list onto the table among the slips of paper, the squat black telephone, the Waterford sugar bowl, the ashtrays. "How can anyone *think* in here?" She moved closer to the window, fanning herself with one hand. The eyelet curtains hung limp from their rods.

"Sit down, young lady."

"I won't," she said. "And besides, I'm late as it is. I've got two shows today and I should have left an hour ago."

"That's all we need," her father said. "The bride swimming down the aisle in her bathing suit."

Peggy narrowed her eyes. Whatever she was about to say, Rosemary knew it would be another mess for her to clean up. "Peggy," she intervened. "We really need to finish this."

"Then plan your own wedding, why don't you?" Peggy darted through the door into the hallway. Her feet clacked rapidly up the stairs. Their father wasn't far behind. Soon enough came the clinking of the stopper in the crystal decanter, then the decanter's lip against the rim of a highball glass.

Her mother pursed her lips. Any mention of Rosemary's wedding put the same queasy expression on her face. "I'm sure she didn't mean that," she said. "It's just nerves."

Rosemary gave her own grim smile and retrieved the scattered slips of paper, one for each guest who had circled Peggy's big day on the calendar. Rosemary's wedding day hadn't had the mayor, the borough president, or a single city councilman. It hadn't had much of anything. The service was conducted in a small side chapel used for baptisms, and was followed by a somber lunch at an Italian restaurant. There hadn't been time to get a proper wedding gown made, and even with alterations, the gown her own mother had worn twenty-five years earlier would never have fit her. She settled for something off the rack in Bloomingdale's bridal shop. As the pinch-faced clerk rang up the purchase and stowed the gown in a pink box, she stared rather obviously at Rosemary's midsection. But for all the humiliations surrounding her not-so-big day—and there were plenty—what Rosemary remembered most clearly was the weather: piercing cold beneath a crystal-blue sky, the kind of cold that brought sharp tears to your eyes and sucked the breath out of you. As they exited the chapel, the wind came hard off the Hudson and absolutely ransacked them; it pushed through their coats, riffled their pockets, snatched at hats and scarves. It was the first time that Mr. and Mrs. Martin Dempsey had stepped into the light of day, and no doubt Rosemary's mother saw it as an omen, an ill wind to chill their hearts and remind them what comes of giving in to fiery passion.

But that's not how Rosemary saw it. The wind hit her and she laughed, high and joyous. It was an odd thing to do with everyone else so stoic and resigned—everyone except for her and Martin. When she laughed he took her hand and he kissed her. Not the chaste kiss they had exchanged in the chapel in front of a small knot of friends and sad-faced aunts. This was a full-on-the-mouth kiss and it thrilled her the way that blast of cold air had. Her parents heard her laugh, they saw the kiss, they did not approve—but what did she care? She was a fallen thing in their eyes, never to be made whole. Through long weeks of shame and tears, she had seen herself as they saw her, but in that moment she was free. The life that came next would be hard, but it would be hers—hers and Martin's. She had crossed over into a country from which there was no return, and if it was the custom of this land to kiss your husband in broad daylight, buffeted by a wind that burned your flesh but made you feel alive, then so be it. They would cross the border, hand in hand.

IN THE LIVING room, which Birdie insisted on calling the parlor, Dennis Dwyer poured himself a drink. He'd learned long ago that if you kept the booze in its bottle, you looked like a drunk, but if you emptied it into a fancy cut-glass decanter, you were a man who appreciated the finer things in life. He knocked the first back in one go, and as the heat spread down his throat and through his limbs, he stared into the glass as if it contained more than a space for his next drink. His second was bigger than the first and as he raised it to his lips he became aware that he wasn't alone. Kate had commandeered the sofa—which Birdie called the divan—and was lining up a row of straw-haired dolls in pinafores and crinolines. She worked methodically, her little mouth quietly shaping some nursery rhyme, or else a conversation between her and the dolls. Dwyer stared at her, waiting for her to notice that her grandfather was in the room. She worked her way down the line of dolls, patting some on the head and poking others in their glassy, unblinking eyes. When she reached the end, she turned toward Dwyer and pasted on a big toothy grin.

Dwyer sipped the second Scotch. The girl still had that frozen smile on her face.

"What are you looking at?" he said.

She shrugged, a big stagy shrug—the Our Gang movies, that's where that one belonged—and turned back to her dolls. Dwyer had another sip and eased himself into the armchair, which Birdie hadn't yet come up with a better name for. He regarded the drink in his hand. He would nurse it, make it look like his first.

Why did each daughter's wedding have to come with such a bitter taste? Years ago, he had steeled himself for the sucker's bargain you made when you threw a wedding: the women make all the decisions and you write the checks. And then on the big day you walk your daughter down the aisle and hand her over to some sweaty-palmed happyjack. You get her back for one dance at the reception, you make your toast, and you watch your wife cry her eyes out all day long and into the night. Fine, he got it. There were even moments that he regarded as his by right, those rituals that he looked forward to performing. The stately walk into the church, the toast—he had never been much for dancing—those were all things he could do, and do well. Birdie's crying was something he would have to endure, but there would be her sisters, those old biddies, to help absorb some of the tears.

He hadn't counted on the fiasco with Rosemary. Knocked up by that piss-poor Irishman, fresh off the boat and looking to stick his thing into the first American girl stupid enough to open her legs—and that girl had been his Rosemary, whom he'd raised to be better than that. Loads better. And a musician! Dwyer knew that Martin spent his time with the coloreds, so what could you expect? If Rosemary had been looking for a way to put a knife into her father's heart—to pay him back for setting her curfew too early when she was at St. Barnabas, or for telling her she had to go to Mount St. Vincent instead of one of those New

England colleges where the girls ran around with Protestants or else with each other (he'd heard those rumors)—well, mister, then she had found it. And it wasn't exactly a private disappointment, the kind where you can close your door and keep it in the family. Was there anyone in the Bronx who didn't know that Dennis Dwyer's daughter had gone to the altar with a bun in the oven? By God, that had cost some votes. He tried to explain the hurry-up wedding as two crazy kids in love— *They'll drive you nuts, what can you do?*—but once the baby was born you just had to do the math.

Dwyer did his level best to make them look respectable. He even offered that filthy mick—his son-in-law, if you could believe it—a job in the Department of Public Works. And the little nobody turned him down cold. The runt said *Thanks but no thanks* on the job, as if it were beneath him. Men, real American men who were twice as good as him, were standing in the street begging for work, and little Martin Dempsey tells Dennis goddamn Dwyer that he's going to keep blowing his horn till all hours with a bandstand full of Negroes beating out jungle music. That's going to put food on his daughter's table? And that's going to raise his grandchildren?

More than once he had thought about closing his doors to them— closing his wallet, too—and telling Rosemary that she had brought enough shame on the family to last a lifetime. But blood ran thick. Blood bound you together with all of those who shared your name and it made the things you felt—love and anger and disappointment, mostly—stick to you like glue. There were claims of blood that even he was powerless to dissolve, but he knew that there was more to it. He knew that if he cut off Rosemary and her ill-conceived family, they were sure to fall, and fall far. And he knew what it would do to him to hear stories circulating about his daughter living in some cold-water tenement in Harlem, dumped by her deadbeat husband and shacked up with some other musician—only this time, a colored one. That was sure to put him in his grave. At the very least, it could cost him an election. He deserved better than that.

Peggy's wedding was supposed to be different, a rare chance at a do-over that would erase, or at least outshine, the first Dwyer family wedding. The church and the banquet hall would be a one-two punch of flowers and ribbons, champagne and chandeliers, silk and chiffon, and a cake that was bigger than the tenement where Dennis Dwyer's parents had raised their eight children. But more than all of that, there would be a guest list that would testify to the place of the Dwyers in the hierarchy of the unruly kingdom of the Bronx. He wanted La Guardia there, sure, but more than that he wanted Edward Flynn, who had been for twenty-five years the king of the Bronx power brokers. Flynn wasn't even fifty yet, and already he had been the chairman of the county Democratic Party, the secretary of state for all of New York, a member of the Democratic National Committee, and a boon companion of FDR himself.

But they had all screwed Dwyer, and none worse than La Guardia—the same "Little Flower" who had practically begged Dennis Dwyer to throw his weight behind him in his first bid for mayor. Dwyer had taken a big risk: La Guardia was a Republican, for Christ's sake, and the mayor knew he owed Dwyer, and a dance with the bride was one way he was supposed to make good on that debt. Not because Dwyer had any interest in seeing his little Irish rose in a clinch with that runty Italian, but because having the mayor make time for the wedding would show a banquet hall full of voters, officeholders, and party operatives—not to mention everyone who saw the photo that was sure to run in the society pages of the *Bronx Home News*—that Dwyer was a man with influence. A man who could not be ignored. But La Guardia backed out, and then to rub salt in Dwyer's wounds he appointed Flynn the city's ambassador to the World's Fair, which would require Flynn to squire the royals around when he should be toasting Peggy's future.

Dwyer briefly considered changing the date of the wedding—"Damn that La Guardia," he had said. "Doesn't he know the king and queen don't vote!"—but he ran up against the limits of his own power: the church was triple-booked on every other Saturday in June, and the club didn't have an opening until the end of September. Even Dennis Dwyer couldn't push another bride and her family of registered voters out of their reserved and deposit-paid spot. Every other option smacked of the kind of pasted-together wedding that they had been forced to organize for Rosemary. No, Peggy's wedding needed to be set in stone, proof that certain events could be planned, anticipated, and held in abeyance until the appointed hour. In a stab at finding a silver lining, he also convinced himself that there was political hay to be made here: for years to come, Dwyer would tell his constituents the story of how he was invited to meet the king and queen—which indeed he had been—*But I said, No, thanks, Your Highnesses, that's the day* my *princess is getting married.*

Dwyer knew already how things would play out on his princess's wedding day. Just as he was leading her down the aisle in front of a crowd of nobodies, some Young Turk at the World's Fair with his eye on leapfrogging Dwyer would be pouring his smooth talk into Flynn's ear. He'd wonder out loud, *Where's Dwyer? Didn't he make the cut?* And if somebody said it was his daughter's wedding day—if they remembered that much—that would just start the talk all over again. *Wedding, huh? You heard about his older girl, right?*

FROM ABOVE, WITH its circles and spokes of names, the dining-room table looked like some kind of delicate machine. Each lacy white cog could be jammed by a stray touch or blown apart by the slightest breeze. Peggy had left for the fair, and her mother was supervising the cleanup of glassy-eyed dolls that Kate had dragged downstairs and scattered across the parlor. With the dining room quiet and his temper cooled, Rosemary's father fixed his eyes on the jumble of seatless guests and half-filled tables.

"Maybe you had it right all along," he said. "You saved us this headache, at least."

Rosemary sighed, closed her eyes for a moment. "I think I've got this figured out. I'm going to move the Quinlans to table three. The across-the-street Kellys move to six. And Aunt Bridget moves to four, with the Beauchamps. That just leaves the Boston aunts."

"The nuns?"

"They aren't actually nuns."

"Never been married, always in black—might as well be nuns."

Rosemary smiled in spite of herself. She wanted her father to know that he had crossed the line, yelling and cursing. She didn't want Kate to hear that kind of language from her grandfather. A smile was a reward he didn't deserve.

"Ah, Rosie. This could have been yours."

Her smile collapsed. "Not now, Dad."

"I'm not just talking about the fancy wedding. You could take this Halloran kid and turn him into a congressman, maybe even governor."

"What happened to mayor?"

He winced and stuck out his tongue. "He doesn't have the balls to be mayor. Even you couldn't do that for him."

"I'm sure Peggy will get him where he needs to go."

"Congressman," he said. "That's still on the board. Peggy knows enough to get him there. Still—it should have been you."

"I don't want to marry Timmy Halloran. I picked Martin—"

"You didn't pick—"

"—because I love him. You need to know that. I married Martin because I love him."

"Rosie, Rosie, Rosie." His face broke into a toothy, yellowed smirk. "Don't pull that crap on me. You're better than that. At least, I thought you were."

BIRDIE DWYER HAD said good-bye to Rosemary and given each of the girls a kiss. She was already worried about the older one: too much of her mother in her and look where that had led. Too much time around men, especially men like her father—that had been Rosemary's problem. A man could tell himself that life was one big pleasure palace built just for him, but women were supposed to know better. Rosemary thought like a man, she had mannish habits, mannish appetites. It wasn't something a mother was supposed to think about her own daughter but there it was.

Peggy could be brash and you wouldn't call her ladylike, but she knew how to attract the right kind of attention. Men liked her and she liked men, but she also knew that they were good for only so much. Peggy, like her mother, knew you couldn't trust them, couldn't be friends with them. It wasn't their fault and it certainly wasn't yours; it just was. But Rosemary—well, sometimes Rosemary seemed too eager to be one of the boys. She knew too much about baseball and politics, and not just the sorts of things that appeared on the front page of the paper. Rosemary knew who ran the Sanitation Department, and whom he had supported for county sheriff, and who his wife was, and why the wife couldn't possibly sit next to Aunt Pauline at the wedding.

Dennis had gotten his hooks into her from the start, dragging her in front of his cronies from the time she was four to recite the starting lineup of the Yankees or the past ten mayors of New York. These memory games had become his favorite party trick. Dennis imagined that her cutie-pie act smoothed his own rough edges in the minds of voters and potential patrons, but Birdie knew it never worked that way. Rosemary had never been cute. It was unnerving, really, having a child rattle off the names of everyone on the city council when she should have been dressing up dolls, hopscotching on the sidewalk, and hiding from her blustery father.

And maybe college had been a mistake. Birdie thought it would keep her busy with something other than her father's latest campaign. She would meet other girls who would bend her interests in more realistic directions: dances, marriage prospects, the business of running a family. But the only thing those years at Mount St. Vincent's did was make Rosemary restless—she complained about the nuns, about the other girls, about the Fordham and Manhattan boys who circled the campus like sharks—and then at the graduation dance she fell for that Martin of hers.

Maybe that had been for the best. It wasn't like suitors were lining up at the door. Boys didn't know what to make of her. She was either their pal or a way to get closer to Peggy. Rosemary was too quick, too sharp, when she talked to boys her own age. She thought she was having fun with them but men bruise easily; Birdie had tried to teach her that. Couldn't she see it in her father? He let on as if he liked roughhousing, but only as long as he was the one landing the punches. He was like bone china: hard to the touch, but brittle. Fragile, even, if you didn't handle it properly. But Rosemary, for all her book smarts, never really understood men. Not the way a woman is supposed to.

Maybe if she and Dennis had had a boy. That might have made Rosemary realize she wasn't her father's son and that there was no point in pretending. It's not like they hadn't tried—God, how they'd tried. She lost one before Rosemary, then two more between Rosemary and Peggy, then the last one when Peggy was barely nine months. That time almost did her in, and afterward Dr. Reimer said that they should be done—that they were lucky to have the two girls and it was best to count your blessings and not your losses. She never asked if the doctor did something to put a stop to it or if her body called it quits. There had been so much blood that last time, so much more than any of the other times. And who knows, they could have all been girls anyway, and then look where they'd be: four more Rosemarys or a houseful of Peggys. That wouldn't have made life with Dennis any easier, to say the least, and what would it have done for her? It was best not to think about what might have been. *If it's to be, it'll be.* That's what her mother had taught her. And so Birdie felt responsible for Rosemary, but only so much.

THE PLAZA HOTEL

NEW ROOM, SAME OLD man: Michael's jailer or doctor. The angel or the devil. Michael still hadn't cracked that mystery. It had been a few days since he'd first seen the man on the boat, but they had docked and disembarked and there had been a ride in a car. They were in a city—if he was forced to guess, he'd say New York, but there was another mystery for you. What were they doing in New York?

The old man wasn't offering any answers. He stared at Michael and tented his fingers on the ridge of his heron's-beak nose, as if whispering secrets to himself. They were in a stalemate—the old man on a white-and-gold sofa engorged with stuffing and Michael adrift on a great raft of a bed, where he'd been coming in and out of wakefulness all morning. Each time he woke he peered in the old man's direction and there he was, with a great thatch of white hair sweeping up and away from his angular face. As soft and cloudlike as his hair was, his spectacles seemed cut from iron. They framed those agate eyes, which danced from boredom to bemusement to consternation. If he didn't know better, Michael might think that he was just an old man contemplating a snooze or a snootful of brandy.

Since their earlier encounter, when the old man had opened his mouth and emitted a sound like hell's own bells, Michael had not attempted to engage him in conversation. The man ignored him and he ignored the man. He hadn't heard the Noise, not in its full force, since the man had last opened his horrid mouth, but he was still plagued from time to time by hammer-to-the-temples headaches and edge-of-the-cliff vertigo that made it impossible for him to fix his attention on any one thing, including the passage of time, for very long.

Michael's mind had always been prone to wander—a cause for rebuke from his priestly schoolmasters. His mental rambles were slow and leisurely; he could spend an afternoon pondering the way the light played on the surface of a stream, or devising a more scripturally illuminating homily about the woman who meets Our Lord on the road to Emmaus, or imagining a host of scenarios in which he and Eileen Casey were caught in a rainstorm and forced to take refuge in the Cooneys' barn. He could work through all the possible directions that such an episode could lead, even though thoughts of Eileen were constant reminders of the weakness of the flesh and made up a sizable percentage of his weekly confessions. Often it was only the cane across the back of his neck that called a stop to such voracious flights of fancy.

But he could no longer sustain such efforts. His mind had become like a hummingbird that bobbed from this bloom to that; he sipped but never drank too deeply. It was another by-product of whatever had befallen him, one that he hoped would fade in the days or weeks or months ahead. But this ongoing visitation had him worried that rather than ascending into better health he was spiraling into the abyss.

He marked time this way: Before the Noise and After the Noise. The line between the two epochs of his life was a ragged gash in his memory. The Noise had obliterated his sense of time on either side of the event. On the border of the Before side, he was in a church, he remembered that much, with his brother Francis (he had awoken one morning on board the ship with a full and sudden knowledge that the Ginger-Haired Man was his brother). At the back of the church stood a man in dark blue serge—a uniform, it seemed—and throughout the Mass, Francis would look over his shoulder at the man, who never once sat or knelt. Incense rose from the altar. There was a boy in a cassock and surplice, and an old priest with a purple stole. The After period began in fragments: Francis's face streaked in black; the ceiling of an automobile with the blue sky edging through the windows; the smell of brackish harbor water momentarily swept aside by a gust of sharp, sweet salt air. These events raced by in a whoosh that filled his ears, like the tail end of a comet that had smashed his life in two. He wasn't so much deaf as deafened, as if he were subjected to the endless hollow moan of a conch shell the size of a castle. He had tried to speak but could not tell what sounds, if any, came out of him. He tried to read but the letters refused to make sense. He could see them just fine, but felt like he was stuck in the moment right before the symbols could be deciphered, each word forever on the tip of his tongue. Writing posed a similar hurdle. As he moved the pen, the ink flowed onto the page and never stopped moving. It was animated, restless, and he hadn't yet found a way to fix the letters—letters he could not read—in place.

Michael was snapped from his reverie by a sound. The old man cleared his throat and before Michael could react—the Noise was coming, he was sure of it—the old man spoke. "Are you going to stay in bed all day?" The man's voice was scratchy, as if from disuse. He cleared his throat again.

"Are you going to scream at me?" Michael said.

"Do you want me to?"

"No. But that's what you do."

"I hardly think so."

"But—on the boat."

"I was speaking then, just as I am now. Perhaps you weren't ready to hear me."

Michael considered this. He rapped his knuckles against the headboard. No sound. "So why are you the only one I can hear?"

"I don't know," the old man said. "But you are apparently the only one who is aware of my presence. Here and on the ship, I pass unseen and unheard."

Michael sat up fully in the bed. Someone had dressed him in paja-mas. He didn't remember dressing himself before bed, and now that he thought about it, he didn't remember arriving at this new place. There was the boat, then the car, the city streets, the light glancing off the windows on the tall buildings, the lurching stop-and-start of the car in traffic—more cars than Michael had ever seen—and then here he was.

"May I ask a question?" Michael said.

The old man raised his eyebrows. He was open to questions.

"Are you a ghost?"

The old man looked startled, as if the thought had never occurred to him. He held up his hands, examining his palms and the liver-spotted skin that lay creased along his knuckles. He stood and crossed the room to where the morning sun backlit the drapes. Through a gap where the drapes parted was visible a broad swath of green, the tops of trees, and an expanse of lawn that stretched into the distance. The old man gazed out the window for a moment before turning to face Michael. "I'm not comfortable with that term," he said. "But I think that's the simplest answer."

Something about the way sunlight hit the man's face connected the pieces in Michael's jigsaw memory. He had seen this man before—not in person, but somewhere. It had been a photograph in a news-paper. A large picture, black-bordered and surrounded by type.

"Hold on, now," Michael said. "Are you Mr. Yeats, the poet?" Wil-liam Butler Yeats—Nobel laureate, spiritualist, and one-term senator of the Irish Free State—had died in France in January. His picture had been in all of the papers.

The old man seemed to consider this question with great serious-ness. He looked out the window at the riot of green and the brick-and-stone towers that picketed each side of the park. "I was," he said as if astonished by this news. "And now I am again. Or perhaps I have always been—it's a difficult question."

"One more," Michael said. "If you don't mind."

Yeats shrugged.

"What are you doing here?"

"That," Yeats said, "is a question I cannot answer."

FRANCIS KEPT PROMISING Martin a big surprise, but already, every step on the way was like something out of a dream: His brother shows up out of nowhere and tells him that his father is dead, and suddenly they are in a taxi bound for the Plaza Hotel, all while Martin in his exhaustion was teetering between drunkenness and incipient hangover. With each city block, the soft hands of gin and vermouth loosened their tender hold on his head and surrendered him into the rough grip of a vindictive headache.

A white-gloved hand, a sleeve swaddled in gold braid—this is what Martin saw when they came to a halt under the Plaza's dark blue awning. He stepped out onto the sidewalk and peered up at the stairs leading to the front doors, each flanked by a man in the hotel's gold-and-blue livery. He wished he'd had a few more hours of sleep, wished he'd shaved before they left the Bronx, because he must look like a man who'd been through the wringer. But here at least he could be grateful for the quality of his clothes; these were not doors that a man entered without a high gloss on his shoes and a knife-edged pocket square. He gave his hat a rakish tilt, hoping to make himself appear less like riffraff and more like some dissolute playboy returning to his bed after a night in one of the city's private casinos.

As Martin prepared himself for this masquerade, Francis gave him a shove. "Step to it," he said. "And for Christ's sake, mind your manners. They all think I'm a feckin' peer." All that time in jail and Francis still said *feckin'*—a child's curse, the thing you said when you feared your granny might be in earshot.

Francis glided through the front doors without a glance at either of the doormen. Martin was pulled along in his brother's wake, his fingers at the brim of his hat in a quick show of thanks.

The lobby was a blur of mosaic tile and gold-veined marble columns. They stopped briefly at the bronze-backed front desk, where in a bristling Scottish burr Francis requested, and was handed, the key to his room. As the doors to the elevator spread wide, Martin's eyes darted to its operator, then to Francis. The operator's uniform matched the doormen's—gold braid, brass buttons, epaulets—but his hat wasn't the mock sea captain's topper that the outside men wore. The elevator man's was a smaller affair, like one belonging to a bellhop in a movie, or an organ-grinder's monkey. *Poor sot,* Martin thought.

"Good morning, gentlemen," the operator said as the doors closed.

"Seventh floor, my good man." Francis fixed his eyes on his reflection in the polished surface of the interior door.

The Scottish accent, the "my good man"—it was too much for Martin. "Christ, Franny. What's this all about?"

Francis raised one eyebrow and with a slight upward tic of his chin indicated the elevator operator. "All in due time," he said, pronounced it as "Aul en doo taim."

"What you're up to? New York. The Plaza. This can't be real."

Francis gave the operator a conspiratorial wink. "It's quite simple," he said. "His Lordship decided you were having too much fun in the Colonies. Hard liquor. Loose women. Fast horses—but not quite fast enough, eh, my boy?" He winked again at the operator, playing to his audience of one, before returning his attention to Martin. "As the hunting season had come to a close, I was dispatched to collect you and return you to the bosom of your family. And not a moment too soon, by the looks of you." Francis reached for the lapel of Martin's jacket, rubbed the cloth between his fingers, and smirked. "Yes," he said, "a sea journey is just the thing to restore a man whose luck and good health have deserted him—don't you agree, my good man?" he asked the operator.

The operator looked startled. "Well, sir, I'm not much for seafaring—"

"Yes, quite," Francis said. "My sentiments exactly."

"Is that your big surprise?" Martin said. "That you've escaped from the madhouse?"

"Fitzwilliam, please," Francis said, "you know what the doctors have said about losing your temper."

The operator announced their arrival and drew open the doors. Francis dug into his pocket and withdrew a coin, which he placed with some ceremony into the smaller man's palm. "I trust I can be assured of your discretion concerning my brother's condition," he said. "I wouldn't want loose talk to jeopardize his...prospects."

"Of course, sir," the elevator man said. "No loose talk, sir."

"Splendid." Francis took Martin by the arm and escorted him into the hallway. He waited for the doors to close, for the hum of the motor at the top of the shaft, before addressing his brother. "Look here," he said. "If you're not going to play along in front of the hired help, then you can at least keep your gob shut."

MARTIN HAD SEEN plenty of hotels. During his early days in America, he had barnstormed with territory bands, playing grange halls, mountain resorts, beachside dance halls, and country clubs all across New England, the Catskills, the Poconos, and the Jersey Shore. The sleeping arrangements were like barracks—four men to a room, often two men to a bed. The musicians crashed from sheer exhaustion after a day on the road and a night of playing sweet, hot, and everything in between for a pack of sweating small-town jitterbugs. But even those crummy rooms were a treat: no bandleader would spring for a hotel unless they were booked for a two- or three-night stand. Mostly they played one-nighters, and that meant they finished their set, struck the bandstand, stowed the instruments, and got back on the bus for the long ride to the next town. Martin slept sitting up, head to the window, or else leaned forward with his head pressed to the back of the seat in front of him. He was stiff and sore all the time, and the only remedy for the ache of the long nights and the cramped quarters and the lousy road food was the short spell onstage giving the locals more than they could handle, sending them home more wiped out than the band.

Now Martin played nightly in the lounge of the Kensington Hotel, just a few blocks south and west of the Plaza. The Kensington was quality, but it wasn't the Plaza. The walls here were as pale as the sand on a secret beach. The hallway carpets, pretzel-patterned in red and gold, gave a spring to a man's step. The world outside might still be hanging on by its fingernails but inside the Plaza all was safe and serene, and that was a luxury.

Francis fit the key into the lock and paused. "Ready for your surprise?" he said.

"Just open it up."

He turned the knob and stepped through, waving one arm like the ringmaster in a circus. Martin followed the sweep of his hand and there on the sofa was his brother Michael. He knew from Michael's letters that he was no longer a boy—boys didn't fill their typewritten correspondence with references to the Seven Sorrowful Mysteries— but this older version of Michael looked like he hadn't grown so much as been stretched into a taller, ganglier version of the boy Martin had known. Michael's attention was focused on a gaudy gold-and-white chair in one corner of the room. He seemed to be rehearsing a part in a play, running through a silent pantomime of hand gestures and cocked-head glances. Martin called out his brother's name, but Michael ignored him. Martin repeated himself, louder this time, and clapped his hands together. "Michael!" he said. "Is it really you?"

Michael's gaze remained fixed on the empty chair.

"You didn't think I'd come all this way and leave him rotting in that poxy monastery?" Francis said.

"Michael," Martin said again, and then turned to Francis. "What's wrong with him?"

"He can't hear a thing," Francis said. "Deaf as a post, and all because —"

Michael suddenly wheeled around and, seeing Martin, shook himself like a man coming out of a dream. A look of confusion gave way to a smile that bloomed across his face. He leaped off the sofa and pulled his brother close.

After a moment's hesitation, Martin returned the embrace. "It's good to see you," he said, then stepped out of the hug and took Michael's face in his hands. He leveled his gaze at his brother and repeated, slowly: "It is so good to see you."

Michael nodded, his eyes shining with tears, and slapped Martin on the back.

"Franny, what the hell?"

"I told you I'd explain it all in due time."

"Will you stop it with the due time — what in hell happened to Michael?"

Francis crossed the room. On a silver tray, a decanter and an ice bucket flanked a huddle of highball glasses. "Care for a drink?" he said.

"It's ten in the morning," Martin said.

"So that's a no?" Francis lifted the lid on the ice bucket. "Can you believe it? No ice. Plaza Hotel, my arse." He filled one of the glasses halfway and settled himself on the sofa. Like the other furniture in the room, it was upholstered in white and trimmed in gold. The cushions were so thickly stuffed that Francis barely dented the surface. He stretched one arm along the back of the sofa, a pose that suggested confidence, even nonchalance. "Don't hesitate to pour yourself a small one if you feel the need. And I'll apologize in advance for the quality of the liquor. I'd have asked for Powers, but it would have blown my cover, so I told them to bring Scotch."

"Franny," Martin said, "for Christ's sake—"

Francis held up one hand. "What happened was this."

IT STARTED WHEN a note from the parish priest in Ballyrath reached Mountjoy informing the prison's governor that Francis Dempsey Sr. had died. Loads of men had been denied furlough for a mother's burial or a daughter's wedding, but unbeknownst to Francis, the governor made arrangements for him to attend the funeral. When it was settled, he called Francis to his office, a sternly whitewashed room around which were hung lavish still lifes, all painted by the governor's wife. Francis did not know why he had been summoned, and as he watched the overhead light play off the older man's bald dome, he considered who might have informed on him, and for what real or imagined offense. After a final jagged signature, the governor placed his pen on the blotter and turned his attention to Francis.

"Inmate," he said. "I regret to inform you that your father has died. Mountjoy Prison is sorry for your loss."

"My father? But how—"

"No talking, inmate," said the warder at his side.

"Are you mad?" Francis was addressing both of them: the governor with this story about his father; the warder for saying he couldn't speak at a moment like this.

The warder reached for the short truncheon he carried on his belt, but the governor waved him off. "You have been approved for a furlough," he said, "to attend your father's Mass of Christian burial."

Francis struggled with the basic facts that had been presented. His father? Dead? But how, and when? The governor, who was not in the habit of offering condolences, recited the details not of his father's demise, but of the furlough itself. They were to depart in the morning at half six and were expected to return that same night. Francis would be permitted to wear the clothes held for him in the storeroom, which were the clothes he had worn when he was processed into Mountjoy, but he would be required to have his hands shackled during the duration of his time outside the prison walls. If he made any attempt to escape or in any way delay his return, he would face the full force of disciplinary action: solitary confinement, a month on the paltry No. 1 Diet, and additional time added to his sentence.

At the end of this recitation, the governor turned toward Francis. "Understand one thing, inmate: This isn't for you. It's for your father. You're a disgrace to his good name."

This was the last in a chain of half-sensical comments directed at Francis about his father during the time he spent in Mountjoy. Most of the old-timers had given him a wide berth, muttering about *Dempsey* this and *Dempsey* that. Francis had assumed there was something about himself that rubbed the codgers the wrong way. More than once, he would put the question to a man: *What problem have you got with me?* Most would cut their eyes and shuffle off; others would tell him, *I'm not afraid of you, so you know.* It was the raving of lunatics, men who had spent too much of their lives staring at prison walls. Their only fun was in taking the piss out of the younger ones.

Francis arrived for the funeral in the back of a car from the Mountjoy motor pool driven by a warder who had complained bitterly through the hours it took to ply the winding country roads connecting Dublin to Ballyrath. The warder was a city boy, and every glimpse of cottage or pasture sent him into fits of boredom, rage, and derision. The pastor wouldn't allow a shackled man to serve as pallbearer, and after much hectoring (by the pastor) and grumbling (by the warder) and chafing of wrists against iron (by Francis), the handcuffs were removed. Francis took his place at the casket, where he was given a rough embrace by Michael, who had been granted a day's leave from the seminary. It was the first time the brothers had seen each other in the flesh in almost two years. Michael's eyes were red-rimmed and swollen, but he gave his brother a wan smile. Michael looked so small, as if he were melting from the pain of losing his da. Francis stretched out his arm and wrapped it around his brother's shoulder, pulling him close, something he couldn't have done with handcuffs on. He had spent a year and a half locked up in a cage made of stone and steel, and when he could finally stretch his arms it was only because his father had died. He couldn't make sense of that. His father couldn't be dead, because as long as he had known him, his father had always been alive. In that grim logic of grief, he caught himself wondering what his father was going to do when he found himself in that coffin. There would be hell to pay, that was for sure.

But meanwhile here Francis was, out of jail and in his own clothes, back in Ballyrath, his father dead, and Michael dressed in the gown of a priest. He couldn't sort out what was real from what was a dream. His only guide was the raw, hollow ache in his chest. The pain would tell him what to believe.

Michael had been driven to the funeral by Brother Zozimus, whose principal task was to read the mail of the seminarians in pursuit of any impure thoughts, words, or deeds. He took up a place at the back of the church, kneeling on the stone floor throughout the Mass, while the Mountjoy warder lingered just inside the church's arched double doors, smoking his way through a pack of Silk Cuts. The brothers sat side by side in the first pew.

At the end of the Mass, the pastor trod down the aisle and the mourners followed in his incensed wake. On the front steps, a crowd gathered, many of them locals who had attended the funeral out of obligation to the man who had educated their children. Others had come out of simple peckishness for any break with the routine of a Tuesday in May. Among the mourners were a fair number of strangers, hard-looking men who had sat apart from each other, scattered around the church as if magnetized against contact. The warder watched the sluggish procession and grew gradually more agitated as neither of the Dempseys passed through the low-slung arch. One of the strangers, a man with red-blasted cheeks beneath a flat black cap, told him the boys were lighting a candle in their father's memory before an image of the Sacred Heart. Another said the priest had asked Michael to retrieve another censer from a cabinet in the sacristy. The crowd milling about the doors seemed in no hurry to transport the coffin to its final resting place. The minutes ticked by, punctuated by the tolling of the bell overhead. The only two who seemed impatient for the reappearance of the Dempseys were the warder and a young woman dressed all in black. Both craned their necks to see over the heads of the throng and into the shadowy vault of the church.

Inside, a group of the hard-looking strangers drifted to the front of the church and formed a knot around the Dempsey brothers. The condolences were brusque—"I'm sorry for your loss," each said in turn— but the men stared at the boys with an intensity that was hard to ignore, scanning the brothers as if seeking to square the cast of their eyes or the shape of their noses with memories of their father's own face.

One of the men leaned in to Francis and in a raspy stage whisper said, "Sure you're not going back to that jail, are you?"

Francis thought the man was trying to lighten the mood with a joke. "Have you got a better offer?"

The other men laughed grimly, but no sooner had Francis spoken than a plan began to take shape.

"Say good-bye to your brother and go," the man said. "We'll slow down that screw."

"Go how?" Francis said.

"The Brother's keys are in his car," Michael said. "But you're not going without me."

"Good man!" one of the strangers spat.

"Your father's sons!" another said.

The first man pushed a folded paper into Francis's hands. "I drew this up during that frightful eulogy. It'll take you to a safe house where you can sort out your next move."

"Where are you sending him?"

"Not the place in Ardagh? It's been donkey's years since anyone—"

"No, no—"

"Not Westmeath? That was a shithole twenty years ago. Can't imagine what it's like—"

"Will you cut it?" the first man said. He stabbed the paper with a stubby finger. "Follow the map." A network of pencil lines, boxes, arrows. "That's Limerick, that's Glenagoul, and that line's the road to Cork. Take the turn for Castletownroche, and when you're halfway there, look for the broken arch, the white barn, the red door."

"A red door? He'll never—"

"Take it and go!" He pushed the map against Francis's chest, then burrowed in his pocket for a handful of coins and a few banknotes. "Come on, lads," he said. "For the orphans' fund."

The eyes of the men were aglow. They were on a mission—an escape, a rescue operation, call it what you will. It was a return to younger days when they had all been soldiers and believed that a better, brighter world was one well-placed shot away.

"WHO WERE THESE men?" Martin said. He was hunched forward on the sofa, following every word.

"That's just it," Francis said. "Had to be friends of Da from the Cork days."

"Da was never the having-friends type."

"Well, there were a lot of them—tough-looking yokes, too."

"They must have been from the university. Old professors, come to bury one of their own."

"They didn't look like teachers." Francis spun the Scotch in his glass, contemplating its movement. "I have to ask, did you ever wonder if Da was involved in any IRA business?"

"Da hated politics. And politicians even more."

"I'm not talking about politics. I mean fighting. Things got awfully hot in Cork."

"Mam was mad about speeches and rallies, but Da? He was no soldier."

"You're sure of that? You'd remember best."

"Not a chance," Martin said.

"Wait till you hear the rest."

FRANCIS AND MICHAEL were bent double, picking their way through the headstones behind the church and making for the line of cars along the road. Both saw the mound of fresh dirt, the newly cut sides of the hole where the coffin would soon be lowered. "I'm not dropping you off at the seminary, so you know."

"I'm done with all that," Michael said. "Didn't you get my letters?"

They found the seminary's automobile, a black Vauxhall Cadet polished every weekend as part of the students' regular contribution to the upkeep of St. Columbanus. Francis ducked into the driver's seat and quietly pulled the door shut. Michael lingered outside, peering over the roof at the throng outside the church doors.

"Come on," Francis said. "Now or never, Michael."

Michael spotted Eileen on the fringe of the crowd, and as soon as he saw her, she turned and looked him full in the face, as if she'd heard him calling her name from someplace deep within. It had always been that way—from the time they were tykes right up until the moment she told him that there was no hope for them, that it was settled, that she would marry that old codger Doonan. But now his eyes were on hers, just like in the days before, and her mouth formed a single word: *Go!* For his sake and for hers. *Go!*

Francis echoed the same word—*Let's go!*—and then Michael was in the car and the car was moving and they were off.

In the commotion that followed it was discovered that Francis or

Michael or some co-conspirator had nicked the keys from the ward-er's automobile as well. He tried to commandeer one of the other cars to begin pursuit, but none of the locals had driven to the church—Ballyrath was no bigger than a postage stamp, and few people owned cars—and after the out-of-town mourners hustled to their cars and fidgeted with their coats and trousers, they reported that their keys, too, had been stolen. After an hour's delay, the warder finally waylaid a truck used for the delivery of peat and set off in pursuit. The head start alone was sizable enough but the Dempsey brothers also had the advantage of having grown up among the lanes and hedgerows around Ballyrath, and they drove like madmen drunk on the prospect of the freedom that lay ahead.

"I believe we're both outlaws now," Michael said.

On the run in the Vauxhall, they were no longer Francis and Michael Dempsey, they were Frank and Jesse James. And they weren't bumping over a rutted backcountry road in the middle of Ireland, they were racing across the high plains outside of Carson City or Dodge or Tombstone—some frontier town whose name Francis had dredged up from the cowboy novels that formed the bulk of the prison library.

"Da'd murder you for reading that tripe," Michael said.

"I heard Yeats himself loved cowboy stories, so what's the harm?"

"Yeats is dead."

"Well," Francis said, "so is Da."

Though they wanted to imagine that some lean-boned sheriff with a drooping mustache was gathering a posse to hunt them, they knew that they had only the massed forces of the Roman Catholic Church and the newly christened Republic of Ireland at their backs. For the first time in their lives, the brothers gave thanks that Ballyrath was so far off the map of twentieth-century progress that there wasn't a telephone within miles, but they knew that eventually word would reach the outside world that an escaped convict and a seminarian–cum–car thief were on the loose. Until then, they had to achieve some distance from the scene of their escape—a difficult proposition on roads unbroken by alternate routes and hemmed in by bristling hedges, where they could be stopped cold by a single donkey cart turned sideways in their path.

Once the flush of excitement started to wane, they were confronted with the reality of being on the run and mostly penniless on an island that required money and legal papers to depart. In search of a less conspicuous mode of transport, they stopped east of Athenry to trade the Vauxhall to a pair of traveler folk for a dilapidated Morris Minor. "Smells like priests," one of the men said, and Francis had to agree with him. The Vauxhall had the stink of hair tonic and candlewax on it. Though they were fleeced in the deal, the brothers fired up the engine and, lured by the comforts of the words *safe house,* followed the map south.

IT DIDN'T LOOK like much upon their arrival, but maybe that was the point. It was an out-of-the-way house down a long lane off a back road—the kind of place that no one would simply stumble across. Had they known where they were going, or had their map been more than an old man's half-remembered cartography rendered with a nubby pencil on a pension-check envelope, they could have made the drive from Ballyrath to the house in six hours. But the map, the swap with the travelers, the detours when they feared driving too close to towns or police barracks—all of it added up, and by the time they steered the Morris Minor, a desperate machine with a fly-pocked windscreen, up the dirt track that led to the house, it was long past midnight. The only light came from the half-moon and the car's headlamps, which Francis aimed at the front door and left on as they exited the car.

Sure enough, this was it, red door and all. A long stone cottage topped by a mangy thatched roof. The door itself was stout, ribbed with iron bands, and absolutely immovable.

"Would've been nice of him to mention that," Francis said. "Maybe take a moment from his lousy mapmaking to jot down a note about where to find the key?"

The windows seemed equally impregnable. Thick shutters latched from the inside betrayed no hint of light in the cottage. All of this contributed to the sense of this safe house being extremely safe, snug, and secure—provided you could ever get in. Michael suggested a search of the Morris Minor for a jack or a pry bar, anything they could use to jimmy one of the shutters or, if necessary, smash a window. Francis had to admit that his lock-picking abilities weren't up to this door. It was a skill he had tried to acquire at Mountjoy, but given that anyone caught practicing on the cell doors faced a week in solitary confinement, his education had been more theoretical than applied.

Taken together, the Dempsey brothers were an unlikely pair of housebreakers. Francis wore the suit he had been sentenced in—a suit that had sat, poorly folded, in the jail's storehouse since the first day of his incarceration. Gangster-inspired, with broad lapels, chalk stripes, and a double breast, it was not a suit made to convey the innocence of its wearer. Francis thought the outfit made him look dashing; the judge thought it made him look guilty. Francis's companion in this halfhearted assault on the locked door, meanwhile, was dressed in a narrow, inky-black cassock studded with buttons from toe to notched collar.

Francis's clumsy efforts with the door were interrupted by a voice from the darkness: "What do you want here?"

Both brothers' shadows, outlined by the car's headlamps, jumped like puppets in a children's theater. "Who's there?" Francis said. "Show yourself."

"Move on," the man's voice said. "You've no business here."

"We were sent," Michael said. "Broken arch, red door. We have a map."

"Don't show him that," Francis said. "He's not supposed to be here, either."

"Give the map to me." The man emerged from the darkness behind the house, his hand extended.

"We're to stay," Michael said. "Collect our bearings."

"No one's staying here."

"But you are."

"Well, I'm the only one."

With a scrape of wood against the stone threshold, the massive front door opened wide enough for a man's head to poke through the gap. "Who's out there?" he said, squinting into the headlamps.

"And that one," Michael said. "That's two of you."

"It's my place," the first man said.

"Why should we believe you?" Michael said. "You lied about being alone."

There were in fact four men at the house, each thrown into a state of great agitation by the arrival of strangers. Three of the men had spent a month ensconced at the Factory, as the IRA called its clandestine bomb-making facility, developing munitions for the Sabotage Campaign, the IRA's latest plan to bring Britain to its knees. Until today, they had received only a single visitor, a quartermaster from the Army Council who had relayed instructions to guide their work and a timetable for completing their assignment. Although he would not admit it, the quartermaster had also come to see whether or not the three had blown themselves to bits. But now, in the past twenty-four hours, the Factory had become a hive of activity. Early in the morning a car had arrived, disgorging two rough-looking fellows and a man called Finnegan who ran this entire section of the country for the IRA. One of the bruisers stayed behind, keeping close watch on a stoutly made strongbox, while Finnegan and the other drove to Cork for meetings with other higher-ups.

Francis and Michael knew none of this. As they stood outside in the spring night, chilled and tired, they knew only that their safe house—this hastily packaged gift from the men at their father's funeral—would not be a place where they could quietly sort out their next move.

"So the first one," Francis said to Martin, "starts going on about us bringing the *gardai* right to their doorstep, how we're going to get them all hanged—like I'm some kind of eejit who doesn't know how to hide my tracks. Meanwhile, they've got the house packed with gelignite and paxo and all manner of nasties. They're raising a ruckus about me and Michael and telling me to get the goddamn car away from the house and so I get back in to move it and right in the middle of all this commotion one of the bombs goes off."

"That's what happened to Michael?"

"Not just to Michael. All that was left was a pile of stones—and Michael in the middle of the wreckage."

"You brought our brother to a bomb factory?"

"We didn't know it was a bomb factory. It was supposed to be a safe house."

Martin put his hands over his face. He was exhausted, but there were questions he needed to ask. "And the IRA men? What happened to them?"

"I tried to see if there was anything to be done, but—" Francis shrugged. "And it was all I could do to find Michael. Limp as a rag, he was. I swear I thought he was dead. But I lifted him up and he was breathing, barely. And then next to him I see a strongbox lying on its side in the stones and the burning thatch. The lid was smashed to pieces and it was packed full of cash—British pounds, American dollars, even some German notes. I figured either I take the money or let the first man on the scene help himself to it."

"So the bomb just—exploded," Martin said. "And you had nothing to do with that?"

"I had words with them, but nothing more. And if they were such lousy bomb makers that a few choice words could set off the whole works, I don't think I can be blamed for that."

"I'm just trying to get this straight. You left a houseful of men dead, and you made off with their money?"

"I didn't kill them, Martin. Their own bomb did that. And would it have been better if I let the police find the money?" Francis rubbed his chin. He needed a shave. "To hell with them—they almost killed Michael. I'm looking at the money as compensation. And if the money was for this cock-and-bull bombing scheme, the real question should be how many lives I've saved by depriving them of their funds."

"Jesus, Francis, they're going to come after you. Every one of them. The police, the IRA, the FBI. Take your pick. An escaped convict whose bankroll oh-by-the-way is courtesy of the IRA? God only knows how you even got into the country."

"Money opens a lot of doors," Francis said. "And to keep them open, I've been telling folks I'm some kind of aristocrat. Earl of Glamis, Thane of Cawdor. It's brilliant."

"Earl of—why didn't you just tell them that you were the king of England?"

"Too easy to figure that one out. His picture is everywhere."

Martin stared at his brother, dumbfounded.

"Come on, Martin. Glamis? Cawdor? I cadged it all from *Macbeth*. It's not real."

"Those *are* real places, you idiot. *Macbeth* is practically a history play."

"How can it be real when it has a ghost in it?" Francis stood, uncertain at first where to go in this vast room. Of course: the bar cart. He dribbled another measure of the Plaza's Scotch into his glass. "I may be an eejit, as you say, but even I know that there's a world of difference between a history and a tragedy. Tragedies are make-believe, and all the interesting ones die in the end. In a history play, the clever ones survive."

Martin was ready to go another round with Francis—what was his plan in America? What were they going to do about Michael?—but then he noticed Michael had drifted toward a far corner of the room and was staring intently at an armchair in front of one of the windows. As Michael moved closer to it, he cocked his head from side to side and moved his lips, as if whispering to himself. "Hold on," Martin said. "What's he doing?"

"HAVE THEY ALWAYS been like this?" Yeats said.

"So I've heard. I was only seven when Martin left for America."

Yeats shook his head as if in disbelief that this was what the afterlife offered: a seminary dropout and his two bickering brothers. It wasn't the first time Michael had seen that look. The more he told Yeats of what he could remember of his own personal history—his mother had died when he was an infant, his schoolmaster father had raised him and his brothers in the country, he had suffered some unknown misfortune—the more dour and distracted Yeats became, as if perpetually asking himself, *Is this really it? This is what comes next?*

Yeats removed his spectacles and buffed the lenses with his handkerchief. He did a thorough job of it, giving more time to the effort than seemed necessary.

"Can I ask a question?" Michael said.

Yeats glanced up from his task and squinted at Michael. His face had the naked, mole-like look common to people who have removed their eyeglasses.

"Seeing as how you're dead, sir, and composed, I would assume, of some sort of spirit matter, do you really need those glasses?"

Yeats turned the frames over in his hands, studying the arms, the hinges, the lenses. He placed them with some ceremonial grandeur—slowly, meticulously—on the bridge of his nose and secured them behind his ears.

"Yes," he said. "I do need them."

"To see?"

"I need them. Can we leave it at that?"

"But are they necessary?" Michael said. "Or is your attachment to them merely sentimental?"

"Why do you assume that sentimentality and necessity are incompatible?"

"How's that again?"

"There are times," Yeats said, "when sentimentality *is* necessary."

MARTIN AND FRANCIS had called a truce. Martin was too tired and Francis had announced that his bladder was full to bursting—though he had offered to continue their conversation so long as Martin didn't mind him unbuttoning his trousers and having a slash right there on the carpet. Martin put his head back on the sofa and pressed his palms to his eyelids. The hangover was gaining steam, and arguing with his brother wasn't any help. This was not the way he had pictured their reunion, although if he had been honest with himself, he would have admitted that, yes, this was exactly how things were likely to go.

As Francis pissed loudly into the toilet, he tried to tally how many cups of coffee he had bolted down before striking out for Martin's apartment—three? Four? He didn't even like coffee; he was hoping only for a stronger jolt than the thin-boned American tea could provide. They had been in America for two days and the quality of the tea had been one of the few disappointments. He could have gone straightaway to find Martin, but he figured it best to give himself a couple of days to get settled and for Michael to continue on the path to better health. The sea air had been good for him and city life had been even better. When they had set out from Cobh, Michael was a shell of himself. He could hardly walk ten feet without help from Francis. But two days of room service and plush beds—cheers to the

FC Plan, once again—put some flesh on his bones and even a bit of the old sparkle in his eyes.

As for Martin, he was an odd duck when it came to questions of family loyalty, and Francis had been unsure how he would respond to the train of illegality that Francis was dragging behind him. So far Martin had taken it all in stride, or as much in stride as Francis could have hoped for. But how would Martin have responded if Francis had told him the truth? That when Francis had been ordered to move the car, he had not only had words with one of the bomb makers, but had scuffled with him? And that when the first man had tried to settle the fight with a punch to Francis's midsection, Francis had sent the man reeling inside, and slammed that iron-ribbed door, and somehow the whole works blew up? Francis had already spent the intervening weeks asking himself if things could have gone differently if only he had been more careful. He didn't need Martin asking the same questions and coming up with his own answers. And whether or not he told Martin all there was to know about the event, the essential truth remained the same: Ireland had dealt the Dempsey family one more kick in the balls, but this time—through Francis's quick thinking and selfless devotion to his brother—he had made it the occasion of their triumphal flight from their cruel, capricious homeland.

If it all sounded like something out of a true-crime novel—another staple of the prison library—then there you had it: life imitating art. Or maybe this was what life did best, drop you in the middle of a story that you'd have a hard time believing if you saw it between the covers of a book. Even Francis himself had trouble keeping it all straight: mystery men from his father's past, hand-drawn maps, stolen cars, an IRA bomb factory, a trunk full of banknotes, American heiresses, fancy ocean liners.

But now that Francis had finally brought all the Dempsey brothers together again, he was ready to enjoy himself. There was a barbershop off the lobby, and that would be the place for a shave. Hot towels and lather, the straight razor against his neck. He hadn't had a chance to treat himself since they arrived. Sure, last night's dinner had been steak and a bottle of Bordeaux, but it had been room service, a pale shadow of what he imagined the full restaurant experience would be. He wanted waiters, busboys, a maître d' to consult about the merits of the Pomerol versus the Haut-Médoc. He had a necktie he'd been saving for the right occasion, one he'd picked up on the ship during the Atlantic crossing—who knew there would be a tailor on board, exclusively for the first-class passengers?—and this first Saturday in New York was just the time for it. The Dempsey brothers were reunited and that was cause for celebration. They would start with a fine dinner, where they would fill themselves with porterhouse steaks and martinis, and then Martin could take them to a real nightclub. He was a musician and must know a thing or two about how to have a good time—or at least where a fellow could go to have one. Francis wanted to hear jazz music and he wanted to drink a Manhattan with a cherry as big as his fist. He wanted to see girls dancing in nothing but feathers and glitter, their eyes rimmed in black. He wanted bright lights and brighter music, gin and cigarettes, lipstick and smiles. He wanted a night that bled into the next day, a party that never stopped.

There was a depression on, here as back home, but not for a man with money in his pockets. In the Ireland he knew, the sense of squalor, of dinginess, of glamourlessness, was omnipresent. There were greater and lesser degrees of it—he had run with a posh crowd in Dublin before his arrest—though you could never entirely escape its damp touch. But here? It had taken Francis only a day in the States to see that when so many were poor, his money and his title gave him a special glow and granted him access to a world that others could only dream of. A depression didn't mean the extinction of comfort and luxury. They still existed in abundance, but it was a bounty available to a select few. He thought of that Walter fellow on board the *Britannic,* going on about how the crash had acted like a sieve, culling the ranks of the truly rich. Francis had nodded in sage agreement, even backed it up with a sly wink, but underneath, other ideas roiled: *You fat filthy bastard,* he had thought. *Give me half a chance—I'll show you how to thin the herd.*

Now here he was. The seventh floor of the Plaza Hotel. His face was framed by a gilt-edged mirror, like a portrait of some distant, wealthy relative. *Charming bloke, my great-uncle. Fought with Wellington at Waterloo. Quite, quite.* Francis withdrew a diamond pin from his jacket pocket and slid it into his lapel. He had lifted it from Walter the night after their dinner, when he found him legless-drunk on the casino deck. Walter got off easy, Francis told himself. Could have pitched him overboard. He smiled at the memory of it and pointed his finger gunlike at his reflection. *Your money or your life. Your money and your wife.*

He readied himself for more questions, but on reemerging from the bathroom he found Martin fast asleep, his chin on his chest and his legs forming a bridge to the marble-topped coffee table. His breathing came slow and regular, bracketed by a ragged snore on the inhale. Michael had returned to the sofa; he was perched on one arm, examining his brother's profile. He looked better than he had in ages. Like his old self again.

"Let's take a walk," Francis said.

Michael didn't answer—not that Francis had expected he would. His younger brother stared intently at Martin, a look that Francis took to be happiness. He had brought Michael here and now he had given him this gift of his oldest brother. If Michael could speak, Francis was certain he would say something like *Thank you, Francis, for bringing us back together.* It almost made Francis mist up just thinking about it.

He boxed Michael on the shoulder to break whatever spell Martin had over him. "Come along, brother," Francis said. "Let's take Manhattan."

FORDHAM HEIGHTS

PARKED DOWN THE BLOCK from the house he'd visited the night before, Cronin had to admit that he'd gotten rusty. Worse, he'd been careless—careless, impatient, stupid—to go knocking on the door so late, but he had spent the day tracking down every M. Dempsey in the phone book and by ten at night he was tired and angry and that was the wrong way to go about this sort of business. When the old woman came to the door, he was sure he'd turned down another blind alley, but then she opened her craw and said Mr. Dempsey wasn't at home because he was a musician and kept odd hours. At the mention of music, Cronin knew he had his man. Now he could only hope he hadn't spooked Martin and sent Francis into hiding.

He wouldn't have been so careless in the old days, but now even his hunches were failing him. Of the almost one hundred and fifty Dempseys in the phone books of the five boroughs, there were no Martins and only three M. Dempseys: one in Brooklyn, one in the Bronx, and one on Staten Island. It should have been easy enough. He started early Friday morning in Brooklyn, but four hours in front of a brownstone on Prospect Avenue revealed the mystery M. to be Mae Dempsey, a member in good standing of the ladies' auxiliary at Holy Family Roman Catholic Church. Cronin's next roll of the dice took him to Staten Island and, really, he should have known better. What kind of a musician lived on Staten Island? A ferry ride and a long walk put him on a leafy street in front of a two-story wood-frame occupied by the middle-aged Malachy Dempsey and his unruly brood of tow-headed sons. Cronin heard them whooping it up from halfway down the street. It had been a long way to go for a quick answer to his question.

He should have started with the Bronx—the borough was lousy with Irish—but for Cronin, the Bronx was a landscape of pits and snares. It was the terrain of his past. Back in Prohibition days, Gavigan had knocked heads with bootleggers big and small trying to chisel off little pieces of business, nowhere more so than on the west side of Manhattan and up and down the Bronx. Whenever there were heads to be knocked, it was Cronin's job to do the knocking, and now the thought of running into men with scores to settle had spooked Cronin into staying clear of his old stomping ground. He knew, deep down, that the M. Dempsey he was looking for was the one in the Bronx, but he had been foolish enough to believe—worse, to hope—that this job could be easy, that it wouldn't force him to go straight into the maw of the bad old days.

Cronin had been jumpy since he stepped off the train at Grand Central. The press of bodies on the platform, the steam and the darkness and the shrill whistles of the conductors, and the jostling of the porters and the garbled voices on the loudspeakers calling out departures—it had nearly sent him into a panic. For five years, he had been softened by the sound of wind ruffling the birch trees. He was buffeted only by the flanks of the cows, and snugged close at night in the bed with Alice. On the platform, feeling every eye on him, he couldn't help jerking his head this way and that, though he knew it was likely to get him noticed: it's the nervous man, the one who most wants to be invisible, who is spotlighted in the crowd. He settled himself as he moved up the staircase and into the vaulted concourse, where he navigated the thinning crowd and pushed through the door onto Forty-Second Street. Amid the splashes of neon and the million-bulbed marquees, he walked west through Times Square, then crossed

Eighth Avenue, moving like a man who would brook no nonsense from pickpockets or stickup men. He gripped tight the handle of the valise and struck toward the river, walking past storefronts locked up against the night's rougher traffic. Yellow light spilled onto the street from an all-night hash-and-eggs joint full of cops and cabbies. He passed a bar that seemed darker on the inside than the street itself, and then another, and another. In any one of those bars could be a man who had spent years rehearsing to himself what he would do if he ever came across Tom Cronin, unarmed, on a dark street. The bars could be full of such men.

He did not wander aimlessly; this was no nostalgic tour of his old haunts. He knew well the spot where Gavigan had said he could retrieve an automobile: a warehouse in the West Forties that at midnight still echoed with the sounds of cars and men—slamming, cursing, rattling, laughing. The syrupy tang of motor oil, the whiskey of petrol, the haze of exhaust: gouts of it billowed from the open bay of the garage. Half of the building was a taxicab company. Cronin's car would be in the other half, the one whose entrance faced away from the street and smelled of fresh paint and larceny. Inside he found a man in striped blue coveralls peering into the open mouth of a Buick. Cronin waited for the man to slam shut its hood.

"I'm here about a car." Cronin's voice sounded small in the sudden quiet, but it had the intended effect: the other man—a kid, really—startled.

He was a beanpole, all straight lines and angles. His knobby wrists poked from his sleeves like a scarecrow's. He tried to play off his flinch as something else, shooting his cuffs, straightening the collar of his coveralls, like a man going out on the town. He gave Cronin the once-over. "Oh yeah, and who are you?"

"That's no matter," Cronin said. "I'm here to pick up a car."

The kid smirked. "And I'm just gonna hand over the keys?" His eyes swept the top of a battered tool bench that ran the length of the

Buick. A wrench. A tire iron. A ball-peen hammer. Cronin took it all in.

"Gavigan sent me," Cronin said. "So, yeah, that's what you're gonna do."

"Gavigan, huh?" The kid picked up a rag and scoured his blackened hands. "Wait here."

The name was like gravel in Cronin's mouth, but it was proof, if he needed it, that Gavigan could still open a few doors. It was a name he had hoped never to speak again, but there were worse places to find out if the currency of Gavigan's name had kept its value. If some hard-luck case with a score to settle thought twice about potshotting Cronin because he feared what Gavigan would do, then the name was doing its job.

Stretch reemerged from a small room at the back of the garage with a clipboard in his hand. He muttered under his breath—*Gavigangavi gangavigangavigan*—while he flipped through yellow pages lined in blue. Without looking up, he said, "Are you...Cronin?"

Gut-punched. That's how it felt to hear his name spoken so freely. Had Gavigan really been so reckless?

The kid seemed unfazed. To him, Cronin's name was a word on a sheet of paper, nothing more. He held out a pair of keys ringed to a leather tab. "Back there," he said, cocking his head to the right. "Packard. A black one."

Cronin took the keys. The kid was barely in his twenties—too young for Cronin to have crossed paths with him. And he would have remembered someone so lanky and skittish. He was like a character out of a children's book: the marionette who cuts his strings and gets a job fixing cars.

"Can I see?" Cronin had already reached out and had a tight grip on the clipboard, his fingers marking the page. He wanted the puppet to know that he would not win a tug-of-war against flesh and blood, and that with the keys in his hand, Cronin no longer needed him for anything.

"Sure, buddy," he said, relinquishing the clipboard. "Knock yourself out."

It was all spelled out in a hasty scrawl: *Thurs./Fri. Cronin, pickup for G.* The *G* was circled, apparently the kid's effort at a coded message. Cronin tore off the page and stuffed it into his pocket. He thought for a moment about threatening the kid, promising some terrible punishment involving the tire iron and a pair of pliers if he breathed a word about his visit, but it would only make him more likely to talk, to test the weight of Cronin's name.

As Cronin turned the key and the car came to life, he wondered again what Gavigan could have been thinking to bandy about his name so carelessly. Or maybe it hadn't been him at all. When did Gavigan take care of such details? It must have been that Jamie, the one behind the wheel of the car, where Cronin had once sat. Because this was the kind of thing Cronin himself would have done: Send a message in letters twenty feet tall to some reluctant stooge about just how precarious his position was. That was a message to keep a man focused, to make him work with a sense of purpose.

Now it was Saturday and Cronin was back in the Bronx, parked on a street of narrow lots, each house leaning into its neighbor. The days away from the farm were already piling one on top of another. He had arrived late on Thursday, spent Friday morning in Brooklyn, then wasted the afternoon on a fool's errand to Staten Island. He should have called it quits and started fresh on Saturday—he had barely slept on Thursday night, tossing and turning in a dollar-a-day flop on a bed that sagged like a sailor's hammock—but there was one Dempsey left and Cronin was eager to bring a close to this mad business. He was working on the assumption that Francis had made contact with his older brother, that he might even be in cahoots with Martin, and that the dead men in Ireland and the quick turn toward America might all be part of a Dempsey family revenge scheme—a scheme that would lead them to Cronin and the farm. So he had rushed it, and if last night's foray had tipped off the Dempseys, then Cronin just might have banjaxed the whole operation.

Slumped behind the wheel of the Packard, his shirt plastered to his back and his collar chafing him like a yoke, Cronin thought again of Gavigan. Of how he'd appeared at the farm, acting as if finding Frank Dempsey's wayward son were Cronin's responsibility. But what did Gavigan know? He had never even met Frank Dempsey. He knew him only by his legend—first as a hero of the cause, then as a sticky problem that had to be solved. Cronin knew them all, though it had been a long, long time since he'd set eyes on Frank or Bernadette or their boys.

It was Gavigan's mention of music—of the oldest boy being a musician—that had first sent a shock through Cronin's veins, a shock he hadn't quite shaken in the days since. Of course his mind went straight to Bernadette—to Mrs. Dempsey. God, what a beauty, and God, what a voice! All through the war, she had offered music lessons from the family home, just down the street from the university where Mr. Dempsey taught, and where Cronin worked for the grounds-keeper. When the Dempseys took notice of him, he was flattered by the attention. Even then, he saw the couple through a golden haze: These were educated folks who organized marches and published articles in the nationalist newspapers, and now they wanted Tom Cronin, with his turfy fingernails and his three years of schooling, to join them. They invited him to meetings where the talk was all about the struggle against the English, about the need for Ireland to be free. There were men at those meetings who had survived the Easter Rising and they spoke of how they had struck the match and watched the fuse burn for years and now it was time for the powder keg to blow.

Cronin had never cared for politics, but these meetings fit his own life into a bigger story: Hadn't his own brother died in the Great War, fighting for the same empire that oppressed them all? The Dempseys were the first to make him feel like he had an important part to play in building this new Ireland, like he was the man to put the muscle behind these speeches and grand plans. If he was a little bit in love with Bernadette Dempsey, what was the harm in it? Everyone loved her. When she spoke, she could outpatriot any of the men. And when she sang one of the old songs, all of their eyes shone with tears and their hearts filled with rebel blood.

Cronin had a memory from those early years of young Martin plinking out a tune on the piano. The boy couldn't have been more than nine or ten at the time, but it was brilliant to watch his little fingers running up and down the keys. His mother stood behind him and beamed, her lips moving silently as she counted out the tune. Her hair, coppery red and lively as silk, was pinned up and away from her face, with a single strand dancing against her swan's neck.

He stopped himself short. He didn't deserve these memories, not when he was the one who had put her in the ground, who had robbed those boys of their mother's love. The war against the English ended but it seemed only days before it became a war of Irish against Irish, and in that war Frank Dempsey chose the wrong side—he stayed loyal to Michael Collins, the Chief, who had made the bad bargain and left them short of the full freedom for which they'd toiled. Cronin stood with the men who wanted full payment for the blood they had spilled. They had no time for talk of a three-step path to independence or of an Irish Free State. They wanted a completely free Irish Republic. What Cronin couldn't stomach was the notion that he'd risked eternal damnation in service of a halfhearted victory. He wanted to punish Frank Dempsey and the men like him who'd put Cronin's soul on a scale and shown him how little it purchased. It should have been a simple enough task, the kind of job that Frank himself had trained him to do, but Cronin had botched it. The bomb in the car was meant for Frank. What business did Bernadette have taking a drive so early in the morning? Where could she have been going?

The click of a woman's heel on the front stoop shook Cronin out of his reverie. He hadn't noticed her in the rearview mirror or through the windshield when she crossed the street two cars ahead of him but suddenly there she was, struggling up the front steps with a baby in her arm and holding a little girl by the hand. The baby could have been Gracie and though the girl was younger than Henry, with the car windows down in this awful heat, Cronin could hear her peppering her mother with the same sorts of questions that his Henry had for him. If Martin Dempsey lived here, then this had to be his family, and the sight of them stickpinned Cronin to his seat. Here he was, thinking about the men from his past who could bring sorrow to his doorstep and about the sorrow that he himself had wrought, while this family before him, one very much like his own, could not see the monster lurking at their gate. He sat in the car, sweating more than ever, and composed a silent litany. *Lord, protect those in that home who are innocent. Lord, let me not be the agent of their undoing. Lord, though I am full of darkness, help me to restrain the evil I carry within me.* But as soon as the door closed heavily behind the woman and her children, his thoughts returned to Alice and Henry and Gracie. They were the ones he would make any bargain to protect. They were the ones who deserved his prayers. Why was he wasting his breath on strangers?

He mopped his face with his handkerchief and added a final line: *Lord, if I must act, understand what I do and why it must be done.*

MIDTOWN

FRANCIS DIDN'T CARE WHERE he and Michael were going. As long as he was moving, life was grand. Since he had left the prison, where the best you could hope for was walking in circles, he had been on the move; whether by car, by ship, by taxicab, or even by the power of his own feet, his momentum had been constant. In the hotel with Martin he had felt like he was back in Mountjoy, with the four walls and the questions and Martin looking right at him. But Martin was snoozing and Francis had had a hot-lather shave followed by a lunch in the Oak Bar that could have filled five men, and now he was out on the street with Michael in tow.

The city was a revelation. Energy pulsed up through the sidewalk, propelling each of his steps. Everyone he passed seemed to feel it too. They moved quickly and with purpose. The men's suits were new and sharply tailored, like the uniforms of palace guards. The women beamed, their eyes bright and their bodies surging beneath summer blouses and close-cut dresses. It was only the first week of June, but the city was alive with the promise of summer: the air was warm but not humid, it kissed rather than stifled. In Dublin, every soot-stained façade—every English-built edifice rechristened in the name of the new Ireland—glowered at you, asking what business you had there. *Eyes down and move along,* that's what the streets of Dublin said. It was a city of iron railings and weathered brick, and the people didn't fare much better than the buildings. The worst parts of the city were overrun with thick smoke and women gone toothless by forty from too many children and not enough decent food or fresh air. The men, even in the best parts of the city, were angry-faced and closefisted, desperate to protect whatever they had carved from the nation's piss-poor larder. But why think of Dublin here? If Dublin was hunched and cowering, then New York soared and carried the spirits of every man and woman with it. It was a city that said *Look up!* A vertical city, a transcendent city that set the mind on higher thoughts. Sure, times were hard, but New York at its worst was leagues ahead of Dublin at its best—and when had Dublin ever seen its best?

As they left the shelter of the hotel, there loomed behind them a sparkling equestrian eminence: a rider erect in the saddle, a goddess heralding his arrival. There were no somber marble wreaths, no veiled women forming a train of weeping and regret—even the horse looked haughty. Francis threw an arm around Michael's shoulder and propelled him across Fifty-Seventh Street, dodging taxicabs and plunging into the scrum of pedestrians moving in the opposite direction. New York might be beautiful but if you stopped to admire it, you were cooked. Each new block was an island, each street a narrow ocean. As you put the last block behind you, each crossing washed you clean. Who had time to dwell on the *then* when the crush of bodies forced you to pay attention to the *now?*

Michael took a deep breath. It seemed years since he had been outside and under his own steam. The city itself had reanimated him, and now it carried him along through a fairy-tale world: inside every window sparkled constellations of diamonds. Even the windows were outlined in gold. Up the façade of one building, gold tracery followed the angles of each window, scrolled around the doors, and illuminated a set of small stone figures carved into the cornice of the entryway. Michael tugged on his brother's sleeve and pointed to these bird-bodied, lady-headed Harpies baring their teeth and talons. Francis smiled back at Michael. Their father had drilled enough of Homer and Virgil into them that he could tell a Harpy from a Fury at forty paces.

They walked down Fifth Avenue, drawn into the crowd, and all around was glittering commerce. Department stores rose like palaces, their windows offering a peek at the treasure hoard of the king. BERG-DORF GOODMAN and BONWIT TELLER were chiseled in stone and scripted in gold. Their great revolving doors admitted a steady flow of pleasure seekers and disgorged an equal number of treasure takers. In the windows the mannequins, calm and composed, enacted scenes from a better world. Blank-faced, they danced in chiffon summer gowns or lifted champagne flutes above a picnic basket, their arms showcasing the freedom afforded by a light summer frock. The sun was high in the sky and everything sparkled—the windshields of the taxicabs, the chrome details of the fat black cars, the high windows of the towers that lined the avenue. They were in a city of glass and white marble, bleached and made clean by every sunrise. It was the city of the future that the adverts for the World's Fair promised.

Francis hadn't come to America looking for anything more than an escape from the mess he had made in Ireland. But strolling through the city gave him a thrill. He wasn't just watching this parade of opulence, he was a part of it. He and Michael could be hiding in some rainy hovel right now, dreading the kick at the door that would signal the end. But he had chosen a different sort of refuge, and damn him if the idea hadn't been the best he had ever had. They had a room at the Plaza, fine clothes, and enough money to bluff their way into any corner of the city where their feet could carry them. Even Michael seemed enlivened by the shine of the street. His eyes darted skyward, his cheeks were flushed with the glow of good health, and his mouth fairly gaped.

But what had caught Michael's attention wasn't the bared legs of the mannequins or the walnut-size diamond in the window of the jewelry store or the way that women not so subtly sized up Francis (he was a handsome fellow, and the suit gave him the aura of wealth and good breeding), nor was it the yellow taxicabs and the beetle-bright cars that lined the avenue. He was taken in by the sight of a worn, red-stone church looming on the next corner. Its carved steps led to an entrance that was austere in the extreme—a rebuke to all of this shimmer and bustle, but one that must have been issued years earlier, preemptively. The church had long ago set an example that none of the newer buildings cared to follow. For these new buildings, the trick was to seem permanent and fundamental to life while at the same time projecting an air of modishness. Each was a temple not merely to the current moment, but to the coming season. The future. The church, however, was plain, but on purpose, not because of a lack of funds or imagination. It seemed as if it had been built and then abraded with copper-wire brushes to deny itself, even in the first moments of life, any sense of freshness, any of the vanity that came with the new. It had all the shine and polish of rumpled butcher's paper. Michael imagined an interior of white walls and simple wooden pews. Presbyterians? It seemed the sort of church that they would build: a monument to self-denial surrounded on all sides by the serious business of making money.

Michael wished he had a notepad—he wished he could still write!—so he could jot all this down for his next visitation from Yeats. Maybe Yeats wouldn't care to read the finer points of difference between one church and another—wasn't Christianity just another source of metaphor for modern poets?—but maybe he would make something of the red-stone church's down-the-street neighbors. A Gothic-spired cathedral flying the papal flag faced off across the avenue with a massive bronze Atlas bowed under a steel-ribbed globe. Farther ahead, a golden giant fell while a fire crackled in his hand, and behind him a bearded eminence used his burning fingers, sextant-like, to measure the darkness. Above this figure rose the tallest tower Michael had ever seen: a slim sheaf of unbroken lines that soared into the cloudless blue.

This wasn't sightseeing; it was an extended hallucination. A city of golden doors and particolored churches, of Titans who had populated the myths of Michael's childhood, symbols of state power and godly authority and freedom and rebellion and punishment. He wanted to take Francis's sleeve and ask, *Can you see this? Is this only in my head?* But he knew that Francis would only give him that patient, pitying look. Yes, he would have to ask Yeats about all of it, and as he formulated that thought, he had to laugh. *I'll ask my ghost to decipher my hallucination. Brilliant. Just brilliant.*

For the second time that day, Martin found himself on the IRT bound for home. On his early-morning ride he had been drunk but happy. Now, his hangover had caught up with him. It had been lurking in the shadows, waiting for Martin to doze, and though he had made it wait and wait—perhaps the only benefit of staying up through the night and deep into the next morning—a hangover was a patient creature. Martin's head was as brittle as a rusted bell and his limbs were sapped by the burn-off of the adrenaline that had hit him with the sudden appearance of first one brother and then the other.

When he had awoken at the Plaza, with no sign of Francis or Michael anywhere, he could almost believe that it had all been a dream. Had he come to a party at the Plaza last night, blacked out, and imagined the whole thing? That was a more plausible explanation than finding his brothers in New York, living like a couple of millionaires on holiday. A quick search turned up a few suits hanging in the closet, along with a collection of plaid waistcoats, which jibed with his memories of Francis and the Scottish alias. Martin pissed in the toilet and checked himself in the mirror haloed by bulbs. There was no denying it—he looked like hell. He had all the charm of an unmade bed. He collected his hat and as an afterthought scrawled a note, which he propped on the desk in the suite.

F & M

Dinner at my place. Tomorrow at 4:30.

Meet your American relations!

—M

On his way out of the lobby, he was asked by the porter if the gentleman required a cab, and for a split second Martin considered it. Then he thought of Rosemary. If she saw him putting a dent in their grocery budget to pay a cabbie, she'd have his head.

Rosemary. She would be wondering what had happened to him. What a story he would have for her: Francis and Michael in New York City, the Plaza Hotel — but what was he to tell her about the circumstances of his brothers' escape? That was a question for another time. It was all too much for now, past midday on a Saturday when he hadn't truly slept since Thursday night and in the meantime had traveled from the Bronx to Broadway to Harlem, then back to the Bronx and from there to the Plaza Hotel. At least he wouldn't need to be back at the Kensington in time for tonight's show — but there was another bit of news he had to break to Rosemary. She would have more than his head when he told her he'd quit playing for Chester.

And then there was his father. Da was dead. Martin stared at the train window now, mirrorlike in the darkness of the subway tunnel. All around him mothers fussed with children, and men and women talked and laughed or carried on whispered arguments, but Martin tried to quiet his mind and let silence lead him toward an answer to the question that had tugged at him all morning long: *How do I feel about this?* He certainly didn't take any delight in his father's death — he wasn't a monster — but was he saddened by the news? He felt a weight in his stomach and a light and empty space in his head. It wasn't sadness so much as a gnawing uncertainty, or the awareness of a distance between how this news should make him feel and how he actually felt. Martin had known the moment he left Ireland that he would never see his father again. Shortly after he had landed in New York, he wrote to say that he had arrived safely, to convey an address where he could be reached, and to explain as best he could his reasons for leaving. Looking back, he would guess that the letter was probably too grandiose—more manifesto than *Remember me, dear Papa*—but he was nineteen and drunk on America. His father sent a terse reply, which brought to an end the correspondence between father and son.

This didn't seem a fitting memorial. Quarreling with a ghost about who was to blame for the failure of their correspondence and, to be honest, for so much else. They were headstrong, the both of them, and Martin had been so preoccupied with his plans for America, and then by the place itself, that he was quick to consign his father to the ash heap of things he had left behind when he sailed from Ireland. His father was an item on a long list of failings and untenable situations, or, to give him his due, he was a *force* that had kept Martin mired in a life he did not want, and which he believed he could escape only through careful planning and great effort. Any contact with his father threatened to pull him back to the old country, the old life. Or so he had told himself. *Why,* he reasoned, *should I carry with me into a new country, a new life, this anger and guilt*—the guilt itself engendered by the anger he directed at the old man? Better to forget it all, or treat it as some fever dream that had plagued him for a time, but would recede from memory as the sun rose and a new day began.

The train rocked on its rails, slowing into one station before speeding toward the next. What would his father make of this—dead more than two weeks and Martin still arguing his case? It wasn't as if he knew nothing of his father since his departure. Traces of life in Ballyrath had made it into Michael's letters: his father had taken ill two winters ago but had regained his health; Mrs. Greavey, the woman who took care of his cooking and washing, had procured a nanny goat, believing as she did that goat's milk was the key to a long life, but his father could not develop a taste for it; the O'Brien boy had demonstrated great potential with his Greek, almost as much as Martin had once shown. This news was accompanied by a heartfelt wish—Michael's, he assumed, and not his father's—that Martin had continued his study of Greek, as the consequences of wasting such a gift were well illustrated in the parable of the talents.

Maybe this was a fitting memorial: Da knew better than anyone else how hard it was to break off a conversation simply because death had intervened. Hadn't their mother remained a constant presence in his life? Hadn't his efforts to escape from his own sorrow and guilt and anger—at the world for taking her, at God for letting her go, at Bernadette herself for leaving him—driven him to move to the farthest point on the island from the car wreck that had killed her? That was the shocking part about the cause of his father's death: his heart. Martin had long believed that his heart had already been blown to bits the day their mother died. If he had managed to preserve some piece of it for himself, he had never let his sons see it.

He had hoped the train would give him a few quiet moments to think through the events of the day, and look where it had gotten him: worked up into a lather about a life he had left behind. His father was dead, and Martin could think of no way to mourn him.

SUNDAY
JUNE 4

IN CHURCH

IN THE PARISH CHURCH in Woodlawn where she had made her First Communion, knelt through confession and Stations of the Cross, and lit countless votives before the statue of the Blessed Virgin, Rosemary had always had her favorite saints. Agnes with her lamb, Stephen and his pile of stones, Lucy with her eyes on a plate. She had no interest in the pious men in their broad red hats and their dusty books; even stained glass couldn't brighten their sour faces. The popes' crowns all looked like hard-boiled eggs and the nunnish wimples were proof that these moldy old men had never gotten outside to mix it up with the crowd. Rosemary preferred the virgin martyrs to the doctors of the church any day. Hadn't Saint Catherine of Alexandria argued with the king's philosophers until they chopped off her head with a sword? That was going to be Rosemary when she grew up, or so her younger self had thought. She wanted the forthrightness and the refusal to give an inch, but now, kneeling in prayer in this foreigners' church in Fordham Heights, she wondered if she had taken on the suffering but forgotten to ask for the glory, the grace, or the clarity of purpose.

But who was she to be picky? Any saint here would have to do today, because Rosemary had plenty to pray for. She wanted patience for the next round of wedding planning, but then what was the point of praying about the wedding, or her sister, or her parents, now that Martin had come shambling back into the apartment looking punch-drunk and poorly shaved, telling her that his father was dead and his brothers were in town and the youngest was in some kind of state and the two of them were holed up at the Plaza—the Plaza, could you imagine the cost?—and right at the end, almost like an afterthought, mentioning that he had quit Chester's band? And over what? The songs didn't *swing*?

Perhaps she could look to Saint Monica, patron saint of wives, but prayers to her tended to be pleas for forbearance, and Rosemary wanted more than forbearance. And there was always Saint Jude, who handled lost causes. But it hadn't gotten that bad. Not yet.

She knew that once you married a man, you were tied to him for good or bad—sickness, health, richer, poorer, till death did you part. A husband's good decisions could make your life easier, and his bad decisions, or bad habits, could absolutely ruin you. She had seen it in her parents' home and had vowed that she wouldn't fall into the same trap. Her father was a blusterer and a bully. He made enemies, he stepped on toes, he took from men the things he had it in his power to take and he gave to men what it benefited him to bestow. That was politics. And her mother, who had hitched herself to him when the two had little in life, had become an imperious, lonely woman. Suspicious of people who had less, resentful of those who had more. Did she have anyone she could count as a friend, a confidante? Or did everyone fear that sharing the least bit of their own troubles with Birdie Dwyer would surely find its way back to Dennis, whereupon it would be filed away until it was useful? Still, her parents had mounted a charge that got them most of the way to the top. It was a good life. Most had far less. But it wasn't a life that Rosemary had ever wanted for herself.

She had gone and hitched herself to Martin, and for all that was good about him—he was no blusterer, no bully—he had proven himself to be capricious at times. She knew that men made decisions for their own reasons and you hoped that you could fit those decisions into the life you thought you were making, but she was starting to see that life was like being handed the ingredients one at a time for a meal you were supposed to make, never knowing what was next. You might start with a chicken, a few carrots, a sack of potatoes, and think, *Now we're getting somewhere*—but the next three items would be a bicycle tire, a top hat, and a bag of penny candy, and you had to figure out how to use it all. There was no chance to slip any of it into the trash, or set the hat on your head, or pretend you never saw the tire.

Martin claimed he had a plan and maybe that was true, and maybe it was even a good plan. But a good plan—a truly good plan—wouldn't have left Martin out of work, wouldn't have left her wondering how on God's green earth she was going to square their expenses in the black-bound ledger where she tracked every nickel spent with the grocer, the butcher, the butter-and-eggs man, the cobbler who would fix the heel on the old shoes she would wear to the wedding.

A truly good plan—one that would be good for her, too—wouldn't need to be cloaked in secrecy. Because if it was truly good, Martin would have been bursting to tell her all about it. He would have talked to her about it over his cup of tea, after the girls were in bed, on one of those rare nights when he was home instead of at the Kensington or somewhere on Fifty-Second Street or in Harlem. They could have formulated this plan together. She thought again of the kiss outside the chapel on the day they'd gotten married. Was she wrong to see that as a promise? Or just wrong to think that promises couldn't be broken?

MILES TO THE south, on the island of Manhattan, in another church of the same faith, John Gavigan bowed his head in prayer. The priest had raised the Host and it was a time for all good Christians to fall to their knees, but if Gavigan perched his wrecked skeleton on the padded kneelers for even a second he would need to be lifted back into his seat. So he would risk blasphemy to save himself from that humiliation.

He bowed his head and turned his thoughts to his own mortal end. He wasn't bloody-minded but seeing Tommy Cronin again had gotten him thinking about how the time had passed. For a dozen years, Tommy had been faithfully at his side. Gavigan's shadow, they called him. And then one day he was gone, and with his disappearance some of Gavigan's foes whispered that Gavigan was get-able. That Cronin hadn't been just a shadow but a shield. Here Gavigan was, though, years after Cronin had walked off his post, and no one had gotten him yet.

Most of the men he had known in life had not made it this far. The loudmouths and the brawlers, the ones who were too quick to provoke or too bullheaded to ever back down, were the first to go. They seldom made it out of their teens, which was the Decade of Not Being *Too* Stupid. Then you're in your twenties, the Decade of Hustle, where you've got to keep your eyes open for every opportunity, whether it knocks or not. That would get you into your thirties, the Decade of Luck. Gavigan had seen plenty of guys who were full of get-up-and-go lose it all because they picked the wrong side of a turf dispute in the old neighborhood, or got swept off to Rikers Island for not bribing the right cops (or for trying to bribe the wrong ones), or claimed too big a slice of some union's bankroll only to find out firsthand how many bodies you can hide in a building's foundation, and how quickly the concrete sets. You saw enough of that and you realized you had to find a way to bleed the luck out of the system, to make it all about the right decision instead of the wrong one. That's when you entered the Decade of Being Smart, and if you knew what was what, you kept being smart for the rest of your life. But if you were no good at being smart, or if you were one of those guys who had been lucky and who thought that the luck would never run out, then you became one of the men whom Gavigan sheared like sheep, taking from them year after year, until they were good for nothing but mutton.

Gavigan had made it. Through all the traps littering the streets of the city, he had made it. But now, as his knees turned into rusty hinges and his lungs filled with a vile sludge, he had begun to wonder what all the decades of hustle, luck, and smarts had gotten for him, and what relics of his trials and victories he would leave behind. He had never had a wife, never had children. He wasn't about to make like his fancy-pants neighbors and leave what he had to build a museum full of watery French landscapes or hand it all over to the opera, where the rich sat bawling in their seats while some fat Italians screeched about lost love.

He had hoped to make his mark with this Ireland business, bank-rolling the operation for going on forty years: the Easter Rising, the War of Independence, the anti-Treaty side of the civil war. He was convinced that none of it would have happened without the money and the guns and the yet-more-money he had dispatched to the Old Sod. His mother had raised him on stories of the Famine, the shame of the workhouse, uncles led in chains to Australia, a hunger so raw no lifetime could ever satiate it. But it wasn't the old stories alone that had raised the banner in his heart. Just before the turn of the century, as he began to get a little money in his pockets, he had taken his mother to the Odeon in the old Five Points neighborhood to see one of the great Irish tenors. The performance turned out to be some kind of Fenian fund-raiser and while the singer caught his breath, another man took the stage and gave such a fiery recounting of the sins against the Irish people that Gavigan pledged himself right then and there to the cause of a free Ireland. It wasn't long before he was meeting at white-tablecloth steak houses with the up-and-coming class of Irish-Catholic merchants and lawyers—the strivers of New York with their fine suits and Jesuit manners, men who would have otherwise looked down on a gutter rat like John Gavigan. Only now they were drooling to get their hands on the money he could give to free Mother Ireland from British rule. When it was guns they needed, Gavigan knew how to get them, and when they needed men on the docks who could label rifles as machine parts—well, Gavigan took care of that, too. But what did they need from Gavigan now? Did they come to him for his general's eye for strategy, his banker's eye for business, his soldier's eye for knowing when to pull the trigger?

No, Lord, they want none of that. Only my money, Lord, to spend on schemes that don't have a snowball's chance in hell—forgive me, Lord, but I sometimes lose my temper, just as You did when the money-changers took over the temple. And I know how that is, Lord, when you're trying to stay true to the cause but all around you is incompetence and idiocy. I know a thing or two about staking out turf and keeping it yours, but does that get me listened to? It sure as shit does not. And forgive me again, Lord, for my rough language but You know that I am an uncouth soul, and You seem to love me for it anyhow. So thanks there, too, Lord.

This was the part that burned a hole in his gut—because what had their years of ignoring Gavigan's best ideas gotten the Irish? Only a piece of the island, with a big bite taken out of the top. He for one wasn't going to say that was good enough and call it a day. The south had purchased its independence—*And goddamn it, they hadn't even gotten that, not all the way*—and the price was the blood of every northern republican trapped in servitude to an English king and subject now to constant persecution by the murderous Ulster unionists, who were more determined than ever to keep themselves in the fold of the empire. Having been deserted by their cowardly, self-satisfied brothers in the south, the Catholics in the north were both poor and powerless. He thought his money had built a generation of revolutionaries, but they were content to be a nation of civil servants. They had sold their own kin for a comfortable pension.

And even the IRA, the ones who were supposed to finish the job come hell or high water, had fallen into weakness and disarray. He had urged and argued for something big, something that would kick the English square in the balls. Kill the whole cabinet in one swipe! Instead, they had launched this pitiful Sabotage Campaign, with its bombs in mailboxes, bombs in trash cans. It was an annoyance, nothing more. Gavigan called for an all-out assault on the north, a coordinated strike that would be the signal for a larger uprising. Just what they'd intended in '16, only better organized, with enough guns and men to force Parliament to throw up its hands and say, *Enough is enough! These Irish will never be quelled!* But no. The Army Council knew best. Gavigan told them they were mad and worse, that they had no stomach for a real fight. But still he opened his wallet because without him there would be no action at all.

And will you look at what's happened now, Lord? This little nobody walks in and robs them blind and then lights out for America, his pockets full of my money. So now it's up to me, once again, to clean up the mess they've made. Stupid fucking micks. Pardon my language, Lord, but it's true what they say: Every Irishman worth a damn has either emigrated or been executed. The simpletons who stayed behind need constant supervision.

Gavigan still dreamed of one last score. Something so big that it would sweep away the small-timers. And if it wasn't going to come from Ireland, then the American-born Irish would show them how it was done. There had been chatter around New York a few years back about flying a plane across the Atlantic, Lindbergh-style, to bomb the House of Commons. The plan had been to fly from the edge of Long Island, rain fire on the Parliament, and ditch the plane in sympathetic France. Gavigan lined up just such a plane. He found men willing to carry out the plan. But when he laid it all out for his supposed comrades, they balked. *It was just talk,* they said. *Eyes full of stars, heads full of whiskey.* Gavigan knew the truth, that they were scared of their own ambition.

But You know me, Lord. I'm not scared of nothing. Show me a sign, Lord, and I will not let You down. You have given me some good times on this earth, more than a man deserves, but if You give me one last score before we meet face to face then I will die a happy man. I've never asked for anything it wasn't in Your power to give, and to be honest, I have tried my best to take care of myself and go easy on the asking. So if You can see Your way to helping me go out a winner, then we can call it even. Amen.

FORDHAM HEIGHTS

MARTIN AND ROSEMARY'S OLDER daughter, Kate, had been perched at the front window awaiting the arrival of these strange new creatures, her uncles, and when she saw the taxi at the curb, she sent up the alarm: "I see nuncles! The nuncles! The nuncles!"

Martin tromped down the stairs to meet them, and moments later, Michael and Francis, their arms brimming with presents, pushed through the front door. Before Mrs. Fichetti could interrupt the reunion, they swept upstairs for a round of introductions: brothers to their sister-in-law, uncles to nieces, and nieces to uncles. Francis gave a broad smile as he sized up Rosemary: Dark hair and a pretty face, though she looked a bit too serious. Still, she had a nice bosom and a slim figure, even after the two babies. *Good fun to be had there,* he thought. *Well done, Martin.* He had never known Martin's type of girl. There were so few options among the country lasses in Ballyrath, and anyway Martin had always seemed more interested in music than girls. He wasn't going to tie himself down while his sights were set on America.

Michael was tottering under the weight of a giant bottle of champagne—"It's bigger than Evie!" Martin said—and as Michael was relieved of the bottle, Francis began dispensing presents. For Rosemary there was a brooch from Henri Bendel, which she said was too extravagant, all the while pinning it smartly to her blouse. For Kate, a Madame Alexander doll. "My baby!" she cried with rapturous glee when the box was opened. And for the littlest Dempsey, a silver teething ring in a powder-blue Tiffany box. Evie took hold of it in one fat fist and began madly drooling. Francis patted his pockets in a show of forgetfulness—"Now, what have I got for Daddy?" he said, winking at Kate—before producing another Tiffany box, this one containing a tie clip made up of thin lines of silver dotted with quarter notes. Francis beamed throughout this Santa Claus in June ceremony while Michael stood by his side with his alert, happy-but-not-idiotic smile, a look he had been practicing in the mirror that morning.

Martin's smile was more pained as he tried to tally up the dent his brother's largesse had made in the budget for Michael's medical care. Michael himself looked like a little boy dressed up for some fancy family outing: his aunt's wedding, his brother's First Communion. With his thin neck, large head, and black hair pomaded flat against his skull, he resembled a dapper, man-size lollipop.

Michael hadn't known where they were going, but the pieces were falling into place. Martin had sent him a photograph of his family and here they were in the flesh. The wife was Rosemary, the daughters were Katherine and Evelyn. Rosemary seemed nice enough: she'd given Michael a hug and a kiss on the cheek when he entered and had looked at him with pity and concern. He was sure that she had said something kind, something comforting. Once he had been relieved of the bottle, Kate immediately instigated a game of peekaboo with Michael, popping her head behind her father's armchair and then reappearing, her chubby, cheeky face exploding into what he surmised were peals of laughter. He reciprocated with a pop-eyed look of surprise while trying to let on to the adults that he was playing a game and not slipping to some new, deeper level of enfeeblement.

But where was Yeats? Apparently he hadn't made the trip from the Plaza. Perhaps he had become accustomed to the high life. Perhaps Yeats was merely a cantankerous old bollocks who kept his own hours and was frequently detained by the goings-on in the spirit world.

Could any halfway decent medium summon him away from Michael and toward some dimly lit table, where the poet would be put to work pecking out cryptic nonsense on a Ouija board? Or was he right now in some celestial parlor, sitting down for a chat with sharp-penned Swift and mad-brained Blake and poor doomed Keats, talking poetic meter and the oddities of a language in which *Keats* and *Yeats* did not rhyme?

Now he had done it: drifting off, and all adult eyes were on him, wondering what was happening in the head of poor doomed Michael. He looked from face to face, offering a wry smile, a raised eyebrow, a wink for Martin. *I'm still in here,* he wanted to convey. *I just can't get out.*

Rosemary had been curious to meet Martin's brothers, and so far it had been quite a show. Though Martin had told her the outlines of his life back in Ireland, she hoped that meeting his brothers would fill in some of the blanks. She knew that he had been born in Cork, where his father taught at the university. She knew that his mother, a musician of some local renown, had died in an automobile accident when Martin was twelve and that shortly afterward, his father had moved the boys to a remote town halfway across the country. Martin had chafed at small-town life and wasn't much fonder of his father, whom he blamed for uprooting the family while the shock of their mother's death was still fresh.

She knew more of Michael than of Francis, thanks to his letters. She couldn't follow most of Michael's theological meanderings, but truth be told, neither could Martin. And as tight as their budget was, she tried never to begrudge the twice-yearly payments they made to the seminary: Michael had a vocation, a calling from God, and that was not a thing to be questioned. Francis, who was harder to figure, was the one who gave Martin fits. Rosemary and Peggy had their differences, but Martin and Francis were oil and water, or, as Martin had said, chalk and cheese.

And now they were all together for Sunday dinner. As Martin settled everyone around the table—the girls arrayed on one side and Francis and Michael along the other—Francis insisted that they pop the cork while the champagne was still cold. He'd had the concierge procure the bottle and pack it in a bucket filled with ice, but the ice had melted and the bucket had been abandoned on the front stoop. Rosemary brought four glasses from the kitchen and Francis chuffed the cork, letting it ricochet against the ceiling. Champagne frothed from the mouth of the bottle and when each had been served, they raised their glasses.

"What shall we toast?" Francis said. "To families reunited?"

"To a speedy recovery for Michael," Rosemary said.

"To the memory of Francis Dempsey, may his soul rest in peace," Martin said.

Francis did a double take straight out of a holiday pantomime. "I'm not dead yet," he said.

"*Ach,*" Martin said. "Show some reverence."

"Says the man who missed his own father's funeral."

Rosemary interrupted before the brotherly rough-and-tumble became any rougher. "Tell me, Francis," she said. "What sort of funeral did your father have?"

"Oh, it was grand," he said. "Father Hogan was his dour old self. Ashes to ashes and all that. Lengthy eulogy on the noble service Da performed all those years, educating the sons and daughters of Ballyrath, bringing the light of knowledge and so on and so forth. Da would've hated it."

"Father Hogan getting the last word," Martin said. "That should've been reason enough to keep Da going for a few more years."

"It was never a fair fight between those two." Francis dropped his voice into the gruff bark that best matched his father's tone. "In a battle of wits, that man is completely unarmed."

"That's the real reason he didn't want Michael in the seminary," Martin said. "He was afraid he'd turn into a little Hogan."

"Instead of a little Da."

The three of them turned toward Michael, who was making faces across the table at Kate. He seemed to sense the pause in conversation and the turn of all the adult eyes toward him. He straightened in his chair and resumed slicing a piece of roast beef.

"Michael wasn't the only one who disappointed him," Martin said. "A university professor, and what did Da get from his sons? A musician, a convict, and a priest. I don't know which of us he thought was the worst."

"He'd been a classmate of Joyce's, for God's sake!" Francis said. "He never liked the gatch on that one, though. Always mincing around, giving out about God and art. And don't get him started on what that fellow did to *The Odyssey*!"

"Do you mean *Ulysses*?" Rosemary said. "Have you read it?"

"Only enough to know which pages to show interested buyers. Too bad for them the rest of it's all whinging about lemon soap and kidney pie."

Rosemary stifled a laugh. "Oh, there's more to it than that," she said.

"So you've read it?" Francis looked impressed. "Quite the libertine you've married, Martin."

There was a knock at the door, one that started and did not stop, and all Martin could think was that it was Mrs. Fichetti, come to complain about the racket. But this racket was his family. He was ready at last to give her an earful. He turned the knob and yanked the door open.

"Thank *God* you're home!" Peggy's voice filled the apartment as she brushed past Martin, dropped her purse on the armchair, and made for the dining room at top speed. "I just *had* to get out of there!"

"Hello, Peggy," Martin said to the open, empty doorway.

"I swear I'm going to call it off." Peggy was speaking to no one, to everyone. "I'm going to call off the whole thing—oh, hello!" She'd expected only Rosemary and the girls, but here was a big redhead and another fellow who looked like a smaller version of Martin. "Oops, I've barged in," she said, pulling at the fingers of her gloves; *gloves,* even in this heat. "I'm *so* sorry—but you will not believe what it's like over there. I had to make a getaway!" She tossed her gloves on the table, narrowly avoiding the gravy boat, and flopped into Martin's chair.

Rosemary shot her a look of concern. "Who else canceled?"

"It's not that," Peggy said. "It's just Mother. And it's Daddy. I'm not going to waste another minute thinking about it."

At the sight of Auntie Peggy, Kate started announcing the details of a donnybrook she had witnessed in church that morning: a boy in the pew in front of them had punched his younger brother during the kiss of peace, and the younger boy cried so much that his father had to carry him out of the church. Kate had been telling the story all day—twice already to Michael. Her voice had only one volume, and she was a champion hand-waver. "The Italian," her grandfather called her.

Francis stood and offered his hand. Peggy looked like she had stepped from the screen of a Hollywood movie—one of those wholesome American exports where the daughters smile and speak their mind and wear shimmery tops that hint at the shapes of their brassieres. Her hair was a long blond swoop that curled up just above her shoulders, and her cheeks were still flushed from her rapid ascent of the stairs.

Martin brought a chair from the kitchen and as he returned to the dining room was struck by how right and comfortable this was: Rosemary and Peggy and Francis gabbing away, the pantomimed introductions with Michael, Peggy rising from her seat to take Michael's hand between her own, Francis laughing and insisting on a hug rather than a handshake, Kate telling the story—was it the tenth time today?—about the boy in the church, then telling it again, Rosemary leaning over to give the baby another spoonful and the baby smiling a two-tooth smile and sputtering over the soft mashed carrots and the soggy crust of bread from the Italian bakery. This was family, his family. He had been a part of Rosemary's family for four years, but it had never been a snug fit, and sure, he and Rosemary had their own family inside these walls. But here now were the Dempsey boys brought back together, and here were Rosemary and Kate and Evie. His first family—his original family—getting acquainted with his new family, the one he had made for himself.

Francis tried a man's patience, but with Rosemary and Peggy for an audience, he showed that he had charm to burn, and if Michael was silent he was still sweet and he really seemed to be making an effort. Perhaps his brain was intact, and that was a good sign. And then Rosemary. She shone. She was the girl he had fallen in love with, full of bright humor and as quick and sharp a talker as any of the boys. Even Peggy, who could be a piece of work, brought a jolt to the room. Francis and Michael were full of smiles whenever she rolled her eyes and flipped her hair and talked in that way where every thought was a chore and a joke rolled into one. Having two women in the room was just the spark the night needed. They had all been a bit too formal; the ratio had been all wrong, and there were still so many questions surrounding the sudden appearance of the Irish relations. But Peggy's presence made those conversations impossible, and that seemed to put everyone at ease. With her in the mix, the night took on a sudden gabby energy.

Francis loosened his tie, then unbuttoned that ridiculous plaid waistcoat. Before long all of the men were in shirtsleeves, their cuffs rolled to the elbows and their plates doubling as ashtrays until Rosemary said, in a florid, stage-Irish brogue, "What's wrong with the lot of you, were you raised in a barn?" Martin scooted to the living room and returned with two thick ashtrays, a his-and-hers wedding gift from one of Rosemary's myriad aunts. The room filled with a sweet blue haze and the champagne kept flowing. The bottle seemed to have no end.

So there was dinner and then dessert—a chocolate cake, in honor of the reunion of the Dempsey brothers—and then tea, and when that was done Rosemary told Kate to say good night to her father and her aunt and her uncles and she scooped up the baby and brought the girls into their bedroom. Martin reached into the cabinet for the bottle of good whiskey. He brought two glasses back to the table and poured a short one for himself and one for Francis, but before he could cap the bottle, Michael claimed Martin's glass for his own.

Martin started to speak, but Francis cut him off. "Let him have it," he said. "I can't see that a glass is going to do him any harm."

Martin brought another glass from the kitchen, but when he poured his drink Peggy snatched it and raised the glass in a toast to Martin.

Francis cheered her on: "Good for you! That will show the whiskey miser!"

It was something out of the Marx Brothers and on another night it might have been enough to set off Martin's temper, but everything about this night was moving so nicely and he didn't want to do anything to wreck it. "You're devils." He said it with a smile and rose to get a fourth glass from the cabinet.

When Rosemary returned from the girls' bedroom, she found Martin, Francis, and Peggy laughing and talking, with the last of the whiskey pooled in the bottom of the bottle.

Michael's eyes were bright and alive as he tried to imagine the course of the conversation. Without the distraction of voices and laughter, he was able to count how often Francis snuck a look at the nape of Peggy's neck, at the tightness of her blouse. He saw too how Peggy let her gaze linger a little too long on Francis, how she batted at his arm with her brightly polished nails.

Peggy was asking herself why she didn't spend *more* time at her sister's place. She'd never seen Martin so loosey-goosey, and this Francis was a hoot. Who knew that Martin's brother would be so much fun? Martin was nice, and it was neat, she guessed, that he stuck with his music when a lot of others would have taken whatever job Daddy offered them, but he came across as kind of stuck-up, as if he was judging you and you were always coming up short but he would never tell you what you needed to do to pass his stupid test. No, Martin was great for Rosemary, but there was something unsettled about him. Like he was always going somewhere but had lost the address.

Now Peggy had discovered this brother of his whom she'd barely known existed. She had heard that Martin had family in Ireland, but the only brother he ever mentioned was the younger one studying to be a priest. But Francis. He was the type that her father called a good-time Charlie. (That's what he'd called Martin when he found out Martin was a musician, except that as far as Peggy saw, Martin rarely looked like he was having a good time.) But you only had to spend a few minutes with Francis to see that he knew how to have fun. Just look at that giant bottle of champagne! Now that was how you started a party!

Her fiancé, Tim, was a sweetheart—the sweetest!—but if Peggy had pointed out a bottle like that to Tim, he would have said, *Who could ever drink that much champagne?* Or would have wondered how much it cost. Or complained that champagne gave him a headache. Peggy decided right then and there that she wanted a bottle just that big at her wedding reception—and if they made them any bigger, then *that's* what she wanted. The single biggest bottle of champagne that anyone had ever seen. People would laugh at the very sight of it, and for months afterward and maybe even for the rest of their lives they would tell the story of the biggest bottle of champagne they had ever seen. And the kicker would be that they could say that it wasn't just the biggest they'd seen—it was the biggest they had ever tasted. Because that's what Peggy would do: before the toasts started, she and Tim would uncork that bottle like it was a cannon and all the guests would fill their glasses. What could be more fitting than that? It would be beautiful; symbolic, even. And for once it would be nice to show everyone that every day didn't have to be about cutting corners and doing what's practical and for God's sake don't waste anything. For one day they would have this bottle full of more champagne than anyone had ever seen and they would drink it dry.

"SO WHAT'S A typical night like around here?" Francis said. They had moved their drinking into the living room, a few feet farther away from where the girls were sleeping. The radio played and Francis held his glass to the overhead light, where it glowed like honey. "I picture bathtubs full of gin, Duke Ellington and his colored dancers dropping in at all hours, rent parties that have the neighbors calling the police—"

"What exactly have you been telling them?" Rosemary said to Martin. "I really want to hear more about these dancing girls."

"The only girl who's been dancing around here is Kate, though I'll admit that getting her to keep her shirt on and her skirt down can be a problem."

"Come on, now," Francis said. "You must go out on the town. Nightclubs and ballrooms are Martin's places of business."

Martin and Rosemary exchanged a look and a movement of the mouth that wasn't quite a grimace but certainly wasn't a smile. There hadn't been many nights out lately, they allowed, not for the two of them together.

Peggy clapped her hands. "That's what we should do! Dancing! I want to go out dancing."

"It's a Sunday night," Rosemary said. "And you're getting married in six days."

"Exactly," Peggy said. "You just said yourself that once you get married, you stop having fun."

"That's not—"

"So where should we go?" Francis said. "Where's the tip-top for dancing in this town?"

Peggy's eyes were aglow. "The Savoy! Let's go to the Savoy!"

"For crying out loud," Rosemary said. "You can't go to the Savoy!"

"Why not?"

"Because if Mom and Dad find out that I let you go to Harlem on the Sunday night before your wedding, they will kill you, and as soon as they're done with you, they'll kill me, too."

"What's all this about you *letting* me go? You sound just like *them*."

"I'll keep an eye on her," Francis said.

"I don't think it's such a good idea," Martin said.

"I managed jail without a scratch. I think I can handle myself in a dance hall."

"You were in jail?" Peggy's face flushed. "Do Mother and Daddy know about that?"

"Jesus Christ, Franny. Will you watch what you say?"

Rosemary took hold of Peggy's arm. It was the same pincer grip she used when Kate misbehaved in a department store. "They don't know, and they can't know."

"Oh my God—"

"You can't say anything. Ever."

"What's all this?" Francis said. "I'm not ashamed—it's our narrow-minded, priestly government that should be ashamed."

"What did you do?" Peggy said.

"He didn't *do* anything," Martin said. "What I mean is, he's not a thief or a killer or—"

"I was practically a political prisoner."

"Oh, Janey Mack," Martin said.

"Here's what we can agree on," Rosemary said. "Mom and Dad are never to hear a word of this."

"Because Martin is ashamed of his own brother," Francis said.

"Because I'm not my in-laws' favorite person, and having a convict for a brother isn't going to help matters."

"Do I look like a convict?"

"Not at all," Peggy said. "You look like a gentleman."

"It's nice to know there's someone in this family who thinks so."

"Now, if it's okay with you old married folks, this gentleman and I are going dancing."

While Francis reknotted his tie, rolled down his cuffs, helped himself to another slice of cake, and even ventured into the kitchen to pick at the few scraps of roast beef that had escaped his plate, Peggy ransacked Rosemary's closet for something to wear. She complained in an offhand way about how out of date, and also how large, Rosemary's clothes were, before finally settling on a dress that Rosemary had bought right before she found out she was pregnant for the second time and which she had never worn. Out in the living room, it was decided that Michael would stay at the apartment and that Francis would escort Peggy home from the Savoy—midnight at the latest!—but that he was not to have any contact with the Dwyers.

"Stay in the cab when you drop her off," Martin instructed his brother. "Just to be on the safe side."

"Not very gentlemanly," Francis said.

Once Peggy was safely deposited in Woodlawn, Francis was free to spend the night with Michael in the living room—"Fat chance of that!" Francis scoffed—or return to the Plaza.

Rosemary seemed as resigned to this course of events as Martin was. She knew Peggy, and knew that trying to keep her from going her own way would only stiffen her sister's resolve. It had been like this for years, back to the days when they shared a bedroom and Rosemary took it on herself to shield Peggy's shenanigans from their parents. Nights when the house had the hollowed-out calm of a bell that has finally stopped ringing, Peggy could open the door, slide through a span no wider than a fist, and move from inside the house to outside in the interval between one breath and another. From their bedroom, Rosemary imagined her sister's bare feet on the flagstone path, Peggy with her shoes in her hand and a boy waiting, always a boy waiting, around the corner or in a car that would coast for two or three houses before roaring to life—every boy a Romeo snatching his Juliet from under Mr. Capulet's whiskey-blasted nose.

Peggy was always back in bed before Rosemary woke up, having drifted in as quietly as she'd left, and when the girls were called to breakfast, Peggy was the one who was chipper, refreshed, and rested. Rosemary would be worn down by a lousy night's sleep, her dreams tortured by what-ifs—because if Peggy was the carefree Juliet, then Rosemary was the nurse, the maidservant, the worrywart older sister.

FRANCIS AND THE blonde were gone and Rosemary had gone to bed. In the living room, Michael sat up with Martin, who was gamely trying to mime a series of questions. *Would you like a drink?* was easy enough, but how was he to suggest a cup of tea? After a flurry of half-hearted attempts to shape a kettle with his hands, he decided it was best to go to the kitchen for the real thing. Martin paused at the wireless on his way out of the room and switched it on. The light came up on the dial, but after he'd fidgeted with the knob he caught himself and, embarrassed, switched it off.

Michael shook his head, waved his hands in front of him, tried to suggest it was all right, that Martin should listen, but his brother didn't seem to catch his meaning and instead sat heavily in an armchair upholstered in a nubby blue fabric.

This was all getting to be too much. There was so much Michael wanted to talk to Martin about, but when had Martin ever really listened to Michael? They hadn't been face to face in ten years, and back then Michael had been only a little spiv and Martin already fixated on his dream of America. Michael had tried through his letters to give his brother a sense of his life and of himself, but that attempt had been banjaxed by unbroken codes and bollixed lines of communication. Martin might have read the words, but he didn't really read the letters. If he had looked closely, the code would have offered itself up for the cracking. Michael couldn't make it too obvious, for fear that Brother Zozimus or one of the other priests charged with monitoring the correspondence of the seminarians for blasphemous, prurient, vulgar, scatological, or otherwise unwholesome content would consign the letter to the basement furnace. Still, Michael had hoped the tone of his letters would be enough to alert his brother—his actual, flesh-and-blood brother—to the presence of hidden messages lurking in the typewritten pages: the perils into which Martin placed his soul by attending the cinema (*a place whose interplay of light and darkness approximates the fires of hell and the shadow cast by the refusal of God's mercy*); the sinful nature of jazz music (*a bestial rhythm which inspires gyrations that taunt all notions of Christian purity and mimic the seizures of the possessed whom Christ Our Lord exorcised*); and the flesh- and spirit-rotting qualities of strong drink (*a poison that seduces the body and debases the soul and deprives men of the ability to govern, with firm hand, their animal nature*). Martin couldn't think he was serious about any of it. Michael figured his brother would have a good laugh at each month's tortured missive, and then enjoy some cryptographic fun unearthing Michael's dispatches from the front lines of pastoral education: PRIESTS OLD AND DAFT, STUDENTS YOUNG AND DAFT, or HAVE I MADE A MISTAKE? PLEASE ADVISE, or MY GIRL, MY GIRL, WHY HAVE YOU FORSAKEN ME?

Michael began to realize with the passage of time and the receipt of too many stale, codeless replies that while they may have been born of the same parents, he and Martin were strangers. Even when they'd lived under the same roof, Martin was always off practicing in some empty shed, or in the shell of the great house over the hill, a once-grand manse that the locals had burned during the war to settle accounts with their landlord. And when Martin wasn't blowing that clarinet of his, or wrestling with the pub's rickety upright—the only piano in town—then he was working to put aside a bankroll for his American plan. Now here they were, face to face, and both were struggling with anything more complicated than a yes-or-no question. More than that, Michael couldn't deny the way his own brother fidgeted in his chair, uneasy with the presence in his own home of poor, young, damaged, God-mad Michael.

It was too much. Michael stood quickly—and so unexpectedly that Martin flinched—and moved to the wireless. He punched the button, and the golden half-circle of the numbered dial glowed. One hand was on the webbing that covered the speaker and when the signal popped, Michael felt a pulse under his fingers. He turned the volume knob and the pulse became a thrumming—his hand was like an insect's antennae. He could feel the music, the pounding of the drums, the buzz of the horns, pinpricks from a piano. He closed his eyes. He didn't want any interference. He imagined that if he could force all sense impressions to enter through a single door that he could concentrate the experience and feel it more vividly. Sound was nothing more than vibrations and here those vibrations came into his hands, as if he were a blind man reading the humped code of a Braille page. He could have hummed the tune. He could have sung along. And then he lost it.

His eyes snapped open and Martin was at his side, one finger pressed to his lips, the other hand cutting the volume to nil. Michael felt hollowed out, but his brother only pointed to his wristwatch, then put both hands together, as if in prayer, and laid them on the side of his head. *Quiet. It's late. Everyone is sleeping.* Michael, wounded, nodded. Martin was talking—his jaw was moving and Michael assumed that he was producing words—but Michael could only stare at his own hands.

Since Michael's appearance yesterday, he'd worn a look of blissful perseverance. Martin had wondered if he was some sort of holy fool, offering up his suffering to the greater glory of God. Now, for the first time, Michael looked like someone from whom every treasure he'd ever carried had been snatched. Martin touched Michael's shoulder, enough to get his attention, and began to play the air in front of him as if it were an invisible piano. With the fingers of his right hand he worked the valves of a make-believe trumpet. He took Michael's hands in his own and placed them back on the speaker, and as he punched the button, the eye of the wireless glowed again. Martin nodded *yes-yes-yes* and that idiot's grin came back to Michael's face and he smiled and nodded back, a mirror of his brother, and squeezed Martin's hand. Having Martin understand meant the world to him.

Michael could feel the music coming through the speakers again, but the song had changed. This one was a light rainfall on his palms instead of the thunderstorm of the earlier tune, but he could feel it, could almost hear it, and he had been so parched for sound that even this quieter number made his senses bloom. He closed his eyes and leaned, stock-still, against the cabinet. Martin stayed with him, his hand over the other speaker, trying to feel what his brother felt.

An hour later, Michael was alone, the apartment dark. Martin had mimed sleep; it was becoming a game for the two of them now, not the earlier grim attempts at communication but a contest to see who could out-charade the other. He left the room and returned a few minutes later with a pillow and a bedsheet for his brother. Michael wondered if this meant that Francis wasn't coming back. Had Michael been exiled from the fancy hotel? Had this been Francis's plan all along: to convey Michael to the United States and deposit him with Martin? Had he been traded, if only temporarily, for the blond girl? On the sofa, Michael knit his fingers together and webbed them over his still-full belly. He rested his chin on his chest and closed his eyes.

When he opened them—ten minutes later, maybe an hour—Yeats was sitting in the same chair Martin had occupied earlier in the night.

"Where have you been?" Michael said.

"I was going to ask you the same question."

"I've been here for hours."

"So have I." Yeats made a steeple of his long fingers and tapped them against the bridge of his nose. "This Bronx is a very strange place."

"Only the Bronx?" Michael sat upright on the sofa. He ran his hands roughly over his face, shaking off the last traces of sleep. "Mr. Yeats, I can't make sense of a single moment I've spent in America. And I've got a theory I'd like to run by you—about your nature, your origin, the substance of your being—but you have to promise not to take it personally."

Yeats crossed his legs and sat back in the chair.

"I've been speculating that you might be a figment of my imagination. That your apparent presence is the result of some psychological or physical injury that I've suffered—an injury which has rendered me somehow off balance, mentally speaking."

"You're saying I am a delusion."

"In a manner of speaking, yes. And you must admit that if our roles were reversed, you'd be asking yourself the same question."

Yeats seemed about to answer, but paused and composed himself. "Why is it so difficult to accept that communication is possible between the spiritual and material planes?"

"I don't deny it at all. But the sort of visitation I'm familiar with is Virgin-Mother-on-a-mountaintop, not dead-poet-in-New-York."

"And yet, here I am." Yeats stood and began pacing the room.

For all of his doubts, Michael didn't want Yeats to be a figment; it was more comforting to think that he was a ghost or some other entity from the world beyond. If he was a delusion, then Michael was only talking to himself, although a part of himself that wore a Yeats mask.

But if Yeats was real, then it was a sign that some outside assistance was available. Or perhaps it was simply, and necessarily, companionship—contact with a mind other than his own.

"So tell me," Michael said. "What's so strange about the Bronx?"

Yeats stopped his circuit of the room. "I was in this flat, but all was in a state of flux. The weather changed minute to minute: sun and then clouds, hotter and colder, pouring rain and then blue skies. At the same time, the buildings themselves aged. Freshly laid bricks one moment and derelict the next. I saw this flat as it is now, and as an empty lot, and as a clapboard-covered house. I saw it as a run-down tenement—squalid in its appearance, one window covered in boards, its bricks scored by black smoke."

"A vision of the future, do you think?"

"The future, the past, the current moment. It was as if I were flipping through an enormous book, forward and backward, trying to locate a particular page. It may have been the most peculiar part of this entire experience."

"Simply existing, months after your death—that's not the most peculiar part?"

"Of course not. I expected some sort of existence after my physical death. But this sensation of time, of the way it fluctuated—it was unsettling." Yeats peered out the window. Across the street, a row of identical houses. Over the roofline, the hazy glow of the Grand Concourse was visible. "Gradually, the pages became somewhat easier to control. I could slow their movement, explore each before turning to another. I have seen many people in this flat, and I have seen inventions that Wells or Verne could not have imagined."

"The future, eh? I've always imagined the skies full of zeppelins, and—"

"It's as ragged as the present. Worse, even. Fires burning unchecked, whole city blocks in ruin. The past, at least, was quieter. This land is newly settled, and you need only scratch away the veneer of asphalt and brick to see the land for what it was. Meadows. Hillsides. Forests. The imprint of mankind's efforts is widespread, but it does not run deep. What was built here could be swept away in no time at all."

Yeats seemed uncomfortable, fidgety even. Michael had seen him sit, legs crossed, for hours on end, but now Yeats paced, shifted, looked quickly in one direction and then another.

"Are these your new accommodations?" Yeats regarded the sofa, the chair where he had been sitting, the oval coffee table. He seemed disappointed by the lank drapes, the faded floral rug, the narrow polished breakfront with its collection of cups.

"I don't know. Francis was here earlier but he left with a woman."

"A woman?" Yeats seemed more interested in this than in anything Michael had yet said. "What sort of woman?"

"A pretty one. She arrived during dinner and later the two of them left. There was some sort of a row about it. She was a bit of a wild one, I think."

Yeats let out a sharp laugh, almost like a seal's bark. "Do you have much experience with wild ones?"

"I didn't spend my entire life in the seminary," Michael said. "And I saw enough to know that she fancies Francis. She kept touching his arm while she was talking to him."

Yeats took in this information and continued his pacing, as if working through a mathematical equation. "Knowing what I do of your brother, and what his inclinations might be in the presence of a wild young woman, it is likely that he is otherwise engaged tonight."

"You didn't see any of this in your giant magic book of the future, did you?"

Yeats stared at Michael for a moment, and then looked away.

"So it's to be the sofa for me, is it?" Michael said. "Well, I've slept on worse."

Yeats ceased pacing. "We *could* strike out on our own."

"Just the two of us?"

"If your theory is correct and I am only a delusion, then it would be you alone."

"It's more of a hypothesis," Michael said.

"I suppose I understand your hesitation," Yeats said. "Perhaps you prefer to be carted about like a child, or treated like an invalid. You are the youngest of the brothers, are you not?"

Michael paused for only a moment before hauling himself to his feet. "So you're going to shame me into action, is that it?"

"That depends," Yeats said. "Have you any money?"

Michael had a few crisply folded bills of uncertain denomination that Francis had given him before their Saturday walk. The money gave him a certain confidence, but there were other logistical difficulties to be overcome when a deaf-mute traveled with a ghost. He thought of the stilted exchange of gestures that vexed him and Martin. "Assuming we can find a taxi," he said to Yeats, "how am I supposed to mime 'big hotel'?"

"Check your pocket," Yeats said, nodding toward the suit coat draped over the arm of the sofa. From the breast pocket Michael withdrew a business card; the gold-embossed crest at the center matched the one on the doors and awnings of the hotel.

"Where did that come from?"

Yeats shrugged. "Perhaps I put it there when you weren't looking."

"You tricky poltergeist!" Michael clapped his hands together. He hadn't felt so full of life, so ready for adventure, since…since any moment he could remember. "Well, then," he said. "Let us arise and go now."

"Are you quoting me to me?"

"One of us was bound to say it. I thought it better for the both of us if I was the one to do it."

HARLEM

THE SAVOY BALLROOM WAS the mecca of New York big-band jazz, the mile zero of swing, the hottest spot in Harlem — "the Home of Happy Feet!" — and it drew dancers from every shade on the color line: black, brown, beige, and white; jitterbugs and Lindy Hoppers; hep cats and duchesses. And the Savoy was all class; men were gentlemen or else they were gone. Charlie Buchanan, who had a tin ear for music but managed every detail of the Savoy down to the three-times-a-week floor polishing, insisted on that. More than once the bouncers — all of them ex-boxers, all of them in tuxedos — had shown an ill-mannered lady-killer to the door, to the sidewalk, and right into the Lenox Avenue gutter. The ladies of Harlem knew they were safe, if safe was what they wanted, and that meant they flocked to the Savoy, which meant that men flocked there double. The Savoy boasted two bandstands, the floor held four thousand, and the music didn't stop until two in the morning — and that was the only math that mattered on a night out in the city.

As Francis and Peggy pushed through the front door and up the staircase that led to the second-story ballroom, Benny Carter was in the house and the joint was hopping. The Savoy was long and narrow — the Track, they called it — and by ten o'clock the floor was packed with couples swinging under the watchful eyes of the bouncers and the dime-a-dance hostesses. Carter was a sax man — one of the finest altos in New York City, and that meant in the world. When he stepped out to solo, the jitterbugs spun faster, black and white pairs weaving within inches of each other. At midnight, the weekly opportunity contest began and the dancers cleared the floor, or as much of it as they could; there must have been a solid few thousand on the Track that night. Pair by pair, the dancers in the competition took the floor and showed what a Lindy Hop could be if only it were given space to breathe and room to fly. Thirty minutes was an eternity for the onlookers to wait their own turn to cut it up again, but who could tear themselves from the spectacle of Carter's orchestra pushing the show ponies and being pushed by them? After each couple finished, the crowd went mad with applause (or didn't) and finally the night's champions were crowned. The winning couple barely had time to embrace and claim their prize before the bandstand jumped back to life, practically midnote, and signaled the crowd to retake the floor and keep stomping until they felt the room shake.

The dancers never let up. They spun and kicked, dipped and swayed, shimmied and sashayed, all propelled by Carter's electrifying arrangements. He ran them through "Blues in My Heart," "Oh, Lady Be Good!," and "I Ain't Got Nobody." But what sent the crowd into a frenzy—and what had been driving the Savoy dancers into a dervish whirl for three nights straight—was a new addition to the band's repertoire: a light, popular tune from a few years back that Carter had reengineered into a full-blown stomp. The original had been breezy, lilting; a melody for whistling on a balmy day in May, with the sun shining and your best girl's hand in yours. Carter had turned the song into a heavyweight-title fight pitting the sax against the trumpet. The horns bobbed and weaved, feinted and jabbed. As the song gained steam they began to assemble combinations: haymakers from Carter's alto followed by a roundhouse from the trumpet. But the kicker, the essential element that drove the dancers into the stratosphere of joy and motion, was a hesitation between each round in this slugfest—the vocal equivalent of the ring girl parading across the canvas with a numbered card held high above her lipsticked smile. At the end of each rapturous solo, Carter leaned in close to the microphone and hissed, "Now *that's* more like it!" It was the only lyric he had salvaged from the song—the tune's title, in fact—and the crowd began to anticipate it, to want it, and so Carter withheld it that much more. The horns would scream and die, the band would crash to a halt, and Carter would slowly draw the microphone to his mouth, dragging out each word as the Savoy faithful whooped and hollered. Just as suddenly as they had stopped, the band would reignite, burning hotter and hotter until it seemed that the ceiling of the Track was about to blow sky-high.

Francis and Peggy had chugged through the first few numbers, feeding on the energy of the other dancers, but as the band tore into this new floor-burner, they retreated into the mob of spectators basking in the union of music and motion. The band fed the dancers and the dancers pushed the band: Hotter! Louder! Faster! The band and the dancers skated together on the edge of the precipice, and the thrill of seeing them, or *being* them, came from the sense that all of this could collapse into chaos but that right now, in this moment, it had not and would not. They were an engine that ran on rocket fuel, the gears in perfect alignment, the pistons humming.

And through all of this, it never once occurred to Francis or Peggy that this song was Martin's song—that what Benny Carter had rearranged was in fact Martin's one entry to the Hit Parade, the ditty that had briefly raised his hopes about a prosperous future, and that now seemed to him like a mirage he had been foolish enough to mistake for a leafy oasis. They'd heard Martin's version as recorded by the Chester Kingsley Orchestra in 1937, but hearing that song in this one would have been like recognizing the face of the model in a painting by Picasso. And in those moments, Francis and Peggy were too drunk and happy, too hot and overwhelmed by the music and the dancing and the play of shadow and light, to trace the ways that Benny Carter had added muscle to the bones of Martin's song.

* * *

OUTSIDE THE SAVOY, in a car parked on Lenox Avenue, Cronin kept an eye on the doorway of the ballroom. If anyone noticed him they tried hard not to show it. A man his size and his color, camped out on the busiest street in Harlem, could only be in the employ of the police or some gangland boss. Either way, he wasn't someone you wanted to cross.

After spying the missus and her children the day before, he'd had to wait only another fifteen minutes before he saw someone else bound for the apartment house. The man crossing the street was unmistakably a Dempsey. His profile gave him away; he was his mother's son and there was no doubting it. Cronin should have felt some satisfaction—he was one step closer to finding his quarry—but all he felt was whiplash. Everywhere he turned, he saw reminders of other places he should be and older times he could not forget.

Cronin was ready to follow Martin wherever he went—sooner or later he would go to his brother, Cronin was sure of it—but hours later, when the last upstairs light was finally switched off, Cronin called it a night. His instincts were failing him. He was rusty, plain and simple. On Sunday, he had returned to a spot down the street from the apartment house and sat watch all through the day, but aside from morning Mass, the Dempseys stayed close to home. He was expecting another wasted day when a taxicab rolled to a stop in front of the apartment and disgorged a stout redhead and his spindly companion, who was coming out on the losing end of a wrestling match with an enormous wine bottle.

Again, it was Bernadette—Mrs. Dempsey—who confirmed what Cronin suspected. She had marked each of her sons as her own. Martin had her face, as did the younger one, who had been a baby when Cronin had—when she—when Bernadette died. Francis was built like his father but he had his mother's wild shock of red hair. It rose above his head like a flame, as though he didn't care who saw it.

Cronin could have taken him, but he stuck to his promise—his vow—to give the front door a wide berth. He didn't approach Dempsey then, just as he didn't approach him later when he came down the steps with the blonde on his arm. If he'd done that, Dempsey and the girl might've made a break for the cab and he might've lost them. It was possible Dempsey had a gun on him—hadn't he left three dead already?—and who knew who this girl was, and whether she meant anything to him. He might use her for cover. Cronin had seen men do that before. Or she could turn out to be a witness, someone who could point the finger at Cronin, and he'd be forced to do something about that.

He could say he was playing it smart, but he knew what Frank Dempsey would say: that he had gone soft. Cronin spots a woman and two children walking up the front steps and suddenly the house and all who enter it are off-limits? It had to be a joke. The old Tom Cronin wouldn't have let a *houseful* of children put him off his task. Hadn't he gut-shot a police inspector in Cork—what was his name? Browne? Yes, William Browne. Hadn't he gut-shot William Browne in the front hall of his own home with one of the man's children watching it all from between the spindles of the staircase? Cronin had waited until the family gathered for their supper—he figured that would be the moment when he would have Browne to himself at the front of the house while the rest of the family feasted in the back. He didn't count on the boy still being upstairs. Hadn't the boy heard his mother calling him down to eat, when Cronin himself had heard her from the alleyway? Why had the boy lagged behind so? It troubled Cronin, the way it happened, but it didn't stop him. And it wasn't as if he noticed the lad's saucer-eyed face only after he shot his daddy dead. First he saw the boy, then he looked Browne square in the eye, and then he pulled the trigger. The boy's shriek followed Cronin down the front steps, out into the street, and down through the years. But it didn't stop him the next time. Or the time after that.

This was why Frank Dempsey had chosen him. Not because he saw

Cronin as a diamond in the rough. Not because he thought the fire of revolution burned in Cronin the same as it did in him and his sainted wife. Not because he liked Cronin, or saw him as a comrade-in-arms and boon companion. Frank Dempsey had singled out Cronin and cultivated him because he knew that Cronin was the kind of brute who could stand at a man's front door with the man's own son looking at him and pull the trigger that would put the boy's daddy in the ground.

It was a simple thing when you considered the mechanics of it, but most men couldn't do it. Their skin went clammy and their hands shook. The gun weighed a thousand pounds and they would stutter and stammer at the point of action. He had seen men piss themselves when they should have been pulling the trigger. But not Cronin. He was a man who could do it, and Frank Dempsey knew that about him. He had read it in Cronin's eyes. He had seen it inked on his skin. He knew it even before Cronin did.

All that he had done before he had done for reasons he could never quite explain, not even to himself. How could he go soft now, when the cause he served was the safety of his own family? No, Cronin had to remind himself that he was still that man, despite all of Alice's talk about him being a changed man. Only the old Cronin could stand guard on the walls that protected the life that he and Alice had built. Isn't that why Gavigan had come for him—because he could do things that other men could not?

Soon Francis Dempsey's moment would come. He had eluded his pursuers in Ireland and for a few days given them the slip in New York, but he had not counted on a man like Cronin coming for him. Dempsey was either brash or stupid or simply naive enough to think that no one would catch up to him, or that going to another country meant leaving his crimes and enemies behind him. Cronin knew better, and the next time he had Dempsey in his sights he would not hesitate. He would follow Dempsey until he came to a rest and then he would swoop down on him like an owl taking a mouse. He would give Gavigan his prize, he would once again wash his hands of all of this, and then he would go home.

PEGGY ASKED HIM where he was staying and he said, "The Plaza," like it was the obvious answer and she said, "You are not," and he said, "Why don't you see for yourself?" and she hesitated for only a second—she was *getting married* in six days—and then she said, "I'm calling your bluff, Mr. Dempsey"—she was getting married in *six days!*—and they were down the stairs and out the door of the Savoy and there was a cab waiting for them, just like they'd called ahead for it. It was eighty blocks to the Plaza but the ride slid by in no time at all. They talked about the music and the dancers, they looked out the window and joked about the couples they saw pressed into each other and the men slumped against walls, and they laughed at anyone who raised an arm to hail their cab. *Sorry, buddy,* they'd say. *Next time, Mac.* Francis practiced his American accent and Peggy laughed so hard her sides hurt. She gave him words and whole phrases that he would mangle with a slow drawl he had learned from watching Gable and Cagney and Astaire and Errol Flynn. She tried out her brogue and it was his turn to laugh.

Before they knew it they were passing the Metropolitan Museum and then the cab was coming to a stop in front of the broad steps of the hotel. He paid the cabbie, he held the door for her, and when the porter tipped his cap to Francis, he remembered—*Angus, I'm Angus in here*—and he gave the man a bob of the head and he and Peggy crossed the lobby, lights ablaze but otherwise empty, hushed for a moment by the after-midnight grandeur of a Sunday that had turned into Monday. Peggy kept expecting him to turn back and she almost laughed again when she heard him use an even funnier accent at the front desk, but the man behind it only nodded and handed over a room key with some degree of ceremony, and then they were on the elevator and in the hallway and then the key was in the lock and they were inside, alone together.

Six days. She was getting married in six days. And yet here she was, in the Plaza, long after midnight with a man she hardly knew. She'd been sparring with her parents for months about seating charts and centerpieces and wedding showers and the stupid World's Fair. Tim had been at the DA's office all weekend—he was *always* at the office— and she had begun to wonder if this was the life she was walking into. They weren't yet married—*six days!*—and already Tim had stopped courting her, *wooing* her. He wasn't treating her like his sweetheart anymore. He was treating her like a wife. And it wasn't that she wanted him around all the time (who could stand that?), but every now and then she wanted a night out, a bouquet of roses, a velvet-skinned box with a jeweler's name stamped in gold letters. There hadn't been any of that since they'd announced their engagement, and she was beginning to feel like she was little more than the porcelain bride standing on top of the cake. She had a place to be and a role to play, but no one expected her to talk, to move, to ask, to want.

When Francis closed the door, she turned into the darkness of the room, which wasn't just a room, but a whole suite, with a big window that looked out on the park, and at this time of night the park was an inky lake surrounded on all sides by city, or else every window and streetlight was a star and the park was a hole in the night sky, and you only had to reach out your hand and you could touch that void and disappear into it. Life as she knew it had become stretched and thin and she had slipped through some tear in the fabric and found herself here with him. Francis had a big grin on his face. She had called his bluff and he had shown her four aces, a full house, a flush—that was it. Francis held a royal flush and she didn't want to say another word in her own voice or in a funny accent or in any language at all. She walked slowly toward him and when they were face to face she put her arms around his neck and his hands went to her hips and she drew his mouth to hers.

MONDAY
JUNE 5

MIDTOWN

Monday morning, and Lilly awaited an audience with another man at the Foundation. She wished she felt more lively, more ready to make her case, but last night she had ventured as far as Harlem and by the time she returned to her studio it was long after midnight. Even on a Sunday, incandescent bulbs had pulsed on the dance-hall marquees, illuminating the faces of young men and women dressed for a night on the town. She hadn't time to develop anything, but she had high hopes for a few of the shots: a darkly radiant woman checking her reflection in a shopwindow, red lipstick poised at her puckered mouth; a man with coppery skin, his hat rakishly askew, pausing to buff his two-tone shoes with a handkerchief; a white couple at a ballroom entrance where the man, a strapping redhead, grinned goggle-eyed at the lights swirling overhead. Later, just as she was preparing to leave, she snapped a shot of a lone white man behind the wheel of a parked car, staring balefully at the same ballroom entrance.

This was the New York that Lilly had come seeking—a city of stolen moments and sidelong glances, back streets and narrow alleys. She wandered Chinatown at night, among the restaurants scrawled in neon and the dark shops with their jars full of mystery: shaggy tree bark, tendriled mushrooms, a root that resembled a withered hand. Or alone in the Bowery among the hollow-cheeked men so worn down by life that even the once-sharp hunger of their eyes had gone dull. Or roaming the docks that jutted into the Hudson, where she once had come upon two men, their hands in each other's trousers, coiled in a rough embrace. Camera at the ready, Lilly stalked her subjects along the marble-faced avenues of Wall Street and among the market stalls of Little Italy. It was on the street that you could see people as they really were, but only if you knew how to look, and when. And Lilly knew. She had the eye, the sense of timing. She waited for those moments, often in great crowds, when people believed that they were insulated by anonymity, and so they dropped the masks they wore in more direct encounters. A friend of hers in Paris had painted his Leica black in order to make it less obtrusive. A secret eye. He didn't want the glint of chrome to alert his subjects to the presence of a camera. But Lilly didn't need any of that trickery. People were willing to overlook a woman with a camera, especially if she was no great beauty. And if they did see her, she was easy to dismiss: just some tourist. What harm could she be?

For all of her success, even Lilly would admit that this was not the life her parents had imagined for her. Lilly's father had been the director general of a large dye factory, where he spent his days poring over ledgers and finalizing order sheets. The Great War had been hard all around, but Meyer Bloch's factory had produced the dye used in half the uniforms of the Austro-Hungarian army and so the family had prospered. Even as that prosperity waned in the postwar years, Lilly's mother maintained their home as one of the liveliest salons in Prague. Artists, musicians, writers, and hangers-on filled the grand house as Madame Bloch puppet-mastered conversations, arguments, liaisons, house concerts, and exhibitions. She often explained to Lilly the vital role of the patron, and how it was her calling to transmute the base coin of industry into the pure gold of art. It had been her mother's great wish that Lilly would follow in her footsteps, and throughout her youth, Lilly had accompanied her mother on trips to Paris—always Paris—to find which way the winds of culture were blowing. Every gallery in the City of Light knew Madame Bloch and knew not to waste her time with Monet, Seurat, or you-must-be-joking Corot. She sought only the new, she had a discerning eye, and she could negotiate a sale the way Talleyrand hashed out a treaty. Madame Bloch imagined that one day Lilly would marry well, recharge the family coffers, and devote herself to her own style of alchemy—curating not only art but artists.

But Lilly did not want to curate, to collect, to purchase—she wanted to make. If her mother's genius lay in her ability to recognize art that would matter (or that she would *make* matter), Lilly's talents lay in sensing the moment and having the reflexes to capture it. She had first tried her hand at painting but was soon seduced by photography. Perhaps it was because her mother had so little interest in this field; the camera, to her, was nothing but a machine for creating ghastly portraits drained of life and color. To Madame Bloch, there was something too coldly industrial about the camera for its products ever to be elevated into the leafy glade of art. Only a painting—an image filtered through the mind of a true artist—could depict the soul of its subject. Could a photograph match the raw beauty of a Schiele portrait? Or Matisse's riots of color and shape—could those be re-created on a sheet of chemical-soaked paper?

Lilly could not be dissuaded, and her choice of the camera over the paintbrush may have been an unspoken oath of allegiance to her father. While she loved her mother—and she did love her, everyone loved Madame Bloch, who allowed no other choice, with her grand manners and vast expressions of delight, her life lessons cast into compact aphorisms and her freely offered pronouncements, her stock of stories and her devil-may-care generosity—Lilly's father offered a simpler and more doting kind of affection. Lilly knew he cared for her, even if he never said it in as many words. He could have come out against her attending the Arts Academy, but did not, could have forbidden the installation of a darkroom in what had previously been a linen closet, but did not. Photography was somehow a recognition of the role of industry—dirty, smelly industry—in making her who she was. From a cocktail of toxins and metals, her father extracted money, her mother a persona, and Lilly—a reason for being.

At twenty, Lilly had set out for Paris, where her mother's reputation allowed for a rapid entry to salons and ateliers. A canny gallery owner whose country home in Brittany was largely funded by Madame Bloch's purchases introduced Lilly to Man Ray, and in the years that followed she sought out others whose experiments, in studios and on the street, extended the borders of what film could be. All the while, her mother fretted that entering the art world as an acolyte rather than a patron would only doom Lilly to the role of dilettante, hanger-on, or—horror of horrors—muse. Madame Bloch had had the misfortune of meeting many self-styled muses over the years—they were a necessary inconvenience if one was to consort with artists—and found them to be a generally hysterical lot. More than once, a teary, bandit-eyed girl had come to the house begging to know the whereabouts of some painter Madame Bloch had hosted the previous week, and who had left it to his patron to break the news that he had already returned to Madrid or Paris or Moscow or Berlin. Madame Bloch did not want her daughter among this disposable, pitiful tribe.

Lilly had also grown up around these women and had seen them transformed in weeks or months from *my muse* to *that impossible woman,* had seen these men of genius flee Prague while their muses' bellies grew big and their hearts broke wide open, and she set rules for herself to avoid their particular fate. Not that she was a nun during her years in Paris and elsewhere. In time, her predilections became a running joke among her circle, for though she served as apprentice, student, amanuensis, and sometime model, she would not sleep with other artists. As she had once told a friend, she drew a strict line between the darkroom and the bedroom.

But that life, that world—it was all gone or quickly going. It had been years since Berlin, Munich, and Vienna had purged themselves

of degenerate art and the degenerate artists—her friends and rivals—
who created it. Surely Prague would be next, and while Paris was
still Paris, it was foolish to believe that could not change in one blink
of the camera's eye. The poison was sure to keep spreading. Who
was there to stop it? She often wondered what her mother would
have thought of this latest turn of events. Madame Bloch never considered her salons to be merely some rich lady's exercise in luxury and
self-congratulation. No, her efforts among the avant-garde were more
than a private indulgence. They were a bulwark against idiocy. Art, to
her, was a light in the darkness, and if it burned brightly enough it
could dispel the dark forces altogether. Such a funny thought for a
woman who saw herself as a latter-day Medici. When had one of
Raphael's frescoes ever stopped the Florentines from marching against
Pisa, or kept the Spanish from the gates of the Tuscan republic? Lilly's
mother had been lucky enough not to live to see one of her most cher-
ished values overthrown by columns of brown-shirted troops marching, unimpeded, across the Charles Bridge.

Lilly wasn't an idealist, and she didn't see a virtue in walking boldly
into the lion's maw. If the lion wanted to eat you, it would eat you—
and how then could you continue to create? With the collapse of Mr.
Musgrove's plan, and the likelihood that she would have to leave New
York after all, she had begun to wonder if there would be some way to
jump ship in Marseille and make her way to Paris. But France was in
no hurry to draw in Europe's outcasts and oppressed artists. If her
family still had money, there might have been a way to gain entry
through doors otherwise locked, but her father had died years ago
and when the board of directors learned just how expensive Madame
Bloch's art collecting and artist-supporting had become—and of the
debts that Meyer Bloch had accrued to make both possible—they
shut off the flow of funds that had nourished Madame Bloch's *künst-
lergarten*. The house had to be sold, and Madame Bloch decamped to
a flat in a once-fashionable district now known for its faded charm

and the poor water pressure of its pipes. Toward the end of her life, she was selling her greatest finds for a pittance just to keep the lights on. When her mother died last year, Lilly had been back in Prague for only six months, watching her mother struggle against emphysema and the indignities of an empty sitting room and walls that grew more bare with each month's rent.

How would she have made it through those months without Josef? She had been in Barcelona running with a crowd of journalists and war photographers, then bounced back to Paris, where she continued her street photography and began to experiment with frank, unadorned portraits. News of her mother's rapid decline had brought her home, where Madame Bloch commented frequently on how much her daughter had aged in the intervening years and confided to her that her looks (which Lilly questioned) and talent (which her mother questioned) could be used as bait for only so long. Lilly's chances of snaring a husband to support her and restore the Bloch family's curatorial prominence were dwindling with each line on Lilly's face, each night she wasted in the darkroom, each painting that disappeared from the apartment's walls.

It was on a rare night out at the Café National, after a heated argument with a group of drunken surrealists—why did she always find herself tangling with surrealists?—that her friend Magda introduced her to Josef, a lawyer and a columnist for one of the city's antifascist newspapers. Lilly, an incorrigible skeptic when it came to love, arrived back at her mother's flat completely smitten. Josef was dark and small, almost waifish, but he was lively and funny and when she spoke he seemed to be weighing the value of every word she said. Within a week he had met her mother and Lilly never would have guessed what a blessing that would be. On the first night he visited the flat, Josef plunked himself down on a sofa and argued—seriously and jovially— with Madame Bloch for over an hour. They shared a few opinions on art—Braque was a genius, Dalí a charlatan—but were at loggerheads on music and theater. Madame Bloch was annoyed by Brecht, whom Josef revered as a giant. After that first night Josef became a regular fixture in the flat with its musty, faded wallpaper and haphazard assortment of furniture salvaged from the former Bloch manor. He would often arrive when Lilly was not at home and banter with Madame Bloch until she returned, after which he and Lilly would meet friends at the Café Slavia or take in one of the American or French films playing at the Cinema Julis at Wenceslas Square. Sparring with Josef—educating him was how she saw it—brought Lilly's mother great pleasure, even if she was loath to admit it. *Oh, that boy,* she would say. *Where does he get these ideas?*

Lilly's mother had died in December, and it was only a few days after her burial that word reached Lilly that she had been offered a grant by the Foundation. She had made an inquiry in the late spring, back when she was still in Paris, and only now, in the depths of the Prague winter, did she receive a letter from the woman who had taken over her Paris flat informing her that a man called Musgrove had been trying for months to contact her.

A WOMAN WITH platinum-blond hair poked her head into the lounge where Lilly sat and told her that it was time. She led Lilly down a hallway to a door that looked much like Mr. Musgrove's except for the name stenciled in gold on the lustrous wood: Crabtree. It was not a name that suggested good fortune.

At first glance, Mr. Crabtree's office was much like Mr. Musgrove's: a broad, dark-stained desk; a plush carpet in a golden hue that matched the name on the door; and a tall window that looked out into the blue sky, far above the buildings below. But where Mr. Musgrove's office was dominated by a Matisse odalisque that he had bought from the artist himself, this office was a *Wunderkammer* devoted to the American West. On one wall, a tableau of cowboys on horseback raced at a breakneck pace among a horde of long-horned cattle. The stuffed head of a thick-tongued bison hung above the door. A console table supported a shirtless, breechclouted Indian who knelt before a sacred fire while bronze smoke wrapped its fingers around him. And on the credenza behind Crabtree's chair, a war bonnet adorned the head of a blank-faced mannequin. With its spiked plumage and riotous tail of black and white feathers, it looked like a demon bird perched above the shoulder of its captor, Mr. Crabtree.

Lilly began by explaining her predicament and the promises made by Mr. Musgrove. Didn't the Foundation, with its money and its board of directors whose names were cast in solid-gold letters, have the power to make calls, to pull strings, to grease wheels, to cut red tape, to employ any of the metaphors Mr. Musgrove had used in reference to his efforts to extend her visa and allow her work to continue? He had even said it would be possible to bring Josef to America, because wasn't Josef—a champion of the downtrodden and an enemy of the occupation—equally deserving of the Foundation's largesse?

Invoking the name of Mr. Musgrove and the promises he had made did not endear her to Mr. Crabtree. At first he smirked, as if wondering what else Mr. Musgrove must have pulled, greased, or otherwise employed on her behalf. Then he explained to Lilly that European art was not his bailiwick, and that he was generally opposed to the idea of expending the Foundation's munificence on living artists. It made them soft, he believed. Complacent. And as for the program run by Mr. Musgrove, there had been discovered certain improprieties—financial in nature—in addition to the air of moral perfidy that now hung about the whole operation. Despite his expansive vocabulary and the frequent digressions in Mr. Crabtree's disquisition, the message was easy enough to grasp: Lilly's connection to Mr. Musgrove had been transformed from lifeboat to lead weight.

Still, she invited Mr. Crabtree or whoever replaced Mr. Musgrove to visit her studio and see her work firsthand—to see that he and the people he represented had gotten their money's worth. She had spent the days since her last visit to the Foundation organizing her studio in preparation for just such a visit. She should have been packing but she couldn't bring herself to do it. To box up this life here would be to admit that she was really leaving, and that her plan to use New York as a refuge had failed.

Mr. Crabtree glanced at the address listed in her file and startled, as if some stench had risen up from the pages. "That is not a respectable neighborhood," he said. And then: "You simply cannot live there."

But that was exactly what she had been doing for the past three months: living in her studio, taking pictures of strangers, walking the streets of this glowing coal-dark city. Meanwhile back in Prague, Josef existed in some half-state, wondering when the next directive would come from the Castle. Would he be forced to move again? Where could he go? And where could he not go? One landlord had already asked him to leave. He was becoming too outspoken, too notorious. In his last letter, written almost a month ago, he had begged her to stay in New York. *Save yourself from this madness,* he had written. *Allow me to know that you, at least, are safe.* She didn't even have a reliable address for Josef, yet she continued to send letters, sometimes three or four a week. Lilly had placed her hopes in some imagined neighbor at Josef's old flat, someone who would see the pile of feathery blue airmail envelopes with their eagle clutching a cracked bell and would know how to reach Josef. It was a fantasy, she knew, but believing in this kindly neighbor was easier for her than not writing at all. That would have been to admit more than could be spoken. And now as the weeks wore thin and the date on her return ticket became more stark (less than a week!), contacting Josef became a practical matter as well. Where was she to find him? What would she do when she returned home? Was it still her home?

She reached again for something Mr. Musgrove had told her, though she knew better than to attach his name to the thought:

161

Hadn't the Foundation had great success these past five years in bringing to safety in the New World people like her, like Josef—artists,
writers, public figures facing persecution by the enemies of culture?

Mr. Crabtree rubbed his eyes wearily. "Have you been the victim of
persecution, Miss Bloch?"

"My country was invaded by—"

"But do you have reason to believe that you will be persecuted on
your return?"

"The whole country is being persecuted," she said.

"We can't exactly relocate all of Czechoslovakia to the United
States." He chuckled, amused by the thought. "Where would we
put it?"

Lilly had a notion about where he could put it, but a daughter raised
by Madame Bloch did not say such things aloud.

"Miss Bloch, the government of the United States does not grant
visas lightly, and we at the Foundation need to keep our powder dry,
so to speak, for those truly deserving cases. At the current time, we've
no evidence that you face any direct threat upon your return."

"Mr. Crabtree," she said, almost in shock; how plainly did she need
to state this? "I am a Jew, and you're asking me to return to a city
under the control of the Nazis."

"Yes, and I understand that carries with it certain...*complica-
tions*," he said, "but are you an activist of some sort? Perhaps a communist, or—"

"I am an artist."

"Is your art political?"

She shook her head quickly, trying again to find the words to com-
bat this madness. "To ask if art is political—that means everything,
and nothing."

"Cryptic answers aren't going to help your case. The men the Foundation has resettled can point to very specific instances of persecution. One man was barred from employment at every university in

Germany. Another had his laboratory ransacked by hoodlums on the payroll of the party. Another had his home burned. He lost his entire library." He sat back in the chair, the eagle-feather headdress looming over him. "Has anything like that happened to you or to this Josef?"

"He has been evicted from his apartment. He has lost his job."

"Times are hard everywhere," Mr. Crabtree said.

"He did not fail to pay his rent. He was forced out, by the occupation. And Jews have been barred from practicing law."

"But you yourself—have you faced—"

"I left Prague one week before the Reich invaded."

Mr. Crabtree squinted, either deep in thought or in search of relief in the painting of the cattle drive. The lead cowboy jutted his chin, one hand squashing his hat to the top of his head. With his other hand he lashed the horse's shoulder with the reins. "Here's an idea," he said. "Why don't you return as scheduled and reconnoiter the situation?"

"Reconnoi—"

"Yes, take the temperature of Prague," he said. And if it happened that Prague was, in fact, running a fever, he said, then she and Josef could prepare for a more orderly departure. She could again make application to the Foundation through one of its European offices— one that hadn't been shuttered in the past few months due to *the situation,* as Mr. Crabtree referred to it—and in no time at all Lilly and Josef would be walking arm in arm in Central Park. When that happened, and Mr. Crabtree believed it would, the first order of business would be to find them a more respectable neighborhood. Because she couldn't live where she was living. It just wasn't possible.

Except that it was. She had proven it. But what she didn't know was whether it was possible to live in Prague.

Not for the first time she wished that war—a recognizable, guns-and-tanks-and-aerial-bombardment war—had broken out, and that return was impossible. Then the man with the office full of eagle feathers and buffalo heads and beaded belts and tomahawks would understand, and levers would be pulled and ears bent and chips cashed to keep Lilly in New York and to extract Josef from Prague. But this half-lit war, this agreement not to call it what it was for fear that the name would force some necessary action, required Lilly to participate in a lie that Mr. Crabtree was eager to spread: that things would be different at home, but only by degrees.

FIFTY-SECOND STREET

Eᴌsᴛᴏɴ Hᴏᴏᴘᴇʀ ʜᴇʟᴅ ᴛʜᴇ last note and wouldn't let it drop. When the sound from the golden bell of his trumpet ceased, the song would end—and no one wanted that to happen. This was the last rehearsal before their one and only gig and the eight men on the bandstand wanted to savor every note. They had been meeting once a week for the past three months and after the second session it was clear that they didn't need to rehearse: they were all pros, and any pro worth his salt could motor through a wedding repertoire on four hours of sleep, half a hangover, and nothing but the opening key to guide him. They had taken a few weeks to rev up these tunes, to add more verve than your typical wedding band could muster, but the set list had been settled by the end of March, and the band that Martin had assembled turned its attention to music built for nightclubs and ballrooms. Every rehearsal began with a warm-up, a play-through of two or three songs for the reception, each one set to simmer. But it never took long for one of those wedding songs to metamorphose into something wondrous. Teddy Gaines on the drums would pick up the pace, demand a solo, and take this locomotive made of shining brass and polished wood down a different, more thrilling line. Or Hooper, on the trumpet, would turn a quick flourish into a fanfare. The band responded every time. They knew the rules of the game. *We'll see how long we can go with that wedding-party music but sooner or later— and please, Lord, let it be sooner—someone is going to ring that bell.*

So it was a game, but it wasn't a joke. How could it be, when Martin treated each session like the second coming of Benny Goodman at Carnegie Hall?

The others in the band saw how much it meant to the little guy, and if they thought he was crazy to take it all so seriously, they kept it to themselves and played along. At first they figured he was trying to make nice with his wife and score points with his in-laws, Bronx big shots who had the juice to make life's bitter pills go down that much easier. But that was hardly enough to make each man pour his heart and soul into a three-hour set for a clutch of half-drunk Irish squares who wouldn't know Lester Young from Coleman Hawkins and who would probably use the same hateful name for them both. No, they showed up on time and rolled up their shirtsleeves in the afternoon heat at the Dime, a shoe-box club on Tenth Avenue—the western frontier of night-town—and played with everything they had because they knew this band could swing. Martin had assembled the group from the hottest spots in the city: these were men who regularly played the Roseland and the Famous Door, Café Society and the Hickory House. He had ventured as far as Minton's, the Harlem hot-house where cutting contests sorted the wheat from the chaff. These all-night jam sessions let him see what these men could do when they were playing under their own steam rather than the baton of a bandleader, and after weeks of praising, cajoling, and pleading he had assembled the best band that his small budget could buy. It was one advantage of the hard times and the skinflint wages paid by most bandleaders: horn players were always looking for something on the side.

Once he had the crew lined up, Martin went to work shaping the set list. His charts—the written arrangements that brought together, page by page, the parts that each musician would play—looked like the scrapbook of a mental patient. They were scribbled on cocktail napkins and butcher paper, on the backs of receipts and in the margins of the *New York Post*. Only in the past two weeks had he transcribed onto neatly lined pages his hurried quarter notes for the saxophones, the mirrored notes of the trumpets, and the low, insistent halves of the bass. He had thought of this as his chance, for one afternoon, to play these songs the way he heard them in his head, but what came out in these noontime rehearsals was better than he had ever imagined.

While Martin had thought he would be leading the way—isn't that what the bandleader did?—he quickly learned that he was playing catch-up. Men who could hold their own at Minton's were already taking jazz music to places it hadn't yet been. Still, he was the one who had brought this group together. Hadn't he seen plenty of bands full of talented players that somehow never clicked, whereas this group found its groove in a matter of weeks? He must have had something to do with that. Even if he lacked the angel's kiss that elevated Duke and Basie to the jazzman's Olympus, he could still set the direction and let the players take it from there.

Yes, Martin was on to something, and it was the sound of the band that had pushed him to walk out on Chester. These Monday sessions were proof that he wasn't just imagining what he could do if he was the one counting time and building the set list. Since last week's rehearsal, he had bounced between light-headed joy and a sour stomach of dread: How could it be that this band would only live for a day, a musical mayfly, and then disappear? Every man in the band had another regular gig. Martin had already been forced to replace the trombone when Joe Falco went off for a three-month stand in the Poconos. And Hooper, his ace trumpet, had a gig at the World's Fair that he hoped to flip into a seat in the house band for *The Hot Mikado,* which was moving this month from Broadway out to the fairgrounds.

But Martin had a plan—his own top secret plan—and he hadn't mentioned it to anyone. It was too far out in the world of what-if, a sunshine daydream locked up tight against the cold rain of reality. But over these past few days that lock had begun to turn and the tumblers to fall into place. He had set it in motion by quitting Chester's band. *Click:* the first number in the combination. Then there was the news, delivered today by half the members of the band, that his song had been rearranged by none other than Benny Carter and was driving the dancers into a frenzy at the Savoy. It was a sign that Martin's star might again be on the rise, and — *click* — that was the second number. And then there was this band, his band. They had been working toward this moment for months, when they would move beyond being musicians playing a session to being a real band. In a session, some-one was always gassing around, showing off. It was a ragtag business, playing for the joy of it. But now the band had come together. No doubt about it, this band could really swing. *Click:* the last number in the combination.

So this was Martin's plan: Saturday wouldn't be the end, it would be the beginning. He had learned plenty from his early days in Amer-ica playing one-night stands with nonstop touring bands, and then later with Chester during their summer tours. He knew the towns where a band could play to a packed house and then do it all again in the next town over. It was a dog's life, to be sure, but they only had to keep at it long enough to make a name for themselves. And with the way Hoop was blowing that horn, the way he absolutely tore apart "One O'Clock Jump," and with the bandleader being the man who had written "That's More Like It," well, that was a sure bet in Mar-tin's book. They would blaze a path across the territories and then return in triumph to New York, where they would settle in as the new house band at somewhere like the Pennsylvania Hotel. It sounded crazy to be thinking about the Pennsylvania, which had been Basie's spot for years, while the band was sweating through its paces at a hole-in-the-wall like the Dime, and that was one reason he hadn't breathed a word of it. But hadn't Benny Goodman been ready to break up his band in the middle of their marathon cross-country tour?

It had been a complete wreck right up until they went to L.A. for one last show at the Palomar, where they blew the roof off the place. That success, broadcast live around the country, carried them back to New York like conquering heroes, and it had been nothing but gravy for those guys ever since.

But he was getting ahead of himself, because sure, there were hurdles to overcome.

Martin knew that before the band played a single note at the reception, half the crowd would already be in a lather. What kind of joke was this? Colored musicians? An integrated band? The wedding guests would have a laugh if Martin were to assemble an all-white band and put them in blackface. That would be a gas. *Like dancing at the Cotton Club,* they would say. But this? He could already imagine the look on Dennis Dwyer's boiled-potato face. And he hadn't told anyone. Not Rosemary, even. She would only argue him out of an idea that he knew was a good one, but it was Rosemary, after all, who had recruited Martin as the bandleader, and hadn't he taken to the job with gusto? Had he complained, even once, about the wedding?

And then there was the long-term plan. Rosemary wouldn't exactly go wild about Martin being out of town for weeks, maybe months, at a time, but if that plan got them out of Mrs. Fichetti's and into a house of their own, then all, he supposed, would be forgiven. More and more since the baby was born she had been giving out about his late nights and the hours kept by a musician, but isn't that what she'd signed up for when they married? He had to believe that what really troubled her were the close quarters with a nosy landlady always looking over her shoulder. If she had her own place to mind, she wouldn't care if Martin was on the moon five nights a week.

Getting Hoop and Teddy Gaines on board was also going to take some doing. Even if Hoop complained that his current gig was a strait-jacket, a straitjacket kept a man warmer than no jacket at all. And there could be other hurdles. Even in New York, there were ballrooms that wouldn't book mixed bands, and he'd heard it was ten times worse down south, where there was loads of money to be made playing one-nighters. It was hard to figure, but Martin was confident he could sort it all out. Times were changing—when Benny Goodman jazzed up Carnegie Hall, Basie and Fletcher Henderson and plenty more joined him on the bandstand, and hadn't the crowd applauded like mad? He was also counting on Hoop's wife, Lorena, to help her husband see the light. Hoop was always telling Martin that she could sing like an angel, and if the band took off, it could mean steady work for both of them—and maybe being together on the road would smooth out the rough patches. In a different life, Rosemary would make a crackerjack tour manager. There was no one better at keeping all of the i's dotted just so. But you sure couldn't put your wife and kids on the road with a crowd of musicians. He wasn't raising his girls to be tinkers.

He could feel it now, closer than it had ever been. On Saturday everyone would hear it and they would all know that the group was too good to break up. That's when Martin would lay it all out for them. The Martin Dempsey Orchestra would spring fully formed from his head and they would march out together, ready to take on the world.

WHEN THE LAST note ended and brought the rehearsal to a close, there was a hush, then a collective intake of breath. Someone cursed, with reverence, for the sound that had filled the room. Only then did they realize just how much they were sweating in the narrow, lightless confines of the Dime. Stretching like men coming out of trance, they staggered off the club's one-step riser and went in search of the jackets they had shucked off, the shirts slung over music stands.

Teddy Gaines came out from behind the drum kit and leaned against the piano. "Word is you gave old Chestnut your walking papers," he said.

"I did," Martin said. "Just so." A nervous smile tricked the corners of his mouth, as if this was a joke he hadn't gotten used to telling.

"This here'll be something new," Hooper said. "I never played with a bandleader who'd lost his mind."

Gaines and Exley, the bass player, both guffawed. They had been thinking the same thing since the news broke of Martin's midsong departure.

"Come on, now," Martin said, fishing a slender chrome case from his pocket. He deftly removed a cigarette and laid the case on the piano. "It's the sanest thing I've done in a long while."

"So what was it," Hooper said, "the steady paycheck got you down? Tired of playing on the radio all those years? Too many rich folks buying you drinks?"

"You know there's more to it than that."

"Do I?" Hooper helped himself to a cigarette and the use of Martin's lighter. He took a few languid drags.

"Could you do it?" Martin said. "Play that la-dee-dum night after night? There's no life in it."

"There's no life in starving either."

"You're worse than Rosemary."

"Rosemary must be a saint. If I quit a gig like that, Lorena would cut off my balls and throw them in the river."

"I thought she did that the day you got married."

Hooper laughed. "You might have balls, but you've got no brains. You don't like what Chester's cooking? Clean your plate and when the job's done, go to Minton's, or to Monroe's, or do what we're doing here—just play. You think I'm living my dream, playing for the squares at the fair? But I'm getting paid to play, and there's plenty who can't say the same."

Hooper was trying to keep it light but he knew he was lecturing. He could already hear Lorena's voice in his head. *Life lessons from Professor Hooper,* she would say. *Thank you, Dr. Know-It-All.* She could make it sound like a joke, like a pet name even, or she could make it clear that he was working her last nerve. But it was a hard habit to break: when you're the oldest of six, you grow up telling everyone else just how it's going to be.

Hooper shook his head. "Maybe I'm just as crazy as you—letting you talk me into playing a party for a bunch of drunken white folks."

"They won't all be drunk," Martin said. "Not at first."

Hooper mopped his forehead with his handkerchief. Futile. Both the rag and his head were soaked.

"You really think this is going to work?"

"It's going to be grand," Martin said.

"I don't know what world you're living in, but it's not the real one."

"You don't think we sound brilliant?"

"We're better than brilliant. That's not the part I'm worried about."

"You could have said no."

"I guess I'm not living in the real world either."

MARTIN HAD PLANNED to stop at the Plaza after practice. As far as he knew, Francis and Michael had come and gone in the night without making a sound. The only sign of them in the morning had been a pillow and a folded sheet on the sofa, and that giant bottle of champagne, empty in the kitchen. But with the news that his song was lighting up the Savoy, he had a new mission: to visit every music store between Midtown and Harlem. If the sheet music was selling, then that was a sure sign of success. And if they'd stopped carrying the sheet music last year? Then he'd tell the clerks to put in a rush order, because his song was sure to be the biggest hit of the summer.

On his way out the door, Martin was stopped by the Dime's owner, Artie Gold. Artie usually passed time at the Monday rehearsals at a round table at the back of the club, tallying last week's receipts and gabbing with the men who delivered the essentials: ice, beer, linens, seltzer.

"Looks like you're developing a fan club," Artie said.

"Is it the beer guy?" Martin said. "Or is it the iceman? I tell you, the icemen love us."

"No, you dope," Artie said. "Didn't you see who I was talking to? That was John Hammond."

Hammond's name knocked the wry smile right off Martin's face. Every musician in New York City—in the whole Western Hemisphere— hoped to catch the eye of John Hammond. One nod from Hammond was a ticket to the top; just ask Billie Holiday, or Benny Goodman, or Basie himself. The word on the street was that Hammond had paid out of his own pocket to install the air-conditioning at the Famous Door during Basie's long, legendary run. That's how badly he wanted Basie to make a splash, and it was just the kind of thing Hammond did for his musicians. But folks around town also called him the Undertaker, because just as likely as not, when you saw Hammond in the audience he didn't have his eye on you—he was there to tell your bandleader about his latest find, some kid fresh off the train from Chicago who was perfect for the seat you were currently occupying.

"Hammond?" Martin said in disbelief. "Here?" He was sure Artie was pulling his leg, but what if—

"He caught your last number and he wanted to know where he could see the whole act. I told him you were just a bunch of shoeshine boys I let play on Mondays out of the kindness of my heart."

"You didn't!"

"Of course I didn't. Sheesh. I told him you had a wedding up in Woodlawn—when is it, Saturday? Leave me an address and I'll pass it on."

"Why don't you give me his number and I'll ring him up? No need for you—"

"Yeah, it doesn't work that way," Artie said. "Just don't get your hopes up, okay? He's a busy man. And Woodlawn? Sheesh—that's like the other side of the moon."

Don't get your hopes up? Martin's hopes had never been higher. Quitting Chester's outfit, then hearing about his song at the Savoy, then feeling the band in full swing—he had all the numbers in the combination that would unlock his future. On Saturday the door would open wide, and John Hammond himself would be waiting on the other side.

THE PLAZA HOTEL

IT WAS LATE IN the evening when Michael got out of bed. His clothes from the previous night were still pooled on the floor: his jacket near the bedroom door and then his trousers and then another step to his tie, his shirt. The shoes, like Mr. Yeats, were nowhere in sight. If the bed had been three feet farther from the door he would have collapsed on the carpet—that's how exhausted he had been when they had reached the hotel in the early-morning hours. Still, he was shocked that they had found the place at all.

When they'd crept out of Martin's apartment, Michael on tiptoe and Yeats in an insubstantial shuffle, the mantel clock registered ten minutes after three. Michael had realized during his Saturday stroll down Fifth Avenue that he could still tell time—the meaning of the short and long hands had not been lost in the fog that still obscured letters and numbers. He had since made a point of seeking out clocks, whether on lobby walls or church towers. This was something he could know. This was proof that he was still a part of the delimited world.

The street outside Martin's apartment was occupied only by bent-necked streetlights, and when Michael asked Yeats the way to their hotel, the old man seemed puzzled. He took a few steps to the right, then paused and muttered to himself. He turned left but lacked the conviction to take a step in that direction.

"Are the pages on the big book of time turning again?"

Yeats nodded gravely.

Michael scanned the row of houses that ran the length of the block. A lightbulb burned in only a single window. The rest of the buildings were dark. He could imagine that in each house a family slept untroubled by the waking world. "Sure it's fine," Michael said. "It's all peace and quiet."

"For now." Yeats blinked hard and again looked right, then left. "This way."

On the Grand Concourse, trucks bearing ice or bundled newspapers or bottles of milk trundled into the city. Two taxicabs rolled past, their drivers nodding at the wheel, before Yeats told Michael to raise his hand to signal for a ride. A third car jerked to a stop at the curb.

As they entered the cab, the driver turned his squashed face toward Michael and mouthed some variation of *Where to, buddy?* Yeats advised Michael that this would be the time to give the man the card in his pocket. Michael did as he was told and sat back with a look of satisfaction on his face. He was insulated from the grumble in the man's throat, the chewed-over words about the middle-of-the-night Bronx fare who was too highfalutin to speak to a cabbie.

When they arrived at the hotel, Michael handed the driver one of the bills in his pocket and kept his hand out, awaiting the change that the driver grudgingly provided. Then he was out of the cab and up the stairs, and he was sure, for a moment, that as he exited the cab he saw the woman from last night—the pretty one, the wild one—ducking her head into the same car he had just vacated, and he was about to call this fact to Yeats's attention, but when he turned his head one way Yeats was gone and when he turned quickly the other way, the weight of the day and the night and the spectrally assisted travel from the Bronx to Manhattan descended suddenly on his shoulders. He caught a last glance at the taillights of the cab—was Yeats now traveling with *her?*—just as a man in livery tipped his cap and pulled open the door, and then he was inside again, crossing the lobby, brightly lit against the predawn gloom.

The man behind the desk nodded to him and turned toward the vast bank of pigeonholes where the room keys were kept. With another nod, the man handed Michael his key, and with a sweep of his arm indicated the location of the elevator. In the elevator, Michael showed the key with its numbered tassel to the operator, and then the doors were opening and he was following the hallway to his room. The weight on his shoulders grew heavier and his head began to cloud and he was through the door and across the sitting room and into his bedroom, where he shucked his clothing article by article, and when he felt the mattress against his shins he let himself fall.

Now it was sometime in the evening, the sun low in the sky but still a long way from setting, and he was alone. Abandoned, even, but— *what's this?*—not forgotten. In the center of the sitting room was a wheeled cart topped by two silver domes. Under one was a fat T-bone steak and under the other some sort of…well, what? It was a large white orb, perhaps some kind of gigantic onion, with concentric rings of scorched brown marking its lines of latitude. Michael prodded it with a spoon, which revealed the surface to be hard and stiff. A more deliberate jab with the spoon cracked the shell and unleashed gobs of vanilla ice cream. Oh, heaven! He spooned mouthfuls of ice cream flecked with sugary meringue into his mouth. Had he for one moment thought badly of Francis for leaving him alone? If he had, then all was forgiven. Michael settled onto the sofa, and alternating bites of beef with half-melted ice cream, he was certain that Francis was the greatest brother that a brother could hope for.

FIFTH AVENUE

Martin kept asking Francis, What's the plan? But there wasn't any plan beyond the FC Plan, and that was working like gangbusters. The money and the clothes and the air of well-bred Scottishness had led to the *Britannic* and its first-class dining room, which had led to the Plaza and now to his next destination: the Binghams. Yesterday he had received a card, creamy paper embossed in gold with the family name and address. On the back, in a chain of tight curlicues, Mrs. B—Delphine, he was supposed to call her—cordially invited Sir Angus and his brother Malcolm to dinner on Monday evening. Even Francis, who had never been formally invited to anyone's home for dinner, could sense a tremor of urgency behind the invitation. Who dined out on a Monday? Could they really be so worried about losing their monopoly on the attentions of their young Scottish aristocrat?

Michael, who had been crashed out in bed all day, would have to stay behind. Martin must have dropped him earlier, and all without waking Francis, who had slept until noon, and who could blame him? Blame the gallons of champagne and whiskey at Martin's, the dancing and the gin at the Savoy, the frenzy of the Lindy Hoppers, the return to the Plaza with Peggy. God, that Peggy! She was another one of the spoils of the FC Plan. He hadn't even given her the Scotsman act, but the sharp suit and the giant's bottle and the fat roll of banknotes had certainly promoted his cause. Hadn't she called him a gentleman? Would any of it—this life he had led since fleeing Ireland—have come to pass if he had been the flat-broke brother of Martin, camped out in some cold-water rooming house or sleeping on the tatty floor of Martin's apartment? Not one bit of it.

And now it was on to meet the Binghams. Given the family's acres of jewels and their months on the Continent, he assumed the Binghams lived fairly high, and friends in high places were the best kind to have. That was one of the central tenets of the FC Plan, or would be, if he ever took the time to write it all down. But when had there been time for anything since the accident? When had Francis had a single moment to sit down and plot his next steps or investigate this persona he had patched together? There was so much he didn't know about Scotland, and America, and New York, and this business of being an aristocrat. All he could do was steal a few hours on the ship and at the Plaza poring over recent issues of *Harper's Bazaar, Town and Country,* and *Esquire,* imagining these to be a *Burke's Peerage* of the American ascendancy. From these he gleaned that the New World's aristocracy could be cracked with the right accumulation of steel mills and coal mines—as long as the source of one's wealth was obscured by the sheen of daughters schooled in French and sons who wore white jumpers and rowed for Harvard.

To prepare himself for an evening with the Binghams, he had tried to concoct a few stories to burnish his own lordly bona fides, but the best he could manage was some family lore about his great-uncle Mad Fitz, who had acquitted himself so honorably during the Boer War—or should it be the Crimean? Single-handed defeat of spear-wielding Zulus, or the capture of an entire Russian regiment? Or was it the Turks? Tennyson had written a poem about someone the English had fought, but here was the downside of being raised in a flyspeck of a town where your father was the only schoolmaster: if he didn't teach it, you didn't know it. As for Francis's education after his exit from Ballyrath, English military history and Victorian poetry hadn't been a part of the curriculum. He knew a great deal about books considered too immoral for impressionable Irish minds, knew how to pack salacious French postcards between black pasteboard covers so that they resembled hymnals, knew how to smuggle condoms past inspectors and how to relabel cheap claret as grand cru Bordeaux. He had specialized in luxury goods, or goods that gave the illusion of luxury and sensual abandon. But these weren't the sort of stories to impress the Binghams.

Francis checked one last time on the still-snoozing Michael and a few minutes later stepped into a taxi called by the shrill whistle of one of the Plaza's stewards. Rung by rung, through the Sixties and Seventies, the cab climbed the ladder of streets that jutted eastward from the park. Down each one Francis saw a row of low, elegant buildings in shades of white and gray, like a mouthful of strong, square, American teeth. Iron scrollwork danced up the steps from sidewalk to front door, stood guard along the squat parapets, and swept basketlike below the windows, as if to catch the overflow of abundance that spilled from the homes of the city's first citizens.

Not until he reached the address printed on the card did he realize that the Binghams' house wasn't a house at all. It was a mansion— no, a palace. It wasn't *at* the corner of Seventy-Eighth and Fifth, it *was* the corner of Seventy-Eighth and Fifth (and Seventy-Ninth, too). From a block away, the building looked like it had been constructed from spun sugar and marzipan. In the late-day sun, the marble walls blazed a brilliant white. It was the white of a welder's torch, of a star tethered to earth. The top of the building stretched skyward in a riot of turrets, arches, towers, and other architectural excesses that Francis lacked the vocabulary to name. Any casual passerby would be overwhelmed by the froufrou and the frippery—all those details that made the Binghams' urban château seem like the product of a young girl's fevered imagination. But closer inspection revealed not a fairy-tale castle but a fortress. Beneath the whipped-cream cupolas were battlements that no siege engine could assail. The foundation was granite and the roofline bristled with sharpened iron rods bent to seem as harmless as licorice sticks, but woe to the barbarian who tried to storm this castle; *tant pis* to the prisoner who bided his time in this bastille.

Francis was greeted at the front door by a middle-aged man in a stiff black jacket, a man he almost addressed as Mr. Bingham. Before Francis could commit his first faux pas, the man took his hat and ushered him into a foyer floored in checkerboard marble. Twin staircases snaked upward to right and left, meeting in a center mezzanine that oversaw a chandelier as wide as the crown of a chestnut tree, each leaf filigreed in gold. The ceiling soared to a fluted dome suspended above the foyer like a giant seashell. On each side of the staircase, wall niches displayed busts carved in black or white marble—gods or emperors or members of the Bingham family, for all Francis knew. The butler opened a set of doors twice as tall as Francis and indicated with a nod of his head that he was to enter the room. As Francis crossed the threshold, the butler closed the doors behind him. The back wall of this new room was bookshelves, floor to ceiling, each volume bound in red leather and embossed in gold. Painted on the ceiling was a woodland scene, nymphs in flight, their loose hair covering their most interesting bits. Before he could give it a more thorough inspection he heard a mild *ahem* from another quarter of the room.

He turned toward the source of the sound and a smile leaped to his face. Mrs. Bingham was perched in the center of a sofa, cloudlike in her gown, her hair set with silver combs. Anisette was on her left, her pose suggesting that she was aiming for demure but her smile so broad that she seemed ready to burst. To the right of Mrs. B sat a young woman whose face was caught between a sneer and something more like idle curiosity: *You've got two minutes; impress me or go home.* No one spoke. This was a scene that Francis was meant to admire. He would have tested their resolve—checked his wristwatch and counted up the seconds, just for the fun of it—but he feared that Anisette couldn't withstand the strain.

He clapped his hands together and time restarted. "My dear ladies," he said. "This is indeed a pleasure. Familiar faces in this strange land! What a delight!"

"Your Lordship—" Mrs. Bingham began.

"Please, we're friends. Friends call me Angus."

Francis closed the distance between them—his feet did not make a sound on the thick Persian carpet—and took her hand, planting a quick kiss on her index finger. He needed to work on his hand-kissing. He had only seen it done in the movies—posh yokes were made for kissing hands—and of course in church, where the target was some bishop's fat golden signet. He next pivoted toward Anisette, whose hand was already extended, and offered a quick peck.

Mrs. Bingham introduced her daughter Félicité, two years Anisette's senior. Félicité sat back and extended a long, reluctant arm toward Francis. She had completed the transformation of her sneer into something more complicated, something both haughty and sporting. Here was the girl at the carnival who deigns to try the ring toss, because really, how difficult can it be? As Francis leaned in for the last round of hand-kissing, a door in some distant arrondissement of the library slammed shut. Félicité jerked her hand midkiss, popping Francis squarely in the mouth.

"What did I miss?" A creaky, metal-on-metal voice came from the back of the room. "He hasn't seduced my daughters yet, has he?"

Francis could taste blood in his mouth. The older sister had really let him have it.

"Oh, Emery," Mrs. B said. "Don't embarrass our guest."

"That's what he's here for, isn't he? To make off with one of the girls? Well, Your Lordship, which one is it going to be? Both of them are pretty enough. The younger one is sweet but a bit too flighty if you ask me. And this one's got her head screwed on straight but she has a sour disposition."

His voice filled the room, but Emery Bingham was not a big man. He was compact and old, whittled down by time. He could have been Mrs. B's father, perhaps even her grandfather. He looked a bit like a terrier at a dog show, prettified with his close-cut suit and his blunt beard — his mustache an iron-bristle brush that hid his mouth completely — but beneath the veneer he had a lean frame and a killer's eyes, quick and hungry. The best efforts of the city's tailors and barbers could not change what he was: a creature bred to enter dark, tight spaces and emerge with his prize clamped between his teeth.

"Let me get a good look at him," Mr. Bingham said. "Ever since you got off that ship all I've heard is tittering about Sir Walter Scottish."

"Father," Félicité said. "Please don't include me in their nonsense."

"You'll have to excuse Félicité," Mrs. B said, with a curt clearing of the throat: *Don't ruin this for your sister.*

"She doesn't like to see anyone happy," Anisette said. "Not even herself."

If the Binghams had been set to simmer, they now threatened to reach a boil. The tableau was more vivant than ever. Francis stepped back and took a second look around the room, with its wall of books, endless carpet, nail-trimmed wingbacks with their undented leather seats, and the ceiling and its scene of Arcadian cavorting. The satyrs were shaggy-jowled, and wasn't the leader of the goat-legged pack the spitting image of a younger Mr. Bingham? And the nymph at the center of the composition, the one whose wicked smile spurred the satyrs to their mad pursuit and whose hands made such a lackluster effort to conceal her abundant charms — didn't she look more than a little like Mrs. B?

"What a show we're putting on for our guest!" Mrs. B said. She reached a hand to each of her daughters in a way that would have evoked maternal pride if not for the white-knuckled grip she had on their wrists. The Bingham daughters composed themselves. This was a skirmish they had been waging for years, and one that they were a long way from resolving. They folded their hands, now free of their mother's grasp, and put on small patient smiles while their eyes darted to ensure the other was observing the truce. The dustup with her sister had cooled something in Anisette, who looked less eager to gobble up Francis. Félicité, however, had gained a spark. Whether it was the sheen of action or simple schadenfreude, whatever she had robbed from her sister, she had added to herself.

Mr. Bingham gloried in the whole scene. The rapid boil, the flushed cheeks, his wife's iron hands, all of it provoked real joy in him. No smile was visible beneath his brambly beard, but his eyes had the same mad glint that Francis had seen first in Anisette and then in Félicité. It must have come as a disappointment to him when the butler entered the room and announced that dinner was served. Mrs. B and the daughters rose as one and slowly disentangled themselves from each other. Sharp limbs and thorny stares softened. Bright smiles replaced pouts and glowers.

Mr. Bingham, rocking on his heels, was the last to leave the room. He had kept a gimlet eye on Francis, had seen the way he took in the books, his daughters, the ceiling. Now he too looked up and let his eyes trace the curves of the nymphs. There was his Delphine leading the charge (she always led the charge) but she wasn't the only woman he'd known whose likeness graced the mural. That had taken some doing—keeping Delphine in the dark about the models he had hand-picked and sent along to that crazy Belgian painter—but it had been worth it. Good times to think back on during sleepless nights. But that sort of fun was all in the past. The only one enjoying himself now was that woolly-legged bastard on the ceiling, though even he was trapped forever in the moment before he got what he wanted.

* * *

THE MEAL PLAYED out like an arcane ritual meant to appease a voracious culinary god—one whose chief commandments were quantity, variety, and luxury. It began with balled cantaloupe served in tiny silver bowls, then progressed to a chilled cream of tomato soup—an acknowledgment of the blistering sun that had set aglow the walls of the Bingham manse. As the ladies pecked at the bits of cold fruit and soup, talk turned to the can't-miss sights of New York: Had he taken a stroll in the park, or seen the Metropolitan Museum? No? Then Anisette would have to show him around. Mr. Bingham ignored the conversation and the dishes before him; melons and tomatoes were children's food. His mood improved with the presentation of a Halifax sole, which he smothered in sauce béarnaise, followed by a braised Wiltshire ham. Each course was announced by the butler, like the acts in a vaudeville show. The meat was accompanied by a cart of vegetables: cauliflower in hollandaise, green beans amandine, potatoes Parmentier. While the Binghams picked at their plates, Francis finished every morsel he was served. He assumed that each course was the last—meals in Ballyrath and Mountjoy had been single-plate affairs—but when a roast Philadelphia capon in bread sauce was presented to the table, he began to see himself as a steer being fattened for market, a goose being stuffed for Christmas dinner.

At the mention of Philadelphia, Francis asked if the dish was in honor of their dinner companions on the *Britannic,* the Walters. He was trying to sound waggish. High-born gents in the movies always seemed to be displaying their waggishness.

"Oh, that awful woman," Mrs. B said, and she and Anisette shared a laugh. Félicité rolled her eyes in annoyance at another of their Grand Tour in-jokes.

Without looking up from his plate, Mr. Bingham spoke between forkfuls of delicately ribboned ham. "These Walters? Were they Americans?"

"The worst sort," Anisette said. "Loud and mean and—"

Mr. Bingham's fork clattered to his plate. He pointed at Anisette as if she were exhibit A in an argument he had been having with his wife. "A little time in Europe and already she's starting to think like one of them! First it's her fine British gentleman, and now she's going on about 'the worst sort' of Americans."

"Daddy, I was only trying—"

"Before this goes a step further, I want you lovebirds to listen to me." Mr. Bingham jabbed his finger again at Anisette, then wheeled toward Francis. "Do you want to know what sort of American I am? I'm the sort who's not looking to trade a lifetime of hard work for the deed to a run-down castle full of nothing but history and bad debts."

All eyes were suddenly on Francis. He was puzzling over *lovebirds* and Mr. B's *Before this goes a step further* and wondering just what *this* was. Certainly he was game for a little flirting with the young Miss Bingham, but it seemed that the Bingham family had been buzzing about a much more long-lasting connection in the days since the *Britannic* had docked. This was a new development in the FC Plan. He didn't know how long he could sustain being Angus MacFarquhar, but looking around the dining room with its piles of silver, its bottles of Bordeaux, its gilt-framed landscapes, and then at the spray of diamonds on the necks of the younger Binghams, he was willing to keep it up for a while. Right now, he needed a way to say neither yes nor no.

He dabbed at the corners of his mouth. *Bonhomie,* he told himself. *Aim for loads of bonhomie.* "There's no need to worry, sir. Our castle is in tip-top shape, but I must confess it's not mine for the trading. My older brother is the heir. Second son of an earl is about as lucky as the fourth son of a baker."

While Mr. Bingham swallowed a mouthful of ham, his eyes made it clear that he had more to say. "That's not exactly settled, is it? Let's say your older brother drops dead. Doesn't that make you the heir?"

Now it was Mrs. Bingham's fork clattering to her plate. "Emery! Really!"

"I have a right to ask! It's a strange way of life—idle days spent wishing bad fortune on others."

"Sir Angus would never wish bad fortune on his older brother," Anisette said. "Just look at all he's done for Sir Malcolm."

"I'm saying it's a bad system that ties your fortune to an accident of birth and not your own efforts. Just look at their king. Two years ago he was a duke. Father on the throne and older brother ready to take over. And now he's the one with his face on all the coins. But did he do anything—he, himself—to improve his lot in life?"

"He didn't have to," Mrs. Bingham said. "It was all that Simpson woman's doing."

"Don't blame her," Mr. Bingham said. "She saw what she wanted and she got it. That woman has gumption to burn."

"Is that why they burned witches?" Félicité said. "Because they were so full of gumption?"

"You'd best steer clear of fires yourself," Mr. Bingham said to his older daughter. "You've got at least as much gumption as that Simpson woman."

"If that's what that dreadful woman has," Mrs. Bingham said, folding her hands in her lap, "and what Félicité has, then I hope our daughter's gumption comes from your side of the family."

Anisette had followed this latest turn in the conversation with a tight-lipped set to her mouth and a few nervous glances at Francis. "Oughtn't we to refer to her as the Duchess of Windsor?" she said. "Wouldn't that be proper, Sir Angus?"

"You can call her what you will," Francis said. "But, please, just call me Angus."

Mr. Bingham turned from Félicité to Mrs. B. "Don't go playing the nun," he said. "When my Sarah passed, you staked your claim and staked it quick." The bristles of Mr. Bingham's mustache hid a smile.

"Yes sirree, you were on your guard for anyone with the claim jumper's eye. I could tell stories — "

"That's quite enough, Emery." She may have sounded shocked, but she could not forget the ferocity of her younger self — eighteen years old, a nurse to the first Mrs. Bingham in the final months of her decline, clearing the way of better-bred rivals.

"This is my point," Mr. Bingham said. "You can't blame the one who's willing to take what he — or she — wants. The world's full of namby-pambies waiting for a handout, whether it's from FDR or Joseph Stalin or Jesus Christ. But the joke's on them. The winners aren't the ones who *get;* they're the ones who *take.*"

"That's an awfully cruel world you're describing," Francis said in his plummiest Angus accent.

"It is a cruel world!" Mr. Bingham's fist banged the table. His wine jumped in its crystal goblet. "Maybe you can't see it from the walls of your castle, but I guarantee you this: somewhere in history, you had a great-great-grand-someone — the first in your line of dukes or earls or what have you — and he started with nothing in this world but a knife in his hand." Mr. Bingham gripped his bread knife with a balled fist; no longer the family silver, it was a dagger, a shiv. "And one day he spied some fat lord sitting pretty in his own tip-top castle, and when that man turned his back, your ancestor — God bless him! — made him pay for his carelessness. You and yours have that man to thank for all that you have."

Francis knew that as Angus, he should speak up on behalf of divine right or noblesse oblige or the class system or some such nonsense. But Mr. Bingham was describing a universe that Francis knew, a universe whose rules Francis was desperately trying to turn to his advantage. Wasn't this the FC Plan writ large? Francis had been dealt a bad hand but right when he could have called it quits, he had decided to make a go of it. To reach for the knife. To show a little gumption.

"Now look, Emery. You've offended our guest."

The collective stare of the Bingham family was again on Francis.

"Oh, not at all." His voice nearly cracked, he was so giddy. "Not at all. Only I was wondering, Mr. Bingham, whom do you have to thank for all that *you* have?"

Mr. Bingham's eyes narrowed. His life had been built brick by brick, course by course, on a series of men slower, kinder, weaker, or less willing than Emery Bingham to do what was necessary. How many handshake deals had he broken? As many as there were men stupid enough to make them. How much had he taken without asking? All of it. You asked only for the things that you were too weak or too poor to get on your own. Bingham was the cardsharp who wins a big pot and then uses his stack of chips to bully the others—to bet more than they're willing to call, to bluff past their ability to check. Bingham had never checked in his life. He raised every hand. But where had that first pot come from? Had it been luck? Had he been smarter than the other strivers? Had he simply outworked them? Had it been fate, or God's will, that had set this life in motion?

It started with that first big strike, copper where no one was looking for it in the Montana Territory. He had been living in a hole in the ground for months—an actual, literal hole, with a piece of canvas stretched over the top that couldn't keep out the rain, much less the cold or the rodents that gnawed at the rotten grub that passed for food. He was nothing but a brash troublemaker who had dug more dry holes than any other starry-eyed prospector for a hundred miles. When he hit the jackpot, he was digging on land he didn't own without a dime to pay the claim fee. He knew that as soon as he brought the first lump of ore into the assay office, the hills would be crawling with miners with more money and better connections. Instead he brought a sample to a man in town—a small-time pimp—and promised him a 50 percent stake in exchange for seed money to get the operation up and running and on the books. For six months he fended off his partner, arguing that start-up costs—men, mules, equipment—had consumed every penny he'd harvested from the ground. *Starting a mine ain't cheap,* he said. Then, before his partner could beat him to it, Bingham signed up a lawyer and paid off a judge who declared the agreement null and void and then prosecuted the man for pandering, the first time in the history of the territory that anyone involved in an industry as vital as prostitution had been jailed. By the time that man was released, Roundtop Mining, Bingham's new outfit, owned half the town, including the two biggest brothels—one for workaday miners, the other for pit bosses, business owners, and other professionals flocking to the nascent boomtown. Had that man—Dawkins, yes, that was his name—had Dawkins been a victim of Bingham's quick, sharp knife? No, he'd been a fool with more money than sense. All Bingham had done was correct the imbalance.

"Enough of your men talk," Mrs. Bingham said. "Maybe the world is a horrid place, but not here and not now. We have a lovely visitor who has come to us from far away, and just in time to celebrate a great event for our two countries. Did we tell you, Sir Angus, that we're going to be presented to the king and queen?"

"Not me," Bingham said. "I'm not going to stand around in a monkey suit so that I can bow— "

"Daddy, it's not just his king," Anisette said. "It's his family."

"Inbreds, all. That's what I was— "

"Emery, please!" Mrs. Bingham's eyes flared. "The queen is his cousin."

A knot formed in Francis's stomach. When had he said that? Had he gotten too drunk, too carried away, during dinner on the *Britannic*? He sputtered, tried to form a thought that wasn't pure gibberish.

"Don't be so modest, Angus," Anisette said, flushed with pride at her offhand use of his first name. "You're among friends."

"Yes, Angus." Félicité perched her chin on the same fist that had caught Francis in the mouth. "Do tell us all about your cousin the queen."

Mrs. Bingham had leaned toward her husband and was talking to him in a rasping whisper.

"Speak up!" he said. "I can only follow one conversation at a time."

"Earl. Of. Glamis," Mrs. Bingham said, loud enough for all to hear. "His father is the Earl of Glamis. That's where the queen grew up—Anisette saw it in *Life* magazine. There was a picture of her there with her girls. Reminded me of my own little lambs."

"Yes, Glamis," Francis said. Had Martin been right, then, about *Macbeth* being a history play? It was another failing of his father's classics-heavy curriculum, which offered no preparation for life in the twentieth century. "Of course, it's a large family, as you can imagine, and none of us ever expected that she would be the queen."

"How wonderful," Anisette said. "You simply must tell us all about her."

"Yes, you simply must." Félicité's eyes raked across Francis. She toyed with a necklace freighted with diamonds.

"We don't know each other terribly well," Francis said. He cast about for something to say. This was not one of the anecdotes he had prepared. "There is a story about her dressing me up in doll's clothes when I was a wee babe. But the truth is, you've forced me into something of a confession. You see, the queen has always been known for being very good, but I must confess that for a brief period, in my misspent youth, I went out of my way to be quite bad. And so it was to the family's advantage to keep me as far from Her Majesty as possible."

The queen talk had rattled him. (Curse that Shakespeare—but wasn't it his own fault for trusting an Englishman?) He hoped that by confessing to being a reprobate of unspecified depravities, he could align himself with Mr. Bingham and the elder Bingham daughter, and that by claiming to be a reformed soul, he could further ingratiate himself with Mrs. Bingham and the younger Bingham daughter— though it seemed Anisette needed little else to deepen her swoon.

The smiles on the faces of each of the four Binghams showed the success of the plan: approving, conspiratorial, sympathetic, enraptured.

"I imagine," Mrs. Bingham said, "that you will be among the party at the British Pavilion?"

British Pavilion? They kept lobbing haymakers at him. It was all he could do to ward off each blow. "That hasn't been decided," Francis said. "As I said on board the *Britannic,* my brother's medical care must be my chief priority. I wish this were an entirely social visit, but unfortunately..."

At the mention of his brother, smiles melted into furrowed brows. While Anisette asked questions—And how is Sir Malcolm? And what have the doctors said?—Mrs. Bingham briefed Mr. Bingham and Félicité on poor, deaf, mute Malcolm (so brave, so young, so tragic, so et cetera).

When Mrs. Bingham learned that his brother had not yet seen a doctor, she insisted that Sir Angus take him to her husband's personal physician. "I will call Dr. Van Hooten myself," she said. "You will see him tomorrow—just name the time and it is done."

Francis was going to dodge this latest jab just as he had the others. Who knew what the doctor would uncover and how quickly his suspicions would be reported to the Binghams? But the truth was that Michael did need to see a doctor—and why not a rich man's private physician? Wasn't it exactly what he had told Martin he was planning to do? Michael's well-being had to be more important than any ruse Francis was perpetrating on these most genial hosts. If this doctor could help Michael, could get him back to where he once was, then it was worth the risk of being exposed to a family of oddball millionaires. Francis had enough from the strongbox to reinvent himself again, if necessary. Now that he and Michael were in America, they could go anywhere, become anyone.

With the question of the appointment with Dr. Van Hooten settled, Mrs. Bingham again steered the conversation to their impending presentation to the royal couple. It was the first item on the monarchs' agenda after their arrival at the Trylon and Perisphere: they were to be seated on a dais while members of New York's elite were introduced. The Binghams had secured four spots—"Humbug to that!" Mr. Bingham reminded her—and in the absence of a male escort, which seemed quite, well, indecorous, Mrs. Bingham wondered if there would be any way that Sir Angus would do them the very great honor of accompanying them—that is Mrs. B, Anisette, and Félicité— through the receiving line?

Once he had unwound Mrs. Bingham's syntax and saw plainly the question within, Francis smiled more broadly than any of the Binghams. What a lark this was! Dinner at a mansion, a besotted heiress, a millionaire's private doctor, and now a meeting with the king and queen of England. They'd never believe a word of this at Mountjoy. He raised his glass to mark the occasion—to solemnize this contract he was making with the Binghams. "I would be delighted," he said. "Absolutely delighted."

Francis had his FC Plan, but Mrs. Bingham had her own plan in mind. Earlier in the day, she had thought it enough to be escorted to the royal visit by a cousin of the queen, a cousin the queen might even recognize and ask to come closer for a chat, after which she would ask, "And who are these lovely women accompanying you?" That would be enough, she believed, to burnish the social luster of the Bingham name. But now, to be the woman who effected a reconciliation between the Rose of Scotland—that's what they'd called her in *Life* magazine—and her cousin, once the black sheep but now the protector of his wounded brother (also a cousin of the queen), why, this would be a triumph that would echo through the generations. It would rankle those society matrons—hags, every one of them—who still, after decades, talked about the cheap Canadian tart who had snared the Copper King, and who spoke coldly to her, if at all, and spread wicked gossip about her daughters. And if all went well—if it went *extremely* well—then these same ladies would soon beg for the chance to sit in her parlor and ask, "Will Anisette's wedding be in New York, or will you go to Scotland?" She was getting ahead of herself, she knew, but she could sense something building between Anisette and Sir Angus, and the night hadn't yet reached its final act.

THE FOOD AND the talk and the effort of being Angus MacFarquhar had left Francis both exhilarated and drained. And so when Mrs. Bingham escorted him from the dining room, he hoped that she was leading him out. Instead, she guided him toward a wide arcade that drew him deeper into the house. Anisette had preceded them through the door by a few steps but had disappeared. Félicité had loudly announced that she was retiring for the night, claiming a headache that was simply annihilating her. Mr. Bingham had remained at the table, waiting for some phantom final course that only he could see. Francis and Mrs. B passed through a vaulted gallery packed with milky, vacant-eyed statues. Amid the tangle, Francis caught sight of a huntress, a limbless Athena, a dying Gaul. Down another corridor, he spotted a billiard table as wide and green as a football pitch, while another door opened onto a cavernous ballroom with a floor like a mirror of black glass.

"We have a little treat for you," Mrs. B said as she turned the knob on a final door, this one into a conservatory populated by a large wire-strung harp, a spinet, a cello, and a grand piano cut from the same brilliant stuff as the ballroom floor. A viola leaned skeptically in one corner, and he knew without being told that it belonged to Félicité. All around the room, music stands sprouted like thick, fat flowers and in front of one of them, arranged in a row, were three wingback chairs, one of which was already occupied by Mr. Bingham. Apparently there was a more direct route to the conservatory, one that didn't include a winding tour of the treasures of Bingham Castle. Francis saw that he was being courted, enticed to say yes to questions as yet unasked. And if a bargain was in the offing, then one more jeweled coffer was about to be opened before him: Anisette reappeared, a violin in one hand and a bow in the other.

Francis now saw why Félicité had been so quick to call it a night. Here again was Anisette in the spotlight, though the spot being lit was beginning to look less like a stage and more like a sales floor. If the marble walls and pencil-point turrets and the gold leaf and the polished mahogany and everyone-gets-their-own-meat and right-this-way-Your-Lordship weren't enough, then this latest exhibition would prove that the Binghams' prize canary could sing and not just look pretty on her gilded perch. Somewhere deep inside his meat-stuffed and wine-glazed heart, Francis couldn't help feeling sorry for Anisette. So much effort expended to catch the eye of a prince who was in fact a lowly pauper. Or was he? Francis had a bankroll; seed money, really, but it could be enough to get started. He had watched the way Mr. Bingham gripped his knife while he spoke of fat lords and their castles, and he surmised that Mr. Bingham himself had gone from nothing to this vast pile of something. And now Francis had only to endure the scratching of horsehair on catgut to move a step closer to—what?

He again considered that this game of make-believe was in truth another in the string of risks that had carried him from iron handcuffs to silver cuff links. The wheel of fortune kept calling him a winner, and every time his number came up, he risked it all on the next spin: the escape, the accident, the *Britannic*. Big gambles paid off even bigger. So maybe it wasn't just the Binghams' good graces that he needed to win. They had taken a shine to him, and now here they were, practically begging him to carry off their daughter. Saying yes was a preposterous gamble, but saying no was pure idiocy.

As soon as Francis and the elder Binghams were settled, Anisette propped the violin beneath her chin and without a word or a glance at her audience she launched the bow at the strings. Francis had braced himself for an onslaught but he was immediately enraptured. The first note was a starter's pistol in a musical steeplechase that cleared every high note without pause and let out on long runs that would have been called daring if Anisette weren't so obviously and firmly in control of the tempo and the timbre. While her hands worked their expert magic along the body of the instrument, her face remained calm, even placid, but it was her eyes; oh, those eyes! It wasn't just that they burned hot—though the look on her could have melted steel—it was that they were active and searching in a way that Francis had never seen before. Not from Anisette. Not from anyone else he could recall. Her eyes narrowed and then bloomed. The pupils were pinpricks and then vast pools of inky black. She was pushing herself through a journey—racing through sunlight, clouds, another sunrise, then nightfall—and bringing them all along with her. Mrs. Bingham inclined her head to one side, a slight smile on her lips; Mr. Bingham's eyes were shut, either in sleep or in reverie. Perhaps they had grown accustomed to Anisette's abilities, the way that people who live by the sea can forget that the sunset over a blue-and-foam bay can rend your heart with its raw beauty. But Francis was transfixed. When Anisette finished the piece with a sudden thrusting flourish, his hands broke unbidden into applause.

Mrs. B startled and Mr. B, roused from a postprandial nap, shook his head and looked crossly at Francis. The clapping seemed to break whatever spell had possessed Anisette, and with a winsome smile and a blush she was the Anisette of earlier: uncertain, eager to please— almost as if she too had been roused from sleep, mid-dream. Francis made a show of folding his hands in his lap and the elder Binghams resumed their poses—benevolence for her, somnolence for him. Anisette again raised the violin to the crook of her neck. She took a deep breath and the change came over her eyes once more.

Her encore worked the slow, sad, rough-throated end of the instrument. The bright sparks of the first song had faded, but they had lit something hard and slow to burn, like a coal fire that could glow all night. Anisette swayed, as if the violin were tethered to distant bells that tolled with each subtle pull. *Like this,* Francis said to himself. *I could spend the rest of my days like this.*

He was certain that he'd heard this piece of music before, but he could not remember where and neither could he put a name to it. He had gone rusty after his time in Mountjoy, which was a shame because one of the great benefits of life in Dublin in the years before his arrest had been re-immersing himself in music. He had met or maintained close relations with many of his best customers at the Opera House. It gave the whole operation a touch of class, he believed, that he could take orders between acts of *Rigoletto*—and it gave his clients the comfort of working with someone of obvious taste and refinement. *Francis, have you any more of that cognac? Francis, can you get me that novel by Huxley? Mr. Dempsey, has your man any more of those photographs—for a friend, of course?* His business concluded, he would settle into his seat. There were even times when an aria brought him close to tears, when an ingenue soprano sprung the lid on a boxed-up memory of—that was it.

This tune that Anisette was playing, with its achy questions, its plaintive appeal; he remembered now that he had heard it as a boy, in the house in Cork, when his mother was still alive. There had been a crush of people in the parlor—the big bodies of adults, a thicket of legs and skirts. A man was readying himself to play the piano. A young woman, a student of his mother's, stood beside him with a violin and with a nod the two began the same piece of music that Anisette now drew from the strings of her instrument. Francis's mother stood behind him, her hands on his shoulders. The perfume she always wore smelled tangy and floral. From the pressure of her fingertips—right, then left, right, then left—he could tell that she was swaying to the music, counting time as her pupil worked through the soaring trills and sudden choking stunts.

There was the taste of plum pudding in his mouth, Martin stood next to him, his father was somewhere in the room, there was a fire in the grate, and then his mother's voice was in his ear, framing the words *Kreutzer Sonata*. Her lips were so close that he felt the shape of these strange sounds as much as he heard them, as if she had spoken to him in a made-up language. He licked the last sticky crumbs of the pudding from his fingers and leaned back into the taut orb of his mother's belly. This was in December 1921, St. Stephen's Day. Michael would be born in March. She would be gone in August.

Francis was only nine when Mam died and Da whisked them out of Cork and off to Ballyrath. He knew things about his mother, factual things—she had red hair like his, she had a beautiful voice, she had gone to Boston to study music before she met Da—but he had trouble remembering her face. He had few clear memories of her that he could call up and peruse at will. Those days, and his mother, came only unbidden and in flashes.

Anisette stopped mid-measure, the bow shrieking against the strings. Her hair had come loose from its combs and the color burned in her cheeks. "Angus." Her voice cracked, a broken whisper. "Is something wrong?"

Before he could answer, Francis realized he was crying. The tears had been pouring out of him and now he snapped the square from his pocket and mopped his face. When he rose it was on unsteady legs. The night had started as a lark but here, in its closing hours, it had taken on a profound weight. His eyes met Anisette's and for a moment it was as if they were alone, exposed to each other. He feared that anything he said would banjax all his efforts to pass himself off as not-Francis. In that moment he did not have the strength to pretend. He had not come to the Binghams' seeking anything more than a night out and a chance to climb a rung or two on the social ladder, but here was Anisette, with depths to her that he had never guessed, and all around her shimmered a memory of long-ago days.

His throat parched, he quickly thanked the Binghams for their hospitality, for the use of their doctor, for making a stranger feel so welcome in this great city. The darkness pressing against the windows reminded him that it had been hours since he had abandoned Michael with no one to mind him but a beefsteak and a bowl of ice cream. Michael with his queer expressions, alternately dazed and rifle-sharp, as if there were something in the room that demanded his full attention: the chair with the fleur-de-lis fabric, the drapes that framed the view of the park, the painting of a bowl of pears. Michael needed tending.

He had planned to walk the twenty blocks back to the hotel in order to unwind the restlessness in his legs and sort through the welter uncorked by Anisette's performance. A Highland tradition, he was going to say, to get a good leg-stretching after a hearty meal, but the truth was that he was destroyed. When the Binghams insisted on having their driver bring round the car, he graciously accepted, and in minutes he was rolling down Fifth Avenue.

If only he could talk to Michael. They'd had only one day together before the accident, but it was time enough to see that his little brother, who'd been a child, really, when Francis had made his way to Dublin, had grown into someone who could ease Francis's loneliness and make him feel a part of something. Michael would love to hear about the Binghams, richer than Midas and madder than hatters, falling all over themselves to make sure that Sir Angus would escort them to the royal ball. The Michael he had gotten to know in the Morris Minor would have had a good laugh at that.

ANISETTE SAT AT her dressing table, thinking about the wedding. Oh, it would be lovely! She already had the dress, and they had decided ages ago which flowers she would carry in her bouquet. Not that she wanted everything to be exactly as they had planned it last year.

Hadn't Maman said that they would find someone better for her in Europe? An Italian count or a Polish prince, that's what Maman had said, though Father hadn't liked the idea of another Catholic in the family—a palace coup, that's what he called it. Still, anyone in Europe would have been better than the best New York had to offer. Look at what a mess that had been. If she had gone through with it, she would still be in her newlywed year.

She thought it was all going to be so nice but then her intended went and tried that horrible business. She could still smell the drink on his breath, the reek of gin. He had started kissing her, late on the night of the Christmas party at his parents' home, but the kisses became cruel. He bit her lip, hard enough to draw blood, and when she shrieked he put one hand over her mouth and the other under her dress. He said filthy things to her, with his hand going up her thigh and his mouth hot against her unwilling ear. She struggled, she kicked at him, but he persisted, and only when she managed to pull her face away and scream long and loud did he finally stop.

"You're right," he'd said, wiping his mouth on the back of his hand, "let's wait. That way the wedding night will be full of surprises."

She couldn't get those words or his leering smile out of her head. Both had followed her out the door and all the way home, ten blocks in the bitter chill. It was that night, crying in the tub, that she told her mother she never wanted to see him again. Not ever. Anisette knew that the trip abroad had been planned to escape the chatter that echoed from Park Avenue to Scarsdale to Greenwich. She didn't know about the sizable payment and the use of the villa in Cuba that kept her intended from contributing to the chatter.

Angus, though. Angus was kind, genteel, sensitive—nothing like that other one. Of course she had known him only a few days, but what she felt for him ran deeper than anything she had felt before. He was polite and clever and he looked after his brother and he had been so careful not to tell tales about the queen. Hadn't he said it himself? That he had once been bad, but he had changed his ways, and become good?

There was something familiar about Angus, but until tonight she hadn't been able to put her finger on it. It was during dinner, as he sparred with Daddy about sharp knives and Scottish hills, that it came to her: Robert. Her brother had been her protector, her pal. He was eight years older and had been like a favorite uncle. Or what she imagined it would be like to have an uncle. (They never spoke of Maman's family, and Daddy's other children—her half brothers and half sisters—were old people themselves; older even than Maman. They lived out west, in places Anisette had never visited, and there was never any talk of them coming to New York.) When Anisette was a little girl, her nurses had been a succession of pinch-faced matrons— pretty nurses made for bad marriages, her mother said—and whenever they grew cross with her, Robert was the one who could charm them out of their foul humors. He had also been her champion and chief advocate in the long-running wars with Félicité. How many times in her childhood did he rescue her from a bout of hair-pulling or free a doll held hostage by her older sister?

She had often thought of Robert after that awful Christmas party. He would have taken care of everything. Robert would have heard her scream and stormed in, and with one punch sent her Intended to his knees. Then with a few razor-sharp words, Robert would have shamed him in front of all the guests. In another age, it might even have come to a duel—with Robert victorious, of course—and Anisette wouldn't have minded that one bit.

But Robert had been gone for so long. He had been sent off to Yale—*for polishing,* her mother had said—and for the first two years he sent funny letters and packages full of her favorite lavender candies, and he visited on holidays and played college songs on the piano. Anisette would take the harmony while Félicité sulked and made faces in the corner. But over time the letters dwindled and the visits grew less frequent. Robert and Daddy began to argue terribly, and shortly after his graduation, the visits stopped. There was still the occasional letter, but where he had once sent jokes and silly doodles, his notes now asked only for her to argue on his behalf to Father: to beg him to support Robert's scheme for diamond mines in Rhodesia, or bananas in Nicaragua, or rubber plantations in Java. Whenever she tried to raise his name in the house, Father grew vexed and Maman's eyes filled with tears. She had once heard Félicité say, with a note of envy, that Robert had gotten so polished at Yale that he slipped away entirely.

She didn't want to let Angus slip away. Saturday seemed an awfully long time to wait to see him again, so she would have to find another day — and soon. Hadn't she been bold enough to knock on the door of his stateroom so late at night that he had already dressed for bed? Her mother would fret and Félicité would sneer and Father would scoff, but Anisette would be bold again.

TUESDAY
JUNE 6

THE PLAZA HOTEL

CRONIN HAD FOLLOWED FRANCIS Dempsey and the blonde back from Harlem on Sunday night. The Plaza had been a surprise, but then Dempsey was full of surprises: the fancy clothes, the giant bottle of wine, already a girl on his arm, and now a night at one of the poshest spots in the city. Cronin had seen petty criminals like this before— yokes who would clean out the till of a speakeasy and go on a spree. Fresh pair of shoes. New hat. Drinks all around and always the best woman they could afford. Yokes who believed that a pile of stolen cash conferred protection not just from life's hard knocks but from the dollar-a-day avenging angels on the payroll of the local bosses. It always ended the same way: their battered bodies would turn up behind a row of trash cans, stripped of life and those flashy shoes.

But this Dempsey was up to something bigger. Early in the morning Cronin had seen the blonde leave the Plaza in a rush, and at the very same time, the littlest Dempsey, the one who'd been only a baby back when Cronin knew the family, swept into the hotel. So this was their hidey-hole? And then that same night Dempsey was off for hours at some Fifth Avenue mansion, only to return in a Rolls-Royce polished to such a shine that it seemed to move invisibly, reflecting the night and the street lamps. The eagerness, the hot certainty that Cronin had felt outside the Savoy to swoop down on Dempsey and dump him with Gavigan, had mellowed into caution. Gavigan wanted Dempsey found, but that wasn't quite the same as saying he wanted Dempsey brought to his doorstep. Plus, as the days ticked by, Cronin was start-ing to think that Dempsey wasn't acting alone. He had someone look-ing out for him, guiding him, and that must be what was giving him such blithe confidence. Cronin knew the feeling, had once basked in its warm glow himself. For many years he knew what it was to live under Gavigan's umbrella, back when that meant something. There were many who knew Cronin to be untouchable, for fear of what Gavigan could take from them, and many more who kept their dis-tance from Gavigan for fear of what Cronin could do to them. But this Dempsey? He had the IRA after him, and the Irish police—whatever they were worth—had to be aware that they had let one get away, and yet here he was, swanning around the city like a gentleman on holiday. He was either a worldly fellow, clever and confident, or the biggest dullard to have set foot in the city in years.

Tuesday morning came and Cronin sat on a bench, his back to Cen-tral Park and his eyes on the Plaza, waiting for Dempsey's next move. This was what Frank Dempsey had taught him. To be patient. To know a man's route footfall by footfall. You didn't ambush a man by following him; you had to be in front, awaiting his arrival. How many times had they lain in wait, ready to ambush a British patrol, only to abandon the attack when the conditions weren't in their favor: the Brits were meant to be on bicycles, not in lorries; the patrol was sched-uled to cross the bridge at half twelve but arrived early, before the rifles were in place. Seize the day, Frank had taught them, but don't force the moment. Better to wait than to stumble. The men in West Cork had said it best: The purpose of the flying column was to exist. There was nothing to be gained by a glorious defeat. So he had waited patiently for Francis Dempsey, but his patience hadn't yet paid off. During the war they would observe a target for weeks before carrying out a strike. It was important to know routines, numbers, armaments. A man's habits were his undoing. There had been an officer in the Auxiliaries who kept himself under lock and key in the barracks—

never went out on patrol, never took part in operations, never walked alone through the city. Even on Sundays, he had an armed escort to church. Except—except his escort left him at the church gate and it was twenty steps from the gate to the stone porch that fronted the church doors. And one day on those steps, as the bells rang overhead to announce the Mass, Cronin and a fellow called Devlin approached the officer on the steps and fired two shots from their revolvers, Devlin into his gut and Cronin into the side of his head. He was dead before he hit the stones and Cronin and Devlin were gone before the bell had stopped tolling.

But this business with Dempsey was different. Partly because it wasn't an out-and-out hit but a kidnap, which was loads more difficult. In a hit, you only had to pull the trigger and be on your way, but to grab a man and deliver him without too much commotion was a job of work. A man who thought he was fighting for his life could be a whirligig of kicks and punches, eye gouges and foot stomps and knees to the groin. And who knew what surprises Dempsey carried in his pocket? Cronin had seen men gutted with a sharpened screwdriver, blinded by a ha'penny nail.

Aside from the difficulty of the task itself, there just wasn't time to plan it out properly. The Bronx one day, then Harlem, then the Plaza, then the Upper East Side? Cronin couldn't yet find a pattern, and every day left Alice and the boy and the baby exposed, unguarded. It hadn't been like this in the old days, when no one waited for him at home. There had been only the operation, the orders, the cause. Other men had families and he saw the strain it placed on them: the worry of being away from wife and babies, the fear of what would happen if the Black and Tans, knowing that you were planning ten ways to put them in their graves, went calling on your wife. Cronin never had to worry about any of that, but now everything was different. He had been five days away from Alice and each day hung on him like a length of chains. She was a capable woman, but this business with Dempsey and Gavigan—this was a different order of trouble. This was a world she did not know, a world that Cronin had hoped she would never see.

CRONIN CROSSED THE street, leaving the park for a walk-by of the hotel. Just as he reached the middle of the road, with cabs on each side honking at him, the two brothers sauntered down the front steps and ducked into a waiting taxicab. He cursed his luck. His car was all the way on the west side of the park and a man dressed like Cronin could not expect the bell captain to hail a cab for him. He took a deep breath. They would return, but for now he had the hotel to himself. As the Dempseys' cab lurched into the morning traffic, Cronin reached into his pocket for one of Gavigan's crisp ten-dollar notes. He approached the bell captain and held up the bill.

"The man who's after getting in that cab," he said. "He dropped this when he reached in his pocket for your tip."

Hesitation—no, calculation—was visible on the bell captain's face. Shock that a man in a farmer's going-to-town suit wouldn't just pocket such a windfall, mixed with larceny as he wondered how to keep the tenner for himself.

"Will I drop it at the front desk for him?" Cronin said, thickening up his brogue. If Alice heard him and his *after getting in that cab* and his *will I,* she'd say he sounded like he'd just gotten off the boat.

Confronted by this earnest, honest country bumpkin—an immigrant, no less—the captain reached for the brass pull that opened the door. "Right this way, sir," he said.

The *sir* reminded Cronin of the way the chemist always called Henry *young man* whenever the boy was given a chance to choose a piece of penny candy. A compliment that put you in your place.

"You can tell them at the front desk that the money belongs to Sir Angus. They'll know what to do."

Of course he wasn't staying under his own name, but Sir Angus? As he crossed the lobby, Cronin asked himself again if this Dempsey was a canny bastard or a complete nutter. At the front desk he related the story and proffered the ten.

"You're a good man," the desk clerk said. "I wish there were more like you in this city." The clerk slid the ten into an envelope and paused before he sealed it. "May I tell His Lordship the name of his benefactor?"

"I'm only doing what any man would have done," Cronin said, an answer that provoked a smile, a silent cousin of the bell captain's *sir.* *That's right,* Cronin thought. *Just a simple man, here to see the sights.* He made sure to gawk at the ceiling and at the broad entrance to the Palm Court, with its lush greenery bursting from gold-glazed pots, but kept an eye on the clerk as he turned and slid the envelope into the warren of pigeonholes on the wall behind the desk. Cronin leaned in and squinted: room 712.

"If you'll pardon my asking," Cronin said, "the man outside called the owner of that banknote Sir Angus, and I couldn't help but notice that you called him His Lordship. Is he some kind of royalty?"

The desk clerk chuckled and leaned toward Cronin, as if taking him into his confidence. "We treat all of our guests like royalty," he said. "But the MacFarquhars may just be a little closer to the real thing."

"How about that?" Cronin said. He nodded to the man—oh, they were the best of friends now—and forced a knowing wink. What would Alice say if she saw him gabbing with clerks and carrying on like the village idiot? "Well, then, I'll be on my way," Cronin said. "Wife'll be wondering where I've run off to."

The clerk smiled and Cronin smiled back. His face was going to ache for days after all of this smiling. But now he had it: a name and a room number. He could give Gavigan a map so simple that even that skinny shadow of his could follow it straight to Francis Dempsey. He felt in his pocket for the keys to the Packard. He was ready to pay Gavigan a visit.

PARK AVENUE

THE CALL HAD COME at nine in the morning. Dr. Theo Van Hooten had finished his breakfast and was beginning his perusal of the morning newspapers—he had four dailies delivered, including the afternoon edition of the *Herald,* and over the course of the day he would work his way through each of them. He did not read every word—he had little interest in business news and had never been much of a sports fan—but he often read three or four accounts of the major stories of the day. The papers today were abuzz with news of Saturday's royal visit: a parade up the West Side Highway, a party at Columbia University, lots of pomp and circumstance at the World's Fair, and then dinner with the Roosevelts in Hyde Park. He read all about it, with a singular focus that he could never muster in the old days, back when he was actually out in the world, among people caught in the great gears of history. It had been a dozen years since he'd walked in that world, since he'd taken the position as private physician to Emery Bingham, a wealthy man from one of those vast, rectangular western states that Van Hooten, for all of his education, could never quite remember. The job had come with many benefits but a single condition: That if he was summoned by the Bingham family, on the telephone whose number only the Binghams knew, he must answer. Failure to do so would result in his immediate dismissal.

Van Hooten had not thought much of it in the early years. For a doctor with his background—Harvard education, residency at Johns

Hopkins, partnership in a private practice on Park Avenue, all by the time he was thirty-five—jobs were easy to come by. He would have enjoyed a broad safety net except for one troublesome fact: Van Hooten despised the practice of medicine, a revelation that had come to him only after he was too far along in his professional life to seriously consider other options. He saw his days laid out in front of him, a night gallery of sunken chests and drooping scrotums, phlegm and sputum and milky discharges of uncertain origin. He had thought that by treating only the very wealthy he would insulate himself from life's danker unpleasantries, but his years on Park Avenue had taught him that although the rich might be better perfumed than the poor, shingles was still shingles, a hemorrhoid still a hemorrhoid. Moreover, quitting the profession in disgust was simply not possible. Van Hootens had been doctors since at least the time of Rembrandt. The old Dutch master himself had included a distant Van Hooten forebear in *The Anatomy Lesson,* the man's pointy blond Vandyke practically twitching in excitement at its proximity to the flayed arm of the convict. No, abandoning the only profession the Van Hootens had ever known would have required that he admit to himself and all those around him that he had failed miserably, and publicly, at a career in which he had shown such promise.

So when old Mr. Bingham fell out with the senior partner in the medical practice and Mrs. Bingham asked if Van Hooten would be interested in becoming Mr. Bingham's personal physician, he leaped at the offer. One patient, even one as elderly and potentially infirm as Mr. Bingham, was just what this doctor ordered. Given Mr. Bingham's disdain for doctors, Van Hooten figured that he would see his one patient for an annual physical and in between he would be left to a life of semi-luxury—and except for that one codicil in the contract, he would have done exactly that. Theatergoing, speakeasy-visiting, opera-loving, socialite-wooing—all that and more could have been his, if the Binghams had not insisted that he be available to them at any minute of the day or night. They made use of this privilege only rarely, and it was always the missus—only the missus—who called. But had he not been in the apartment when those calls came, the job would have been forfeited, and he would have found himself back at the old practice, examining the lugubrious bulge of an inguinal hernia, exploring the mungy contours of a gangrenous foot, or debriding the bedsores of some sodden-fleshed dowager.

He still dreamed of a steak dinner at Delmonico's or a martini and a raft of littlenecks at the Oyster Bar, but the same thoughts left him in a bitter sweat. Even a trip down the elevator and into the lobby could spell doom. He was haunted by the sound of the phone ringing in the empty apartment.

In the past decade, he had left the apartment no more than a dozen times. Almost all of his excursions were for the Bingham père's annual physical, which Mrs. Bingham insisted upon and which always led to the same conclusion: that Mr. Bingham was an unwilling patient with the constitution of a petrified tree stump. Time and Bingham's own cussedness had abraded whatever soft tissue had once clung to his frame, leaving a sentient, rocky core.

During Van Hooten's confinement, the big events of the day—the stock market crash, the election of FDR, the end of Prohibition, the rise of the New Deal—were little more than headlines to him. A woman named Foster arrived every morning to prepare his breakfast and tend to his laundry. She set the coffeepot, scrambled his eggs, buttered his toast. Dinners came delivered from a rotating cast of restaurants; the food would arrive in the lobby in folded paper cartons, which a doorman would then ferry to his door. Liquor and other essentials—books, record albums, stamps, typewriter ribbons—came by similar means. Every year a tailor visited to measure him for custom shirts and suits that almost no one would ever see, while a barber arrived every other week to trim his thinning hair.

His friendships had fallen away years ago—few, then none, wanted to spend hour after hour in Van Hooten's apartment with never the prospect of a night on the town. He had long abandoned any thought of a wife and children. The demands of family life could only distract from his duties to the Binghams. His dealings with women, like all of his encounters, became transactions. He placed a call, a woman arrived, and the night ended with the payment of a fee. But in recent years, even sex had lost its appeal. The same squeamishness that had driven him from the medical profession had overwhelmed whatever lusts resided in his heart. His one remaining source of pleasure was chess. He was currently involved in more than a dozen games, all carried out by mail.

When the telephone rang that morning, Van Hooten had not set foot outside the apartment in nine months. The shock of the ringer jangling in the hallway almost sent his second cup of coffee into his lap. The telephone sat on a console table in a spot Van Hooten had calculated was the center-most in the apartment, equidistant from the bedroom (he slept with the door open), the bathroom (he had not had a satisfying bowel movement since 1927), and the living room (he listened to the phonograph only at very low volume). He raced to the receiver, a heavy black thing that he lifted with a mix of fear and gratitude. The call could only mean that Mr. Bingham had taken ill, and that Van Hooten must venture out to attend to him. O blessed day!

But no. Mrs. Bingham informed Van Hooten that he was to be visited that morning by a Scottish lord whose younger brother needed medical attention. He was to do everything in his power to assist the young man, who had suffered some grievous harm of uncertain diagnosis.

"He's a medical mystery," Mrs. Bingham said. "But we believe that you're just the man for the case."

The kind words from Mrs. Bingham did little to soothe his disappointment. He so badly wanted to go outside. He kept a freshly pressed suit, a clean shirt, and a new tie hanging in the wardrobe, ready for a venture into the city. He had already promised himself that the next time he was summoned by the Binghams, he would insist on walking back to his apartment, rather than being taken door to door by the Binghams' driver. But that was for another day. Today, he would have visitors.

THE DOORMAN RANG him at ten sharp, and presently there were two gentlemen at his door—a strapping redhead and a dark-haired stripling. Van Hooten knew that his social graces had gone rusty, and after a quick exchange of greetings with the redhead, he guided his guests into the library. The bookcases were lined with medical journals—row upon row of bound volumes—but it had been years since he had kept current with the literature. Most of the articles dealt with conditions too boring or, more frequently, too horrid to contemplate. He was fond of reading the evening newspapers in his library, but he had made sure to tidy these up before his patient arrived. He wanted the report back to the Binghams—he knew there would be a report—to mention how serious and even scholarly Van Hooten could be.

"Now, how is it that I can help you?" Van Hooten said when his Scottish visitors were settled.

Francis explained that three weeks prior, his brother had suffered an injury that left him badly damaged: deaf, mute, and mentally... scattered. He smiled apologetically at Michael as he relayed his medical history. Damaged, scattered—these were terrible things to say about one's own blood. When Van Hooten asked the cause of the injury, Francis hesitated. "I'm going to have to take you into my confidence," Francis said. "The circumstances of his injury—they're complicated."

Francis had thought this through over his morning pot of tea. He needed a story that struck close to the truth if this doctor was to make an accurate diagnosis. He had told anyone on the *Britannic* who asked that his brother had been injured while foxhunting—trampled by a horse or some other plausibly aristocratic mishap. But would an actual doctor note the absence of a telltale hoofprint on the side of Michael's head? Would he report his suspicions to the Binghams? Or simply misdiagnose Michael's condition? If there was a way to sort out what was wrong with Michael, Francis did not want to scuttle it with the wrong sort of half-truths and outright lies. And so before he began, he asked the doctor if he knew anything of Ireland's recent history.

"I confess I do not," Van Hooten said. During the years he had spent in the apartment, the newspapers had been full of FDR and the WPA, Hitler and Chamberlain, the Lindbergh baby and the Dionne quintuplets. News of the quints had especially troubled him. He still shivered whenever he thought of the poor doctor who endured that delivery. More like the work of a veterinarian, if you asked him.

Freed by the doctor's ignorance from any strict adherence to facts, Francis spun a tale of his brother's recent visit to Ireland, where he had been the guest of wealthy landowners who, for the sake of discretion, Francis could not name. These friends had maintained their vast holdings despite the turbulence of the past two decades, but lately had drawn the ire of a splinter group of malcontents who advocated returning the land to the so-called common people.

"Bolsheviks?" Van Hooten said.

"*Irish* Bolsheviks."

"I had no idea."

"Oh, they're out there. And these particular Bolsheviks detonated a bomb on our host's property. My brother, quite unluckily, was near the site of the explosion, which razed a small cottage."

"He doesn't look too badly damaged—from the outside, I mean."

"That's why we came to see you," Francis said. "To find out what happened on the inside."

"Yes," he said. "The inside."

Van Hooten hefted a gleaming otoscope and peered into each of Michael's ears. He noted that both eardrums had been ruptured. Then he studied Michael's eyes, the way they followed a pencil he drew back and forth across the young man's field of vision. He ended each phase of the examination with a short *hmph,* as if time and again he were surprising himself with one of his findings. Van Hooten had Michael remove his shirt in order to get a better listen to his lungs. There were no problems with his breathing, but his torso was speckled with scratches and fading bruises outlined in yellow and purple— proof of the Bolsheviks' handiwork.

As he examined Michael, Van Hooten chatted idly—sometimes, it seemed, to himself, and other times directing a question at Francis: How long had he been in New York? What were his impressions of the city? How had he come to know the Binghams? When Francis mentioned meeting Anisette and Mrs. Bingham on the transatlantic crossing, Van Hooten dropped his stethoscope. He made no move to pick it up.

"The Binghams were in Europe?" Van Hooten said. "How— how—how long were they away?"

"Two or three months, I suppose."

Van Hooten was short of breath. Mrs. Bingham had been out of the country—she had been across the ocean—for two or three months? Two or three months when the phone would not have rung. When he could have left the apartment, left the building, even left the city. His mouth was dry, his fingers numb.

"I—I wasn't aware of that," he said, the words barely audible. When the older Scotsman asked if his brother could get dressed, Van Hooten could only nod. The younger one buttoned his shirt, tied his necktie, and wandered out of the library and into the hallway. "Is he capable of being on his own, unsupervised?"

"He's not an idiot," Francis snapped, then cleared his throat to regain his composure. He had almost said *eejit*—a dead giveaway for anyone who knew how to tell a Scottish lord from a boy raised in the Irish countryside, though Van Hooten probably wouldn't have noticed.

Francis's tone brought Van Hooten back to the room, the examination, the case before him. He retrieved his stethoscope from the floor and placed it on the table with the other instruments, then withdrew a notebook and pencil from a drawer. He asked if Michael suffered from headaches or other signs of physical discomfort.

"He has fits," Francis said. "Less now than right after the blast, but he still gets them. Very bright lights can start him squirming, and he's liable to faint straightaway."

"Has he complained of any other symptoms?"

"How's he to complain? I told you, he hasn't said a word."

"Can't he write?"

"Not since it happened."

Van Hooten hummed again. The news of the Binghams' overseas jaunt had rocked him, but now he was warming to the task at hand. This was the side of medicine that he had always enjoyed: the way that each answer opened the door to other questions, after which you chose the questions that would get you to the next set of answers, followed by more questions, until, like the letters of a crossword puzzle falling into place, you would have a rational diagnosis. For Van Hooten, a diagnosis was a holy grail in a world that resisted reason, a grail reached by treading a cleanly paved mental pathway rather than mucking about in the soupy fens of the body for an answer. In this case, he had precedents, not only general principles, to work from: Hadn't he seen plenty of cases like this during the Great War? Blank-faced boys whose eyes could never alight on any one thing for long, or whose gazes were permanently fixed on some distant point no one else could see. Of course a blast could rupture the eardrum and send the tiny bones of the ear sprawling helter-skelter. He had seen plenty of men who would never again hear the anguished cries of their brothers-in-arms, or their sweethearts' voices, or the stirring tones of the songs that had sent them off to Europe in the first place. He had seen men so badly shell-shocked that they ceased speaking for good. Nor was this young man's inability to read and write unheard of for a wartime casualty.

"Assuming that his hearing does not return—" Van Hooten said.

"Are you saying that it won't?"

"This type of injury—hearing loss resulting from a single catastrophic episode—is, I must tell you, often permanent. The eardrums can repair themselves, but the real damage runs deeper."

Francis wanted to be shocked by this. He wanted to express outrage that the doctor was so quickly settling for this fainthearted diagnosis. Surely there must be something that could be done: some procedure, some bit of arcane medical knowledge, that would make Michael, well, Michael again. But a part of him had known from the beginning that what had happened to Michael could not be unwound.

"As for the cognitive issues—the reading and writing—it's possible that those can be reversed. Given time and the proper treatment."

"And what would that—"

From somewhere in the apartment came a rapid-fire clacking—like gunshots or tree branches snapping in a storm. The two men followed the sound into the dining room, where Michael sat before a typewriter, his gaze fixed on the wall and his fingers working madly at the keys. He was surrounded on all sides by chessboards. The table, the sideboard, even a few of the chairs were covered with them. On each board, a miniature skyline of royals and their courtiers fanned out in elaborate formations of attack and defense. Vanquished pawns, rooks, bishops, and knights littered the gaps between the boards. And with each fervent punch of the keys, the pieces on the nearest boards jumped.

"Stop that!" Van Hooten shrieked. "Stop!"

* * *

WHEN MICHAEL HAD set out with Francis that morning, he had no idea where they were going. Perhaps a return visit to Martin's apartment? Another amble down the broad street of jewelers and churches? For the life of him, he could not figure out what they were doing in New York City. Had he played any part in planning this voyage? Had they come only to visit their brother? Did Francis have some new occupation that had posted him, in high style, to New York City? That last option seemed the least likely. Francis had been in prison — that much Michael remembered — but had he been released already? Was the pit in his memory so wide and so deep that it contained all of Francis's prison time within it? As the cab navigated the traffic, the two of them sitting side by side, Michael was struck suddenly with an image of his brother's profile in another automobile, at another time. Francis was at the wheel and the engine whined with exertion and beyond the open window lay rolling hills quilted in green and bordered on all sides by stacked-stone walls. Francis wore a blue suit and Michael was swathed in a cassock that went from his notched collar to his scuffed black shoes. Wind poured into the car — he felt it stiff against his face, rich with the smell of wet grass — and he was hooting in mad celebration. *I'm free,* that's what he'd been thinking. *I'm free!*

Whatever he was remembering, it was before...before...before the Noise, and the constant silence, and Yeats, and New York City. The moment in the car, racing across Ireland, was on the far side of the lost time. If he could only concentrate and connect this moment to what came before and what came after, he was sure that he could reassemble the shattered jigsaw of his memory.

The taxicab came to a lurching halt in front of a tall building on a boulevard lined with other tall buildings. Francis took Michael's arm in his and ushered his brother into the lobby, where they were met by the doorman. In his epaulets and high, gold-braided hat, he looked like a general stripped of his medals. Then: elevator, corridor, middle-aged man with wispy blond hair, handshake, library, his feet on an Oriental rug. All of it passed in that echoless silence that made him feel as if he were floating. He had never realized how much he counted on the sound of his own footsteps to make him feel grounded, sub-stantial, alive.

When he looked up from the carpet's pattern of lotuses and twisted vines, he found Yeats leaning amiably against the wall in the corner of the room. The table next to the poet held all manner of polished medi-cal devices: a stethoscope, a tiny mallet, syringes in four different sizes, a circular mirror attached to a leather strap. The blond-haired man—*A doctor,* Michael said to Yeats, *finally!*—peered at Michael from a variety of angles. The doctor's mouth moved, Francis moved his lips in reply, and so it went.

"What are they saying?" Michael asked.

"They're talking about people you haven't met."

"Shouldn't they be talking about me?"

Yeats shrugged. Noncommittal.

"Does he know what's wrong with me?"

Again, Yeats shrugged.

"Worthless," Michael said.

"Are you referring to me or to the doctor?"

Michael shrugged.

Yeats pursed his lips, a sour-apple expression that Michael had come to know too well. When the poet was displeased, he made no effort to hide his feelings. He removed his glasses and while buffing them with a handkerchief, he wandered out of the room.

"Now where are you going?" Michael said. He followed Yeats out of the library and into the parlor, a musty, tomblike space occupied by brocade furniture tricked out with bronze nail heads and gold cord. The walls were hung with gilt-framed portraits of stern, shaggy-cheeked men, and women bound up in wimples and forbearance.

Beneath the portraits, Oriental rugs abounded. The room was equal parts Ali Baba and Oliver Cromwell. The dining room was decorated to a similar standard. Its claw-foot table could seat six, the gloomy breakfront displayed a family fortune in silver platters, and on the walls were more lace collars and blanched faces. But it was a dining room in name only: a man would be hard-pressed to find space among the chessboards for his morning tea and toast.

A typewriter crouched at one end of the table, a neat sheaf of carbons next to it. Michael had little interest in chess, but he was drawn to the typewriter. It was similar to the model he had used at St. Columbanus to compose his coded letters to his brothers. He sat and tapped his fingers against the keys, but so faintly that the levers lay idle. He closed his eyes and in his head, he recited words, then sentences, and let his fingers find the letters. Muscle memory. He could feel it.

Opening his eyes, he saw Yeats with one hand poised above a white queen. "Hey," he said. "Don't touch that."

"It'll be checkmate," Yeats said. "Or did you have another move in mind?"

"It's not your game," Michael said.

"Go back to your typing."

Michael again scrutinized the machine with its bristling ranks of keys. Isolated as they were, one letter to each black button, he could make sense of them. The letters seemed to pulse and flex, to come apart at the corners, but then to pull themselves back into shape. Here was an *E,* there a *D,* lower down an *N.* Once combined into words, the letters ceased to make sense—on restaurant menus and shop signs, they slithered and separated, forming new glyphs he could not decipher. But he thought again of that feeling of muscle memory. If he could find the *G,* then he would array the fingertips of his left hand to one side of it and his right would find its place two keys over. Brother Bartholomew, who had run the office at St. Columbanus, would be proud of how easily Michael fit his hands to the task. He deplored the way that educated men used their fingers to chicken-peck the keys into submission, and would not abide typists who stutter-stepped through their work. Michael drew one sheet from the stack next to the typewriter and wound it into the cylinder. Slowly at first, and then with speed and authority, he began to type.

> michal dempsey
> michael dempsey
> michasel dempsey

Yeats looked up from another chessboard. "How am I supposed to concentrate with that pounding? And the bell is quite distracting."

"Come over here," Michael said. "I want you to see this."

"I know what a typewriter looks like. George had one just like it." Yeats again reached for a chess piece—a bishop this time—before yanking back his hand.

"You need to tell me what I've typed. I might have found a way out."

"Out of what?"

"Of myself."

Yeats slowly came around the table, his limp more noticeable than before.

"Now watch this." Michael was feeling cocky and took a chance with the Shift key.

> Willliam butter Yeast
> William Butler Yeates
> William Butler Yeats is a stodgy old git

"What do you see?"

"Names, and then a poor attempt at literary criticism. And it looks like we have company."

As Francis and the doctor entered the room, Michael locked down the Shift key and typed in a mad rush.

WHAT HAPPENED TOME?
WHAT AAPPEED TO ME
WHAT HAPPENEND TO ME?
WHAT HAPPENED T

Van Hooten darted across the room and stilled Michael's hands on the keys. "Oh, look what you've done!"

Michael freed his hands and beckoned Francis to come to him, but Francis smirked and gave a slight shake of the head. Francis had diagnosed this doctor as a nutter and was ready to be on his way. He made a *Let's go* motion with his thumb. Michael stood reluctantly and shuffled to join his brother.

"You look as if you've got your work cut out for you here," Francis said. "And we really must be going."

Van Hooten looked from his chessboards to the brothers. This was a bad ending to the examination, and he was suddenly nervous about what his guest might say to the Binghams. Would he say the doctor had treated him rudely? Or that he had been unable to offer a proper diagnosis? Van Hooten couldn't allow that to happen. It could mean the end of everything.

"Please be sure to give my regards to the Binghams," Van Hooten said. "And if there's anything else I can do for you—anything at all— please don't hesitate to ask."

"I'll be seeing them on Saturday at the fair," Francis said, "and I'd be most happy to report any progress you've made on my brother's case." There had been talk during the examination of specialists— men who studied the ears, the throat, the brain—who could be consulted on Michael's behalf. Francis wanted Van Hooten to know that he expected this information posthaste.

"The fair?" Van Hooten said.

"Yes. I'm to accompany them to meet Their Royal Majesties." As soon as the words were out of his mouth, Francis wondered whether he should have said *Royal Highnesses* instead. He needed to figure out his formal modes of address before he stumbled into another Earl of Glamis situation.

"Of course," Van Hooten said. "All of the best families are meeting the royals. Isn't that just what the *Times* reported." It was difficult to tell whether Van Hooten was speaking to himself or to Francis. With each line, the doctor recognized, his voice was growing fainter, as if it had turned inward. Spending so much time alone had made it difficult for him to tell the difference between talking aloud and talking in his head. Often he caught himself midthought and wondered, *Did I just say that? Or merely think it?*

Right now, all of Van Hooten's thoughts were focused on Saturday, and the few hours of freedom he would enjoy. The papers had published an exhaustive schedule of all the events around the royal visit; surely he could expect the phone to stay silent for hours. He could go out for lunch, or walk in the park. He could go to a museum. How he longed to wander the galleries of the Metropolitan, to see the bright colors of Titian and Raphael. He had enough dour Flemish shadows right here at home; he wanted color and sunshine, beatific faces that had never known the depredations of time.

"Doctor," Francis said, and then again, louder. Van Hooten looked as if he'd been shaken from a dream. "You spoke about proper treatment for my brother. Where could such treatment be found?"

Van Hooten stumbled through a list of names, only to realize that it had been years since he had been in contact with anyone in his profession. How many of the doctors he once knew had retired or moved to other hospitals, other cities? With great effort, he tried to put aside the heady prospect of a few hours' furlough on Saturday—what about a musical? He had read the reviews of every show on Broadway in the past decade—and promised Francis that he would make calls, provide references, and pave the way for them. "We'll get to the bottom of this," he said as the brothers exited his apartment. "And do enjoy yourself on Saturday. It promises to be a great day for your country and for ours—and just a lovely day all around."

GRAMERCY PARK

GAVIGAN HAD BEEN TROUBLED by strange dreams. He woke in a sweat, stiff-limbed and sore-headed, the sheets in a pasty tangle. Firing up his engine was difficult on the best of days, but on mornings like this he felt just how much this life had cost him. He moved like a man waist-deep in a river whose current was against him. Every day his lungs filled with a vile yellow sludge that could find release only through strenuous fits of coughing. It was a dog's life, but it was life and that was better than the alternative.

He sat, with no small effort, and tried to bring focus to the particulars of the dream. A waste of time. His dreams always dissolved in the light, leaving an aftertaste that could sour his mood for hours to come. In last night's shadow play, he had been double-crossed. He didn't remember how or by whom—not that it mattered. He wasn't some loon who believed that dreams could give him the straight dope on his waking life, but still, that sense of betrayal clung to him as he extracted himself from the sheets. Nothing rankled Gavigan like disloyalty, and to wake with thoughts of a Judas kiss—that was a hell of a way to start a Tuesday.

At this hour the house should have been ticking like a Swiss watch, steady and almost imperceptible. Helen would be making the porridge and putting the kettle on to boil. In another minute Jamie would ascend the carpet-wrapped stairs to tap at the door with an *Anything*

I can do for ye, Mr. Gavigan? That Jamie was a queer one: he had a sixth sense that alerted him the moment Gavigan opened his eyes. It was never the knock at the door that woke Gavigan, but as soon as he was awake, Jamie was there; he never kept his boss waiting. He was steady, that one. A soldier to the end.

But this morning it wasn't the soft knock that he heard first, it was Jamie's voice raised and then another, buffeting it: Tommy Cronin's. If Tommy was downstairs, there could be only one reason. And coming so early in the day was proof positive that Tommy was eager to get back to that farm of his, with his wide-hipped country wife and that plump baby he'd put in her. Gavigan had had a good laugh about that: Tommy Cronin, a man of the earth, on that tumbledown homestead out in the boonies. Gavigan couldn't think of two nights in a row in his whole life that he'd spent outside the city. He was Manhattan to the bone: born and battle-bred in Five Points, he'd made his name in Hell's Kitchen and come to roost at this spot in Gramercy Park.

Half the reason he'd moved here was that people like John Gavigan weren't supposed to live in Gramercy Park. It was reserved for the posh set: fancy-pantses and silver-spooners, book readers and theater-goers. Dutch Protestants, English Protestants, people so rich they had no need for God. That crowd had put up a statue in the park of an actor whose own brother had shot Lincoln. (That was a notion Gavigan could get behind: To hell with Lincoln, who'd made the Irish fight to free the colored. What had Lincoln ever done for New York, anyway?) Living on the edge of the park entitled Gavigan to a key that unlocked the wrought-iron gate—this was no public park—but he hadn't once set foot inside it. What did he care about flowers? All that mattered to him was that he *could*. Back in the old days, Tommy had been the one who slipped in and out of the park. He thought he was sly about it, but Gavigan knew. Thinking back on it, he should have seen it as a sign of things to come. It disappointed Gavigan that the man could have settled for so little; that he had abandoned his post to grub in the dirt with a woman who spooked when a stranger appeared at her door.

The commotion downstairs grew louder. Gavigan hooked a finger into the dressing gown that hung from his bedpost and struggled his arms into it. At the top of the stairs, his hand resting on the banister, he cleared his throat of the dreck that was already creeping into his lungs. A single hacking cough was enough to call a truce to whatever Tommy and Jamie were battling over.

"Jamie," he said. "Is that Tommy Cronin down there?"

"It is, Mr. Gavigan." Never a *yes* or a *no* from an Irishman—*It is; it isn't*. No word for "yes" in the mother tongue; no word for "no," either.

"Has he found Dempsey?"

"He claims that he has."

"Did he bring him here?"

"He did not, sir."

Gavigan coughed, the sound of something thick and wet being torn in half. "Show him to the study. I'll be down in a minute."

THE STUDY LOOKED the same as it had in Cronin's days with Gavigan, the same as it had looked for decades before Cronin set foot in America. It was an odd name for the room; *study* suggested a bookish nook where a man went to ponder questions of science or philosophy. Meaning-of-life-type questions, angels on the head of a pin. But the only studying that went on in this room was of a more personal nature. Gavigan would sit at his big oak desk staring into the face of the man opposite him, a man in a wingback chair who had come seeking something. Gavigan would study this man's face for signs of weakness, for the soft spots that would allow him to push this man in the direction that Gavigan needed him to go. A man might have come seeking a favor, money, or a promise, but Gavigan was always looking into the future, toward the favor returned, the payback, the other side of the bargain, and Gavigan always got back more than he gave. Most men knew this, and whatever relief they felt for having their wish granted was weighed against the leaden certainty that a day of reckoning would arrive. On the rare occasion that a man left that room thinking he'd gotten the better end of the deal, that was a sure sign of his own stupidity, and a guarantee that Gavigan would be rewarded ten times over.

The desk, a stout plateau of dark wood, enforced a distance between Gavigan and whoever sat on the other side. It was the same reason medieval lords had cleared the land around their castles: to emphasize the prominence of those high walls and to give those inside plenty of time to respond to any barbarous incursions. The room itself was festooned with trophies and keepsakes from Gavigan's eighty years. Along the mantel stretched a rust-furred cutlass of Civil War vintage, Gavigan's weapon of choice when he'd been a young brawler battling his way up the ranks of the Five Points gangs. A shelf held a replica of the death mask of Robert Emmet, presented to him as a gift by the New York chapter of the Ancient Order of Hibernians for "diligent support of the cause of the betterment of the Irish people, at home and abroad." Near it hung an original pressing of the Easter Proclamation, slightly singed along one edge. On another wall was a framed and faded handbill advertising a music-hall performance by a Miss Daphne LaVerne (née Dorothea Gianopolis), the only, and unrequited, love of a much younger Gavigan. Behind the vast desk, daubed in muddy hues of brown, sage, and ocher, peered out a portrait of Gavigan's mother. She had refused to sit for the artist—*Who am I to put on such airs?*—and so the rendering was based on a single meeting between the painter and Meem Gavigan, dead now these twenty years. If the portrait didn't look much like her, it managed nevertheless to capture her defiant heart, her scorching humility.

Cronin had never liked this room. If the house was a tomb, this was the chamber that held the corpse. The light that filtered in was pallid, apologetic. In the old days, Cronin would position himself in a chair in the far corner, off the shoulder of the supplicant. It comforted Gavigan to know that Cronin was there in case one of his visitors ever got too full a head of steam. Not that force was ever necessary. Cronin's presence alone guaranteed that the conversation never went above a simmer.

Alone in the room, Cronin wasn't going to take his old post in the corner but neither was he going to sit in the wingback. He stood, one hand on the chair, as if posing for a portrait—the kind where the chair is occupied by the loving and loyal wife, a baby balanced on her knee. Cronin had never had such a picture taken with Alice and the children, but when he returned home he would insist on it. Let Alice laugh. He wanted a family portrait.

Gavigan, on stiff legs, was preceded into the room by a heavy-bosomed woman with hair the color of iron. She carried a tea tray that chattered with each step. When she set it down on the desk, the steam from the teapot sent a pang through Cronin. His first cup of tea, prepared by Alice each morning after he came in from the cowshed, was one of his great daily pleasures. He missed it, just as he missed everything, everyone, at the farm.

The woman looked casually at Cronin—another of Gavigan's boys—before the snap of recognition showed.

"If it isn't the ghost of Tommy Cronin!" Helen, that was her name. She had worked for Gavigan even before Cronin came to the house. A nurse in the Great War, she had more than once stitched up Cronin after a night had gotten rough. "I thought you got away clean," she said, "but here you are again."

"I won't be long," Cronin said.

"So you say," Helen said, and closed the door behind her.

Gavigan dropped himself into the chair behind the desk. He nodded toward the setup of cups, saucers, sugar bowl, creamer. "Help yourself, Tommy."

"I'll just be on my way," Cronin said. "I'd've left already but your man was in a tizzy, wanting to make certain that the job was done."

"And is it?"

"You asked me to find Francis Dempsey and I've found him. I've all the details right here." He withdrew an envelope from his pocket and skidded it across the desk. Gavigan ignored it.

"It's interesting to me that you think of it as asking. As if you've done me a favor."

"Call it what you will. It's done."

Without a knock, Jamie burst through the door, a newspaper in his hand. "Mr. Gavigan," he said. "There's news you should see."

"What is it?" Gavigan said.

Jamie shot a look at Cronin—he wanted Cronin out of here almost as much as Cronin himself did—and handed Gavigan the morning newspaper, spatchcocked around a two-column story on page 8.

DETROIT, June 5.—Federal agents tonight took into custody Sean Russell, a reputed leader of the outlawed Irish Republican Army, and were reported holding him incomunicado. King George VI and Queen Elizabeth are due in Windsor, Ont., across the Detroit River, tomorrow.

The Free Press said Joseph McGarrity of Philadelphia, who accompanied Russell, was known as an I. R. A. leader in the United States. He was not held, however.

As Gavigan read, his jaw began working over some problem, grinding away at the inside of his cheek, his dentures, his own manky tongue. "This happened yesterday?"

Jamie gave a curt nod.

"And I wasn't told? I have to read about it in the newspaper?" The dream again. The double cross. If it wasn't someone trying to get the upper hand, then it was some joker trying to cut him out entirely.

"I see you have business," Cronin said. "So I'll be off."

Gavigan hauled himself to his feet. "You're not going anywhere!" He tossed the newspaper at the desk, where it clattered against the tea tray's stock of silver and porcelain. "Just look at that!"

Cronin waited a beat before picking up the paper. Russell, McGarrity, Detroit, King George. Were these men, and Gavigan with them, still fighting the old battles?

"Do you see what I mean?" Gavigan said.

Cronin answered with a blank stare.

"What were they doing in Detroit?" Gavigan said. "With the goddamn king and queen just across the border?"

Jamie eyed Cronin, leaned in toward Gavigan. "Russell and McGarrity have been out raising money," he said. "We knew about that—"

"You think this was a coincidence? They just happen to be in Detroit, in spitting distance of the king and queen? They've got a plan in the works. I can feel it. And I can tell you this, too. It's another of their half-assed schemes. They jab and they jab but they never throw the knockout punch. They're flyweights in a heavyweights' game."

"Look here," Cronin said. "This has nothing to do with me. I did what you wanted, now—"

"No!" Gavigan pounded his fist on the desk. His face was a livid, angry red. "You've been a part of this for twenty years! You do not get to walk away again!" A chain of racking coughs tore through Gavigan, threatening to shred him from the inside. He took one of the teacups and hawked a fat gob of phlegm into it. The coughing had exhausted him, and when he spoke again it was close to a whisper: "There's too much we don't know. We've got Francis Dempsey, the son of a traitor. He busts out of jail and makes a beeline for one of our garrisons. Which he destroys. Which kills three of our men. And from which he loots thousands of dollars—thousands of *my dollars*— meant for Russell's godforsaken Sabotage Campaign."

Another fit of coughing ripped at Gavigan's lungs, forcing him to sit heavily in the chair. Once he had regained his breath, he continued connecting the dots: "Then this Dempsey—this nobody—gives the slip to every IRA man in Ireland and sets sail for America. Where at the same time Russell and McGarrity are on tour, thumbing their noses at the king and queen of England. And I'm supposed to believe that this is all a coincidence? That it's nothing but dumb luck?" Gavigan hauled himself to his feet and paced unsteadily behind his desk. "It stinks to high heaven," he said. "We don't know if Dempsey is working for Russell or some other faction. Holy hell, he could be working for de Valera or the Brits, for all we know." He put his hand on the desk, steadying himself.

"This isn't my fight," Cronin said.

"You've got a short memory," Gavigan said. "If nothing else, you owe it to those still in the field finishing what you started."

A short memory. Gavigan could be in the funny papers with a line like that.

Gavigan lowered himself into the chair. Beneath his old man's wattles, his jaw tensed and relaxed, tensed and relaxed. "Tommy," he said, "bring in the Dempsey boy, but stash him somewhere out of the way."

Jamie spoke up. "I can take it from here. If the information checks out, it'll be easy work."

"Your man's right," Cronin said. "I'm done here."

"You're done when I say you're done." Gavigan spat the words. "And if I have to send Jamie and half a dozen men like him back to that country shithole to find you again, it's not going to be a social call like the last time."

Cronin thought of the revolver, which Alice had stashed at the bottom of his valise. It was a Webley, taken from an officer of the Black and Tans ambushed by Cronin early in the war. Cronin had used it to grim effect in Cork and later, in Gavigan's employ. Even if Alice had kept it, how could he expect her to use a thing with such a dark history?

"Until I know what's what, you don't leave this city," Gavigan said. "Now go and get Dempsey. Let's see what he has to say for himself."

THE FARM

O F COURSE HE HAD his secrets. Alice knew that. Despite all that he had told her about his past, about his life in Ireland and then in New York, and about the things he had done that still forced him bolt upright in their bed in the middle of the night, she knew there was more that had been left unsaid. And what he had told her hadn't come easily. Tom wasn't a big talker. He was the strong, silent type and that was just fine with her. But in the early days, when they were getting to know each other, when she realized only after the fact that she was falling for him, they told each other things that they would have kept quiet if they'd had any idea that life would bring them where it did: a man and a woman with a little boy and a baby and a farm to run. If you wanted to catch the eye of a fellow, you didn't flaunt your fears and your past mistakes, just like a fellow never told you the worst in him if he had any thoughts of winning you over. But she had played by those rules once before, with her husband. She had been full of coy looks and giggles, he had played the devil-may-care Romeo, and look what it had gotten her.

It had gotten her Henry—that's what she had to remind herself of whenever she started thinking about the mistakes of the past. At that moment, as she hung the laundry on the line, Henry was scattering chicken feed from a bucket half as tall as he was. He had dragged the bucket from the barn with great effort, but not once had he asked for help. The first sentence out of his toddler mouth had been *I do it,* and at five, he thought himself no less capable of running the whole farm, if need be. She could credit or blame Tom for that. Tom was a capable man and never one to ask for help, either. Not for the first time, she tried to imagine Henry's life without Tom. Would it have been worse for him to grow up with his own father or with no father at all?

Alice should have known better, but what was the use of piling up all of the things that she should have seen, should have known, should have done? Jimmy had been a few years ahead of her in school, one of those boys who from a distance seemed to move through life with an easy grace. She saw that ease and wanted to wrap herself in it, to drown in it. She wasn't a layabout; far from it. She balanced the farm and schoolwork and cooking and cleaning, and when graduation came, her life was the farm and the house entirely—that's what life had in store for the only child of a dairyman, a girl whose mother had passed when she was only thirteen. But nothing seemed to weigh heavily on Jimmy's shoulders. When the mood struck him, he fixed cars at his uncle's shop outside Poughkeepsie. And when another mood blew in, he would spend the day fishing Wappinger Creek. His life was carefree and Alice let herself believe that once they were joined together, she would learn the secret of this free-and-easy style.

Only up close did Jimmy's ease reveal itself to be laziness, a weakness that permeated his bones. She should have guessed at it, should have wondered why all the girls who were his own age passed on him when they began pairing up with boys, choosing ones who were more solid, more ambitious, or more willing to be pushed by the women in their lives. Instead, Alice thrilled at her good fortune when Jimmy's eye alighted on her, as if he had been waiting for her all along, as if life had kept him out of the clutches of those girls who cut their eyes at Alice when she first appeared in the passenger seat of the Model A or shared a Coca-Cola with him at the counter of the Taghkanic Diner, Jimmy's jacket draped over her shoulders. Later she would wonder if that look from the other girls wasn't jealousy but pity. They knew what was coming, but Alice was a farm girl, not a town girl, and so, not being one of them, she was left to care for herself.

Her father had seen it in Jimmy and warned Alice, but was there any girl who listened to her father about love? That's what she believed she felt: love. And love doesn't think about making a living, doesn't ask if your dear one is ready for a life of rising before dawn and mucking out the barn and trudging through the pasture in the pouring-down rain when one of the cows doesn't return at nightfall. Love doesn't care about any of that, but life sure does. Jimmy kept telling her that life would be against them until they could sell the farm and make a go of things in town. An automobile shop, that was one of his ideas. A gasoline pump out front, a garage where he could fix cars, and a small café where she would serve coffee and sandwiches for city folks out for a drive in the country. A little bit of this, a little bit of that, and that's how they would make ends meet. He made it sound like a real adventure, people coming from far and wide to fill up their tanks and sample a slice of Alice's famous apple pie, but it troubled Alice that his dream depended on—required, even—the dispossession or death of her father before it could be launched. In the meantime he made no effort to prepare for any kind of future. He saved no money, did nothing but grumble about living in the house of his father-in-law, and called himself a slave on the old man's plantation. That the plantation was no more than a hundred acres of grass and rock and woods in a remote corner of Dutchess County never seemed to dampen his sense that they could someday sell it for a small fortune and really start living.

Until then, living was precisely what they weren't doing. Alice and Jimmy seemed trapped in a half-life where little by little they stopped talking to each other, stopped going on picnics by the river, stopped going for drives to Rhinebeck or Millbrook or Pine Plains, stopped doing all of the things they had done before they were husband and wife. Alice had held out against Jimmy's pleas throughout their courtship and saved herself until the wedding night, and for a while after the big day they'd had a real honeymoon of it. He couldn't keep his hands off her and she was happy to have his hands wherever they wanted to roam, now that she was Mrs. James Swain. But as he grew more surly, more cramped in the second-floor bedroom, he turned away from her at night. How could he be expected to be in the mood, he protested, when his wife's father was downstairs, in the room below theirs? It was unnatural. But without steady work for Jimmy, that was life.

After a year of this not-living, and then another year of it, he announced that he needed to go on the road to see if prospects were better in some other place. Christmas had just passed and during the holidays Jimmy had run into some old high-school pals back in town to visit their folks. One day he told Alice that a buddy of his had work for him in Worcester, and the next day he said that he might try his luck with one of his pals on the docks in New London. He was tired of waiting for life to come to him—by which Alice figured he meant that he was tired of waiting for her father to die—so he was going to go out and make a life for them. Except it wouldn't be *them*, not yet. It made no sense to take Alice with him until he could get settled (never mind that she could outwork him any day of the week). In the meantime, he would send back money and sock away the rest for their future. That was the plan, and the glow it cast filled him with an energy he hadn't shown in a long time. His was the nervous twitch of the horse who has been loaded into the starting gate and who awaits the bell that will release him into a sprint.

The whole idea of it made Alice's stomach tighten with dread, but for a week he talked about the jobs he might find and she teased him about city girls taking advantage of her country mouse, and she washed and folded his clothes and packed them neatly in their one good suitcase, the one they had bought for their honeymoon trip to Narragansett Bay. Jimmy worked around the clock to get his Model A up and running. The car had been gathering dust in the barn for more than six months now. The repairs were minor, but how was he supposed to find the time for it when her father was always on him about the cows, and what was the point anyway—where did he and Alice have to go? Now, though, he was in a fever to get the engine humming, and on a Sunday evening—he had skipped church that morning—he turned the crank and the Model A was ready to move. He seemed about to hop in and drive off right then and there, with the sun setting and the trees reaching their frozen fingers into the sky, but Alice brought him in for dinner and told him he would need a good night's sleep before he set out to seize that new life for them.

It was a good night. Instead of rolling toward the wall, he turned to her in bed and his hands were all over her and Alice thought, *Yes, this is just what we need,* but she also feared that Jimmy's hunger for her wasn't that of a man saying, *Oh, how I've missed you,* but instead, *Once more, for old times' sake.* In the morning she made him breakfast but it was an effort to keep him at the table, so eager was he to set out. She cried and he told her not to be silly, but the tears kept coming and his mood darkened. He knew that she knew, and he wanted to be away from the scene of his crime. She dried her eyes on the cuff of her sweater and folded her arms tight against the January cold. Jimmy started the Model A and drove away from the farm. Alice waved to him but instead of returning the wave or sounding the horn or shimmying the car side to side in a woozy farewell, as he used to do in their courting days whenever he drove off, he only laid his left arm along the door and tapped out some rhythm with his hand—a victory march, or the signal for a retreat, or just some ditty that stuck in his head when his thoughts should have been on the wife he was abandoning and the baby that would grow in her belly.

That baby was currently squatting among the chickens, engaged in a heated conversation with a Rhode Island Red. Henry had assigned names to every animal on the farm, even the ones that Alice had cautioned him not to get too attached to. She remembered when she had been about his age, finding out that the main course of their Sunday dinner had only twenty-four hours earlier been a fine white-feathered chicken she had named Pearl.

Alice removed a clothespin from between her teeth and called to Henry. "Is everything all right over there?"

It took him a moment to finish what he was saying to the chicken, but eventually he stood and trotted toward his mother. "Little Orphan Annie is not a nice chicken," he said emphatically. "I put out lots of feed, but she won't eat it. She just kept pecking the other chickens."

He was shirtless in overalls, with bits of feathers and feed in his hair. A real farm boy, down to his boots. He had a pair like Tom's—he'd insisted on it, even though the ones at the shop were two or three sizes too large. Alice smiled at him, at his little boy's body growing out of those giant-seeming feet, and swept the hair from his eyes. He had pale, straw-colored hair, like she'd had as a girl. Her father had pointed that out right after Henry was born. As if the strong resemblance to her somehow erased Jimmy's role in bringing Henry into the world.

Alice knew Jimmy was gone for good and only halfheartedly went through the motions of wondering when she would hear from him again. It gave her something to think about, something to distract her from the fears that came with carrying his baby. *Their* baby, not just his, but Jimmy was gone, so maybe just *her* baby. She had prayed for this since her wedding night—a baby, and then many more to follow—but she had never imagined herself deserted, doing it alone. Hoping for letters, for money, for Jimmy's return—it wasn't for her benefit but for the baby's. The baby deserved better than to be born into a broken family.

Things got worse before they got better. One morning her father didn't come in for breakfast and when she trudged out to the milking parlor—seven months pregnant, her feet swollen and the rest of her dripping sweat in the Indian summer heat—she found him on the concrete floor, looking like someone had flattened half his face with a shovel. A stroke, the doctor said, not big enough to kill him but bad enough to confine him to his bed, his speech garbled and his body half frozen. She put up a notice in the post office offering board and lodging and a small wage for farm help, and after two weeks she got her first and only reply: on her doorstep stood Tom Cronin.

And then things got better. Not quickly, and not all at once, but Tom's arrival brought a steadiness to the farm that hadn't existed, she had to admit, since before she had married Jimmy.

Tom could be gruff, and quiet, but over the table they started to talk. He spent time with her father, sitting with him in front of the woodstove and telling him of the day's work and making a plan for the day ahead. In time he told Alice about the life he'd left behind, and she told him about Jimmy and how she'd been too blind to see what was plain to everyone else. One morning when Tom had started the milking and Alice was tending to the baby, her father put his one good hand on her arm and said, "Marry that one." When she reminded him that she was already married, he shook his head with great effort and said, "Good as dead."

Soon her father passed and it was just the three of them. She had named the boy Henry, after her father, and though Tom was shy with the baby at first, he came to treat him like he was his own son. The women in town started to talk—*Look at her with no husband and that man always around*—but Alice had long since learned not to listen to town girls. When the second baby, a girl, came along, she was a new beginning. Grace, they named her. The world could think what it wanted.

"You're going to need a bath tonight," she said to Henry. Her fingers were gritty from where she had touched his hair.

"I don't want to take a bath," he said. "I want Tom to come home."

He had been talking about Tom's return—wondering, asking, pleading—from the moment they had left Tom at the depot.

"And what if he came home and found you smelling like a chicken coop? What kind of welcome would that be?"

Henry eyed her quizzically, puzzling over hidden chains of cause and effect. Was it possible that taking a bath could trigger Tom's return? Or was this a parent's trick to get him into the tub, with nothing to be gained for himself? Taking a bath. Not taking a bath. It was a big risk either way.

Alice wiped her hands on her apron and told him to run along. Grace would be up from her nap soon, and she hadn't yet finished hanging the sheets. As Henry sped away, she said to no one but the laundry, "I want Tom to come home, too." It had been almost a week and she hadn't heard a word from him. She knew that he had not left her, and she believed that if anything terrible had happened to him, somehow she would know. She had no choice but to wait for him to appear at the door as he had done before, all those years ago. And when he did, she would take him in her arms and know that it was him, her Tom, and then she would slap him once more in that big ugly mug and tell him never, ever, to make her worry like that again. She hoped it would be soon. Henry missed his Tom.

BATTERY PARK

LILLY DID NOT LIKE boats and the way they troubled her stomach and pummeled her sense of balance. During the crossing from Europe, she swore she could feel the chug of the engines and the slap and surge of every wave as the ship bobbed on the uncertain waters of the Atlantic. So why, then, was she queuing with crowds of tourists—mothers and fathers sweating in the noontime heat, children crying as ice cream cones melted down their fat pink fists—to board a ferry for the Statue of Liberty? The ferry looked like a child's toy among the ocean liners. Even at the dock, it sputtered and belched black smoke into water choked with the refuse of the earlier tourist hordes. As her foot touched the deck, the ferry lurched and she placed a protective hand over the body of her camera. Before she could get her bearings, the others jostled past her for space along the rail and she again asked herself what could have compelled her to make this journey. But she knew: it was Josef's fault.

Lilly and Josef had made a twenty-item list before she left Prague: Things for Lilly to Do in New York. Josef knew that she would devote all of her time to her work. Yes, she would explore the city block by block, but she would seek out its forgotten corners, and she would do it with a camera around her neck, on the hunt for the next shot. Her late nights would not be spent at the city's hottest nightclubs; she would not drink gin and dance to jazz among tuxedoed gangsters. No, she would spend her nights in her darkroom, getting drunk on the fumes rising from the developing tray. Josef had spelled out this vision of her time in New York and Lilly couldn't disagree. To save her from herself, he had started the New York List with items culled from Busby Berkeley movies and a brochure printed by the Foundation. WELCOME TO NEW YORK! was emblazoned in bright red letters across the first page. The inside was a slick, linear map of the city, all bright colors and sharp angles—a city of candy and chrome. Numbered dots signaled the can't-miss attractions, each briefly and ecstatically described.

> *The Museum of Modern Art: The world's newest great museum!*
> *Chinatown: The mystery of Old China in the middle of Manhattan!*
> *The World's Fair: The World of Tomorrow is waiting for you! (coming April 1939)*

"It's going to be waiting a long time for me," Lilly said. "Can you imagine the crowds?"

"That's why you go," Josef said. "The crowds. The energy. And when you come home, you can tell me what the future looks like."

They were sitting on the sofa in Josef's apartment—the one that he would be evicted from in May—and as he wrapped one arm around her and drew her close, she pressed her head to his chest. They stayed that way for a moment, and then a moment longer. She could feel his heartbeat. "I don't care about the future," she said. "I just want today."

All through dinner that night, Josef continued to add items to the list. *Tea in Chinatown*, he wrote. *The Statue of Liberty. Top of the Empire State Building. Walk across Brooklyn Bridge.*

"What's so special about a bridge?" she said. "And what is Brooklyn, anyway?"

"It's the place on the other side of the bridge," Josef said. "You

don't have to go there, but the bridge is very famous. Sometimes lunatics and the brokenhearted jump off it."

"To their death?"

"I assume so."

"Are you trying to get rid of me?"

Josef left it on the list, with one notation: *Walk across Brooklyn
Bridge (do not jump!).*

Lilly stubbed out a cigarette and surveyed the ever-growing list.
She wasn't a tourist. She was going to America to work.

Josef laughed at her haughty expression, her defense of her art.
"Upon your return, I am going to require thrilling stories about your
adventures in America," he said. "If I ask, 'What did you do in America, my darling?' and your only answer is 'I took photographs, my
pet,' then I am going to be very, very disappointed. And very bored."

Lilly still had the list. She carried it with her on the ferry, just as she
had carried it all over the city, in the hope that she might stumble across
one of Josef's planned destinations. The list was in his handwriting, and
along with the few letters she had received and one photograph—Josef
smiling behind a cloud of cigarette smoke, looking quite dashing—it
was all that she had of him. How could she have taken only a single
photograph of Josef? She had come upon him talking and drinking
with friends at a café near the Liberated Theater and before he saw her,
she had framed the shot and clicked the shutter. But only that once.

There were twenty items on the list and she had crossed off only two.

On Monday, just before her appointment with Mr. Crabtree, she
had found herself on the sidewalk trying to believe it was still possible
to save Josef despite Mr. Musgrove's flight to Mexico or wherever fate
had whisked him. She took the list out of her purse as a way to fortify
herself, and the first words she saw, in Josef's abysmal handwriting,
were *Shopping on Fifth Avenue.* She had scoffed at that one. "Home
to the world's most exclusive retailers," the brochure had called Fifth
Avenue, and even Josef had laughed. "Someone had better tell Paris

they've been supplanted," he said. But there it was on the list, and here she was on Fifth Avenue. She wandered into a shop a block north of the Foundation's offices and purchased a silk scarf: bold and flame-like, an almost lurid red. It was an extravagance, but she'd been careful with the money the Foundation had given her and if Josef teased her—*You are Madame Bloch's daughter after all!*—then she would blame it on him and his list. And anyway, the scarf reminded her of him, and of the night they had met at her friend's party. They left the party together and walked, late into the night, by the banks of the Vltava. They crossed the Charles Bridge and wound through the lanes that approached Prague Castle. On a silent empty street chalked in gray stone and moonlight, they saw a brilliant red dress draped over the wrought-iron rail of a balcony. Was it drying in the night air? Had it been tossed there in a fit of passion? Was it a signal to a lover to come calling? They had speculated, joked, invented preposterous explanations. The only thing they were sure of was its beauty.

As she walked across the plaza to her meeting with Mr. Crabtree, Lilly had knotted the scarf around her neck—a sort of talisman, a way to keep Josef with her. Why had she become so superstitious these past few days? And what good had it done for her, anyway? After she was ushered out by Mr. Crabtree, Lilly rode the elevator to the lobby stunned by Mr. Crabtree's obstinate conviction that all would be well. Such an easy thing to believe when you could retreat to your office occupied by Indian plunder and emptied of hysterical Czechs who pestered you for favors you were unable or unwilling to grant.

By the time she had reached the lobby, she was shattered and disoriented. She unsnapped the clasp on her purse but instead of retrieving a handkerchief, she came away with the list. At the same moment, her gaze alighted on a sign before another bank of elevators: OBSERVATION DECK. She looked quickly at the list and joined the queue. It wasn't the Empire State Building, but it would have to do. She was running out of time; she needed stories to bring home with her.

The crowded elevator rose and rose beyond any imaginable height. When the doors finally parted, Lilly let herself be swept along through a small room, up a flight of stairs, out a narrow door—and found herself in the very rafters of the city. Below her was the grid of regimented streets, a landscape of buildings topped with water tanks. There, so close she could almost touch it, was the Empire State Building soaring higher still, and there too was the Chrysler Building, which made up in style whatever it lacked in raw height. To one side lay the narrow ribbon of the East River, stapled over with bridges that linked the island to the low, mottled city that spread to the east. To the other side, she saw the Hudson River. It seemed that a running start would allow her to vault across to the limitless expanse of America. In that direction, a person could lose herself; go west and keep going, with nothing to stop you but the Pacific Ocean thousands of miles distant. If she set out that way, who would ever find her? There were so many places to hide.

Hadn't Josef himself told her to stay? His last letter had put it quite bluntly: *I love you but do not return. The city is in the grip of a madness. Even sensible people believe that this is as bad as it will get; that our guests can be resisted, or even overcome.* Josef thought otherwise. He had lawyer friends who worked in the Castle, friends who already knew enough not to be seen in public with Josef—a Jew, a lawyer, a leftist, and a columnist for a recently shuttered newspaper. They had told him that legislation was already being drafted that defined who was Jewish and how exemptions could be granted to those deemed essential. *You will perhaps be surprised to hear,* he wrote, *that I will not be deemed essential.* Farther down the page he wrote, *You are essential to me but not to these idiots. Therefore you* MUST *stay.* A postscript dashed along the bottom of the page told her that this could be his last letter. Censorship had become routine, but he managed to get a friend bound for Zurich to post the letter on his behalf. He signed off, as always, *Your favorite, Josef.*

The ferry lurched as its engines slowed. The boat was scudding toward the pier, and the other passengers pushed past Lilly for a better view of the statue. Lilly was left alone near the stern, facing east, and she could see on the horizon the hot glow of the Atlantic under the midmorning sun. She knew what lay that way. Miles and miles of ocean leading inexorably to a port, a train, a city where everything had changed. She was going back to a place where she could not hide, only disappear; where her papers would allow for only one journey, and one destination. She burned like the morning sun to see Josef again, but for the first time she asked herself, *What if I cannot find him?* What if he was already gone?

Even after receiving Josef's letter, she had never seriously considered the idea that she would stay in America while he remained in Prague. If Mr. Musgrove could not bring Josef to New York, then of course she would return to him. But yesterday at the top of the RCA Building, she had let herself get swept away by the possibility of staying in America—of abandoning Prague, and Josef, too. And now here she was, imagining him gone, or lost forever, as if that would excuse the betrayal taking root within her. She should have spent the day packing for the voyage, preparing to return home. Her luggage was due to the agent no later than noon on Saturday. Instead she had unfolded the list and, eyes closed, chosen the next item. Her finger had landed on *The Statue of Liberty* and now here she was, riding this ridiculous ferry, sick to her stomach and even more sick at heart. Soon she would climb to the crown, and she would look to the east, and when she saw the midday glow on the horizon, she would try not to think of burning cities but of the promise of the next sunrise.

FORDHAM HEIGHTS

FROM THE KITCHEN, MARTIN could hear Rosemary's muffled voice singing the girls a lullaby, "Toora Loora" or "Give Her a Kiss" or one of her own invention that worked each girl's name into the tune (*Katie and Evie are my sweethearts...*). Next came the click of the door and Rosemary's feet on the floorboards, laced through with a melody of *ssssshhhh*s directed at the girls' room. Through the open windows came the murmur, laughter, and shouts of neighbors on their front steps, but in the apartment a sense of calm was descending as the girls eased to sleep.

Rosemary returned to the kitchen to find Martin in the middle of the room, knotting his tie. "You're going out?" she said.

"To the Savoy," he said. "With Francis." Since yesterday's practice at the Dime, he had been eager to hear for himself Benny Carter's reworking of his song. His canvass of the music stores hadn't turned up a mad rush for the sheet music, but it was still early days. A lot depended on Carter and whether he recorded the song, and then on the radio stations and jukeboxes—those that played records by Negro bands. *Your first race record,* Rosemary had said last night. *My parents will be so thrilled.*

Now, as Martin checked the length of his tie and adjusted his pocket square, Rosemary busied herself with drying the dishes. They still hadn't talked about his decision to quit the band, or about his prospects for another job. All Martin would say was that he had a plan.

"Don't you think—" Rosemary stopped herself but then figured, *Just say it*. "Don't you think you should've waited until you were back on the Hit Parade? Then you'd have more options, or you could've asked Chester for a raise." She smiled weakly.

Martin laughed, a harsh bark, full of edges. "You couldn't pay me enough to keep playing that music."

"But wouldn't it have made sense to see where the song goes before—"

"I'd already made up my mind," he said. "The song at the Savoy—that feels like a reward for finally doing the right thing."

"I know you've had a shock these past few days, but we need to think about—"

"Yes, I know. Rent. Food. Shoes."

He made them sound like small things, but a roof over their heads and food on the table—what mattered more than that? "It's not just the two of us," she said.

"Do you think I'd've given Chester the high hat if I didn't have a good reason?" He was losing patience, but trying not to show it. He had almost mentioned Hammond last night, just to prove to her that he was on the verge of something special, but he was so anxious that he feared saying Hammond's name aloud could jinx the whole operation. He'd told Rosemary that he had a plan, and that would have to be enough for now.

"We need—"

"What we need is to move out of this dump," he said. "The four of us squeezed in here, and Mrs. Fichetti always minding our business."

She shushed him, her expression cross, and pointed toward the floor, then toward the open window. She spoke slowly, expecting to be overheard: "Oh, she's lovely. You're just in a contrary mood."

Martin gritted his teeth. He couldn't speak honestly in his own home without the old biddy who owned the place giving them hell. Which meant it wasn't his home. It was just a place he lived, a place his wife liked no better than he did—less, actually, because she spent so much more time here dealing with its summer stifle and winter chill, its smells of someone else's cooking.

From the girls' room came Kate's voice, high and insistent. She wanted something, or someone, and if she persisted she was sure to wake her sister.

"Would you mind?" Rosemary said. "She's not going to want me. Having you home in the evening is a treat for her."

"I told Francis I'd—"

"For her sake," Rosemary said. "And for mine. She'll keep this up all night."

Martin sighed heavily, shucked off his jacket, and draped it over the back of a chair. In the girls' bedroom, a pale strip of light traced the edges of the blackout shade. The longest day of the year was coming, and the sun hadn't yet set.

"You've got to hush, monkey," he said. "You'll wake the baba."

"I can't sleep." She was rolling from side to side on the mattress. Her wispy blond hair was matted to her forehead. Martin had pulled down the upper window sash but the air in the room did not stir. With one pudgy fist, the girl rubbed her eyes, back and forth like rolling a ball. She would soon be fully awake, and he would have to either bring her into the light of the kitchen to keep her from waking the baby, or else call Rosemary in to get her back to sleep. Neither option would please Rosemary.

The telephone rang in the living room, and with the first pulse of the bell Kate winced and scrunched her eyes. It rang a second time and he asked himself how long it would take Rosemary to pick it up—the apartment wasn't that big. Did she expect that Martin would—

The phone was snatched up on the third ring. Martin rubbed Kate's back, but she batted his hand. Too hot. Already the fabric of her nightshirt was damp and clingy. He could hear the murmur of Rosemary's voice, then a sudden rise in volume. She was speaking too loud for this hour, especially with Kate teetering on the edge of sleep.

"I want Mama," she said. "I want Mama to sit with me."

"Mama said you wanted Dada," he said. "That's nice, isn't it?"

The girl scrunched her eyes again. A sour-lemons face. A Mama-not-Dada face.

"Now let's go back to sleepy town," Martin said. "When the sun goes down, we go to sleepy town." He spoke with a lilt, hoping to sneak a lullaby past her.

"No songs," she said. "A story."

"It's too late for a story, monkey. All the little monkeys are in bed, fast asleep."

"Story," she said. "A Ireland story. Like Mama tells."

"What kind does Mama tell?"

"The kind with fairies."

"Oh yes, fairies. Of course."

"And leepercons. But no pookas. Pookas are mean. And scary."

"Agreed. No pookas."

"Mama says Dada is from Ireland. And Mama says you sailed on a big boat."

"I did."

"You came to 'Merica—that's where we live."

"All true."

"And you and Mama fell in love."

"We did. We fell in love."

"And you had a baby—and the baby was me!" Kate's expression was beatific, like an advertisement for baby food or enriched bread. She was the happy ending to the story, the point of it all. She did not know how much consternation had come with her arrival, and he hoped that she never would.

"That's a very good story. I think that's the best story there is." He hoped this would be his cue to say good night, but Kate wasn't done with him.

"Now you tell a Ireland story. A different one."

"Katie, it's late and Dada—"

"Stor-eeeee!"

"Katie," he said, a bit too sharply. "Dada is more of a song man than a story man."

"Mama tells stories. Good stories."

"And that's what makes Mama special, and music is what makes Dada special. Aren't you lucky to have two such special parents?"

Kate looked unconvinced. She looked disappointed. *Not for the last time,* Martin thought. But she had also gotten a few more minutes before bedtime, and that was something.

"Now you have to promise Dada that if I sing you a song you will go right back to sleep. No more of this stay-awake nonsense." Framing it as a deal made him feel like he wasn't indulging her—a common complaint of Rosemary's. So this wasn't spoiling. He and his daughter were entering into a pact. He was teaching her the value of keeping her word.

Kate lay on her back, her head on the pillow. Martin sat on the edge of the bed and smoothed the sheet around her. He swept the wet strands of hair back from her forehead. He didn't spend much time with the girls, and when he did, he was prone to impatience on a bad day and befuddlement on a good one. Most nights, Martin wasn't home until long after the girls were in bed—Rosemary included. When pressed, he had been able to dredge up a half-remembered story from his own childhood, but these required a great deal of on-the-spot invention. Halting improvisations on the theme of leprechauns, fairy folk, pookas, and the other citizens of the invisible, ideal Ireland. He had been twelve, too old for stories, when his mother died, and after her death his father had told a different sort of story anyway—when he was in the mood for stories at all. Gone were the twilight creatures who raided cottages in search of porridge or stockings to mend or the odd infant or two. And gone were the big-boy tales of Cúchulain and Ossian and Finn McCool—the heroes of Old

Ireland who had inspired the creation of the New Ireland. Instead, when it was time to send the boys to sleep, Martin's father had cracked the spines of Virgil and Homer and Herodotus. It was no wonder Michael had turned out so serious-minded—the boy had never had a proper bedtime story in his whole life. That was his father's fault, but it was also Martin's. He could have taken it upon himself to read to his little brother, to soothe the boy who would grow up without any memory of his mother. But he hadn't—not once.

And now here was his own little one. She had closed her eyes but hadn't put to rest the smile of victory, of anticipation.

"YOU'RE NOT GOING to believe this," Rosemary said when Martin returned, blinking in the bright light. "Peggy wants to call off the wedding. She says she's been thinking about it ever since she went out with your brother. Didn't I say that was a bad idea?"

"You did." He poured a glass of water from the tap. "You are a prophetess. The Cassandra of the Bronx."

"Has he said anything to you about Sunday night?"

"Not a word. But I'll ask when I see him." Martin downed the glass of water and retrieved his jacket.

"My parents are going to kill her. Then they'll kill me, and then they'll kill you, and then your brother."

"The streets of the Bronx will run red with the blood of the Dempseys." Martin cocked his head. "Now that's something I could write a song about. They'd be singing it from Bainbridge Avenue to St. Stephen's Green. 'Oh, the blood of the Dempseys runs red in the streets! On account of a blonde with two dancing feet.'"

"I'm glad you think this is funny." Rosemary picked up Martin's glass and began washing it in the sink. "You should see my parents whenever the subject of this wedding comes up. Another disaster for the Dwyer family."

Martin reached for her hand and drew her closer to him. He kissed her fingers, still wet from washing up. "Rose of my heart, I wouldn't change a thing."

She raised an eyebrow and grimaced. Skeptical.

"I sailed on a big boat to 'Merica. We fell in love. We had a baby. And that baby was Kate." He kissed her hand again. "It's a very nice story."

"It leaves out a lot," she said.

"We had another baby. We stayed in love. That's still part of the story, isn't it?"

She ran her fingers through his hair. Jet-black, like Evie's. She did love him, and that should be enough to make the rest of this bearable: the apartment and Mrs. Fichetti, the long nighttime hours when the girls were asleep and Martin was in the city, all that time when it was just her and her thoughts and no one to talk to. She hadn't counted on this being such a lonely life. She had imagined that she would be a part of Martin's world, a world of music and cocktails and men in sharp suits and women in dresses you'd see in the magazines. They'd had that life, both of them, but only for a few months. She still kept the memories boxed up. She took them out and looked them over during the long nights, but lately it didn't cheer her to think of the life they had lived in the not-so-long-ago. Increasingly she felt cheated by the life she lived in the here and now. A life of rent, utility bills, groceries, a tab at the butcher shop, a husband who had quit a good job.

"I know what you're angling for with all of this lovey talk."

"Can't a man tell his wife how he feels?"

"Of course he can. He just shouldn't expect anything in return."

"And what am I expecting?"

"Something that could lead to another crib in the girls' room."

"I'm not thinking about babies, not one bit."

"And that's your problem. You never think about babies until it's too late."

He kissed Rosemary and grabbed his hat. He had been foggy-headed from the heat and shadows of Kate's room, but now he saw it clearly: no wedding meant no reception, and no reception meant no Martin Dempsey Orchestra. "You'll talk to Peggy? Set her straight?"

"I'll do what I can."

"Even if the wedding is off, we can still have the reception, right? No sense in canceling a party. I imagine it's already paid for."

"You just tell Francis to keep his distance. I'll take care of Peggy."

HARLEM

B Y THE TIME BENNY Carter finished his set, Martin was hollowed out. He felt such joy that he had a hand in scripting the wonder he had seen, but it was backed by the fear that he would forever be too slow to catch that train—the one that led to a spot on the really big bandstands. It was always this way whenever Martin saw one of the greats perform. The action on the bandstand was a bracing, eighty-proof shot of inspiration, but it triggered in him a furious despair. It was as if he was being taunted, but not by Benny Carter. No, sir. Carter was a beacon of pure light and hope. He was everything that Martin wanted to be: polymath musician, bandleader, arranger. Martin's anger was directed at himself, a chastening fire: *Why isn't that me up there?* He had wanted nothing his whole life but music, and yet somehow he had settled: one hit song, a seat in Chester's band, life above Mrs. Fichetti. Is that why he'd left Ireland? Why he'd come to New York? Martin could tell himself that he was still young—not yet thirty—but he had a wife and children and he was just starting to learn that time was the world's cruelest con man, a master of sleight of hand. You look one way and your wallet's gone. You look the other and the clock has run to zero: time's up!

Benny Carter was a reminder—*This is where the bar is set, my friend; this is how high you must climb*—but he was also a rebuke. Martin was taking his shot with his wedding combo, but compared to Carter's orchestra on the stage of the goddamn Savoy Ballroom, with the dancers whirling and air-stepping all around him, he had to ask himself: *Who are you kidding? A wedding reception in the Bronx, in a roomful of political hacks kissing the arse of your father-in-law? And for that you quit your job?* Cheers to him for trying, but how had he banked his future, his family, his life, on that?

When Francis suggested a drink, Martin stumped with him down Lenox Avenue on heavy legs. He knew he had to snap himself out of this funk, but he knew, too, that first thing tomorrow he needed to find whatever work a mortal like him could get to keep the American Dempseys out of the poorhouse. The ballroom bands had finished for the night, and now was the time when players from all over the city came together in jam sessions to see who measured up. Martin and Francis claimed two seats at the bar of a lounge that was just starting to fill and ordered their first round, and when the drinks came Francis paid and offered a toast to his brother, the famous composer.

Martin winced. "So what happened with Peggy the other night?"

"Oh, just a bit of fun," Francis said.

"You know she's getting married on Saturday?"

"And I was only showing her what she's giving up, joining the ranks of the newly wed."

Martin sipped his drink. "About that," he said. "Peggy wants to call off the wedding. She told Rosemary she's not ready to give up... whatever it was you showed her."

"It's an impressive sight, I have to admit."

"Just stay away from her—for my sake. Give Rosemary a chance to set her straight."

"I've no plans for seeing her again. I'm beginning to feel like she was the one using me. Show a fella a nice time, take him dancing and then go back to his fancy hotel—"

"You took her to the Plaza?"

"She thought I was having her on about staying there. Said she was calling my bluff."

"I don't want to hear any more," Martin said. "I don't want to be lying to Rosemary when I tell her I don't know what happened."

With the noise of the crowd roiling around them, Francis confessed that there was another girl who had caught his eye. He spelled out for his brother the meeting aboard the *Britannic,* the dinner at Bingham Castle. "I don't know what it is, but there's something about this girl," Francis said.

"Yeah, she's worth a million bucks."

"She's worth a lot more than that—but that's not it." Francis looked into his glass, swirled the ice in the last drops of Scotch. "Or not all of it. She played the violin after dinner and there was something, well, something magic about it. You'd know the tune. Beethoven, I think it was." He swirled the glass again, then crunched the ice in his mouth. "Do you remember much about Mam?"

Martin rubbed his chin. This wasn't where he'd seen the conversation going. "I wish I could remember more."

"You're lucky, being the oldest. And she doted on you, with the music and all."

"Mam didn't dote on anyone but Da."

"Da," Francis said. "Well. He certainly needed looking after." He caught the bartender's eye and signaled for another round: Scotch and soda for himself, a gin rickey for Martin. "I wish he could have gone out some other way. Him alone, and us scattered to the four winds."

"There are worse ways, I'm sure." Martin bolted down the rest of his drink. "Sorry. That came out colder than I intended."

"Just how cold did you intend it?"

"Look, I knew I'd never see him again. Still, not having him in the world—I don't know what to make of that."

"He didn't pull us out of Cork just to make you miserable."

"I know that—"

"He was heartbroken and he never got over it. Losing Mam like that—well, she's another that deserved a better death."

"A better life."

Francis lifted the fresh cocktail from the bar. "Cheers to that," he said, nodding the glass toward his brother.

"How is Michael taking all of this? He and Da had a lot of years where it was just the two of them."

"Honestly, I don't know what he thinks. About anything. He's been in good spirits since we arrived but I don't know if it's New York or just the passage of time." Francis rotated his glass a half turn but did not lift it to his mouth. He had already told Martin about the visit to the doctor and the promise of specialists to come, all as a way of validating his big-spending, Plaza-living approach to the immigrant experience. "We had a fine dinner tonight and then it was straight to bed for him. For now, I'm just trying to put some meat on his bones," Francis said. "I don't think the priests fed him more than brown bread and weak tea."

"But how long can you keep this up?" Martin dropped his voice to a raspy whisper, though it wasn't necessary. The bar was humming with talk, with music, with the chime of bottles and glasses. "Are you just going to wait until the IRA comes looking for their money? Or for the FBI to figure out they've got an escaped convict on their hands?"

"Fellas run off all the time," Francis said. "And I'm hardly notorious. The police aren't going to wear themselves out because one well-dressed pornographer got away."

"You haven't given it a moment's thought, have you?"

"On the contrary—"

"Well, would you look at what the cat dragged in?" Elston Hooper materialized out of the growing crowd and gave Martin a slap on the back. "I thought this place had standards, but I guess writing the hottest song at the Savoy will open a few doors."

At a nod from Martin to the bartender, Hooper's regular—bourbon and milk—appeared on the bar. Martin looked from Hooper to his brother and hesitated. Was it to be aliases, or—

Francis extended his hand. "Francis Dempsey," he said. "Martin's wayward brother."

Martin would save the reprimand for later. Escaped convicts ought to be a little more careful about advertising their identity, even in an after-hours bar in Harlem. Or especially in an after-hours bar in Harlem.

"I've been telling Martin about the latest love of my life," Francis said, omitting any mention of Michael, their parents, and the possibility that he was being pursued.

It took Martin a moment to realize that Francis meant the heiress and not his sister-in-law. "It's quite a love story," he said to Hooper. "She thinks he's someone else."

Hooper shook his head. "Women always think their men are someone else. They could never love us if they knew the truth."

"Your friend's a wise man," Francis said.

"He's also a man who lives in fear of his own wife," Martin said.

"All smart men fear their wives," Hooper said. "You could take a lesson, Martin. I still can't believe you walked out on—what's his name again? Chestnut Kingfisher?"

"You think that job's so great? Then you take it." Martin extended a palm toward Hooper, offering him a handful of nothing. "Here. It's yours."

"Now, you know Chesterfield would never hire me. He's got all the trumpets he can handle."

The band that night might have been a makeshift operation, but oh, could they play. They jumped right into "Take the A Train," leaving plenty of room for solos and stepping out, before rolling into a smoky, slow-burn take on "Honeysuckle Rose." Between songs, Martin and Hooper settled into musicians' shop talk: who was hot, who was a pretender, who hadn't paid his band in weeks, who was in the market for a new alto, a new drummer, a new bass. Hooper himself had just come from Smalls, where word was spreading about a scorching horn player from Cincinnati. He had just blown into town, and apparently John Hammond was already working his corner. At the mention of Hammond's name, Martin perked up. He still hadn't said a word about Hammond to anyone.

"Cincinnati!" Hooper sounded astonished. "Cinci-goddamn-nati! Bad enough we got guys from New Orleans, Chicago, Kansas City — even Ireland, if you can believe it — trying to take our jobs. Now we've got to worry about Cincinnati. It's enough to make a man give up music and go into the dry-cleaning business."

There was a parting in the crowd as the people packed close to the band made room for a late arrival. The lighting over the stage was a simple affair but someone switched on a spotlight covered with a blue gel, and the mood of the room shifted.

"I knew she'd get here sooner or later," Hooper said. He leaned in toward Francis and stage-whispered: "Now the show's about to start."

Conversations faded and just as the bass player gave the strings a thrum, a voice filled the room, bright and aching all at once: *Sum — mer — time* . . . the rich, plump notes of the bass filled in the gaps she left between syllables, between words . . . *and the livin' is — ea — sy* . . . She started high, then brought it low. She knew the song was as much a celebration as a bitter joke. The room heard it, and didn't they know it, too. Five words into the song and every eye in the room was straining for a glimpse of Lorena Briggs.

HOOPER COULDN'T SAY exactly when he had been swept up in Lorena's wake. He had first met her when he was thirteen and she was just a year or so younger when she moved into his neighborhood after some family trouble in DC. Baltimore wasn't far from Anacostia but it was far enough, and Lorena arrived with a sense of mystery around her. Right away her aunt brought her to the church where Hooper's father was the pastor, and overnight, it seemed, Lorena was the star of the choir. She had never sung in a little girl's crystalline soprano, at least not since Hooper had known her. Lorena's voice could rumble like thunder, flare like heat lightning, and soothe the congregation with soft rain. At first the older ladies in the choir didn't like it, not one bit: *Who is this girl who comes out of nowhere and thinks she's going to be the one?* But they couldn't harden themselves for long against that voice or against the skinny little girl with the ribboned plaits and the grave face. The ladies would cluck their tongues and say that she was an old soul. And with a voice like that but no mama to look after her? The Lord does give gifts but He can ask a heavy price. Lorena had arrived in Baltimore with one aunt, but inside of a month she had fifteen. Later this would make life difficult for Hooper, to have the eyes of so many aunts on Lorena.

At first, Hooper thought she was just another girl who was always at the church—rehearsing with the choir, helping his mother with the potluck, leading the children's Bible study—and anyhow Hooper already had five sisters; he didn't need any more girls in his life. But by the time Lorena was sixteen, she was no longer a stripling girl but a young woman whose body was catching up to that old soul. Hooper wasn't just smitten, he was signed and sealed for life.

Music was the language of their love. Hooper could hear light and dark tones in her voice that no one else could. And Lorena would listen to Hooper work his way up and down the valves of the trumpet, listen to him feinting and jabbing with the trombone, even listen when he mauled the piano like a man who thought the keyboard was the steering wheel of a garbage truck. She was never shy about pointing out his limitations, never just an audience, and certainly never a dewy-eyed admirer. She would listen, seemingly rapt, as a teenage Hooper pumped his way through "West End Blues," doing his best to sound like the second coming of Satchmo, but as soon as he blew the last note she would start with a string of questions that weren't really questions. These critiques had hurt his boyish pride until he realized two truths: one, she was right, almost without fail, and two, she also believed that he could be one of the greats—she just had a better idea of what it would take to get there. And then there was a third truth, which he realized only after he stopped letting his pride get in the way: he saw that she loved him and that if he wanted that love to grow, he had better listen to what she had to say.

It was true that Lorena told jokes on him and often turned to his chorus of younger sisters with a *Can you believe this fool?* look, but she loved him so fiercely that sometimes she thought her body would burn from it. The jokes, the rolled eyes, the *Lord have mercy*s when he told one of his leg-stretchers—those were just the valves that released the pressure threatening to burst her heart. How else could you live with a happiness too bold to be real? How else could you hold on to a love you didn't think you deserved? Lorena had an uncle in Philadelphia who had bought himself an almost-new car, a two-tone Packard, brown and creamy yellow like a cake in a bakery window. The day he bought it, he took a baseball bat to one of the fenders and made a dent bigger than a dinner plate for everyone to see. "Drive around with a machine this nice and someone's not gonna like it," he said. "Now I don't have to worry about somebody else taking the shine off my apple." Lorena thought about that sometimes when she was with Hooper. If she was too full of smiles about this man, the world was sure to take notice. Someone wasn't gonna like it.

When Hooper left for Howard University, Lorena was sure that someone must have seen, and stolen, her joy. Though it was barely forty miles from Baltimore to Howard, Hooper returned only rarely, and his parents made certain to fill his visits with family time. The Reverend and Mrs. Hooper had always been kind to her, but there was kind and then there was kin. She knew they had more in mind for their only son than life with an orphan girl whose parents were still whispered about. "Such a skinny little thing," Mrs. Hooper would say. "And so *dark*." No one saw Lorena shed a single tear when Hooper left town—*You do your crying on your own time*, her mama had told her—and she kept on singing on Sundays like nothing had changed. If people in the congregation didn't notice the knot of hurt that she tied into every song, then they just weren't listening.

Although her aunt didn't like it, Lorena wasn't singing only on Sundays. A man from church had a brother who owned a nightclub that needed a girl singer for the slow numbers, when the couples liked to take things nice and easy, and Lorena had the voice and the bruised heart to make those songs purr.

By his second year in college, Hooper was spending less of his time in his lectures and more of it toting his trumpet to any band on U Street in need of the next Louis Armstrong. The summer after his sophomore year, he signed on with a territory band playing beach resorts and one-nighters from Chesapeake Bay to Sea Island, Georgia. For eight weeks, the band slept on the bus in towns where no hotel would take them. They played for white crowds who paid the price of admission and then spat insults between songs. They played dances where a rope was laid across the floor: whites on one side and colored folks on the other. The band had been booked to play late in the tour at a dance hall that practically straddled the Georgia–South Carolina state line. As they approached the town, a midsummer carnival appeared to be in full swing: a large crowd had gathered, a bonfire sent sparks into the twilight, and children chased each other through a field. The only thing missing was the music.

From the back of the bus, the trombone player, who was always cracking wise, said, "Finally, someone decided to roll out the red carpet!"

But the bandleader, who sat over the shoulder of the driver, got a better look. "Keep driving!" he shouted. He was a steady man, as good-natured as a favorite uncle, and this was not his first tour of the South. His voice cracked when he spoke, and his eyes were fixed on the tree at the center of the crowd. "You just keep driving! There's no show tonight!"

As they drove past the turn that would have brought them into town, Hooper watched that fire burn, watched the towheaded children chasing fireflies on the edge of the vast crowd, and strained to see the terrible weight that hung from the tree's stoutest limb. In the silence that settled over the band, he thought of Lorena; he hadn't seen her since Easter, when she had taken the solo on "Were You There," and now as the bus disappeared into the night, he sat alone in the darkness and felt himself tremble, tremble, tremble. When he returned home, he was convinced of two more truths: his next step musically needed to be away from Howard and in a northerly direction, and life was too short to live another day of it without Lorena Briggs.

By the end of September, Hooper and Lorena were boarding the train to New York City as husband and wife. The Reverend and Mrs. Hooper were capable of moving heaven and earth to bend the world to their will, but even they saw—after a solid week of tears, prayers, and threats—that what bound their son and Lorena was unshakable by mortal force. "I'll give it a year in New York," Hooper told them, "and if nobody takes notice I can always go back to school." The lie, if they chose to believe it, was enough to comfort Hooper's parents that their son was not condemned to a life of barrooms and dance halls. If they wanted to tell themselves that it was all Lorena's fault— that their son had been led astray by a no-account jazz singer with dreams beyond her reach—well, they knew that was a lie, too. Hooper might never preach a sermon but he could play like Gabriel himself. As for Lorena, they had heard her voice; they knew the truth.

WHEN LORENA FINISHED with the song, the crowd clapped long and loud, and then parted as she made her way to the bar. On the stage she looked like a queen in mourning, but up close she was buoyant, even elfin. Her mouth was outlined in red, her eyes shaded in blue, and her skin glowed like molten metal.

She rested her elbow on Hooper's shoulder as if he were a street-corner mailbox and turned her attention on the Dempsey brothers. "Which one of you boys is going to buy me a drink?" she said, and then a half beat later—her phrasing always perfect—she burst into laughter and planted a quick kiss on Hooper's cheek.

WEDNESDAY
JUNE 7

WOODLAWN

ROSEMARY HAD SUGGESTED TO Peggy that they get together at the apartment, where she could keep an eye on the girls while she talked some sense into her younger sister, but Peggy had balked.

"No offense," Peggy had said, "but your apartment is sort of dreary."

"How am I not supposed to be offended by that?"

"It's not like it's a secret," Peggy said. "Mother says it all the time."

Instead they settled on Driscoll's, a lunch spot in Woodlawn where Peggy often met her friends — brides-to-be and newlyweds who lately had taken to sharing strategies for setting up and running a house of your own, free from the interference of mothers, mothers-in-law, or husbands. As much as she felt a sense of duty about setting Peggy straight, Rosemary dreaded the trip into the old neighborhood, just as she dreaded the cost of lunch and what it would do to the budget now that Martin was up to God knows what.

The lunchtime crowd at Driscoll's was buzzing. Formica tables gleamed, chrome shone beneath the counter stools and on the legs of the chairs. Two sturdy ceiling fans beat futilely against the muggy air, busboys in wilted white shirts hustled pitchers of ice water from table to table to kitchen and back. Peggy, already a minor celebrity by virtue of her last name, had achieved movie-star status. With only three days until the wedding, everyone had a question, a word of congratulations, a piece of advice. Those who would be attending smiled and parted with a "See you Saturday," the uninvited tried to ignore the brouhaha, and the decline-with-regrets avoided making eye contact. Rosemary asked for a table away from the window, away from the center of the action, which of course made Peggy pout, but this wasn't going to be a conversation that Rosemary wanted to broadcast along the invisible wires that connected one Woodlawn home to another.

Peggy ordered a Waldorf salad and when Rosemary asked only for an iced tea, Peggy loudly scoffed.

"That's all you're having?"

"Iced tea is fine," Rosemary said.

"It's my treat, all right?" Peggy looked up at the waitress. "My sister will have a patty melt."

"I don't want a patty melt."

"Then a Reuben? How does that sound? Or a Cobb salad—yes, a Cobb salad."

Rosemary had meant to eat before she dropped the girls with her down-the-street neighbor Angela Videtti, but Evie had been slow to wake from her morning nap and Kate had refused, at first, to go to the Videttis. She said Maria, the only girl among Angela's six children, was bossy and would not let her play with her best doll. Rosemary had known that Peggy would raise a stink about her ordering only a tea—Peggy was allergic to anything that smelled of lack, of thrift, of self-denial. But she was hungry and didn't want to make a scene—not yet, at least—so she relented: a Cobb salad.

"Thanks," Rosemary said grudgingly, after the waitress left the table.

"Don't mention it." Peggy was enjoying herself. The little sister picking up the tab.

"So," Rosemary said. "Are you still thinking about calling it off?"

Peggy's smile evaporated. "Maybe. I mean, why shouldn't I?"

"Don't you want to marry Tim?"

"Sure I do," she said. "Just—not now. Not yet."

"When, then?"

Peggy threw her hands in the air. "I don't know. Some other time.

After the fair, how about? Has anyone stopped to consider that I actually *like* the Aquacade, and that maybe I don't want to give that up?"

"I'm supposed to believe you're calling off your wedding to pursue a life in water ballet?"

"I didn't say I was going to do it for *life*, but I like it—a lot!—and going out with Francis made me realize that sometimes you have to—"

"So this is because of Sunday night?"

"It's not *just* that."

"Do you want to tell me what happened?"

"What happened is that I had a wonderful time. And it's been *ages* since I've had a wonderful time."

"Well," Rosemary said. "You only get so much wonderful."

"You sound just like Mother. Maybe I don't want a life like that."

"Your life doesn't end when you get married. That's actually when it starts. Your home, your decisions—and Tim is obviously going places. Dad will make sure of that. You've got plenty of excitement to look forward to."

"Not if I'm stuck at home," Peggy said. "And you're not exactly an advertisement for the exciting world of marriage, with that apartment and your 'just iced tea for me' and never going dancing or—"

"I have the girls to look after."

"But don't you want—"

"You'll understand when you're a mother."

"I don't want to understand. Not yet."

A waitress, her face sheened with perspiration, appeared with their salads. She set down each plate and dabbed her wrist across her forehead. A pointed paper cap sat perched like a crown on her head. Beneath the cap, her hair was combed tight at the sides and pulled into an elaborate bun. Stylish—the hair, not the cap. Rosemary had seen more and more women wearing their hair in that way. Were they imitating some movie star, from a film she had not seen?

"Can I bring you girls anything else?" the waitress said.

Not until she said "girls" did Rosemary take a closer look at the waitress. She was thirty-five, perhaps forty. Threads of gray hair were visible at her temples.

"I'll have a milk shake," Peggy said. "Vanilla, with whipped cream."

The waitress took a pad from her apron and looked to Rosemary. Perspiration stained the armpits of her uniform. *This,* Rosemary caught herself wondering. *Could I do this?* It might become necessary if Martin was out of work for long. But who would watch the girls? Was there someone—Angela Videtti, someone else—whom she could pay to watch the girls while she worked the lunch shift at one of the diners on the Grand Concourse? Assuming she could find someone who would charge less than a waitress's wages? But that was nonsense. She had been to college. She could do better than waitressing, couldn't she? Typist? Bookkeeper? Could she turn to her father to make an introduction? Her parents would be horrified, of course. The final nail in Martin's—

"Ma'am," the waitress said, one eyebrow lifted.

"Nothing else for me," Rosemary said.

"I'm famished." Peggy speared a grape with her fork.

The clatter of silverware against plates. The clink of ice water poured into a glass. The murmur of conversation—*You won't believe…Never in a million years…I told her you play with fire and you're gonna*—spiked with a stifled laugh, or a table for four sharing one bad joke. Rosemary had stopped wondering if the talk was about her. She was old news. There had been other sudden engagements and hurry-up weddings since hers. But she was reminded of why she had moved out of Woodlawn. She missed the neighborhood—she knew every storefront, knew its parks and people—but it was too much her father's place. Her mother's place.

The waitress set down the milk shake, the glass beaded with moisture. A maraschino cherry sank into a dollop of whipped cream. "That will get everyone talking," Rosemary said. " 'How in the world is she going to fit into her dress?' "

"If I have to wear it."

"Yes, if."

"Here's the thing," Peggy said. "You think I'm a child—no, I know you do. And that I don't want to get married because it doesn't look like fun. Which, thanks for nothing. I thought you had a better opinion of me than that. But if I call this off, or put a stop to it for now, maybe everyone will stop taking me for granted. I know this is a chance for Daddy to show off. And Tim expects me to stick with the plan, this weekend and happily ever after. But when I'm at the fair, or out with Francis, it isn't just *fun,* it's exciting, it's *new.* On Sunday night, everyone was happy, and beautiful, and Francis wanted to be there with me and I wanted to be there with him. I swear that half the time I'm talking to Tim, he's thinking about the office, and half the time when he's telling me about his work, I'd rather be out with the girls. I want more of *that* feeling—the feeling of being exactly where you want to be and nowhere else."

"Oh, Peggy. You're about to marry a man who you say you love and who we all know loves you. If he wants to—and that means if *you* want him to—he could make more money than even Dad has ever seen. And he has Dad in his corner, so if he wants to, let's say, be a congressman, he can get there easier than most. Wife of a congressman. You have no idea what you're giving up."

Peggy wouldn't meet her sister's eyes. All of her attention seemed focused on extracting the cherry from the bottom of her glass. "Wasn't that supposed to be your life?" she said.

Rosemary wasn't going to say, for the umpteenth time, that she loved Martin and was happy with the way her life had turned out. Peggy would never believe it, and Rosemary did not need her sister's pity. "Whatever Tim does," Rosemary said, "you will have your own house, your own family, and enough money to get the things you want. It's more than most people could ever dream of—and you want more? Excitement? Applause? To be giddy and half drunk and swept off your feet by handsome strangers? You have more than enough already. You don't get to ask for more."

Not until she stopped talking did Rosemary see the faces turned their way. Perhaps she had been louder than she intended. Perhaps she had pounded her fist on the table. Perhaps the silverware had jumped on the Formica. A few tables over, one of their mother's neighbors had paused in the dissection of a club sandwich. Peggy gave her a prim, patient smile. She might even have rolled her eyes.

"And this just proves my point," Peggy said. "Married people always want to tell you how it's supposed to be, but it's only because—"

"Peggy, stop talking and listen." The waitress had their bill in her hand, but when Rosemary made the silverware jump, she had turned back toward the kitchen. "I'm sure you had a wonderful time on Sunday night. Quite sure, actually. But the whole thing was a fantasy. Francis is a charmer, but a month ago he was in jail, and now here he is, pretending to be a millionaire on vacation. You cannot throw away a life that's right in front of you—a life you wanted with all your heart and soul just last week—" Rosemary stopped. *Fantasy. Jail. Millionaire.* What would Woodlawn make of this?

Peggy leaned in over the table. "I've been thinking about this for a long time. I keep telling you that, but you won't listen."

"I have listened," Rosemary said. "You're tired of getting pushed around about the wedding—I understand that—and you're willing to throw away something you actually want to prove a point. But a wedding is not a marriage."

Peggy sucked the last of her milk shake through the straw. "And maybe there's more to life than marriage," Peggy said. "And maybe there's not. We'll just have to see, won't we?"

(ENTRAL PARK

THERE *WAS* SOMETHING ABOUT Anisette. Francis hadn't been lying about that. And it honestly wasn't the money.

Francis had considered himself quite a ladies' man in Dublin, but he had never gotten involved in anything serious. He was young and in the years before he got tossed into Mountjoy he'd had flash clothes and money in his pockets. He was known around some of the best brothels in the city—clever and kind to the ladies, and willing to spend what he had. His line of work also brought him in contact with well-to-do women who needed him to fetch items they couldn't acquire in Dublin—books, yes, but also luxuries like perfume and silks that were heavily taxed through the normal channels. Their thanks for his prompt attention sometimes went beyond an extra pound or two as gratuity.

But he didn't have any experience that made sense of the way Anisette worked at him. On the ship and at Bingham Castle, he had felt an impulse that he could only describe as protective. He had been warm, enthusiastic, and quick to gainsay those who seemed keen to prick the glossy soap bubble that surrounded her. But that was no more than being polite, wasn't it? He thought again of her appearance at his stateroom door; she seemed completely without guile. She really was concerned about his brother. She really did want to wish him a good night (Mrs. Walter hadn't even bothered with pretense, which bespoke an honesty all its own). But since Anisette's performance on the violin and the way he had looked straight at her, wild-eyed, and she had looked straight back, he couldn't get her out of his head.

Perhaps the Angus disguise was starting to affect his brain. Francis wasn't the type to fall for some doe-eyed ingenue, but maybe Sir Angus was exactly that type. And the more time he spent with Anisette, the farther he fell.

He was probably violating half a dozen rules of etiquette but he sent a card to the Binghams early Wednesday morning asking if Anisette would perhaps be available for a walk sometime after lunch. What he could not say in the note was that he had gone to bed last night thinking of the particular shade of red in her cheeks when she raised the bow from the body of the violin. Or that the first person he'd thought of when he woke that morning was her. Of course he couldn't write any of this, but neither could he believe that he was even thinking it. When had he become such a moony romantic? Half of him—his more cynical side—wanted to see Anisette in order to bring her off the pedestal she had occupied since Monday night. Reality would surely remind him of all the ways that she was just another girl. Lying in bed the night before, he had told himself that jail was the culprit. In Dublin, he had become accustomed to the tender affection of female company, and to have it taken away for so long had made him desperate. His brief encounter with Mrs. Walter had been the uncorking of a bottle that had been shaken for a year and a half. And Peggy was easy enough to explain: ripe and blond and game for anything. Hadn't she been the one who insisted on dancing and on calling his bluff about the Plaza? This attraction to Anisette—as if mere attraction described the space she was taking up in his crowded brain—must have been some pent-up desire, but for what, exactly? Security? Affection? Attention? It was like a toxin in his veins. The strong wine of desire having turned to vinegar from being bottled up so long. But whatever it was, Francis just wanted to see her.

He received a card by messenger less than two hours later: Miss

Bingham *would* enjoy the pleasure of Sir Angus's company. Could he meet her at the Central Park carousel at, say, one o'clock?

He could, of course. And he would bring Michael, too. After the visit to the doctor the day before, Michael had slept through the afternoon. When Michael woke in the evening, he looked ready to take on the world. He dressed himself smartly and the two brothers sought out a steak house where the cuts of beef hung over the edge of the plate. The dinner was splendid, but within minutes of their return to the Plaza, Michael was fast asleep and Francis was off to meet Martin. He had to admit that he'd enjoyed his night out with Martin far more than he had expected. Though the Dempseys had frayed the ties that once bound them, there was something to this business of having brothers that had, in a matter of days, wound them back together again.

ANISETTE STOOD IN front of the carousel, watching the horses leap and circle. The jaunty notes of the calliope burbled all around her, punctuated by the shouts of children. She loved the carousel, the feeling of speed and freedom as it spun, and the music, so bright and full of cheer, rising into the trees. As a girl, she had begged her nannies to take her to the carousel. Félicité had always protested. She hated the carousel, hated the wooden horses who wouldn't tack left or right no matter how hard the rider pressed. Anisette thought this was funny, because her sister was such a great lover of horses now. Well, maybe *lover* was the wrong word. She spent all of her time at the farm in Connecticut in the paddock, jumping and circling. Urging the horses over the bars, speaking to them in a clipped voice that got them to prance and pivot. Did she love the horses, though? She did not baby them, did not coddle them with soft playful tones—but people had different ways of showing love. And maybe Félicité wasn't good at love. Period.

Maman had been cheered by the note from Sir Angus but she feared that Anisette was being awfully forward in telling him to meet her at the carousel. Was she suddenly a barefoot farm girl, meeting some local swain at the county fair out of sight of her ma and pa? She was to remember herself, her mother said. She was to remember what Sir Angus might perceive as proper or improper behavior for *a suitable match*. Anisette had blanched at the words. Of course she had thought about it, and so, clearly, had her mother, but they hadn't spoken a word of it.

Anisette wouldn't say it directly to her mother but she wanted to see Angus on her own, and that couldn't happen in the house. Father was likely to bustle in early from whatever it was he did all day long— shouting into the faces of men who worked for him; shouting into the telephone at far-off men who worked for him. And there was Félicité, angry and angular and ready to bring out the worst in Anisette just to show her up in front of Angus. But what she really couldn't say was that she wanted to be away from Maman herself. Maman was so sweet, but she had been hovering every moment that Anisette had spent with Angus—except for her sudden, secret visit to Angus on the ship (Maman would have three heart attacks and a stroke if she ever heard about that). More than anything, Anisette wanted to see if Angus was interested in her alone or if it was everything else that had caught his eye: the *Britannic* dining room, the Binghams' house, Father and his copper-mine stories, and Maman, who always knew the right thing to say, to do, to wear. Not that she suspected he was a bad man or a—what did Papa call him? A treasure hunter? Not that he was any of those things, but she wanted to see him for herself and she wanted him to see her as just *her*.

ANGUS ARRIVED AT the carousel with his brother Malcolm and, far from being disappointed that he had brought a chaperone, Anisette was elated. Touched, even. He had held his brother back from the rest of her family and on the ship had kept him hidden from the other passengers while he convalesced. That Angus would want his closest relative to meet Anisette had to be proof of his trust in her, and perhaps of some deeper emotion as well. As he made the introductions, Anisette held out a slender hand, which Malcolm pumped rather vigorously. Angus had described his brother's condition in such dire terms, but here he seemed restored. Perhaps Dr. Van Hooten had found a cure?

"The poor dear," she said.

"He's a fighter," Angus said. "And you wouldn't believe how much he's improved since our arrival. America agrees with him."

Anisette suggested a stroll. In one direction the whoops of children at the playground filled the air. The other way a canopy of trees lolled in the pale breeze. Vendors hawking lemonade and shaved ice did a brisk business. Angus bought three lemonades and offered an arm to Anisette, which she gladly accepted.

They wound through the paths, Francis and Anisette in front and Michael trailing behind, grateful for the lemonade. It hadn't occurred to Francis until they met at the carousel, but this was Michael's first look at Anisette. He seemed pleased to meet her, but what could Francis really decode from a smile and a handshake? And what could he tell Michael anyway? *Best behavior with this one—I'm trying to impress her*? He couldn't ask his brother a single thing.

Francis was aware that all of the inventing he had done on Monday night at the Binghams' dinner table had almost sunk the whole enterprise. Today, he barraged Anisette with questions about herself. In response, he began to hear about nannies and tutors and girls' schools where the students wore white dresses with bright red sashes. Most surprising was the story of her mother, the erstwhile nurse from Montreal. Francis couldn't help wondering what Mrs. B would say if she knew that her daughter had just admitted to His Lordship that Maman was an even commoner commoner than he was. Anisette didn't seem to care a whit. She read romance into the story, the phoenix of love

281

rising from the ashes of the first Mrs. Bingham. Francis saw that he wasn't the first to gate-crash Bingham Castle, but he did not know whether this would help or hurt him with Mrs. B if the news of his own true nature ever came to light. His estimation of Mrs. B, however, increased.

The trio reached a broad paved lane picketed with street lamps and tall trees. Park benches stretched like ribbons the length of the promenade. Children hooted and squeaked through games of tag while mothers tended to a flotilla of carriages, like ships tied up at a marina. Farther down, a man in a squashed top hat played an accordion, clowning for the attention and pennies of passersby. Here and there young couples sat together. A man no older than Francis had his arms outstretched along the top rail of the bench, affecting a pose of leisure in the hope that the woman next to him would sink back just enough for him to draw her in, hand to shoulder. But the benches weren't a spot only for lovers, lovers-to-be, lovers-in-waiting. An old man gripped the edges of a newspaper, holding it inches from his face, as if scanning the pages for hidden messages. A woman in a shabby frock sat farther down the bench, her purse on her knees and her hands folded over the clasp. She seemed to be waiting for a bus that would never arrive.

"This must remind you of home." Anisette pointed to the lampposts: from each one a Union Jack hung lank in the breezeless heat. A sea of red, white, and blue and stripes—nothing but stripes—in every direction. If there was one thing you could say about the Brits, it was that they didn't shy away from excess. *Would you care for some horizontal? Yes, please. Vertical? Of course. And would you fancy some diagonal? Corner to corner, please, and twice over.*

"Well, it does and it doesn't," Francis-as-Angus said. "But I don't think I've ever seen quite so many at one time."

"Not even for the coronation?"

"Of course," he said, with a dry laugh, "the coronation." Yes, the bloody coronation! He had almost Cawdor-and-Glamis'd himself with that slipup. "There is something to be said for all of this enthusiasm. I do think Their Royal Highnesses will appreciate the gesture."

"Oh, you think we're silly. Trying too hard to impress." She was looking up at him from under the brim of her hat, her front teeth sunk into the pillow of her lower lip. Anisette's air of innocence made those lips, so full and swollen, seem almost wanton.

"Not at all." Francis stopped and cocked his head to see beneath her hat. He wanted to see her eyes, wanted her to know that he was being sincere. "It's quite charming, really. You care. You—all of you, the whole city—you want the king and queen, Their Majesties, to feel wanted, admired, welcome. What could be wrong with that?" He really did need to brush up on his forms of address before Saturday: Highness, Royal Highness, Majesty. There were rules for this sort of thing, and Sir Angus MacFarquhar would have known them since the cradle.

"So they're not going to think that we're...overeager?" Anisette blinked. She might have even batted her lashes, or perhaps that was the sunlight filtering through the leaves, or because Francis had seen too many films where Myrna Loy or Carole Lombard had batted her lashes in a moment much like this one.

"Better that than bored, or disinterested," he said. "Who'd wish to come all this way only to hear 'What do *you* want?'"

Anisette giggled, then fell into a more serious mood. Again her teeth sank into her lower lip. She twice started to speak and then abruptly checked herself. She seemed always like a kettle about to boil. "Tell me, Angus. What do *you* want?"

For a moment he thought it was an accusation, like the jig was up. He made a show of mopping his forehead with the back of his hand. "In this weather, an iced gin would be a nice place to start, don't you agree?"

She slapped him playfully on the shoulder in a very un-jig-is-up sort of way. "Now you're the one being silly. I'm serious. When you think about life and everything it could be, what do you want?"

"I haven't given it much thought."

"But you must have!" Anisette's voice was charged, even annoyed. "You must think about the kind of life you want. Do you always want to live in Scotland? What sort of work will you do—or is it crass to suggest that the son of an earl must work? Or is it crass to suggest that you won't?" Anisette's cheeks were flushed pink. The color extended down her neck, blazing against the gauzy cream fabric like a sunburn. "Will you be a bachelor adventurer your whole life, or will you live in a big house full of dogs and children and—"

"Hullo!" he said. "I see that you've given this a great deal of thought."

"Everyone does," she said. "Except for you, it seems."

He had batted away her question as if it were a trifle, but of course he'd thought about it. Francis was full of wanting. All his life he had chased and desired and sought, and getting only made him want more. Playing that hand for higher and higher stakes had spurred him on in Dublin, but since his escape he had been forced to reshuffle the deck. First and foremost, he wanted Michael to be cured, and he wanted not to have been responsible for the accident—the incident— the event that had damaged him. More than that, he wanted for none of it to have ever happened in the first place. But he knew that without the explosion that had nearly killed Michael there wouldn't have been a strongbox, and without the strongbox, there would be no FC Plan, and without the FC Plan... well, he wouldn't be strolling through the park with Anisette, Michael trailing behind dressed like a dapper young dandy.

Francis forced a laugh. "You ask like it's an uncomplicated question."

"It is." She spoke to him as if he were a child, as if English were not his native tongue. "What...do...you...want?"

He could not tell if she was innocent or incredibly forward—if she was a maiden for whom subtext was a foreign language or a bawd who couldn't waste her time with fumbling boys. He'd known madams in Dublin brothels who were less forward in their way of speaking. He thought to parry the question again but something thick caught in his throat. He looked again into those eyes. The truth. She wanted the truth. Had he spoken so much as a single true syllable to her since they had met on the *Britannic*?

"Anisette," he said, "there's so much I want that I can't even find a way to answer the question."

The wall that he had so carefully constructed between Francis and Angus was wobbling. What he had said was true of him—of Francis Dempsey—but whether it was true also of Angus MacFarquhar, he did not know. He had been Angus only for a short time and hadn't expended much effort plumbing the hopes, fears, and desires of the dashing young Scotsman. Angus had come into being as a necessary convenience, a part of the FC Plan, and he was meant to be only temporary, to last as long as the crossing. Francis had never thought about what came after the FC Plan, but now he didn't want there to be an after. He wanted the FC Plan to become permanent: the money and the ease of movement, Anisette and her belief in the future.

"But what about you?" he said. "What do you want?"

She made a show of considering the question, but she must have had an answer scripted and ready to perform. "Well," she said, "I want a lot of things, too. I'd like to get out of this city. Not just for visits to other places, or for the summer. I mean out for good."

"You don't like New York?"

"It's not so much the city itself. It's the people in it—present company excepted."

"Thank goodness for that," he said.

"I want the people I care about to stay close, and to be safe." She thought about her brother. Robert had always been kind to her, but he had gone far away. She wanted him to come home, though she knew there was something about her father that made that impossible, and maybe something about Robert, too. But that was one item on the list: to see her brother again. She would have also liked for there to be a safe place for the people she had met in Europe, because there was so much danger around them. Couldn't one of the more pleasant countries just refuse to take part in any fighting so that everyone who wasn't interested in war could go there?

"I sometimes think about a house on a hill," she continued, "with a broad lawn that goes all the way down to the ocean. The house would be big and airy and full of people and laughter, and there would be children galore and three or four dogs lazing on the porch. And there would be music—lots of music."

"Well, of course," he said. "You have a gift there."

"Félicité is the one with the gift. You should hear her on the piano—except that she never lets anyone hear her play. If there's one person at home, she won't even set foot in the conservatory. God forbid she should bring a little joy into someone's life."

"I don't think she likes me—not even a little."

"Don't let it bother you. She doesn't like me either."

THEY WALKED THE length of the mall, the dappled sunlight playing across the faces of flaneurs, lunch-breakers, time-killers, lollards, and mothers seeking relief from crowded apartments. Children raced from one bench to the next squealing in delight, crying "Cheater!" and racing again. An old woman, pigeon-chested and expensively coiffed, walked a Pomeranian on a thin red leash.

"Oh, how adorable!" Anisette said.

"Yes, and the dog is lovely, too," Francis-as-Angus said.

At the end of the mall, face to face with the busts of the world's great writers, Francis bought a round of shaved ice soaked in flavored syrup: lemon, maple, vanilla. Michael accepted his with a pantomimed tip of the cap, and Anisette took hers with a flourish of her hand—*For me? You shouldn't have*—and a sweeping debutante's curtsy. Michael applauded as best he could without losing his grip on the paper cone.

On the lake below the broad terrace where they stood, young couples sat in flat-bottomed boats, exposed to all eyes but solitary together in the midst of the pulsing city. Another day, Francis told himself, already plotting a return to the park when he could be alone with Anisette. They followed another path that swept past a pond where children and more than a few adults guided model sailboats in a scrambled armada of bright colors and flashing white canvas.

Michael, for his part, was getting tired. Despite the lemonade and the shaved ice, his legs were going wobbly in the heat and his head had begun to pulse. He had perked up momentarily at the sight of the toy boats on the water. In the cloudy haze of silence that wrapped him, he could almost hear the breeze pushing the boats and the water skimming against their tiny hulls. But as the wind rippled the pond, the thousand jagged shards of sunlight snapped him out of his reverie. He didn't collapse, and he counted that as progress, but he was sapped and looked for a shady bench to collect himself.

Still, it was pleasant to be outdoors, to have found this bit of country in the middle of the city. And Francis and this girl on his arm looked so happy. It was undeniable; they both seemed to glow. Michael put his hands to his temples to shield his eyes—like a blinkered horse—and the sight of that happy couple, arms linked, filled the narrowed frame.

Hadn't that once been him? Hadn't he walked by a lake, near home, arm in arm with Eileen Casey? He had, and that sudden certainty was like a key opening a vault where his memories were secured. He had gone out walking with Eileen, far from the eyes of the village. Both of them on errands, but with a plan to meet. They had grown up fast friends, as many children do, though by fourteen, maybe fifteen, they knew it was for life. This one day by the lake—a moment conjured by the sight of Francis and this lovely girl in the soft pink hat—they had strolled with her hand on his arm: a first. The sun was low in the sky. They both knew they would be looked for—well, *she* would be; Michael's father wasn't one to keep a close eye. They walked as near to Ballyrath as they could without being seen together, and at their parting she released his arm, then pulled him to her and planted a kiss on his lips. Before he could respond—grab hold of her, return the kiss—she was already running toward home, laughing and whooping. Michael thought he would burst for joy.

He had recovered this moment, but his mind would not surrender to him the reason they weren't together still. He had seen Eileen, he was sure of it, right before his memory went ragged. She was there, in a crowd, and she was dressed in black. She looked right at him and mouthed one word: *Go!* Was she angry with him? Was she telling him to leave her be?

FRANCIS PUT A hand on Michael's shoulder. Here he was, taking in the sunshine, but he had seen the toll that bright light could exact on his brother: on the ship, on their walk downtown, and now here in the park. Michael had boxed up his eyes with his hands, like a man with a pair of binoculars. They were only a few blocks from Anisette's home, but she had suggested a quick tour of the museum, which rose in front of them like the mausoleum of some fallen hero. Francis didn't think Michael had much coal left in his furnace, but there was bound to be a spot where he could sit in the shade for a few minutes more. Sure enough, there was a bench at the base of the stacked marble steps, under a tree and buffeted by an unexpected breeze. Francis pointed to Anisette and himself, then aimed a finger up the steps. He lifted his eyebrows and held his palms open toward Michael: the interrogative. Michael plopped himself on the bench and leaned back against the wooden slats. With a quick motion of his fingers, he swept his brother and the girl away. *Off ye go. I'll be right here.*

Through the front doors, there were tapestries and bulky statues. Neither had much interest in the art, though. Soon he would walk her down Fifth Avenue and up to the door of Bingham Castle. Even if she were to invite him inside—for tea, for dinner, for that gin he had mentioned—he could not accept. Michael seemed on the verge of one of his spells and Francis had to stop demonstrating to himself (and perhaps to Michael) that he was willing to place what he wanted— thirty minutes more with Anisette, in this most recent case—ahead of what Michael needed: a dark room, a cold towel on his head, and twelve to fourteen hours of catatonic sleep. But Michael was doing so much better, and though Francis knew he would see Anisette on Saturday, when they met the royals, it would hardly be a private affair. Mrs. B would be garrulous, Félicité would be infelicitous, and he and Anisette would get little more than a glance here, a smile there. And after that? There was Martin's question again: What's next? He didn't know about *next*; he could only try to extend *now*.

They wandered through galleries full of paintings, late Byzantine through early Renaissance. Static, gilt-soaked portraits of Christ slowly gave way to voluminous robes, rounded foreheads, pinks and blues crowding out mosaic gold. One painting in particular caught Francis's eye: the ministry of John the Baptist told in a single composition. A path snaked across the top of the canvas, doubled back on itself, and then turned again toward a barred window and a stone wall. At intervals along the path, a wild-haired John appeared, engaging in Baptist-like activities: here standing in the wilderness, locust in hand; there with his bowl, dousing the head of Jesus; past the first turn, taken into custody; and finally, by the cell door, with his head served on a platter. As Francis and Anisette crossed into the next room, saints gave way to citizens: Along one wall, paunchy merchants posed in silk and lace. On the other side of the room, shadows crowded the doughy faces of *bürgermeisters* swathed in black velvet, their white collars immaculate.

"This could be Dr. Van Hooten's flat," Francis said. "He's quite the collector of Dutch faces."

"Oh, dear me," Anisette said. "I completely forgot. Dr. Van Hooten sent a letter to the house, intended for you. I have it here." She opened her purse and withdrew the envelope, creamy, cotton-rich stock, folded stiffly in half.

"The good doctor promised to recommend specialists who could consult on Malcolm's case. Let's see what he has come up with." Francis tapped one edge against his palm and tore a small strip from the opposite side. As he did so, it occurred to him that there was probably a more aristocratic way to open an envelope. The brief letter, which was thick with the credentialed acronyms of the medical profession, referred Malcolm to the care of a doctor at New York Eye and Ear. "Aha," Francis said. But behind the letter was a single sheet typed by hastier hands and annotated in Van Hooten's script: *Your brother's handiwork?* The page began with three attempts at Michael's name before switching to variations on the theme of Yeats:

> Willliam butter Yeast
> William Butler Yeates
> William Butler Yeats is a stodgy old git

"What do you make of that?" Anisette said. "And who is Michael Dempsey?"

Francis pictured Michael in the roomful of chessboards madly pounding on the typewriter. Why hadn't he taken a moment right then and there to see what Michael had written? Once again, he had been too hasty, too eager to pursue his own agenda to put Michael first. Now he held this page in his hand and he was so stunned that he almost answered, *He's my brother*, before recovering: "He's another Irish poet. And now you must forgive me," he said. "I have left Malcolm on his own and really should tend to him. May I escort you to the front steps?"

"You're kind," she said. "But you look ready to jump out of your skin. Go to your brother. I'll spend a little more time in the Northern Renaissance."

"Your parents will think me a cad for not escorting you home."

"Then I won't tell them," she said. "It will be our secret."

He wanted to kiss her—her hand, her cheek, her lips—but he was certain that such a show of affection, even passion, would be too much like Francis and not at all like Angus. Instead he took her hand, briefly, and gave it a squeeze that had to stand in for all the things he had not said and all the kisses he could not yet give.

"Till Saturday, then?" he said.

In response, she pursed her lips into a smile that resembled a kiss, and though he was already moving away from her, he had to wonder if perhaps kissing her in front of all those Dutch faces would have been exactly the right thing to do. But then he was through the low arch and out of the gallery, down a side corridor and quickly descending a flight of stairs that he was reasonably certain would take him to the exit. His hand glided over the polished bronze banister, cool to the touch in the close air, and he saw below the black-and-white scalloped tile of the museum's first floor. As he reached the foot of the stairs he knocked his fingers against the banister, a dull ping, and from over his shoulder came a voice:

"Francis Dempsey."

It wasn't a question, it was a statement of fact, and Francis half turned before he checked himself: *Angus, I'm Angus.* The man who had spoken his name had already closed the distance between them and laid a heavy hand on his shoulder.

In the Scottish accent: "You must have me confused with another—"

"Francis Dempsey," the man said. "You need to come with me."

The man was a solid block, rough-hewn. His voice was Irish—Francis would have said a Cork man, if pressed—but watered down by America, like Martin's.

"I'm sorry, friend," Francis said. "But I've somewhere I need to be."

"You knew someone would come for you. There's an easy way to do this and there's a hard way."

Francis looked over his shoulder, gauging the length of the corridor that led to the entrance hall. The man was stout but he did not look fleet of foot. Francis wondered if he could outrace him to the street, collecting Michael along the way.

The big man let out a breath like a sigh, like he was disappointed or resigning himself to what was to come. He opened one side of his jacket, offering a glimpse of the gun holstered under his arm. "If you run, I'll have a decision to make. Who would you trade yourself for? Your girl-friend upstairs? Your brother, the little one, on the bench outside? Or your older brother, the one in the Bronx with the nice family?"

Francis's mouth filled with sawdust. "You wouldn't," he said, barely a whisper.

The man held his gaze without moving. He seemed not even to draw a breath. "You're coming with me," he said, and when he flicked his chin, Francis began to walk toward the front door, each step as though it were being taken through the dense wet suck of a bog. The man was just over his shoulder, following him down the corridor and into the great hall, as implacable as the statues flanking the room. Francis trod in front of him, his feet grinding the tile floors, searching his mind for something to say that would buy him time or earn him a spot of goodwill. He sorted through questions like a man riffling a deck of cards for an ace. Where were they going? And how were they to get there? And what was to become of—

"Michael," Francis said as they passed through the door and paused at the top of the broad stone steps. "I can't leave my brother alone. He can't tend to himself. He's bad off."

"You should've thought of that before you brought him here."

"It was your own people that did this to him. If you've an ounce of mercy in you—"

"I don't." The man's voice came out through gritted teeth. He scanned the street and took notice of a black car idling by the curb, much to the consternation of the cabs, buses, and other cars that jammed Fifth Avenue. "We're going to walk down the stairs and step into that car, and don't get any ideas."

"You've got this all wrong," Francis said. "If you would only let me—"

"You're pleading your case to the wrong man," he said. "Now go."

IN TRANSIT

CRONIN HAD PLAYED A hunch and the hunch had paid off. Yesterday, Gavigan had given the order to bring in Francis Dempsey, and Cronin knew the old man would be getting antsy. That was a lousy reason to rush and risk botching the whole operation, but it was reason enough. Last night, Cronin had seen the two brothers leave the Plaza around dinnertime and return two hours later. Shortly afterward, Francis departed on his own, by cab. Cronin hadn't bothered to follow him. As long as the youngest was at the hotel, Francis would eventually return. When he saw the two of them cross Fifty-Ninth Street to the park this afternoon, he knew it was time to act. The crowds. The pathways. There would be a chance to catch Francis alone.

From the phone booth outside the museum he had called Gavigan and told him to send a car. Now he had Francis Dempsey, and the two rode side by side in the backseat, bound for a meeting with the man himself. Dempsey appeared white as wax. If he was puzzling this all out in his head, he hadn't yet found any answers. He had been mouthy when Cronin first approached him—full of brio from living like the last great playboy for a week—but only a few words from Cronin had taken the starch out of him.

Those words—threats against the girl, against his brothers, against the family of the eldest—made Cronin sick to his stomach. Alice had told him that he was no longer the man he had once been, and he wanted to believe her. But those words had leaped from his tongue. Words he swore he would never say again had come so easily. And what else would he do to carry out this errand Gavigan had given him? If Dempsey had run, would he have punished the girl? Little Michael, a mere wisp? The whole of Martin's family? He believed he would. If Dempsey ran and by running placed Alice in jeopardy, he would burn the whole city to the ground just to find him.

But now he had Dempsey, and if he had to become this man—his true self, the self he hid from Alice—in order to keep his family safe, then he would do it. The farm was his heaven. He was willing to risk hell later for it. Hadn't he always been a brute? Or was it Black Frank who had made him a brute, and set him on this path? It was under his tutelage, after all, that Cronin had learned the uses of violence. Back home, before he went to Cork city, his mother had called him the gentle giant. When the recruiters from the British army had come to town looking for men to send to the trenches in the Great War, they had picked him out of the crowd straightaway. But no, he said, he wasn't the military type. He couldn't point a gun, pull a trigger— anyone in town would tell you the same. Not Tom Cronin. Sure, there were boys in town who were messers and scrappers and they'd picked plenty of fights with Tom when he was a lad. But they learned quick that if you pushed Tom to his limits he would flatten you. He never started fights, but he sure knew how to finish them.

The recruiters had an easier time with his brother, Jack, who was older and more restless. Christ, he was hard bored living in Glengarriff. Jack took the king's shilling and the promise of a new house on his return, but within a month he was dead. The recruiters came back to try again, to see if Tom didn't want to get revenge on the Turks for what they'd done to his brother. Only it wasn't the Turks whom Tom wanted his revenge on. He would have torn the recruiters to shreds if it weren't for the cries of his mother, but still he roughed them up enough that he had to leave town or else see the inside of a jail for years to come. Suddenly his mam was transformed from a spitfire widow with two grown sons still under her roof to a shrunken old woman with one son buried under foreign soil and another disappeared into Cork, a city big enough for a man to get lost.

A friend of his uncle's landed him a job as a groundskeeper at the university, and it was there that Frank Dempsey began to give a shape to the anger that Cronin carried for the loss of his brother. Cronin knew it wasn't the Turks who were responsible for the dissolution of his family, and from Frank Dempsey, a kind of man whom Tom had never encountered in Glengarriff, he acquired a narrative for fitting it all together, a history that stretched back centuries. Hadn't this sort of thing been done over and over again to men just like Tom's brother? Weren't they always the ones who paid the price? And now Tom had a chance to take part in a struggle against history, to put an end to the endless reaping of the Irish. Cronin's mother might have seen her youngest as a gentle giant, but that's not what Frank Dempsey saw. He looked into the eyes of Tom Cronin and knew he could unlock a terrible energy.

Frank spoke to him in low tones, invited him into his home, prepared him, pointed him in the direction he needed to go. And with each operation that Tom completed, it was Frank who was there to praise him or upbraid him—whatever was necessary to keep him resolute in the cause in which Frank said he was playing such a grand part. But Tom knew he was doing it at the expense of his own soul. Every man grabbed, every shot fired—it reduced him. Frank couldn't see it or wouldn't believe it. He was proud of what Tom had accomplished in the struggle against the old history, and in service to a new history.

Then, before the struggle was over, it was over. The war and Tom's part in it was supposed to free everyone—all of Ireland—from the yoke that had led his brother to his death. But here was Frank telling him that they had done all they could for now. That Collins had signed the treaty, and they would deal with the north and the question of full independence later. That what they had won was enough, for now. Except that wasn't what Cronin had given away his soul on behalf of. How do you trade your soul for a partial victory? He could not stomach it. And when the others who felt the same way got their hooks into Cronin, it was easy to turn him. He had already half turned himself.

Now, almost twenty years later, he had to admit that this was who he was. Black Frank hadn't made him into a brute. It had always been inside him. Frank had just seen that and at least had directed Cronin's grim energy toward something worthwhile. Wasn't it good to fight for freedom? For the rights of a people denied their dignity for centuries? The fact that Cronin later put this same energy into the service of a man like Gavigan—that wasn't Frank's fault. This was entirely of Cronin's own making. And now here he was, still in service to Gavigan, to his system of debts and punishments. Alice said he wasn't this man anymore, but look how easily he had slipped into his old skin.

DEMPSEY DIDN'T SAY a word as they crossed the park, and that was a small blessing. There was nothing a man in his position could say: the wheedling, the false bravado, the efforts to build goodwill, were a waste of breath. Not that Cronin hadn't heard it all. Whether men raged or keened prayers to the Blessed Virgin for her intercession, they all met the same fate.

The car emerged from the park and began working its way to the garage where Cronin would deposit Dempsey and be done. Cronin hadn't even bothered with a blindfold—Dempsey wouldn't be telling any stories, not once Gavigan was done with him. Cronin would have to pat him down when they arrived, just to be on the safe side, though something about Dempsey suggested he was not only unarmed, but completely unprepared for what was coming.

A late train could have Cronin back at the farm before midnight. He would walk from the depot, he had decided, hoping that an hour in the country air would leech the city out of him and give him time to assume the mask of the man Alice believed he could be. Once he was back on the farm, he could climb into bed next to Alice and wake to a hot sun and day of work. He hadn't had a decent night of sleep since he'd arrived in the city, holed up as he was at a cheap dive west of Columbus Circle, within spitting distance of his old haunts and the Plaza Hotel, too. The room held little more than a cot, with a wash-stand and a basin in one corner. Mounted on the wall was a small mirror set in a tarnished gilt frame, and next to the washstand a single chair that a previous tenant had begun to paint canary yellow, only to lose interest or find other lodgings before he could finish.

What business would Dempsey leave unfinished? He was a young man, and given his start in life—good parents, educated people with a fine house near the university—he should have done so much better than this. Gavigan said he was a killer, with a trail of bodies to prove it, but though the color had returned to his face, Dempsey's eyes shone like a frightened rabbit's. Cronin hoped that fear would make him smarter, or at least less foolish, about what was to come—even if all that remained to him was the comportment he brought to his own death. With some effort, Cronin again choked down whatever part of himself felt sympathy, or responsibility, for what would become of Francis Dempsey.

FIFTH AVENUE

MICHAEL AND YEATS WATCHED as Francis and another man climbed into the back of a black sedan. In the moment before Francis disappeared into the car, his head swiveled side to side, searching, almost frantic. Michael stood on the bench and tried to catch sight of the car, already lost in the crush of traffic. "Where is he going?" Michael said. "And where's the girl? Oh, why can't you be a proper ghost and fly after him?"

Yeats ignored Michael and peered at the scrum of cars on Fifth Avenue. He had appeared on the bench with Michael shortly after Francis and the girl had gone inside the museum. He seemed disappointed that he had missed the chance to meet another of Francis's lady friends. "Who was that rough-looking chap with your brother?" Yeats said. "Someone you know, or—"

"I don't know anyone," Michael snapped. "Not here, and not in my own past." The exhaustion he felt earlier had not entirely left him, and the sting of losing Eileen for reasons he could not recall ached like a fresh wound. The hotel seemed a long way off, and after a last glance at the avenue, he stepped from the bench to the sidewalk. He dug into his pocket for the business card of the hotel and held it up for Yeats to see. "Do you suppose we should use this again?"

"No, I do not suppose," Yeats said emphatically. "Your brother has proven himself to be entirely unreliable. If we are ever to make progress, then you and I must take matters into our own hands."

Michael stared blankly. "Progress toward what?"

"The question of my being here. Of my being at all."

"We've been abandoned in the middle of the city and you want us to crack the meaning of life, is that it?"

"There is a reason why I am here and why only you can see me."

"Why must there be a reason?" Michael said, exasperated.

Yeats seemed genuinely startled. "I can't believe I have to explain that to a seminarian."

"I am having a difficult time accepting that there is a reason—not just a cause, but a reason—for why I cannot hear or speak. This is what God wants for me?"

"Who said anything about God? The *spiritus mundi* is bigger than any notion of God. Even the idea of God is a part of the great spirit of the world." Yeats ran his palm over his forehead and up the crown of his pate. Wisps of white hair sprang in unruly directions as his hand passed over them. Michael could sense his frustration. "I am offering you a quest for truth—an opportunity to tear the veil that divides life from death. To glimpse the universal memory that binds us all. And you propose we waste our hours in a gilded cage waiting for your brother to return from his latest assignation?"

Down the block, an older woman crossed the street, holding the leash of a small dog. Looking first at her and then at Yeats, Michael had to wonder whether he was the woman or the dog.

"Mr. Dempsey, my condition and yours require exploration, and there are people in this city who could be of assistance—better, certainly, than that chess-mad doctor your brother brought you to see. During my last visit to this city—made when I was among the living—I met many accomplished mediums. One in particular, a woman called Madame Antonia, had an acute spiritual sensitivity."

"So just fly away without me. Find the nearest crystal ball and start gabbing."

"I would like nothing better, but I remain linked to you."

"And you think a medium can tell you why we're stuck together?"

"Madame Antonia can tell us many things. She also happens to be a specialist in psychical healing."

Michael thought of the bed, the sofa, and the thickly upholstered armchair by the window. He was knackered, and the hotel offered so many places to sleep. But Yeats was right. They were surrounded by mysteries whose solutions could not be found in the hotel. "Fine," he said, "but it's not my psyche that needs healing. It's my ears."

THEY HAD NO business card with Madame Antonia's name and address, and Michael was not going to try pantomiming *Take me to a medium* to a cabdriver. Yeats had a dim memory of Madame Antonia living in the Italian Quarter, as he called it, and an even dimmer memory of this neighborhood being in the opposite direction of the Bronx. An open-topped double-decker idled in front of the museum, slowly taking on passengers, and Michael proposed that they join the queue. When he reached the front of the line, Michael began dumping coins into the till until the driver waved him aboard. He found a seat on the upper level, in the front, and as the bus stuttered its way down Fifth Avenue, he could see the hotel drawing into view. At least they were going in the right direction. From his vantage point he was able to retrace his steps from the Saturday promenade with Francis, and to point out to Yeats the Harpies, the red-stone church, Atlas shouldering the hollow globe. He had expected Yeats to be more impressed by this hodgepodge of myth, story, and symbol, but Yeats seemed too wrapped up in his plans for communing with Madame Antonia. He could only sniff at the statues.

Michael left Yeats to whatever spiritual navigation he was conducting and let himself enjoy the view. Clouds scudded overhead, as if leaping from one tower to the next. As the bus passed the Empire State Building, the city began to change: the buildings were just as densely packed but not so gargantuan, five or six stories instead of thirty or forty. Gone were the gold-lettered shop signs and the windows full of diamonds and silk gowns. They were moving into a place of work, of commerce without glamour. The intersections became crowded with pushcarts, taxicabs, delivery trucks, and people—always so many people—with a hard cast to their eyes.

The bus lurched to a halt, beset by an ever-swelling crowd that filled the streets. The people all seemed to be moving in the same direction, toward a diagonal boulevard that branched at the next intersection. Somewhere there was a parade, a rally, a demonstration. Michael saw men in the crowd carrying placards but their messages of support or protest flowed across the boards like liquid Sanskrit.

"I've been thinking," Michael said. "About the reason for our being linked together. Would you care to hear my theory?"

Yeats looked at him peevishly, then waved his hand in a *Proceed, proceed* sort of way.

Michael proceeded: "As far as I can say, I am Michael Dempsey, raised in a small town in the center of Ireland, and until recently a seminarian. However, everything about my current reality—the clothes, the hotel, being in America—argues that I am not Michael Dempsey. Or not *that* Michael Dempsey. What if I was switched by some act of metaphysical sleight of hand, *Prince and the Pauper*–like, from one world to another—so that right this moment, there's a well-born Michael wondering how he ended up typing letters to the Holy See for Brother Joseph Mary at the seminary?"

Yeats tented his fingers over his nose, his deep-in-thought pose. Michael wanted Yeats to know that he was in earnest. That he wasn't codding. The bus lurched again and came to a halt. The crowd had swollen and from his perch at the front of the bus, Michael could see nothing ahead but the tops of cars frozen in place, even as the traffic lights winked from red to green.

"Oh, it's hopeless," Yeats said.

"You don't think much of my theorizing, then?"

"Not that," Yeats said. "This omnibus. It will be hours before it can get us ten feet closer to our destination."

Taking the lead, Michael disembarked directly into the crowd, then wound his way to the sidewalk. Bodies were packed tight: pedestrians, marchers, onlookers. He imagined the air must be resounding with car horns and curses, chanting and cheering, the grinding of gears and the patter of voices in a hundred—no, a thousand—different conversations, just on this one city block. But all of it passed for him in the same cotton-filled bubble. He sometimes wondered if his feet were even touching the ground. Just as it occurred to him that he had lost Yeats, the poet was there at his left elbow. They walked by rows of shoe-repair and fabric stores, delicatessens and taverns, barbershops and a five-and-dime.

As they fell into step, Michael continued: "This is the part where you come in, Mr. Yeats. We're both in transit from one world to another; from one Michael to another for me, and from life to death for you. We're like two fellows who meet in a train station, each waiting to catch a different train."

Yeats smiled—grudgingly, it seemed, but it was the first time Michael had been able to elicit a grin from the old poet. "You *are* making progress," Yeats said. "You're becoming quite the freethinker. And we are making progress, too. Madame Antonia is this way: I can feel her. A genuine psychic is like a beacon visible to travelers on the spiritual plane."

"We're back to the *spiritus mundi,* aren't we? Well, if you can get us to your Madame Antonia, you'll make a believer out of me."

"It's no wonder you left the seminary," Yeats said. "You haven't an ounce of faith in you."

"I left because—"

The reason, the exact moment, the impetus for all that was to come—it was just out of reach and fogged around the edges. This much he knew: He was in a large room with others dressed like him. Black cassocks, a blackboard, a bald priest, black-bound books open on the desks, black type on white pages. A spring day, one of the first truly warm days of the year, and inside were stone walls and philosophy but outside the sun was blazing and the hills were patterned in green. Another priest, with a paltry spray of red hair, was at the door. He was speaking to the bald priest, who looked directly at Michael and indicated with a curling of his finger that Michael was to rise and—

"I was summoned," Michael said. "Someone came for me and I was sent out."

"Expelled?" It was the most interested Yeats had seemed in Michael's schooling.

"I don't think so. I was sent for, then sent back. My throat was raw and tight. I could taste salt."

"Sad tidings?" Yeats said. "Perhaps some bit of bad news?"

Michael waved a hand to ward off any interruption. He was so close. He pressed his hands over his eyes. One moment of stillness. That would be enough to bring it all into focus. His feet moved automatically beneath him, as if each step were taking him closer to the edge of the pit in the center of his memory. He was about to peer into it and see what had been hidden from him all this—

With a rattling crash, Michael collided with a man stacking crates of oranges in front of a grocery store. Michael windmilled his arms and for a moment managed to keep his footing, but then he stepped on one of the oranges and went sprawling into a box of apples. Fruit rolled in every direction: there were apples in the gutter; oranges were juiced under the wheels of passing cars. Michael was laid out on the sidewalk, his palms and knees badly scuffed. Before he could right himself, the grocer, a big man with a boxer's nose and the arms of a comic-book hero, hoisted him up by the collar. Michael crossed his arms in front of his face to ward off the punch he feared was coming, but the man kept shaking him while his jaw opened and closed in what even Michael could tell was a torrent of curse words. Michael's collar tore loose from his shirt and when the grocer made a grab for his arm—the final prelude to a punch—Michael wriggled free of his jacket and dashed for the intersection. The traffic was against him but he turned his head right-left-right and plunged forward. He was not hit by a cab or flattened by a lorry, and when he reached the next sidewalk, he pressed on, weaving through men and women caught up in the late-afternoon bustle. Only after he crossed the next street did he pause to look behind him. There was no sign of the grocer. Michael slumped against a streetlight, his lungs burning and his stomach ready to empty itself.

He had outrun the grocer but he had also outrun Yeats. He took another deep breath and tried to compose himself. All around him people and cars and buses jostled and he could hear none of it. He could smell hot asphalt and human sweat, the exhaust of automobiles, the dank rot of rubbish bins, and the moldy stink of the storm drains. The subway rumbled beneath the massed drumbeat of the millions walking this lattice of streets. All he heard in his head was a faint whooshing, like the whisper of a seashell, and his ears registered only the muffled pressure of the deep-sea diver. That it was better than the Noise was his only consolation.

He had left the hotel looking like an uptown swell, but now, with his clothes in disarray and blood trickling down his shin, he was beginning to look like a downtown tramp. One pant leg was ripped at the knee. His collar was torn and his shirt was plastered to his sides like papier-mâché. His face was slicked with sweat and his hair roostered off his head.

He figured the best course was to return to the hotel. Let Yeats find his own way back. But when he checked his pockets for the card that had been his ticket home on Monday morning, he found only a few green-inked American dollars. His jacket—that's where the business card was stowed. The only way he would see the jacket again would be to retrace his steps, make a silent apology to the grocer, and offer whatever was in his pockets as payment for the squashed oranges and bruised apples.

"Are you ready to continue our search?"

Michael flinched in surprise, then looked up from dusting off his clothes. "Why didn't you warn me that I was about to run into that ape?"

"You didn't want to be disturbed."

"And you picked that moment to listen to me? We need to work on your omniscience."

The two resumed walking, and although Michael's vision of the seminary had brought him to the brink of so many lost memories, he could not find his way back to that spot. He trailed behind Yeats, growing more certain with each step that this mad errand had been a grave mistake. He wondered, too, where Francis had gone, and when he would see him again. This was without a doubt the longest day of his life—or the longest that he could remember, and it troubled him that the two were not necessarily the same.

The steady, silent march with Yeats wasn't making the time pass any faster. Michael jogged to pull even with the poet. "I have another theory, you know. One that explains your presence, too: Virgil and Dante. A dead poet, a man who has lost his way."

"Don't you find that a bit presumptuous?"

"Casting you as Virgil? I think you've earned it."

"No. Casting yourself as Dante." Yeats walked a few paces in silence, then cleared his throat. "Tell me, Mr. Demp—"

"Michael. It's just Michael."

"When you *could* speak, Michael, did you talk quite this much? And in this manner? What I mean to ask is: Did you drive your friends absolutely mad? Or were you simply without friends?"

Michael stopped. Yeats did not seem to notice and continued walking.

"You can be very cruel, Mr. Yeats," Michael called after him. "Especially to those who you think are lesser than you."

Yeats turned, a sour expression puckering his face. He, too, seemed wearied by all of this walking, and now this unpleasant turn in the conversation. He sucked at the inside of his cheek and gave Michael a slow, top-to-bottom inspection, then resumed walking.

Michael stifled a curse. Whatever he was feeling—anger, sadness, despair—had come on quickly and boiled behind his eyes. Was this another effect of Whatever Happened? He didn't remember himself being so moody, so mutable.

Varium et mutabile semper femina flashed through his head. His father sitting in the chair beside Michael's bed in Ballyrath, reading from a leather-bound *Aeneid* before Michael drifted off to sleep. *Varium et mutabile semper femina.* Hermes says this of Dido—*Woman is fickle, always changing*—when he urges Aeneas to desert her to fulfill his destiny, before she, in anguish, throws herself on the pyre. There was an oil lamp burning beside the bed and his father was hunched low, close to the flame and close to Michael. He read in a steady cadence, first in Latin and then in English. Michael must have been young—not yet ten—because there came a time when his father would read to him only in Latin. But in this moment the house was quiet except for his father's voice chanting dactyls and spondees and the buffeting of the wind against the panes. Outside, the darkness had claimed the house, but inside, Michael was warm beneath his eiderdown and safe in the boats of the Trojan exiles. Da rarely directed conversation his way, and this was why Michael loved to hear his father read: for the uninterrupted presence of his calm voice, untainted by anger.

"Michael," he said. Then again. Then louder, but hoarse, not like his father's voice. "Michael."

Michael shook himself: It was Yeats. Not his father at all.

The details of the memory lingered—his father, the *Aeneid,* the cottage—but he was no longer inside the moment. Did Da know what had happened to Michael? Had Francis notified him? Did his father know that he was the only one in the family still on Irish soil?

Yeats cleared his throat, a habit Michael had grown tired of enduring. "Perhaps I spoke too harshly," Yeats said, "but you must admit—"

"Admit?" Michael said, and here the edge in his voice grew sharper. "I *admit* that I have tried to introduce some levity, to make our time together more bearable, and perhaps even pleasant. But you, however, are determined to increase our measure of misery and isolation by acting at all times like a hoary old bollocks."

"Now listen here—"

"Why should I listen when you've not heard a word I've said in all this time?" Michael wanted his voice to boom, but he was too frail. He was shrill, his eyes wild. He did not care. "I am lost, Mr. Yeats. I don't know where I am or why I was brought here. I don't know where my brothers are, or how to find them. Until very recently, I didn't even know who I was. My past has been lost to me, and I do not know how I came to be the way I am. If you can help me get—get *found*, then by all means, help. But if you're going to sneer down your nose and *ahem* at me, and interrupt every moment that brings my past into view, then please—please—pop off back to whatever celestial sphere you came from. And when you get there, ask them to send Virgil or Keats or Lord Byron in your place. Someone with a trace of human feeling left in them."

Yeats blinked behind the frames of his spectacles. With his beak of a nose, he had seemed birdish, an eagle. But there wasn't anything aquiline about that blink. Owlish, that was the word for it. "Do you suppose," Yeats said, and here his voice came out smoothly, slowly, "that you are the only one troubled by our situation? Some months ago I bade farewell to this world. I had come to the end of my earthly journey and believed that a new journey was about to begin, one which would allow for the decoding of mysteries I had contemplated all of my life. And now I find myself not in some celestial sphere, as you call it, but in a cesspit of a city where my only companion confuses cracking wise with wisdom. And so I too am struggling to maintain my sense of bonhomie, which I will admit was in short supply even when I lived among my dearest friends."

The two stood in front of a weather-beaten brownstone. A pitted terra-cotta balustrade led up to double doors coated in flaked green paint. Beneath the stoop, an iron gate barred entrance to the apartment below. In the front window, lace curtains parted and an old woman peered into the street. When Michael met her gaze, she closed the curtains and withdrew.

"I will make an effort to be more courteous," Yeats said, "but I am certain that our search for answers—answers that will benefit us both—lies this way." He pointed down the street, deeper into the unknown city.

Yeats might have wanted answers to the state of things, but Michael wanted only to get back to the way things were. Not back to the seminary or even to Ballyrath—just back to being himself. If he were to wake tomorrow, his senses intact but no memory of how any of it had happened, he would call off the search, he would ask no questions, and he would merely live.

THE WORLD'S FAIR

AFTER THREE HOURS ON the balcony of the Savoy Pavilion, Hooper's mind had started to wander. Here he was, one of the star
attractions at the World's Fair, but it had to be said: The gig was a
snooze. *What's that you say, Professor?* No sooner did he stretch the
truth—thinking he was some kind of star—than he heard Lorena's
voice in his mind, calling him on it. *Oh, so you're the big attraction?
Don't let it go to your head, Professor.* He knew she loved him, but that
woman could cut him to the quick like no one else. She was the only one
who still called him Professor, like it was his given Christian name. Others had knocked it down to Fess, a mark of honor in its own way (or so
he told himself). You had to be somebody to get a nickname, the kind
that stuck, the kind that other people recognized: Satchmo, Count,
Duke. He had been tagged "Professor" during his first months in Harlem by one of the old-timers at Monroe's. If anyone asked, Hooper said
it was on account of the years he'd spent at Howard, before he left school
to become the next Louis Armstrong. If you asked the regulars at any of
the late-night jam sessions, they'd say it was because Fess Hooper was
always trying to tell you what was what and how to do it properly.

But that was after hours, and this was his day job: five days a week,
dressed like a rail-riding hobo, blowing into a dinged-up bugle while a
pair of dancers gave a preview of what was waiting inside. Paying customers got a bigger, better-dressed band and even more dancers whirling
through the Lindy Hop, the big apple, the mutiny, and other steps made

famous at Lenox and 141st Street. In the front windows of the pavilion, life-size marionettes herky-jerked through the big dances of the day, while along the side, beneath big red letters that proclaimed THE WORLD'S GREATEST COLORED DANCERS, Hooper and his bandmates did their thing. It was jim-dandy with Hooper to make the dancers the center of attention, but he wished that more thought had gone into the music on the balcony—a set list that he had complained was little more than hoots and hollers. So while his horn pumped out one tune after another, his mind would wander away from the pavilion and around the Amusement Zone, where the Savoy jostled for attention with the Parachute Jump and the Drive-A-Drome, Skee Ball and the Silver Streak.

The brochures and the big talkers could say that the mission of the fair was to usher in a new era of peace between nations or to showcase the abundance and industrial might of America's great corporations, but they were wrong on each count. The Amusement Zone was the sticky-sweet, candy-apple heart of the whole operation. Maybe the fair proper, with its Trylon, Perisphere, and Futurama, had its eyes fixed on the world of tomorrow, but the Amusement Zone, with its carnival barkers and twenty-five-cent thrills, was all about the world of today, and offered the clearest picture of what poor, restless, down-at-the-heels America truly wanted. After years of scrimping and making do, America wanted a thrill. America wanted pizzazz. America wanted to have a good time.

Is that all, Professor?

End of lecture, Lorena. And now back to the tour.

Just down the lane from the Savoy Pavilion was Little Miracle Town, with its tiny houses, tiny horses, and tiny people. Around the corner was the Sun Worshippers court, where near-naked white girls lounged on chaises and frolicked among the trees while fairgoers snapped pictures of these free-spirited natural wonders. If that didn't beat all, bare-breasted women posed in the Living Magazines exhibit and twirled in the Crystal Lassies building, and if your tastes ran to the more exotic, there were topless mermaids on one side of the

Amusement Zone and topless Amazons on the other. But he let his mind wander past all of that—just as his feet would follow in another few hours—because even in New York, the powers that be weren't so keen on black folks gandering at naked white girls. Next on the tour were the Chinese acrobats and the Seminole Village, then the two-story chrome cash register that logged the fair's attendance as if every visitor were another coin in the drawer. The tour of the zone always led back to Frank Buck's Jungleland, which was the biggest nonsense of all. Maybe the apes on Baboon Island were the real thing but one peek at those elephants and Hooper knew they were Indian, not African—*You just have to look at their ears,* he had said to Lorena.

Yes, Professor, she'd said. *Gotta look them in the ears if you want to know what's what.*

But that wasn't even the worst of it. Those real live African tribesmen, dressed in leopard skins and beating their conga drums? One of them was a neighbor on 130th, Harlem-born and Harlem-bred.

HE HAD SET it up with the other horn player to cover his Saturday shift so he could play the wedding gig, which was a whole different brand of nonsense. Lorena had already made him promise to be long gone from Woodlawn by nightfall—she knew where the city's color lines were drawn—but the job paid better than a day at the fair and even Lorena couldn't argue with that. He'd heard one of the old lions at Minton's talking about making seventy-five a week when he played with Ellington at the Cotton Club during Prohibition, but no one had seen scratch like that in ages. Nowadays a man showed up from points south, horn in hand, ready to blow up a storm, only to learn a lesson as soon as his feet touched Harlem ground. The clubs where the colored folks had their fun didn't pay much. It was hard to get the big dollars out when the big spenders weren't the ones coming in. The downtown clubs paid better, but they wanted white folks in the seats and white faces in the band; looking out for their own by looking only *at* their own. Sure, there were exceptions: since Basie had held court at the Famous Door, most of Fifty-Second Street had gotten wise and made room for one or two of Harlem's finest on their bandstands. And once you made a name for yourself, there was Europe. Duke was there now, as was Lester Young. Hooper had dreams of a European tour of his own someday, when he and Lorena would sip champagne at the top of the Eiffel Tower. They would raise their glasses in the direction of Baltimore and say, *How do you like me now?*

So you could say that things were changing, but they weren't changing fast, and if you wanted to get into what it was like outside New York—take, for example, Miami, where a black man couldn't be on the streets after nine at night without a note from a white man explaining—

And that was just the sort of lecturing that would put Lorena in stitches. *Yes, Professor,* she would say. *I am taking notes.*

As for this Martin Dempsey, Hooper couldn't tell if he was a joker or just plain simple. Like when Hooper asked him about quitting Chester Kingsley and Martin said, *Then you take it. Here. It's yours,* like that was something that could happen in this world. Like the worst-paid seat in Kingsley's outfit wouldn't bc the best payday Hooper had ever seen. If Dempsey knew what he was saying, then he was cold-blooded. And if he didn't—if he hadn't caught on that the brownest guy in the Kingsley band was maybe half Italian—then he was flat-out ignorant. Or maybe it was because he was Irish. America was a strange land, and it could take a man a while to figure out just how strange.

A bullet-headed white man snapped Hooper out of his mental ramblings. He shouted, "Hey, go, daddy-o!"—trying out the hep-cat slang he had likely read about in *Life* magazine. In his Sears and Roebuck shirt and fresh-pressed trousers, he laughed at his own joke and looked from side to side for a smile or nod or a *You got that right.* Around him, a sea of white faces squinted into the sun and the sun kept right on burning.

Hooper could only shake his head. These folks might bring a taste of the Savoy home with them to New Haven or Pleasantville or White Plains, but they would never see the Savoy for themselves. They didn't know that they were getting but a keyhole view of what Willie and Dolores could really do—and that if you gave them a dance floor and a full band to fuel them, they could do more than dance: they could fly. Sure, Lindbergh had hopped across the Atlantic but these dancers did him one better. They did it without wings.

When Hooper had landed the pavilion job, he thought of it as a foot in the door, but he had been playing in that ramshackle jug band since April and no one had mentioned him sitting in at the Track, no matter how he blew his horn. It was a long way from Flushing Meadow to Harlem and even Hooper's sound couldn't carry that far. Just the other night, after they had run into Martin and his brother at the bar, he told Lorena that maybe he should think about quitting the fair. "Some days I feel like I'm a monkey in the zoo," he said.

Lorena rolled her eyes and gave him that laugh. "Monkeys gotta eat too," she said.

Still, there were times when his mind didn't wander, when he kept body and soul together, shut his eyes, and wrapped himself in the music. Then he wasn't playing outside in the hot sun for sweating tourists who stared and moved on. He was following the bass line like it was a bright path through the darkness and every drumbeat another step forward. The piano was another traveler on that path and sometimes they raced, sometimes they danced, sometimes they walked and told stories—joyous, sorrowful, and shades of blue in between. He wanted to stay in these moments, but these songs had a logic of their own. The Savoy Pavilion had to stick to its schedule: twenty minutes of music and dancing and then the fairgoers had to move on. To the Aquacade or the Music Hall, Penguin Island or Sun Valley, Old New York or Merrie England or, Lord help them, to Jungleland.

THE BOWERY

*D*ON'T STARE, LILLY. IT's not polite. Lilly could still hear her mother's voice whenever she caught herself looking—no, staring—at another person. It wasn't polite, but it was necessary. She walked through the city, patient as a coiled spring for the right gesture, glance, or convergence of bodies and objects. Moments before, on the street outside the Automat, she had found just such a convergence—the fruits of staring, she would happily admit.

She had photographed the man on Houston Street straight on. He'd caught her eye because of the simple irony of his situation: a man with an extravagantly unkempt, almost Prussian mustache, holding a sandwich board for a shop that trafficked in electric razors. Stubble like iron filings clung to his cheeks, chin, and neck. He resembled a penniless officer in a nineteenth-century novel, one of those fat books by some brooding, Christ-mad Russian. The picture was funny, in a quick, droll sort of way, but as she continued to stare at the man, the simple irony began to fade. The sandwich board obscured his body from his Adam's apple almost to the tops of his shoes. There was no visible evidence of arms, hands, knees. Those parts that made him a man—his heart, his gut, his cock—all of it had to be inferred. Which was always true, to some extent; didn't trousers, a shirt, and a jacket require a similar leap of faith? And here was the part that Josef would love: the man had erased 95 percent of his visible humanity in service to a product he either chose not to use or could not afford—but just

315

as the sign rebuked him, he, in turn, undermined it. The photo could be a statement about the ways that industrial capital co-opted the soul while the self sought the means to sabotage—or at least make a mockery of—the terms of its own imprisonment.

Then again, it might just be a funny picture of a man in need of a shave, possibly even a man who couldn't read the words he'd been paid a nickel to promote.

AFTER TAKING THE picture, she ducked into an Automat—not her sort of place, but the broad front window gave her a view of the street that made her feel like she was inside a giant glass camera. Two tables to her left, a woman huffed at a cup of coffee. Lilly's cup from the same urn had come to her watery and lukewarm, but this woman blew on hers like she'd been served directly from a steam pipe. She was small, narrow-shouldered and flat-chested—petite, if you were being polite; mousy, if you were not. She wore a pale blue blouse and her soft, dented cloche was a type that had not been stylish for half a dozen years. The woman's eyes were fixed on a book open flat on the table. It was clothbound, something from the public library, or perhaps one of her own, its dust jacket stored reverently at home where the jostling indignities of the daily BMT commute couldn't fray its crisp edges. She saw no rings on the fingers that encircled the cup. There were no bags from Macy's or Gimbel's, no sacks from the pushcarts, in the empty seat next to her. Had she taken a break from work? Was she stealing a few free moments outside some office, away from the other girls, away from the tyranny of the telephone and the pile of typing and filing mounted on one corner of her desk? And that book: Was it a romance full of white-throated maidens, torn bodices, and roguish highwaymen, all offering an escape from a world of apartments, elevators, bus rides, and outer boroughs? Or could it be a Bible? Was Lilly witnessing devotion amid the grab and gabble of the city? The woman's posture seemed somehow to fold in on itself, as if her shoulders could bend so far forward they would almost touch, like the covers of the book in front of her. All through this examination and dissection, the woman seemed not to feel the hot greedy glare of Lilly's eyes.

Lilly was studying the way shadows pooled in the hollows beneath her eyes when she saw a glint, a sudden flaring of light in all that shadow, that told her the woman was crying—or was about to. It had taken patience and the sustained effort of staring to realize that she had been looking at a woman who did not want to cry in a diner and who blew on her wan coffee not to cool it but in an attempt to stanch the tears that were boiling behind her eyes. Something in that moment of recognition plucked the silver filament that joined Lilly to the woman, and without warning, she raised her head from her book, her face naked and unguarded. The woman appeared startled, embarrassed, and then—what? Angry, wounded, violated? Before Lilly thought to express some kind of fellow-feeling or apology, her hand twitched and the Rolleiflex went *click*.

Lilly turned away, staring now only at the window. The blood thrummed in her veins, but it was not from being caught in the act of intruding on another's privacy. It was because she knew that the shot was a good one, and she was eager to see it emerge in the darkroom. Outside was a tumult of taxicabs and pushcarts and men and women waiting for the crosstown bus, but the window also threw back her own portrait. What would someone see in her? she wondered. What would a casual observer, or a dedicated starer, glean from the exterior she offered the world?

When she turned away from the window, the woman was gone and a young man had taken her place at the table. He was slight, though perhaps it was more charitable to call him trim, or compact, and his table was empty: no cup, no food, no book, nothing. He looked as if he had fallen into some trouble. His shirt was a deep ocean blue but

317

the tails were hanging half out, and the collar was torn like a broken wing. His necktie, a pennant of red silk shot through with bolts of silver lightning, hung askew. But what caught her attention wasn't the quality of his clothes or the state of their disarray. It was the way he stared—yes, a fellow starer—at the chair that sat across from him. There was something tragic about him, alone and disheveled among the shiny chrome surfaces of the Automat but determined to interrogate the furniture. She aimed the Rolleiflex, clicked the shutter, but she was not done with him. Those eyes and the sense he gave of a man who had fallen, or was in the act of falling, made her think of her studio, and her portraits, and how this could give her the one good reason she needed to delay packing for a few hours more.

"IT SEEMS THERE is someone here for you." Yeats pointed a finger and when Michael turned to look, a woman put a hand on his shoulder as if she knew him, and her lips formed some useless words.

She was older than Michael but not old. Her crimped black hair was pulled away from her face. Her eyes were huge and as dark and inky as her hair. She spoke again. She had a full mouth, high cheekbones, and a nose that she must have hated when she was a girl. Michael thought of a shark's fin, the prow of a ship. If he were to share these thoughts with Francis—if he could ever share such thoughts again—his brother would screw up his face and say she sounded dreadful, but she wasn't. She looked regal, possessed of a swift beauty.

Michael managed a smile and the woman sat in the chair next to his. She had given up talking and had taken to staring hard at him. He feared she might think he was a nutter—he said as much to Yeats— and he pointed to his ears and then with both hands chopped the air in front of him: broken, empty, all gone. Then he touched his mouth and made the same sweep-it-all-away gesture. She squinched her eyes (*I understand, I'm sorry*) and he shrugged (*What can you do?*). She

smiled herself and then Michael did the same. Natural and spontaneous this time. The woman had a boxy camera slung around her neck
and after some fussing in her handbag she came out with a fountain
pen and a feathery blue airmail envelope, both of which she offered to
Michael. He shook his head and rubbed both hands over his temples,
and she nodded to show that she understood.

She stood and Michael felt a surge of panic. She couldn't leave, not
when they were getting on so well. But she held out a hand and it was a
hand that said not *Good-bye* but *Come with me* and that's what Michael
did. He looked to Yeats's side of the table for some guidance but the old
man had disappeared. The thought suddenly struck him that she might
be as ghostly as Yeats, which was why she'd been able to grasp his mean-
ings so quickly, based only on a few choppy gestures. But her hand felt
solid enough. Her fingers were long and delicate, though the nails were
blunt. As short as his own, in fact. He held her hand as he rose from the
table and when he was on his feet she took his arm and guided him out
of the diner. It wasn't chivalrous, but he let her push open the door, as a
test. He hadn't noticed Yeats opening doors or moving furniture, and
now that he thought about it, weren't ghosts always moving things
about? The seminarians all believed that St. Columbanus was haunted
by a wax-faced monsignor who had expired over a secret stash of French
smut and by the spirits of novices done in by some fatal combination of
sodomy, spoiled meat, and self-flagellation. Weren't they rumored to
spill books from the library shelves? Hadn't he, late at night, heard a stifled moan drifting from the lavatory, or the stairwell, or the empty room
at the end of the corridor?

SHE WAS BEING pushy, she knew that. Why, she was practically
abducting this boy from the café—an illiterate deaf-mute, of all
things! When she'd first seen the way he stared at that chair, so
intently, she'd wondered if he wasn't somehow addled. But his eyes

had a quickness to them, and who was she to pass judgments about staring? That alone should have told her that the two would hit it off—if that's what you could call leaving with a man, a boy, really, with whom she had never shared a word.

Now she was on the street, steering him arm in arm toward her studio, four blocks away. It was another in a string of bright, hot days. There were moments when the sky was so achingly clear and outlined the rooftops so distinctly that the buildings seemed positively radiant, as if the skyline had been etched with a chisel and thrown into relief by this shimmering blue backdrop. Beneath this sky, the private parks and pocket-size plots burst with flowers that had been gorging themselves on sunshine and heat. Whatever miseries the people on the street nursed in their hearts, they had the consolation of being in a living city, a city that was racing forward. This vitality, which Lilly had so loved, now only reminded her of what she was leaving, and where she was returning to.

Lilly hadn't walked so close against the body of another, her feet falling into rhythm with his, since her last night in Prague. Her friends had thrown her a bon voyage party, where they had made toasts and said sweet and funny things about her, but really she would have preferred to skip it all and spend the night packing and repacking her suitcases and the large trunk that contained her equipment—everything she would need to create a replica of her home studio. The best part of the night was the walk with Josef, after the last toasts and the kisses and the hugs, each with its wet smell of the damp end-of-February air. They wandered away from the restaurant, tracing a languid path toward Lilly's flat. Arms linked, her head against his shoulder, they circled Wenceslas Square, passing the café where they had first met, then strolled to the middle of the Charles Bridge, watched over by bronze saints who raised their hands in greeting, or warning. The night was quiet and the lights glittered on the river. Everything around them was so serene that it was easy to believe the city was sleeping, rather than brooding, and that in that dreamy space they could walk unobserved—feet ticking on the cobblestones, the city theirs alone—to a room with an empty closet and trunks labeled for transit lying at the foot of a soft bed. Her train left the next morning. A week later the Wehrmacht would enter Prague unopposed.

A BLOCK FROM Lilly's studio they passed an empty lot like a missing tooth in a row of dingy tenements. The buildings were bandoliered by fire escapes that sagged into the street, and at the back of the lot, laundry hung in lines above piles of trash. Boys filled the space, yelling and hooting—a baseball game was in its fourth inning and the Giants were staging a rally. Some of the boys were stripped to their undershirts. Others wore knickers and had their sleeves rolled above their elbows. The ground was pounded smooth, and the improvised bases marked a rough-cut diamond: a cigar box for first, a lid from a bakery tin for second, a square of folded and stained canvas at third, and for home plate, a hardback book spread facedown, half its pages torn out and gold letters still visible across its cracked spine.

The pitcher, a gangly kid, went into his windup and fired the ball fast and straight. The batter should have mashed it into the pile of broken furniture and old tires out among the pennants of Tuesday's wash. But he was late with his swing and he popped the ball foul. It went up and up and drifted like a lost balloon toward the street. Michael and Lilly had paused to watch the game and both followed the lazy arc of the ball against the charred brick and scuffed brownstone. One of the boys darted toward the sidewalk, his hand outstretched, as the others cheered or booed him. Michael had never so much as seen a baseball game before, had never caught a ball like this in his life, but he reached out a hand and waited for it, thinking it would settle inevitably into his palm. The boy's world in that moment was the ball and only the ball, and as he neared Michael he lunged and grasped the ball in his open hand, crashing into Michael and sending him sprawling into a pile of bricks and broken timbers.

Michael opened his eyes to shattered brick and splintered wood, and that's when the shock hit him. Déjà vu more intense than any he'd ever felt. Something about these objects, the angle of his view. He saw it all happening again—the bright flash, him reeling, the pieces of what was once a building flying all around him. Was this a memory? A premonition? He tried to hang on to it, to pick it clean of details, but it receded as quickly as it had come. He shook himself and attempted to sit up. The blow had knocked the wind out of him and his arm tingled as though crawling with a thousand ants. He would need to ask Yeats about this. Yeats knew something about visions.

The woman stood over him now, concern written across her face. She shouted and pointed and swatted two of the boys on the head, then pulled them back when they tried to retreat. The boys hauled Michael to his feet and he found that he could stand unaided. He made a show of dusting off his sleeves and adjusting his tie. *I'm fine, I'm fine.* He straightened his trousers and presented himself for inspection. The woman's face softened and with her thumb she dabbed at a spot on his cheek. The boys returned to their game. Michael crooked his arm and Lilly slid her hand around his elbow. From across the street, you would have thought they were sweethearts.

Lilly stopped at a four-story building that ran half the length of the block. A spandrel of soot-blackened terra-cotta crowned the entrance: TAPSCOTT NEEDLE CO. The letters were curvaceous, their serifs blooming into leaves and flowering buds. Flanking each side of the name was a bobbin of thread with a single strand that looped through a needle's eye, the only ornamentation on a building that was otherwise grimy brick and smudged glass. The first three floors were still occupied by the needle trades, though none operated under the Tapscott name. That business had gone bust in 1930. The current tenants made ladies' undergarments on the first floor, men's hosiery on the second, and canvas belts and straps on the third.

On the fourth floor was Lilly's studio, a vast space interrupted only by columns that ran in two rows from one end to the other. The rest was brick walls, wide-planked floors, high ceilings, and a broad bank of windows facing the street. Lilly had done her best to clean the windows with newspaper and white vinegar, but there was so much grit on the outside that she could not scour away. She had planned to use the studio only for her work, but the water closet that she intended for a darkroom included a toilet and a sink large enough to be a tub. She could wash her clothes here, could provide for her hygiene. She had a daybed in the corner farthest from the nighttime lights that bled in from the street and the sun that poured through the windows in the morning. Perhaps it wasn't a respectable neighborhood, but to Lilly, the studio felt airy and full of possibility.

"HAVE YOU CONSIDERED that she may be a harlot?" Yeats said. He was leaning against one of the columns and polishing an apple on his sleeve.

Michael gaped. "She doesn't seem the type—does she?"

Yeats reviewed the facts: Michael had been taken by a woman he did not know to a room in a neighborhood that could be charitably described as seedy. No words had been exchanged, but it was likely that the woman sensed from Michael a certain willingness to be led.

"Janey Mack." Michael's voice was a hot whisper. "A harlot."

"I take it this is to be your first experience of sexual congress?" Yeats took a loud, crunching bite of the apple.

Michael gave him a puzzled look. "My—well—wait a minute: Why are you eating?"

"The fruit plucked from the branch," Yeats said. "The Edenic overtones. I thought you would appreciate the reference."

"Even if you're right about this," Michael said, "you can't stay. That is out of—"

"I'll excuse myself, though I don't imagine it will be a lengthy absence."

Lilly had been sorting through a cabinet where she stored plates of film and the flashbulbs for the mirrored eye that perched above the camera. Now she was at Michael's side. She led him by the arm across the room, away from the door. "If you wouldn't mind," she said. "Could you come over here?"

Michael craned his head back toward Yeats. "What is she saying?"

"Words of love." Yeats took another bite from the apple.

Michael looked from Yeats to the woman's face. In the time they had spent together, he had believed there was some connection between them. He was able to seize on her meaning, and it seemed that she could read him, could know him, without need for words. Now he wondered if all of this had been a deception, merely the tools of her trade. Not that he didn't want to—to—know her. He had wanted this moment—well, perhaps not this exact moment, but the shedding of his virginity, the touch of a woman. It had boiled in his blood for years. He had imagined—he had hoped, dreamed, prayed even—that it would be Eileen. When he thought of her now, her image came in flashes. Her face flushed from running, the wind-flattened grass all around her. Eileen kneeling at the rail to receive Communion, her eyes shut and her tongue out, while he, the altar boy, held the brass patent beneath her chin. Eileen, dressed all in black, her face black-veiled. But when had that happened? He knew the other moments and what surrounded them, but Eileen all in black? Again he wondered if this was a memory or a premonition. Or was it a dreamy reminder that things between them were over, were dead, could never be?

And if all of that was over and done, then why not this? Why not with this woman? Must he be a monk to punish himself? Hadn't he already tried that?

The bed against the far wall was small but neatly made. Michael took a deep breath, let out a long sigh.

He was an odd boy, that was for certain. One minute he was animated and elastic, all smiles and raised eyebrows taking the place of words. She would even have called him quick-witted. He seemed to notice things that others ignored or looked straight through. Hadn't he been delighted, even consumed, by those boys and their game? His eyes had tracked that white ball up into the air, and his face—his mouth an O in wonder—had almost broken her heart. But when they entered the studio he became grave and distracted. His mind seemed to be fixed on a spot on the wall, or one of the columns, or her bed. She steered him to the space where the camera, a large box on a tripod, faced a single chair. With a hand on his shoulder she asked him to sit and it was as if she had snapped him out of a sound sleep. He looked at her and then the chair and then the camera and some knowledge of the situation registered and he bobbed his head: *Yes, yes, yes, of course.* He blushed, and she saw Josef in his features. Dark hair, dark eyes, the angled cheekbones, the high forehead. She brushed a hand over his temples, smoothed his hair. She posed his shoulders, squaring him to the lens, and retreated a few steps to consider the light, his posture, the way to approach this shoot with a subject who wouldn't be able to hear the direction she had given to the others who sat in this spot: *I want you to think of a question you have always wanted answered.* For a moment, his eyes roamed over her face, her body, before becoming fixed again.

"You were wrong, Mr. Yeats."

Yeats stood beside the camera. There was no trace of the apple. "It was a fair guess, given the facts at hand."

"Did you really think she was a harlot?"

"I did," Yeats said. "But I've been wrong about women in the past."

She looked at Michael through the viewer, checked his position in the frame. Her subjects often had dreamy looks on their faces as they pondered the question, wondering either what they would ask or what their answer would be. She wanted to catch him in one of those moments when his eyes danced, absorbing the world around him, but this stare seemed as much a part of who he was as that other side. And she knew she couldn't force it. She never told her subjects to smile, or not to smile, or to do anything but think about the question. It was a way of distracting them from the business of having their picture taken. But this boy was already distracted. She activated the shutter, cued the flash.

Light erupted where Yeats's head had been only a moment before. Michael felt himself swallowed by it. His arms and legs, then his body and his head, all fell away from him. For a moment everything went white, and then all was blackness.

HELL'S KITCHEN

I'M GOING TO STRETCH my legs. That's what Cronin had told the string bean with the ginger hair, the one who'd been so careless with his name that first night in the city.

"And what am I supposed to tell Mr. Gavigan when he gets here?"

"You tell him I'm stretching my legs," Cronin said.

It was a sign that Gavigan had slipped in the past few years: the quality of the men he kept around him. When Cronin had first fallen into his orbit, Gavigan controlled a thriving bootleg-liquor business on the city's west side. He had men on the docks, he worked in cars, had a piece of construction, too. Wherever the money was. He wasn't a kingpin on the order of the bigger Italian outfits, but he had his own domain and he kept a close eye on its comings and goings. Even in the days before Cronin stepped off the train on the way to Albany, though, Gavigan's sphere was shrinking. Repeal had been a blow, sure, and Gavigan had been too old, too slow, too old-fashioned, to make a move into prostitution, narcotics, hijacking. Cronin watched one man after another defect. Indignities were visited upon Gavigan that a year or two earlier would have been Cronin's to punish. Each loss of the empire only made the old man more desperate to keep what remained. Not one to ease himself into the grave, he was sure to go out cursing and thrashing.

In the old days, the kid at the garage would have learned to shut his trap or someone would have dumped him into the river. *Where's Red,* one of the fellas would ask. *Oh, he's walking to New Jersey.* The others on the Gavigan payroll would have had a good laugh at that one.

And then there was this Jamie. He was hard to figure, but Cronin could see he was no fool. There had to be some flaw in the design that had marked him for service to Gavigan instead of one of the bigger players in the city's winner-take-all sweepstakes. Hadn't Gavigan always surrounded himself with misfits, castoffs, men with nowhere else to go? Cronin knew all about that.

Two blocks from the garage, Cronin slotted the coins into a pay phone and put his fat finger in the dial. He still carried the page from the phone book, each Dempsey checked off but one. The telephone rang twice. There was a pause, followed by a faint click—the sound of a woman removing an earring.

When the woman answered, Cronin asked to speak to her husband.

"He's not available," she said. "May I take a message for him?"

Cronin had half a mind to hang up. This was madness, to be calling the Dempseys. "Could you tell him to look in on his youngest brother?" he said finally.

"Is something wrong? Is Michael all right?"

"Just tell your husband that he needs minding."

"Who is this?" she said. "And where's Francis?" The woman seemed to think this was a conversation.

"Ma'am." His voice was like a door slamming. "Tell him this: Michael is at the Plaza Hotel under the name MacFarquhar."

"Pardon me," she said, "but how is that spelled?"

"It's spelled like it sounds," he said. "MacFarquhar. Room seven-twelve. Have you got that? Seven, one, two."

Cronin placed the receiver back in its cradle. He had been grinding his teeth since the moment he'd dialed the first number, and his jaw ached like he'd been socked. Was he ever going to be rid of the Dempseys? Could he ever cut himself free of Gavigan? One led to the other and then it all doubled back to the beginning—Dempsey to Gavigan to Dempsey to Gavigan—until the words melted into one string of nonsense that would echo in his ears as long as he lived.

He wondered if the youngest Dempsey had found his way back to the hotel. How difficult could it be? All he had to do was walk down Fifth Avenue and he couldn't miss it. But he thought again of Francis's panic at leaving his brother on his own. There was something wrong with the boy—Cronin had seen it. He had left the boy exposed and alone once before, back in Cork, and now he had done it again. He wanted to believe that none of this mattered to him, not a whit, but of course it did.

He should call Alice. He had coins enough in his pocket and he had not spoken to her since their hasty farewell at the depot. Her voice would shore him up. Or else it would completely undo him. Right there was the reason he could not call, and there was this, too: Alice would hear in his voice a change. She would hear that Cronin had become a man she did not know. Not that he had changed into something new, but that he was changing back into what he once had been. The man it had taken him years on the farm to un-become.

THE BOWERY

WHEN LILLY EMERGED FROM under the hood at the back of the camera, the boy was crumpled at the base of the chair like a broken doll. For a moment she feared that the flash had been fatal, that the camera had fired some bolt of energy, Tesla-like, into his heart. She looked down at this stranger—his white shirt and torn pants, his limbs splayed and his mouth gaping, his thick shock of black hair tousled across his face—and she gasped: He was the image of Josef. Is that what she was seeing? A vision of Josef's fate? "Josef!" she cried out. "Josef, get up!"

There was a catch in his throat, and his chest rose. Lilly's eyes filled with tears as she knelt beside him. Her sobs shook her to the floor. Yes, she had always been superstitious—a harmless foible, something she and Josef laughed about—but for weeks she had been so desperate for a hopeful sign that her nerves had been rubbed raw. The fate of the world—her world, at least—depended on how many pigeons roosted on her windowsill, and which would be the first to take flight.

Now here was this changeling boy and with one flash of light, the spark of life had almost gone out of him. But what was she to do? She knew no one and had no telephone, and she was certain that if she tried to carry the boy down the stairs it would result in his death or hers. He stirred, his eyes twitching and his lips trembling as if on the verge of speech, but he seemed unable to come to consciousness. Had he fainted? Did he suffer from fits? He needed bed rest, she decided,

330

because really, what other option did she have? As she dragged him to the daybed in the corner of the loft, she imagined what Josef would say about all of this: the absurdity of this boy she had waylaid, the sight of her hauling a stranger into her bed, and even how little of the studio she had reserved for sleeping, dressing, eating. *Ninety-five percent work, five percent personal,* he might have said. *That seems about right—for you.*

Satisfied that her guest was sleeping and not comatose, she went back to work, cataloging the negatives and the rolls of film she had not had the time to develop. She tapped out dates, locations, and brief notes on a typewriter she had purchased cheap at a street market. The Shift key was broken, so all of her letters were lowercase. As each page rose above the platen, she razored it into strips, which she glued to the lids of small cardboard boxes. The boxes were then carefully sorted and stacked inside a trunk, along with the cases custom-made to hold the Rolleiflex, the Leica, the Agfa-Ansco. The trunk was due to the shipping agent by noon Saturday. Her clothes could fit into a single valise.

This labeling allowed her to participate in Mr. Crabtree's notion about life in Prague. She would return to her studio, which would be just as she left it more than three months ago. Nothing would have changed, within the studio or without. Certainly the name of the nation had been effaced, but that was an issue for the cartographers, the typesetters, the sign painters. Lilly would need only to add these newly labeled boxes to the others—from Paris, Spain, Prague, and points in between—and everything would be neat and orderly, all in its proper place.

Sometimes Lilly thought she should board the ship with no luggage at all, nothing more than the clothes she wore. Let her months in America disappear like a dream, so that when she finally awoke in Prague she would have nothing to show for her time away. Perhaps that would make it possible to believe she had never left, but had only slept. With no mementos, no photographic proof of New York's exis-tence, she would have only a head full of dreams so real she took them for true but that, like all dreams, would fade with time.

Or she could abandon the studio and go west—the traitorous thought that had gnawed at her since she gazed out over the city. Disap-pear into America with nothing but the Rolleiflex and a few rolls of film. Would anyone look for her? She could go as far as California— Hollywood, even, where her knowledge of light and shadow could be useful. She would take a new name and sit in the constant sunshine. She would pluck oranges from trees and wear dark sunglasses and rely on the heat and the salt water to purge her memories of Prague. She would be a new person, tied only by her accent to the dark continent where, every generation, old hatreds fueled new wars. *Prague?* she would say while sitting by some crystal-blue swimming pool. *A lovely city. Pity, though. It can't seem to stay out of the way of history.*

There was another option, a halfway option: Paris. While many of her friends insisted that Germany had already lit the match and that one day Paris, too, would burn, others scoffed. Germany might gob-ble up the little nations, they said, might even take a bite out of Poland, but it wouldn't look west. Meanwhile, the French had learned their lesson in the Great War. They would never take the field in defense of Czechoslovakia or any of the other newly hatched nations, these car-tographic daydreams. Perhaps an uncomfortable feeling of stalemate would hang over the Continent and its many flavors of fascism, but Paris would still be Paris. The French bureaucracy, of course, wasn't leaving the fate of the city, or the country, to chance. No visas were being issued at the consulate, and certainly not to residents of former nations now under Nazi occupation. The French were going to sit out this tussle behind the safety of the Maginot Line, and they weren't going to do it with millions of refugees crowding their view of the battlefield.

Weary of typing and cutting, Lilly poured herself a glass of the cheap Chianti from the Italian market. She checked again on her guest, fast asleep in his torn clothes, and then stripped him of his shirt and trousers. With a needle and thread she repaired the knee of the pants as best she could. Her mother would have pulled them from her hands and done the sewing herself, and better: *Every woman must know how to make those minute alterations that make a dress fit her like no other.* Lilly had not cared much. Most of what she'd worn when she was younger shocked her mother with its shapeless, mannish utility. *You can try to dress like a man,* her mother would say, *but I don't know many men with breasts like yours.*

She switched off the lights and went to the window. The flat gray sky was obscured by the haze of the city. Across the street, lights burned in the tall windows of a garment factory during its third shift, and women hunched over their tables, each machine buzzing beside a pile of fabric, one side for the pieces and the other for the finished product. Lilly could feel the same activity in her own building. The floor of the loft hummed with the commotion of the machines. In her first week, the constant tremor had made her nervous—as if something was happening far off but moving closer, little by little. Now, however, she took comfort in that bass-note thrum, when she noticed it at all. It was the sound of women at work when the rest of the world was sleeping.

Sleep. Even Lilly needed to sleep. She crawled into the daybed next to the boy. She was surprised by how little of the bed he took up, and as she lay beside him, listening to the shallow sifting of his breath, she fell into a dreamless sleep.

THE PLAZA HOTEL

MARTIN SPENT THE AFTERNOON and into the evening working his way through the Midtown jazz clubs, dropping in on contacts who might know of a band in need of help: piano, clarinet, sax—he would even play kazoo if the price was right. Plenty of the guys wanted him to describe the look on Chester's face when Martin walked out, but none of them had a lead on an open seat. This business of lining up a plan B that might have to transform quickly into a plan A was going to take time. He wouldn't say a word to Rosemary until he had a concrete answer to the question of rent, food, shoes. And besides, he didn't want her to think he was having doubts about the hush-hush, can't-miss plan he'd been dangling in front of her since Saturday night.

He came home just before eight, expecting to get some credit for not staying out two nights in a row. Instead, Rosemary launched immediately into the phone call, reporting word for word what the mystery caller had said. She had already contacted the Plaza, she told Martin, and had the front desk ring the brothers' room. No answer, but all that meant was that Francis was elsewhere.

"The man on the phone," Martin said. "Was he Irish?"

"He had a brogue," she said. "And he said *minding*—that I should tell you your brother *needs minding*. That's Irish, not American."

"And there's been no word from Francis?" Martin said, but of course there hadn't been. Hadn't he warned Francis just last night that the IRA was sure to come looking for him and for its money?

"I think we should call the police," Rosemary said.

"And tell them what? That a man just telephoned and told me to visit my brother, who's staying at one of the finest hotels in the city?" He imagined the questions the police would ask, and the impossibility of answering them. The money, the aliases, Michael's condition, Francis's whereabouts—the list went on and on.

"Don't you think there's something fishy about this?" Rosemary said.

Of course he did, but he asked Rosemary to let him sort it out. It could all be a joke, a misunderstanding—some pal of Francis who had botched the delivery of a simple message. Francis was probably sitting in the Oak Bar right this moment regaling a Texas millionaire with tales from the Scottish Highlands. Martin hoped to put Rosemary at ease, but as he reached for his hat by the door, his hand was shaking. He gave Rosemary a quick kiss on the cheek and told her not to wait up. "Let me see what I can see at the Plaza," he said, as the door closed behind him.

IT WAS LATE by the time he arrived at the hotel. The front-desk clerk was unwilling to hand over a key to the room, and when he called up, there was again no answer. Martin tried to explain the circumstances— someone had called him to come for his brother, and a deaf-mute couldn't very well answer the telephone, now could he?—but the clerk was unmoved. Considering the hour, he said, wasn't it possible that his brother was sleeping? And wouldn't it be best to wait for His Lordship's return?

If Martin had to locate Francis before he could find Michael, then the hotel bar wasn't the worst place to start. He found a seat, shook a cigarette from its pack, and asked the bartender for a whiskey on the rocks. As he sparked his lighter, he heard a familiar voice from a figure on his right, half slumped over the bar.

"Would you look at the riffraff they're letting in these days," Chester Kingsley said as he hauled himself upright.

Shite. Martin knew that sooner or later he would have to settle things with Chester, but he'd been hoping it could happen after he launched the new band and secured a regular spot in one of the city's best nightclubs. A tall order, but that's how he'd planned it.

"Martin, my boy. We need to talk—man to man." Wednesday was Chester's night off, and he'd apparently been drinking for hours. When drunk, he lost the vaguely British accent he employed on the bandstand to announce each selection—*And now, for your dancing pleasure, a little something called "Moonlight in Vermont."* With one hand on the bar, he ambled unsteadily to the stool next to Martin. He leaned in close, his breath clotted with bourbon and grenadine. "So what's next for the great Martin Dempsey?"

"I'll land on my feet," Martin said, half turning his face away from Chester.

Chester drained his highball and traced the glass in a circle over the bar, indicating another round. "Look here, you're either too cocky or too stupid to see how far you're going to fall—and how long it's going to take you to work your way back up."

"I'd like to make this an amicable parting of ways, Chester."

"So you don't like the music I play? You don't like the way I play it? It's not hot enough? Well, screw you, kid, you know-nothing sack of shit. I'm a king in this town—hell, in this whole country! Every week, coast to coast, people are listening to my music. My music! But that's not good enough for you?"

"Look, it's nothing personal. It's just not what I want to play."

"Oh, that's right. You're the fella who wrote that song that's driving the Negro hordes wild up in Harlem. Is that what I hear? Just don't expect it's going to lead to anything. You might be black Irish but I'll tell you this: Those Negroes stick by their own. Maybe you'll

see a few pennies from heaven, but in a week or two, when that colored bandleader — "

"Benny Carter," Martin said.

"—when that colored bandleader has rearranged some other
nobody's song? You're in for a long dry spell—unless you've got
another hit song up your sleeve, something you've been hiding from
the rest of the world all these years?"

"Like I said, don't worry about me. I've got plans — "

"I'm not worried about you, you dumb shit." Chester sipped from
his fresh drink. "You're a family man, aren't you? Got kids? A wife?
That's who I'm worried about. That's who *you* should be worried
about. You've got mouths to feed and you just gave away the best gig
of your life."

Martin bristled. "Don't tell me how to — "

"Because I've been there. I tell you, I've been there. And not because
I did something as stupid. No, sir. I had the rug yanked out from
under me by the goddamn kaiser himself."

"Okay, Chester. You've had enough."

"Klaus Klemperer," he said. "Did you know that was my name? My
real name? Nobody does, and it's a good thing, what with the shit that's
about to come raining down in Europe." Chester swirled the ice in his
glass like dice in a cup. "My first band was the biggest thing ever to hit
the Jersey Shore. Cape May to the Palisades, Poconos into the Catskills —
oh, we were something. Klaus Klemperer and his Royal Bavarian Band.
Oompah, waltz, polka, Dixieland—we did it all. This would have been
nineteen and thirteen, fourteen, fifteen. Sky was the limit, right?" He
took another drink. "Wrong. Goddamn Wilson sent the boys over
there—'Over There'!—and in one summer, it was all gone."

Chester's eyelids fluttered, and Martin thought for a moment that
his brief autobiography would end with a headfirst dive into the
darkly polished bar. It was just as well. Hadn't he been out all day

trying to gin up a plan B? He didn't need life lessons from Chester or Klaus or whoever he was.

"But I got it back," Chester said, his head snapping to attention. "I got it all back, with interest. You think any of that was easy? Chester Kingsley? The Kensington Hotel? You have no idea what it took to make that happen, you spoiled goddamn brat. You're marching in the parade at the end of the war but you don't know the first thing about being a soldier. And now look at you — quitting with no next thing? Tell your wife I'm sorry she married such a *Dummkopf*."

"I'm not done yet," Martin said, more defensively than he'd intended.

"You're young and you're stupid," Chester said, "and you don't know this, but life will get you. Sooner or later, life will punch you full in the face. It'll kick you in the balls and clean out your pockets. That's what life does. So I gotta wonder, why are you doing it to yourself?"

THURSDAY
JUNE 8

HELL'S KITCHEN

FRANCIS HAD BEEN STEWING in this room for God knows how many hours. It was clear that he wasn't the first man to be consigned to this ramshackle oubliette: a scuff line along one wall marked where other men had angled their chairs, hoping for a few moments of repose before whatever it was that awaited them. It was equally clear that some men had not bided their time with the composure that Francis sought to affect, or else hadn't been left alone for quiet contemplation. Another wall was marked with divots in the plaster that roughly matched the circumferences of fists, heels, heads. The concrete floor was spotted with rust-colored drip trails that Francis had at first thought to be paint before realizing their true provenance. The heavy wooden door, which bore no knob on this side, was scratched and scuffed all over with the signs of futile aggression. A single bulb burned overhead.

The sound of cars, of engines turning over and chassis squealing on their springs, infiltrated the room. Car horns honked in short taps and long, angry bleats. The air was hot and close, thick with the smell of petrol, scalded rubber, and grease. Men shouted not in anger but to be heard over the din of the cars and the hoods slamming and the heavy overhead doors rolling up and rolling down. A tailpipe backfired and the voices fell silent for a moment, followed by laughter, more shouting, men giving each other a hard time. Someone must have flinched, he thought, and now his mates were taking the piss out of him. The voices ebbed, overcome by the grind of gearboxes, revving engines, the clear ping of a wrench dropped on the concrete, the clatter of hubcaps spilling from a precarious stack.

From his ladder-back chair, Francis faced the cell's one brick wall, course over worn and flaky course. He followed the mortar, its network of right angles turning and climbing. The cell in Mountjoy had been built of sterner stuff: quarried stone blocks irregular in size and stacked impenetrably. He had spent hours, days, weeks staring at those walls, wondering how long it would be before he saw the outside again. His sentence was three years but he had known men to have months or years tacked on for misbehaviors intentional or otherwise. From the bottom left corner of his Mountjoy cell, the lowest course had run short block, short block, long block, then long, short, long, long, short. The course above that one went long, short, long, short, short, short, long, long, short. A random assortment, he knew, but over time he started to wonder if maybe there wasn't a pattern—a message, even—in the masonry. Shorts and longs. Wasn't that how Morse code worked? He still carried the sequence in his head.

Steady now. These were the moments when he saw how easy it was to slip into madness. A code in the masonry? The old-timers who walked in circles around the prison yard mumbling to themselves— no doubt they were working out the codes embedded in their cell walls. Anything to occupy the mind, to rescue you from the second-guessing and the desperate loneliness and the endless interrogation of what you shouldn't have done, or what you should have done with greater aplomb to avoid getting caught. Those thoughts could eat you up, turn you inward with never a way out.

But now this place. One brick after another. The pattern was brick, brick, brick, brick. The message was brick, brick, brick, brick. It would be neither an escape nor a diversion. There was only what you had done wrong, whom you had left behind, and who stood to get hurt.

He had known he was being pursued. Of course he had. Hadn't he been running since Ballyrath—and running even faster after the cock-up at the safe house? But he had allowed the immediate and robust success of the FC Plan to lull him into a state of calm. He thought again of the explosion, the disintegration of the farmhouse, the plume of smoke, and the stones and pieces of timber littering the site. And the bodies: three of the men from inside the house. Corpses, really. And then Michael. As soon after the blast as Francis was capable of yoking thought to action, he piled Michael's battered body into the automobile and threw the strongbox into the boot. Before he could crank the engine, a voice called his name—a raspy, death-soaked holler, proof that someone else had survived the disaster. He thought, for a split second, of giving aid, but the crack of gunfire erased that notion. Each volley of his name—*"Dempsey!"*—was punctuated by the report of a pistol. So he had left Ballyrath pursued by the church and the state, and he arrived in Cork with the IRA joining the chase. Was there anyone who wasn't hot to run him to ground?

And now Martin and his family were exposed to this danger. The man with the gun had named him. He knew where Martin lived. How could Francis warn him? And how could he protect Michael?

Ach! He had to shake himself out of this stupor! He had not given up when he was brought in chains to his father's funeral. He had not given up when the bombs laid waste the farmhouse and nearly killed Michael. He couldn't fold now. Hadn't he survived worse? Hadn't he, in fact, prospered?

A bolt was thrown and with a squeal the frame released its grip on the door. It was the big fellow from the museum, only now he had company: a smaller black-haired man with a face like a hatchet blade, all angles and planes, and standing behind them a truly old one dressed as if for a funeral in a gray suit, a coal-dark waistcoat, a flat spade of a necktie, and a plump gray fedora.

They brought Francis into a cluttered office furnished with a battered wooden desk, dusty stacks of carbons, cardboard boxes for auto parts, hand tools, greasy rags, and a map of the city pockmarked with pins. To the right of the desk was a pin-up calendar: April 1938, an apple-cheeked brunette carrying an umbrella and wearing nothing but a pair of bright yellow galoshes—just the sort of item Francis might have procured for a client in Dublin.

The old man lowered himself, with some effort, into the chair behind the desk and glared at Francis. "Do you know who I am?"

"As far as I can tell," Francis said, "you're some geezer who sends his thugs to snatch an innocent man off the streets. I've half a mind to set the police on you."

The old man's lip curled, almost a grin. "You do that, Mr. Dempsey. And then you can explain to the police how you escaped from prison, killed three men, stole their money, and entered the country on false papers."

"That's quite a story," Francis said. "You could take that to Hollywood."

The smaller man cuffed him across the mouth. Francis lunged at him, but the big fellow stepped between the two and pressed Francis flat against the wall. The old man's laugh was syrupy with phlegm. "You think you can fight your way out of here? My friend there made a name for himself in Spain, and Mr. Cronin, who you met yesterday, well—let's just say that his hands have been dirty since you were in short pants. Now sit down. You might have gotten the best of those mopes in Ireland, but I assure you we are a different breed in New York."

As if to prove that he had the situation in hand, the old man told the other two to give him a moment alone with Mr. Dempsey. The two stood outside the windowed door, the little one keeping an eye on Francis and Cronin with his arms folded across his chest.

"So now what?" Francis said. "You're packing me off to Ireland? Sending me back to prison?"

"Who said anything about prison? You belong in front of a firing squad, but the difficulty of transporting you back to Ireland makes that impractical." He let that sink in—let Francis believe that he was getting a reprieve—then continued: "So instead I'm going to have one of our friends there cut your throat and dump you in the river."

Francis looked at the two men standing outside. The big one was thickset like a storm cloud ready to burst, while the smaller one looked like a whip about to crack. He had a feeling it would be the little one.

"You and I both know it's only the matter of the money that's keeping you alive. But I am not a patient man. I'd sooner see justice done than wait to recover what you have stolen."

"I didn't steal—"

"You stole! And you murdered men fighting on your behalf!" He hacked loudly into a handkerchief. "How I wish your father could be here to see this. His own son, a thief and a traitor. It would serve him right."

First in Mountjoy, then at the funeral, and now here—the mention of his father's name brought with it benedictions and curses. When he saw Martin—no, *if* he saw Martin again—he would tell him for certain that Da had been up to his eyeballs in some kind of IRA business.

Gavigan coughed into his fist again and mopped his mouth with the handkerchief. The heat was rising in his face, but why lose his temper in front of this boy? He would be dead in a day. "That money belongs to a cause greater than yourself—and you are going to give us back every penny. It'll be the last honorable thing you do."

"What has that money got you but a houseful of eejits who blew themselves to pieces? That's who's going to liberate Ireland?"

"What do you know about it? A boy who plays dress-up with a pocketful of stolen money? When I was your age I was taking over this city."

"Look here, I'm not a week in this country and every door is open to me. I'm dining with millionaires! I've been invited to meet the god-damn king and queen! They've practically given me the key to the city. Any of your thugs—your soldiers for the cause—managed that?" He ought to shut his mouth now—*Don't involve the Bing-hams, keep Anisette clear of this mess*—but he had worked with men like this in Dublin, in Liverpool, in Belfast. Underworld bosses who sharpened their grudges to a razorous edge and who kept on the pay-roll hard men tasked with settling scores. They respected strength, a clever man who lived by his wits, but as in all things, you had to watch how far you pushed.

"More lies," Gavigan said.

"Ask the big fella. If he's been following me around, then he knows where I was on Monday night. A feckin' castle. And who do you think the family asked to escort them to their audience with the king?" He should have been more cautious, but the words kept pouring out.

"If you think this is going to save you—"

"Saturday at the World's Fair, close as I am to you. Though I expect the setting will be a little more...royal."

Gavigan remembered the folded newspaper, Russell and McGar-rity, the arrest, the king just across the river. "Are you working for Russell?" he said. "Is this what he's been cooking up?"

Francis was baffled. Whatever he'd said had set off the old man. And who the hell was Russell?

"What's he planning?" Gavigan said, his voice stormy. "Is this why he was in Detroit?"

Francis swallowed hard. He had Earl of Glamis'd it again.

"I'll get the truth out of you." Gavigan snapped his fingers and pointed to one of the men in the hall. Within seconds, Jamie was standing over Francis. "Now I'm going to ask you again: Are you working for Russell?"

"And I'm telling you—"

At this Gavigan nodded to Jamie, whose fist caught Francis full in the mouth. He tried to rise from the chair but Jamie hit him just below the eye, and when he tried again, a punch to the gut sent him in a heap to the floor.

"Take our guest back to the closet," Gavigan said. "I need a minute to think."

Gavigan was fuming. He was ready to cut the bastard's throat himself. But then he thought of his Sunday prayers, about having the smarts to make the most of whatever luck threw his way. Wasn't this some kind of answered prayer? Hadn't he asked for one last big score? Now, at the end of his life, God was saying, *Here you go, John. I'm making this one easy for you.*

Because if what Dempsey said was true—that he was going to stand within bowing distance of the king—then he could be very useful. Useful? He was a godsend. He could be the instrument by which Gavigan showed them all how it was done. Russell, McGarrity, the IRA Army Council, those Clan na Gael choirboys who took his money but would never let him enter the rolls of their little club, the whole lot of them. *You understand, Mr. Gavigan, that we can't give the authorities reason to suspect...Yes, Mr. Gavigan, but the practicalities...Of course, John, but the situation is delicate...Thank you, but the time isn't right.* He had carved a slice for himself out of the toughest city in the world and defended it against all comers. Could any of them say the same? Businessmen with clean hands, second-generation soldiers who had been children when the real fighting happened—that's what they were. But when men like Russell and McGarrity looked at him, they saw only a bagful of dollars, and they acted like it was a privilege for *him* to let *them*—these generals, these geniuses—make all of the decisions. They would see what a blow he could strike. It would be his last bold act, a lifetime's work culminating in a thunderbolt. This was bigger than the plan to bomb the cabinet, a louder rallying cry than a countryside uprising. Dempsey would hold the gun in his hand, but it would be the will of John Gavigan that pulled the trigger.

* * *

ONCE JAMIE LED Dempsey back into the room, Gavigan explained how it would happen. Francis would follow through on his plan to meet the king and queen, and when he reached the front of the line, he would level a gun at the king's heart and pull the trigger.

Even Cronin flinched. He looked at Jamie, then back at Gavigan. Had he heard that right?

"Are you completely loolah?" Francis said through his busted lip. "I'm not going to shoot the king."

A gargling noise rattled in Gavigan's throat. Pure disgust with this whinging pup. "If it wasn't for men braver than you, Mr. Dempsey, Ireland would still be in chains. Your father was one of those men, until he turned traitor. This is your chance to redeem him."

"You're mad," Francis said.

"No," Gavigan said. "I'm furious that the sons of the revolutionary generation won't lift a finger to finish the job. That given the chance to strike a blow that will echo through the ages, they fidget like schoolboys. I'm giving you a choice that you were too cowardly to make during your own short, wasted lifetime. You can step up to that so-called king, and you can end his life, or your entire family will pay for your crimes. Your family tree rotted when your father turned his back on his comrades, and that rot has stained you and your brothers. You can purge it by taking action, or I will purge it in the best way that I know how." Gavigan wiped his spittle-caked lips, his sweat-greased brow, and explained: If Francis refused to participate in this plan, Gavigan would be forced to apply added pressure. First, he would bring in the younger brother—

"Michael, is it?"

Yes. Michael would be killed in order to make clear just how seriously Gavigan took this endeavor. If Francis still refused to play his ordained role, then the next to fall would be his brother in the Bronx—

"Martin, am I right?"

And his family. It had been so hot these past weeks. Perfect conditions for a house fire.

Francis felt like a man coming off a three-day drunk. The color drained from his face and beads of sweat prickled at his hairline. He had called Gavigan *loolah* only minutes before, but now it was he who was losing his mind. How had he dragged them into this? Michael, Martin, Rosemary, his nieces.

"To be clear," Gavigan said. "You are not buying back your own life. That is already forfeit. You are playing for the lives of your brothers and their families."

"They have nothing to do with this!"

"They have the misfortune of being related to you."

Francis ran a hand over his scalp. He was soaked on the outside, empty on the inside. "Shoot me," he said. "I'll get your money and you can shoot me dead."

"You are marked for bigger things now," Gavigan said.

"You don't just kill a king!"

"He's just a man. He'll bleed, same as you would. Same as the men you killed in Ireland. The only difficulty is getting to him, and that's a problem you've solved."

"I didn't—" Francis faltered. Did the words exist that could get him out of this bind? "It was your people. They did this. They blew us all up." He licked his cracked lips with a dry tongue. "It wasn't my fault."

Gavigan's eyes glowed. He had been imagining the plan brought to life, but this last word from Francis snapped him back to this room, its heat, the smell of gasoline, the clatter and echo of the cars. "We're beyond fault now, little Dempsey. There is only one question left open: Who else is to die for your sins?"

THE BOWERY

URING THESE PAST FRANTIC days, it seemed to Michael that he never awoke in the same place twice. On one side of the great hole in his memory there were only two beds: the mattress piled high with beardy wool blankets where he slept in Ballyrath and the stiff, narrow cot at the seminary. On this side of the gap were the cabin aboard the ship, the posh hotel, and Martin's couch. If he really stretched his memory, ransacked the scraps of images that brought him to the earliest moments after Whatever Happened, he saw flashes of another room and another bed: a ropy pattern on a chenille coverlet, a window with the drapes drawn, a single line of sunlight on the far wall like a white-hot exclamation mark. He had lain there, in and out of consciousness, pummeled by the Noise and unable to move his head. Things weren't as bad as that now, but here he was in some other bed, and when he thought about how he had gotten here, it was the same old story. The day had ended suddenly, with a crash, and now time had elapsed and he was in a new place.

He used to read before bed. During the years when it was he and his father in the house—Martin long gone to America, Francis seeking his fortune in Dublin—they ended most days sitting before a turf fire, a lamp burning on the table as night sounds settled over the cottage: the wind buffeting the thatch, the hiss of the fire, the delicate tick of the mantel clock. The clock was one of the few relics of their life in Cork. The only items in the cottage that could trace their provenance to the Cork house were small and easily carried, as if they had been snatched from the house as it burned: the clock, some books, a few blankets, a single framed photograph of the family taken with Michael draped in his christening gown. (*They were hoping for a daughter,* Francis had often told him.)

Michael didn't think of himself as particularly happy during those long nights, but seen from this distance those were sweet and peaceful times. Da would be scanning some book of poetry while Michael made his way through the *Aeneid,* or when Da loosened the reins of his nothing-after-the-sixth-century policy, perhaps Gibbon's *Decline and Fall* or, for laughs, some Walter Scott. Was Da at that table now, alone in the lamplight, placing the bookmark among the pages and wondering where in the world his boys were? He and Martin had quarreled so mightily that when Martin finally made good on his promise to go to America, it brought a calm to the cottage. In time Francis grew restless too and rather than fight about it, he simply left. But could Da have ever expected them to stay? There had been some talk of Francis going to university but he showed little interest in formalizing his haphazard education. One day, despite their father's hostility to cities—Cork, especially—Francis announced that he was bound for Dublin and that was that. Michael and Da had an easier rhythm to their time together. Maybe it was because Michael remembered nothing of life in Cork, of how things had been before the accident that took his mother and, Martin always claimed, changed their father in some irreparable way. Ballyrath was the only home Michael had ever known and his father was always the only way that Michael had ever known him.

Would he ever set foot in Ballyrath again? And when he did, would his father still be there, at the table, his book open before him, asking Michael to bank up the fire against the chill of the night?

He had let his mind wander. When he could read before bed, sleep came to him slowly. There was time to reflect on the day that was ending and to think about the day to come. But since Whatever Happened, sleep—the loss of consciousness, really—came quickly and without warning. He didn't even know if he could call it sleep. It was a collapse, a demolition from within. He just hoped that he would continue to come out the other side, bleary-eyed but halfway sane, fortunate to be among the living.

LILLY BUSIED HERSELF with the coffeepot. She didn't have much in the way of creature comforts in the studio: no icebox or stove, and the water pressure in the tap that fed the sink was flaccid and full of stammers and half-starts. But she had to have coffee, and in a hardware store on Delancey she had purchased an electric hot plate and a pot for brewing caffè ristretto. When she'd first arrived, she could keep milk on the windowsill, but the heat of the past month had made that impossible. She brewed a sludgy concoction and loaded it with sugar. It wasn't exactly the Café des Artistes, but it was better than the endless cups of dishwater that Americans called coffee. She caught herself making more noise than usual, dropping spoons and clattering her cup into the saucer, but she could have blown the whole building down and the sound of it wouldn't have roused her guest. The boy was clearly exhausted—he had slept for more than twelve hours—and she had to admit the same about herself. The New York List had kept her on the run, and even when she wasn't in motion, the gears inside her head never stopped turning. But this morning she had awoken refreshed, if not exactly restored. Curled up against her catatonic guest, even in this relentless heat, she'd had her best night of sleep in weeks. Maybe in months.

The boy was awake and on his feet before he noticed that he was without his trousers and his shirt. Lilly stifled a laugh and made a show of placing one hand over her eyes. With her other hand, she pointed to the chair where his clothes were draped. She hadn't removed his socks and suspenders, which somehow would have felt more intimate than stripping him of his pants. He quickly gathered his garments and dressed, then sheepishly presented himself at the narrow table where Lilly took her coffee. She indicated the cup: *Would you like some?* He shook his head. He still seemed disoriented— strange room, strange woman, a new day.

She started to ask a question, then cut herself off. She had plenty of paper, along with ink and charcoal and pencils. If words were going to fail them, then fine, forget words. They would go beyond words. With a few deft lines, Lilly sketched a town house like the ones she had seen on her rambles through the more elegant parts of the city: three stories, with stairs up to the front door and tall windows. If he was from anywhere, one of the brownstones seemed a fair place to start. His clothes were dirty but well made. That shirt had not been fished out of a relief bin at one of the Bowery missions. Lilly pointed to the sketch, then to her guest, and shrugged: *Where?*

He looked at the picture, nodded, then reconsidered: *No-no-no.* He waved a hand over the building, as if to erase it, and began to shape a structure with his hands. Gestures in the air. Lilly handed him the charcoal and pantomimed the act of drawing. His lines were halting, shakily drafted. At first he seemed to be sketching a barn, with high walls supporting a roof that pitched sharply downward at each end. He added a small box along the bottom—if it was a door, it was too small to accommodate horses or cows—and then with a series of slashes across the front he suggested row upon row of small windows. Yes, a sense of scale! A large building, at least ten stories tall. An apartment building? A hotel?

Her guest stopped drawing. He ran his hand through his hair, which now stood out on his scalp in a great unpomaded spray of black. On one of the first nights when Josef took her to the movies in the arcades off the square, he had arrived with his hair gleaming and his part sharp as a knife's edge. But by the end of the short feature, his hair had sprung up, a cockscomb. "Why do you bother?" she asked him. Josef played at being offended. "Being the Clark Gable of Prague doesn't come easily," he said.

MICHAEL SCRUTINIZED HIS drawing. It wasn't a bad likeness of the hotel, with its gables and its mansard roof. But where exactly was it? Somewhere between the park and the statue of Atlas, on an avenue lined with jewelry stores and skyscrapers. He snatched up the pencil and drew two parallel lines beneath the hotel. A road. On the other side of the road he drew a grove of trees with bushy crowns and between them the sinuous lines of the footpaths he had walked with Francis and the girl with the kindly eyes. He then drew a pair of ovals, one floating over the other, and connected these with the poles of the carousel horses. He added a pair of stick-figure horses, though if they resembled any sort of animal, it was more likely a dachshund than a stallion.

"Is that supposed to be our hotel?" Yeats said from behind his shoulder.

"Of course," Michael said, without turning around. He was becoming accustomed to the poet's comings and goings. "Francis must be out of his head with worry about where we—I am."

"Francis can't help us find the answers we need." Yeats walked to the other side of the table, within arm's reach of the woman. He leaned over her shoulder, scrutinizing the sheet of paper. "Madame Antonia," he said. "The map must lead us to her."

Michael let the pencil fall from his hand. "He must be tearing the city apart looking for me—him and Martin, too."

Yeats removed his spectacles. His eyes were hard and black. Gone was the mole-ish squinting; this was the man from the ship. The agate-eyed devil in the moment before the Noise demolished him. "Your brother abandoned you on a park bench—which, I'll remind you, is hardly the first time he's left you alone to attend to his own... appetites, shall we say? Yesterday you said that you were lost, but that map you're drawing will only lead us farther from the truth."

Michael had grown tired of Yeats and his talk of Madame Antonia and the truths she could reveal. But he had a point about Francis, whose disappearances were as abrupt and common as the ghostly poet's, and if there was anything to this *spiritus mundi* business— well, was it any more unlikely than the stories he'd read in *Lives of the Saints*? Michael looked back to the sheet of paper. "And how exactly," he said, "would I draw a map to Madame Antonia?"

While Yeats suggested a new set of landmarks—gondolas, the Leaning Tower, perhaps a rudimentary Colosseum—to conjure the spirit of the Italian neighborhood, Michael made a few preliminary stabs with the pencil: a long, slightly bent hull; a tall fanlike stern. More than anything, it resembled history's least threatening Viking longboat, and though Yeats urged him to add a gondolier, Michael dropped the pencil. If Yeats wanted a gondola, he would have to draw it with his own bony, spectral fingers. Meanwhile, the woman had lost interest in his feeble sketching and refilled her cup from a small metal pot. He caught a whiff of the sharp tang of coffee. Wasn't there anyone in this city who made a decent cup of tea?

LILLY SIPPED AT her second cup of coffee and peered at the mass of lines and curlicues. Perhaps the paper and pencils had been a bad idea after all. But then so had bringing him back to the studio. When she had asked others to sit for a portrait, she offered them a cup of coffee at the end of the session. For the children, she kept a bag of sweets in the cabinet above the sink. Her current guest seemed to fall halfway between coffee and sweets. He had the look of a puppet from one of the Prague street performers: pop-eyed and red-faced, a florid *kopf* on a skeleton's frame. But how could she simply offer him coffee and candy, and then with a wave say thank you and farewell? He seemed in no hurry to leave as he alternately sketched and stared, sketched and stared. As she busied herself in the makeshift kitchen, she snuck glances at the paper. The castle in the forest had been joined by— what? A boat? A snake? A giant swan?

The boy again dropped the pencil, exhausted by the effort of mapping the what or the where inside his head. No, he didn't seem in any hurry to go anywhere. So what was she to do with him? She could bring him to the police; for all she knew, there could be a search afoot for a deaf-mute last seen wandering in the vicinity of the Automat. But the police, no, she couldn't go to the police. She would have to tell them that she had only three days left on her visa. They would require an address. Her name would be marked down in a file. So the police were out, but he could not stay at the studio. This was not the time for taking in strays. It was impossible, all of it. How had she gotten into this mess?

He had looked so—so heartbroken yesterday, and once she had snapped him with the Rolleiflex she wanted more, and so off to the studio they went. He had followed her so willingly and somehow she assumed that after the photograph was taken she would walk him back to the diner, wave good-bye, bid him adieu. But now what was she supposed to do with him? She had not realized just how fragile he was. Whatever secrets brooded within were more than his narrow frame could bear.

LILLY AND MICHAEL stood beneath the elevated tracks as a train pummeled the rails with such force that it rattled Michael's teeth. His hand was in his pocket, fingering the bills that Francis had stuffed there the day before. Had that really been only yesterday? For the first time he wondered if Francis had known all along that they would be separated, and that was the reason he had given his brother his own stash of walking-around money. As they'd passed pushcarts hawking fruit and pickles and secondhand shoes, dirt-caked potatoes and spools of ribbon, Michael trained his eyes on the storefronts and the second-story windows. Yeats had said that in an emergency, any decent medium might do, and that he would count on whatever second sight his ghostly state offered to sort the frauds from the bona fide mediums.

Lilly considered the vast brick building across the street. It stretched half the length of the block, a home for horses in the days before the automobile and now a shelter for men who had found themselves rendered obsolete. One of the arches, built broad enough for horses and carts, had been partially filled with bricks of a different color to create a pair of low doors topped by a hand-lettered sign: MISSION OF ST. JUDE. ALL WELCOME. PRAISE THE LORD FOR HE IS RISEN. LO! UNTO YOU A CHILD IS BORN. MEN ONLY. NO PERMANENT RESIDENTS. Both doors were propped open and with the elevated train having crashed and screeched its way downtown, Lilly could now hear a piano and a battery of raised voices coming from inside. She took Michael by the elbow and steered him across the street toward the swell of what must have been a hymn but which resonated like the grim recitation of a national anthem, accompanied by the heavy plodding chords of a left hand made for bricklaying, not piano playing.

A man stepped from inside and scanned up and down the street, looking for souls in need of salvation—particularly the souls of men who required no permanent accommodation. He wore a dark blue uniform with scarlet piping at the cuffs of the jacket and a matching stripe that edged the trousers from hip to foot. He had pushed back the peaked cap on his head so he could mop his brow with a limp handkerchief. While the uniform was meant to give him a military bearing, he looked instead like an usher in a middling cinema.

All she had to do was hand the boy over to his care. The man would know what to do. The building must be full of strays like this boy, whose wide eyes scanned the cross-shaped sign, the elevated tracks, the scoured-brick façade of the mission, and the row of storefronts on the opposite side of the street: nickel breakfast joint, rag merchant, cigar store, pawnshop.

As they drew closer to the door, other men straggled in. One wore a white shirt stippled with faded yellow spots, and Lilly wondered how long it would take for her guest's shirt to lose its creamy luster. Another man almost collided with her; a turban of gauze covered half his face, and above his eye radiated a stain, black at its center and then red waning toward pink at the edges. Lilly stopped short and the boy caught her by the arm, steadying her. With a nod he indicated the bandaged man and made a comic wince: *Ouch!*

The missionary greeted each man who walked through the door, looking him in the eyes and giving every offered hand a thorough pumping. Some men he gripped by the elbow, others received a pat on the shoulder or a few words of welcome. Some were sheepish in the face of such generosity, others beamed under this moment of casual regard. The boy still had Lilly by the arm and he nodded to her again, but she knew this time he was asking if she was all right. She bobbed her head—*Of-course-of-course*—and took his hand.

She was supposed to be tying up loose ends, putting everything in its proper place—but how could she even think of abandoning him? Besides, she had at least half a dozen items left on the New York List and wouldn't it be more pleasant if she had someone—anyone—to accompany her? If Josef could not join her for tea at the Waldorf-Astoria (no. 8) or a visit to the World's Fair (no. 11) or a movie in Times Square (no. 15), then this boy would have to be his stand-in. He was, in many ways, the ideal companion. He was kind, and his quick action averting a direct impact with the bloody turban proved that he was reliable. He wasn't going to ask uncomfortably personal questions or prattle on with inanities at the Museum of Modern Art (no. 19). If he had a tendency to fall over at odd times, well, she had overlooked worse habits in men in the past.

Lilly reached into her purse and withdrew a pen and a small pad of paper. Flipping past the names of galleries she had visited, phone numbers at the Foundation, the address of the shipping agent, contacts at the Czechoslovakian embassy—when such a place had existed—she found a blank page and drew three choices for the boy to consider: a steaming cup of tea, the Trylon and Perisphere, and a film projector.

YEATS NUDGED MICHAEL. "Now, *she* is an artist. Look at how easily she suggests volume with a simple gesture."

"You're not still on that, are you?" Michael said. "Anyhow, I think she wants us to choose one."

Yeats studied the pictures for a moment longer—neither of them could make sense of the pair of shapes in the center—then stuck out a hand before Michael could select the teacup. "Don't choose," he said. "Take the pen from her and draw exactly what I tell you."

He reached for the pen and after a moment's hesitation, Lilly gave it to him.

"This better not be another gondola," Michael said.

"Draw a palm," Yeats said. "No, not a palm tree. Like this." He held out one hand, as if stopping traffic.

"How is that—"

"Draw."

WORKING SLOWLY, THE boy added a fourth option to her paper: an upraised hand with an unblinking eye in its center. He tapped the picture and, as if apologizing for the drawing and whatever it signified, shrugged his shoulders. Lilly held the scrap of paper until her hand started to shake. To prove to herself that the boy was real and not some hallucination, she put a hand on his chest. She could feel his heart beating in his narrow frame. She could have counted his ribs through the fabric of his shirt.

Lilly had been looking for signs, and here was one worthy of her own mother. Mediums were one of Madame Bloch's great affectations; no grand decisions were made without their consulting the tarot, or tea leaves, or the lines of her own hand. And now, just when Lilly had a choice to make—California, Prague, Paris—here was this strange boy suggesting a visit to her mother's preferred method of guidance.

But why was it even a choice? Josef was in Prague. Despite what he himself had written, wasn't that reason enough to return? Wasn't *he* essential to *her*? Her daydreams this past week had flashed through visions of California—a California imagined by one who had just for the first time seen beyond the Hudson River. She knew what California meant for her: a place of escape, of safety. But it was also a repudiation of home and of any pretense that she was capable of love.

Lilly had passed palm readers' studios throughout the city, had even photographed men and women pondering what their hands might reveal about the future, but now she couldn't, for the life of her, remember where a single medium could be found. She took her hand from the boy's chest and scanned the street from end to end. This did not seem the place for a psychic to set up shop: the men here already knew their fate. Somewhere she had seen a row of gypsy storefronts where dark-eyed women in head scarves smoked blunt cigars. Broome, was it? Or Prince? And then there was Chinatown. Lilly had a mysterious stranger asking to be taken to a psychic, along with an unchecked item on the New York List that read *Tea in Chinatown,* so perhaps they could do both. Two birds, the Americans said, one stone. She took the boy's arm in hers and they began to stroll.

HIGHBRIDGE

LORENA STOOD IN FRONT of a five-and-dime on 170th Street, surveying the cars moving up and down Walton Avenue. All around her, other women in groups of two or three watched the same cars. The paper-bag brigade, some called them, on account of the bags that held their work clothes and their lunches. The Bronx slave market, others said, because it was along this strip of stores that white women in cars—the madams—hired black women by the hour as maids, housekeepers, domestics. Lorena had come out last week, her first time on this corner, but she was new to this part of the city and she had arrived too late. The early-morning rush of hiring had already come and gone, and the cluster of women still waiting made it clear that this skinny little girl would be last in line for any of the madams looking for a few hours of afternoon housekeeping.

Hooper didn't know she was here, but she knew what he would say, she knew how he would feel. That his wife had been reduced to this? If there was anything that would get him to pack up his trumpet in shame and head back to Baltimore, it was this: proof that his plan to be the next Louis Armstrong had failed, and failed so mightily that it had put Lorena on the street begging for work. That was why she wouldn't tell him, and when he asked her what she did all day long, she would keep alive the lie that she was still tending to an old woman who lived on Sugar Hill. It *had* been true, right up until last week, when the woman

361

died and Lorena found herself out of a job. Already she was learning that there were things a wife need not tell her husband.

No, Lorena wasn't going to let Hooper quit on her behalf, and if he tried to quit for his own reasons—well, she might not let him quit then, either. Two years of trying was a long time, but it wasn't long enough to give up on the dream they had hatched in his father's church. If he blanched at the thought of his wife bargaining to clean someone else's toilet, then those were the notions of a man who had grown up in a comfortable house, the son of a minister and a minister's wife. He could afford those notions, but she could not. Work was work, and there was no shame in it. Half the women in Reverend Hooper's choir were domestics, though Lorena wondered now if any of them had to get their work like this.

Was this the price of living? Or just the price of living in Harlem? They had come north, heedless as children—she was just twenty when they arrived, and Hooper only twenty-one. Most days she wouldn't want to live anywhere else. She could feel the energy coming up through the pavement, and all around her was a Black Metropolis. Ladies from Sugar Hill, looking like they'd stepped out of a fashion magazine, walked like royalty to the beauty parlors on Amsterdam Avenue. Up and down Strivers Row, men in sharp suits—the kind she wished she could buy for Hooper—leaned on the fenders of Bible-black sedans. On the streets, children raced fruit-crate go-carts; on the stoops, the West Indian girls chanted and hand-clapped songs that had no end. Boys in caps and baggy pants and girls in hand-me-down frocks called out to the fruit vendors and to the shaved-ice man. Down the block, older men played checkers and gave stern looks to any child fool enough to offer advice. Older women leaned from windows and paused on the sidewalks to carry on conversations about the heat, about the city, about the old men and their checkers. And at night! Night was when Lorena's Harlem really came to life, in endless loops of neon, and in music spilling from the doors of the Apollo, and in the breakfast dance at Smalls Paradise, and in the single spotlight that hushed a crowd and gave a singer her chance to shine.

It was all too easy to get caught up in the dream, but life was no dream. Even if you could find a job, in Harlem the wages were lower and the rents higher than anywhere else in the city. Lorena and Hooper's apartment was two rooms—a cold-water flat, three stories up, with a shared bathroom down the hall. All winter long, the wind seeped through the windows until ice formed on the inside of the glass, and in the summertime the apartment was hotter than a two-dollar pistol. There had been nights these past weeks when they slept on the fire escape. It was all part of the adventure during their first year in New York, but now, as their second year drew to a close, it was starting to feel like the best they could do—and maybe the best they could ever expect.

She knew what Mrs. Hooper would say: Lorena had led her boy down the path to ruin. She saw it in the letters that Hooper's mother sent, full of worry and blessings and the occasional dollar bill. Mrs. Hooper was also fond of including clippings from the *Crisis*, the NAACP magazine—usually the College and School News column and any articles about a Howard graduate who was already making a difference in the world. *Thought you'd like to see this*, she would write along the top of the page. Or, *Wasn't he in school with you?* Even in her antique handwriting, the message came through like a megaphone blast. In the latest packet from Mama Hooper, it wasn't the article that caught Lorena's eye but the advertisement on the back of the page: SUMMER CLASSES AT HOWARD STARTING JULY 1. Hooper could be back in DC earning credits toward his degree instead of sweating at the fair for a bunch of tourists who, as Hooper said, didn't know jazz-all about jazz.

Watching the first of the day's cars begin to line up, she wondered what would happen if she told him that *she* wanted to go back, wanted him to finish school, so that they could—what?—settle down in

Baltimore? Was Hooper supposed to be a dentist, an insurance man, a minister? Maybe in Mama Hooper's dreams, but hadn't they committed themselves to a different dream? Sure they had. It was just that a place in the paper-bag brigade and the Bronx slave market hadn't been a part of that dream.

"You new around here?" An older woman, thickset and swathed in a floral dress, had edged up next to Lorena.

"Not so new," Lorena said. "I was here last week."

"Last week? You were here last week?" The woman tsked and shook her head like she was enjoying a joke Lorena had just told. "I've been working this corner for three years!"

Lorena tried to seem unconcerned. She wasn't going to be bullied to the back of the line today, not when she'd been one of the first women here. She crossed her arms and tightened her grip on the rolled top of the paper bag.

"You're not one of those Father Divine types, are you?"

"I don't know what you're talking about," Lorena said.

"Sure you do," the woman said. "Just last week we ran a bunch of them off this corner and the across-the-street corner, too."

Of course Lorena had seen the followers of Father Divine: they were everywhere in Harlem, on the streets and in front of their restaurants, where you could get dinner with all the trimmings for ten cents less than anywhere else in town. With their shouts of "Father is with us!" they told the world that God walked the earth in the form of a pint-size, bald-headed black man who went by the name Reverend Major Jealous Divine.

"You listen here," the woman continued. "Last week I had a lady in a Cadillac ready to pay me fifty cents an hour for a full day's work, and just as I was fixing to get in her car, one of those Father Diviners comes up and says 'Peace' and that she'll do it for thirty cents an hour. So guess who got the ride? Stealing four dollars from me? That ain't peace! It's war!"

"I sure am sorry to hear that," Lorena said. "But I'm not one of them."

They didn't seem all bad, the angels of Father Divine. Last month Lorena had signed a petition they were circulating to get an anti-lynching law passed. Lorena didn't see much use in it—how could a letter signed by black folks get white folks to stop doing something they wanted to do?—but she didn't see any harm in it either. It was one of the things she liked about Harlem, that everywhere you went you heard preachers and soapbox politicians dreaming out loud about the future. The communists said the workers' revolution was right around the corner and that the days of the bosses were coming to an end. To the sound of tambourines and praises, the preachers said the news pointed to the End of Days and the coming of the Antichrist, while others saw, just over the horizon, the glorious dawn of the Second Coming. The Father Diviners did them one better and claimed that God had already taken up residence on Long Island. But none of those futures, revolution or revelation, made this morning on 170th Street one whit easier to bear.

The woman who had been robbed by the angels wasn't done with Lorena. "I'm keeping my eye on you," she said. "You don't ask for less than thirty-five cents an hour, you hear?"

"Martha, will you take it easy on that girl?" Another woman had joined their conversation. Alva was, in both age and size, halfway between the stocky Martha and the reedy Lorena. She wore a blue dress with a wide white collar and a simple silver cross on a chain around her neck. With the ease of someone who had known Lorena all her life, she placed a hand on her arm and gave her an auntish pat.

"Oh, I'm fine," Lorena said.

"Of course you are, dear," Alva said. "Martha's having one of her moods. Did she tell you about losing that fifty-cents-an-hour job? I'll bet she did."

"I still say that's why we need a union," Martha said. "Fifty cents an hour, lunch, and carfare. That shouldn't be so hard to come by."

Now it was Alva's turn to shake her head. She'd been listening to this union talk from Martha for going on a year. But how could you start a union when you were scrubbing and cleaning all day? And how was Martha going to get any of these girls to say no to forty cents an hour? Or forty-five?

"A union sounds good to me," Lorena said. "Fighting each other for work just makes life easy for the madams." *Good Lord*, she thought. *I sound like Professor Hooper.*

Martha nodded appreciatively. "See? She gets it. And now, if you ladies'll excuse me, I do believe I've got work to do." Martha lifted her bag from the sidewalk and strode toward a red Buick idling by the curb. This was Mrs. Rubenstein, one of Martha's regulars, and the other women knew not to bother—not unless they wanted to get an earful tomorrow.

"That must be nice," Lorena said. "Once the madams know you, off you go."

"And it only took Martha three years on this same corner to make it happen." Alva said it kindly, but Lorena got the message: *Honey, think before you speak.*

Both women craned their necks for signs of cars slowing to the curb. The busiest time was between eight and nine, after the madams' husbands went to work and the ladies began acting on plans for a clean apartment by dinner. Lorena didn't want to look too eager, but she didn't want to miss her turn.

"You're sure you've done this before?" Alva said.

"Cleaned a house?" Lorena stifled a small laugh. "My aunt Hessie wouldn't abide a speck of dust."

"That's a start," Alva said. "But do you know how *this* works?" With one hand she indicated the street, the cars, the paper bags.

"No less than thirty-five cents an hour. I heard it loud and clear."

"That's not the half of it," Alva said. With one eye on the cars, Alva gave a quick lesson in the life of a brown-bag domestic. She started with the basics—settle on the wage before you get in the car, along with time for lunch and carfare home—but there was so much more. Watch out for madams who set their clocks back to cheat you out of an hour. Watch out for madams who offered you lunch—leftovers, always leftovers—and then deducted it from your pay. Watch out for madams who saw phantom smudges on the windows and refused to pay at all, or paid less, or else made you do it all over again, off the clock. And watch out for the men who drove up after the early rush; they had work for you, but it sure wasn't mopping and scrubbing.

Lorena nodded with each item on Alva's list. She saw how this worked: you fought the other ladies for the privilege of making pennies and then you fought the madam to get paid for what you did. It wasn't the first time she'd heard that song. As she listened, she prepared herself for the days to come. Tomorrow she would arrive even earlier, and she would bring a clock of her own—an old watch, or the bedside alarm clock. But more than thinking of the lessons she would need to master in the weeks or months or—God help her—years ahead, she was wondering what Aunt Hessie would make of all this. Aunt Hessie had taught her to scrub a floor until it shone like the truth, but she couldn't have imagined that this was what she was preparing Lorena for when she took her into her home.

Lorena's parents had exited the scene long ago. For a time, her daddy ran one of the hottest speakeasies in the District of Columbia. He was a cardsharp and a pool player, he wore flashy suits and conked his hair, and anywhere he went, that's where the party was. To keep the good times going he borrowed money wherever he could get it. Even when the club was so crowded that he had to turn away business, money was always tight. Lorena's mama was a minor celebrity herself, in her beaded dresses that stopped above the knee and her hair as shiny and marcel-waved as Josephine Baker's. Daddy had once told Lorena that she got her voice from her mother, but just as much as she heard Mama singing, she heard her yelling at Daddy. Hot-tempered,

some people called her. A drinker, said the others. Lorena had a narrow bed in a room that was no more than a closet, and from that
room she listened to her parents rage at each other. Who had he been
dancing with? Who had she been talking to? Where had all the money
gone? And how could he be so bad at cheating at cards when he was
so good at cheating on her? She knew that Mama and Daddy loved
her—she was Lolo, their honey girl—and for weeks in a row, sometimes months, she knew they loved each other, too. Despite the
slammed doors, their fights always ended with them cooing in each
other's arms, promising never again to take a match to love and turn
it into ashes.

It was just after Lorena turned eleven that Daddy disappeared. All
those men to whom he owed money came collecting, and they wanted
more than his cash and his nightclub. He'd been putting them off for
too long, they said, trying to play them for fools. They had decided
that his was a debt payable only in blood. The grief and the bottle
made quick work of Mama. On that morning when she couldn't get
out of bed—when she could barely put two words together—Lorena
had run to the upstairs neighbors first, but they had heard too much
from Mama, and too late at night, to lift a finger for her now. Lorena
raced next door to find a widow who had always been kind to her,
and once that woman saw the state of the apartment, and then got an
eyeful of Mama, she shooed Lorena out the door. That glimpse of
Mama, her satin skin swollen and those bright, dark eyes sinking into
her skull, was the last one Lorena ever got.

Late that same night, an aunt she barely knew claimed Lorena and
took her up to Baltimore. Within a week, word came that Mama had
died, and the hurt of it almost swallowed Lorena whole. She hadn't
even said a proper good-bye. She hadn't said any kind of good-bye at
all. In the years that followed, she worked hard to un-remember that
last moment; to preserve Mama in her memory as the woman with
the lilac perfume dabbed behind each ear, the skin that glowed like

bronze in the sunlight, and the voice that rang out high and then dove down low — like an angel, her daddy had once said, who's down to her last dollar.

Aunt Hessie had pitied Lorena and felt obliged to care for her, and that was more than some girls got. Lorena could have easily found herself with far less. Perhaps Aunt Hessie even loved that part of Lorena that reminded her of the baby sister she had raised, but then hadn't she let Lorena's mother slip away to a life no honest woman should lead? She wasn't going to make the same mistake with Lorena, whose life in Baltimore was school and chores and church and little else. Only in the choir could she raise her voice. Only with the pack of Hooper children could she play like she had back at home.

What would Aunt Hessie, dead these past three years, think of her now? Married to Reverend Hooper's oldest son — that would have been a surprise. But with barely two dimes to rub together, and singing till all hours in smoky clubs? That was just what Hessie had feared.

Still Lorena sang, hoping to turn a song into a set into a regular gig. There had to be a thousand other girl singers like her — coal-scuttle canaries — and who needs you when Ella is at the Savoy and Billie is at Café Society and most of the ballrooms, clubs, and lounges in between have a blondes-only policy for the sole lady on the bandstand? But that was the dream anyway, and some nights it was so close that she could feel it like a spotlight on her face. Then came a morning like this: standing on the curb, paper bag in hand, hoping for the chance to clean some white woman's bathroom, to dust and mop and scrub and bleach until her fingers ached and her knees went raw and ashy. All for a few cents and the chance to do it again tomorrow.

A new car, its chrome grille sparkling like a crown, swept into a spot only a few feet from Lorena. A woman who had been standing in the shade of the awning moved toward it, but Lorena froze her with a look. *This one's mine.* She tightened her grip on the paper bag and smiled her biggest smile, ready for what came next.

LITTLE ITALY

WHERE AMONG THE FRUIT vendors and the barber colleges and the stores selling suits for ten cents, the taverns and the cheap cinemas and the tenements and the sweatshops, had Lilly seen signs for palm readers? She headed west, away from the Bowery, toward the Italian and Chinese neighborhoods, where there was sure to be a fortune-teller wedged between the shrines to weeping saints or ancestors buried thousands of miles away in a land that had once been home. In Prague, there had been a Hungarian woman to whom her mother turned in times of turmoil, and Madame Bloch had always been doubly pleased when voices from beyond seconded an opinion she held. *You see, Lilliana!* she would say. *Even the spirits agree with me!*

A church bell announced that it was noon, which gave Lilly exactly forty-eight hours to get her luggage to the shipping agent. She would have to finish her labeling tonight, and pack the negatives and plates tomorrow, so they could be unpacked when she resettled in Prague. And wasn't that the story that she had agreed to, the one that ended with her safe and sorted in Prague? After a few months or years, she would develop the photographs, and the time she had passed in New York City, back in the ancient days of yesterday, would strike her as strange and long ago.

But there was another story, one in which she listened to the chorus inside her head that grew louder every day: *Stay! If not in New York, then in America. Stay!* She was not brave. She didn't believe that one of her photographs could stop a tank or topple a dictator. Even Josef had joined the *Stay, don't go* chorus. She had friends in Munich and Berlin; she knew the laws that had redefined their lives, and she knew that these same laws would soon surface in Prague. But if Hitler wanted Prague so badly and he didn't want her in it, then she could make other arrangements. She could go to California, or she could simply disappear from her studio one day and set up in Greenwich Village, where she could glut herself on jazz and communism. Change a few letters of her name, become someone new, and hope that the government had more important things to do than find one missing Czechoslovakian. Her nation didn't even exist any longer! How could she return to a place that didn't exist?

But that was all for later. Today she had to find a psychic, an item that Josef would never have thought to include on the New York List.

The boy looked from shopwindow to storefront, searching for the telltale hand and eye. Two blocks down Broome Street, Lilly saw a window with the word TAROT outlined in thick red letters, but when she tried steering him toward the door, he shook his head almost apologetically and kept walking. Another sign promised PSYCHIC READINGS but after a pause, during which he seemed to consult with himself, he again shook his head and moved on.

Michael was convinced that their host would soon lose patience with him, but Yeats persisted in his search for a first-rate medium. If not Madame Antonia, then someone of her caliber.

"These aren't mediums, they're charlatans," Yeats said as they passed a storefront decorated with poster-size tarot cards: the Fool, the Sun, the Lovers. "Sad to say, but the spiritualist community is rife with rascals and frauds."

Michael tried to look sympathetic to the problems besmirching the otherwise sterling reputation of the spiritualists. "So you can smell it on them?" he said. "The *spiritus mundi?*"

Lilly took his elbow and guided him across the street. This was the sign she'd recalled, the one that had flared brightly in her memory when he'd drawn the hand and eye. The building was a narrow tenement next to the shop where she'd purchased a block of flaky Parmigiano-Reggiano and another of pungent Gorgonzola. For the past month, she had subsisted on little more than black coffee, cheese, bread, and cheap red wine. She put her hand on the knob of a door that led beneath the tenement stoop, then turned to him and raised one eyebrow.

"Well?" Michael said.

"It's not Madame Antonia, but it will have to do."

Michael nodded vigorously to Lilly, who gave the door a shove. They found themselves in a cramped anteroom. The red walls were graffitied with standard-issue symbols of the occult: pentagrams, all-seeing eyes, signs of the zodiac, a prime number or two. At the other end of the room, a door that was ajar bore a placard with the words ENTER AND BE KNOWN on one side and WAIT AND BE SILENT on the other. Lilly knocked on the door as she swung it open into a low-ceilinged room hung on all sides with tapestries, velvet drapes, and iridescent bolts of raw silk. It looked like laundry day at a gypsy camp. In the center of the room sat a round table where a candle mounted in the neck of a bottle raised a single weak flame. A damp moldy smell competed with the tang of incense.

Lilly called out a hello. She rapped again on the door, louder than the first time. Behind one of the curtains a pot lid clanged, followed by the sound of utensils being dropped and a muttered curse. A woman emerged, and with her came a billow of steam and the smell of cabbage, onions, garlic, oregano.

"It seems we have interrupted her luncheon," Yeats said.

She was a small woman with a large head crowned with a pouf of black hair shot through with gray. The hem of her black dress, which was buttoned to the neck, swept the floor as she bustled into the room.

She gripped around her shoulders a brightly hued, densely patterned shawl on which tigers cavorted, teeth to tail, and elephants paraded, bearing sultans on canopied palanquins.

"How you get in?" Her voice was like the chirping of an angry sparrow. "The door was locked!"

"It was open," Lilly said, "but if we are intruding—" She laid a hand on Michael's shoulder to turn him toward the door.

"No, no, no," the woman said. "Take a seat. Sit! Sit!"

Lilly and Michael sat side by side at the table, opposite an ornately carved chair. From its upholstered back rose a double-headed eagle whose twin tongues burst through open beaks. Yeats, meanwhile, was inspecting a tapestry depicting a palace scene in some Eastern kingdom: a crowned man sat shirtless and cross-legged on a platform while around him women danced and fruit trees bloomed.

"You wait? Yes? You wait? Then we...begin?"

There was something sardonic in the woman's voice, as if all of this—the tapestries, the shawl, the single candle, the promise of clairvoyance—were some big joke she was compelled to tell. She disappeared behind the curtain and again came the clattering of pots. She yelled twice, quickly: a name, orders being given, in a language Lilly did not recognize. Not French or Spanish or German or Czech and certainly not English. A child's voice argued back—the whining tone of the falsely accused—until a slap and a renewed clattering of lids brought the back-and-forth to a close.

The woman reappeared, her cheeks flushed, and took her place at the table. "Now, what you want?" she said.

Lilly looked at Michael; all of this had been his idea. He sat stock-still, his hands folded in his lap and his eyes fixed on the candle. She tapped his knee but he only smiled at her and then resumed his vigil. The woman looked from one to the other, impatient, her mind clearly focused more on the kitchen than on the goings-on in the parlor.

"I have a decision to make," Lilly said, surprising even herself.

"About him?" The medium pointed to Michael.

"No, he's just—he suggested I come to you."

"So, a decision," the medium said. "Is it a romantic decision or a money decision or ..."

Lilly's mother always said that it was important to tell the medium as little as possible. *Make the spirits do the work,* she had said. Of course, Madame Bloch habitually violated this rule; she couldn't keep herself from talking, in detail, about whatever was on her mind. She barely left room for the spirits to do more than nod in agreement or raise vague, easily dismissed objections.

"Just a decision," Lilly said.

The medium introduced herself as Eudoxia—" 'You-doh-key-ah,' you understand, yes?"—and asked if Lilly had a preference: A palm reading? The tarot? Tea leaves? An astrological chart? She could consult a crystal ball, if that's what Lilly wanted, or even take up the Ouija board, though this last possibility she offered in a way that suggested that the option was exhausting or simply ridiculous.

Again, Lilly looked to Michael, whose attention now seemed fixed on Madame Eudoxia herself.

"Why don't you choose?" Lilly said. "Whatever way works the best."

EUDOXIA DIDN'T KNOW if the woman was challenging her or truly did not care. Many of her customers were simply lonely and tired of wrestling in solitude with some nagging question. *Why can't I be happy? Is she cheating on me—and what's the mug's name? Did my mother ever love me?* They would duck through the door and spill their guts for her to augur by appealing to the tarot or the stars or the lines of their own palms. Eudoxia was good at mixing hopeful prescriptions for future success with painful truths gleaned during the time it took to offer a reliable reading: *Stop expecting so much of life.*

Not yet, but she will stray if you do not learn to trust her. Your mother loved you but didn't know how to tell you. For her regulars, she provided warnings of dangers easily imagined and, with a little effort, avoided. She had learned long ago that she was good at giving advice, though good advice was easy to ignore. But advice backed up by the weight of the spirit world? That was worth paying for.

So here was this woman and she had a decision to make. She had good English but was European—an immigrant like Eudoxia or perhaps only a visitor to the city. The boy, who had not spoken, behaved in an odd manner, and the two did not appear related or linked by love. More would reveal itself. It always did. Eudoxia was smart, and truth be told, she possessed more than her share of intuition. At times, she even suspected that her powers went beyond that—but she wasn't the one who needed to believe. As long as the customer believed, then the rent got paid.

"JUST WHAT ARE you expecting, Mr. Yeats?"

Yeats returned from his inspection of the decor and stood next to the medium's chair, which he eyed with apparent distaste. "The experience can take a variety of forms," he said, "depending on the sensitivities of this medium. Direct drawing, direct voice, spirit photography, even levitation—I have seen all of that and more at séances past."

"That's not what I mean. What are you expecting to gain from all of this? How are you going to find the answers you're looking for in *here?*" Michael worried that the ceiling might come down on top of them. Already it seemed to sag in the middle, and with the walls swathed in fabric, finding an exit could prove difficult.

"This is but the first step," Yeats said. "But if we can use her to reach our host, and through her reach George, then the real work can begin."

First they had set out to find the elusive—and possibly nonexistent—

Madame Antonia, and now Yeats proposed contacting his wife, who by Michael's guess was thousands of miles and one vast ocean to the east. "Why do we need to contact your wife?" he said.

Yeats shushed Michael and pointed to the medium. "I think she is ready."

THIS WAS WHAT Eudoxia proposed: Lilly would write her questions on scraps of paper and then set the paper alight from the candle. As the smoke rose from the dish where Lilly was to place the burning paper, Eudoxia would consult the spirits and communicate their answers to Lilly. It had been some time since Eudoxia had used this method, but it always delivered on the mystery and wonder that most gawkers came seeking from a fortune-teller. Eudoxia also offered her standard disclaimer: that the spirits often answered indirectly, as the truth could never be approached along a straight path.

From a small table on her left, Eudoxia withdrew a sheet of paper and a fountain pen. She tore the paper into strips and handed these and the pen to Lilly. "Write what you want to know," she said. "And then the fire, and then the plate."

Lilly examined the pen in the dim light, then offered it to the boy. She hoped that he would find a way to involve himself in this visit—that he had his own reasons for wanting to consult a psychic. Odd enough to have taken in a voiceless stranger prone to fits of fainting and mapmaking. To have him also turn out to be some sort of prophet, nudging her toward a decision of great magnitude, was more than she could manage this week.

He waved off the pen, leaving Lilly to stare at the first blank scrap of paper. This was preposterous, she told herself, but wasn't it just the sort of story that Josef wanted to hear? Lilly's Adventures in New York, chapter 5: the time she consulted a basement psychic about whether to return to Prague or disappear into America.

In her jagged script, she wrote, *Should I return to Prague?* As the words emerged from the pen, she saw that the ink was red.

Eudoxia's eyes were closed, her hands flat on the tabletop. She inhaled deeply through her nose and then out through her mouth in a rhythm that became like a drumbeat in the room. She looked like an ancient oracle, and Lilly let slip a whispered curse that she'd left her camera in the studio. Lilly held the scrap of paper over the candle and watched as the edges browned, then glowed, then caught. When the flame had consumed half the paper, she set it down in the dish and the smoke wound toward the ceiling.

MICHAEL BECAME AWARE of a pulsing, a rumbling, like waves against rocks, crashing and receding. He feared it was the Noise, coming to lay waste to him, but then he saw the medium inhaling so deeply that she lifted her body away from the table. "It's her," Michael said. "I can hear her breathing." The sound was faint, a background noise, really. But after weeks in a kind of vacuum, even the sound of a single breath was a gift.

Yeats clapped his hands together, more gleeful than Michael had yet seen him. "A proper medium opens a window between the spirit world and the material plane so that voices can flow through her in each direction." He leaned in close to the medium. His lips almost grazed her ear as he spoke: "You must find George!"

EUDOXIA JUMPED IN her chair. The deep breathing was meant to heighten the tension before she began speaking. A dramatic pause, followed by half statements and questions that would lead her, little by little, to a satisfying answer to the question burning on the plate. Long ago, when all of this started, the breathing had helped to ready her for what was to come, but it had been years since she had genuinely felt—what? What had she called it, in the beginning? *Touched* was a word she had used. *Guided,* even. But never *called,* never *spoken to,* never—like this.

She heard it again: *George,* the voice said.

She lunged across the table and gripped the woman's hand. "Who is George?"

"There's millions of Georges in the world," Michael said. "And how is she to know that your George is a lady?"

Yeats waved him off. He placed a hand on the medium's shoulder and leaned in close, unspooling a list of names and then places where his wife might be found: Georgie Hyde Lees. George Yeats. France, London, the tower at Thoor Ballylee, Dublin.

None of it made sense to Michael. Even if the psychic could hear Yeats, how was she supposed to make sense of the poet's babbling? Yeats looked like one of the old priests barking into the mouthpiece of the seminary's candlestick telephone. "And our host is not going to board a ship to France," he said, "simply because some barmy psychic told her to find George."

"You saw her studio," Yeats said. "She's packing for a journey. Who's to say we weren't drawn to her for exactly this reason? The *spiritus mundi*—"

"Enough about the *spiritus mundi,*" Michael said. "You said a decent medium could practice psychical healing. I'd like some of that, please."

George? Lilly didn't know any George.

Eudoxia looked wildly about the room. Was it her daughter, sullen in the kitchen, seeking a child's revenge by interfering with her mother's work? No, it was clearly a man's voice. "I heard *George*," she said. "Does this mean something?"

Tell them nothing, her mother had said, and that was easy enough. She did not know a George.

Eudoxia closed her eyes again, placed her palms on the table, and began her deep breathing, faster and more ragged this time. A presence crowded close to her and with it, once more, the voice. Less distinct than before, but still palpable. Eudoxia tried to calm her breathing, to quiet herself. France? Francis? Yes, another name: Francis.

"George and Francis," she said. "George or Francis? So it is romance—"

Lilly cut her off. "Your spirits are confused. I don't know a George or a Francis. Perhaps this was a mistake."

"No!" Eudoxia reached out again and trapped Lilly's hand beneath hers. "Stay! I—I am hearing a voice!"

"Isn't that what's supposed to happen?"

"Not like this," she said. "*Never* like this. Please, stay."

"WE'LL TAKE CARE of you soon," Yeats said to Michael. "But this is important: George's ability to contact the world beyond was crucial to my work. My vision was our vision, jointly. We undertook the task together, and I need to tell her that changes must be made for the next edition. She must amend those chapters that my current experience supports or disproves."

"Do you think she cares about that?" Michael said. "Her husband is dead. She has children to tend to. Don't you think that's uppermost in her mind right now? And not correcting the number of angels on the head of each pin?"

"You clearly know nothing of my work," Yeats said.

"*Your* work?" Michael had to speak up to be heard. The sound of the medium's breathing swirled around the room, like the beating of a moth's wings against his ears. "You said that a medium could provide me with answers, but all you've done is shout directions to advance your own interests."

"Madame Antonia would have been able to help you."

"Bah!" Michael said. "You only think of yourself. You don't care about me or our host—you didn't even peek at her question, and now there's nothing left of it."

Yeats sighed, exasperated, and poked through the ashes. "It's in German," he said. " 'Should I return to—Prague?' "

"Prague?" Michael said. "That's not a German city."

Yeats put his lips close to the medium's ear and spoke in loud, clipped syllables. "No, no, and *nein.*" He stood and straightened his back, then spoke before Michael could object. "She'll never find George in Prague."

Michael closed his eyes and covered his ears, but the whooshing continued. Then, slicing high above it, a voice he was certain he recognized: *Michael!* His eyes snapped open, but it wasn't Yeats who had called him. Yeats remained at the medium's shoulder and her breathing had become more regular. The ebb and flow of the sound's tide resumed.

Michael!

EUDOXIA RECLAIMED HER pen from Lilly, reached for another sheet of paper, and began scratching madly. The voices had grown less distinct but continued to dictate to her. One moment, the words were as close as a lover's breath on her neck; the next, farther off, as if shouted from a train as it pulled away from the station. She had dashed down what she could: *George, Francis, London, the tower…*

Though Lilly couldn't make out a word of it, she watched with interest as the medium alternated deep breathing with bouts of intense scribbling. "Excuse me," she said. "But does any of that answer my question?"

Eudoxia looked up from the page, and at that same moment the ashes in the dish began to stir. If Lilly had been interested in debunking so-called psychics, this would have been the time to peek under the table in search of some contraption—a foot-operated pump and tube, a small electric fan—that troubled the ashes and made them swirl and rise. Instead, the two women both stared at the dish, unable to move, until Eudoxia broke the spell: "No!" she said. *"No, no, and nein!"*

Though he had taken his eyes off the candle, the boy seemed consumed by some invisible goings-on around Eudoxia. He looked intently at her, then to her right, then back to her, then to her right, as if he were following a heated argument. But as the *No, no, and nein* poured out of her, he clapped his hands over his ears and screwed his eyes up tight.

IT WAS HIS father's voice. He imagined his da on the hill above their cottage, under the night sky, calling out to him. Did he know that Michael had left the seminary, undergone some cruel change, and found himself in a far-off city? Had his father played some part in dispatching Francis to New York to reunite the brothers and seek help for Michael? But how was it that his father's voice could reach him now? Could the cry of a father for his lost son travel on this celestial frequency?

Michael shook his head as the clutter within grew louder. He heard the hazy static of a wireless, the muffled chatter of voices, the singsong of a children's rhyme in a language he could not name. All of it threatened to drown out the cries of his father.

"Mr. Yeats, can you hear this? I'd swear it's my father's voice."

Yeats rubbed his chin, pensive. "I suppose that's possible," he said. "He is on my side, you know."

"Your side of what?"

"Of life. Of death," Yeats said. "He crossed over just—hello, that must be it. You said you'd been summoned from the classroom one morning, given some bad news. That must have been when you found out."

"I don't believe you," Michael said, but already the fact of it had seized him.

"It's not a question of belief," Yeats said. "It simply is."

"But why didn't you tell me?"

"I've only just put it together myself. I've had quite a bit of—"

"My God," Michael said. "Da. Da is gone."

LILLY HAD A resounding answer to one question and a list full of mysteries. She was not to go to Prague, but this came from the same voice that had provided a roster of unknowns: *George, Francis, London, the tower,* and one final addition, hastily scribbled by Madame Eudoxia: *Michael.* She didn't know any of these people, and wasn't the Tower of London the spot where the English kings made people disappear? A place of confinement, of confession, of last nights on earth? Far from a place of refuge, that sounded like the Prague that Josef feared the city would become.

And what was she to do with the boy? She realized now that she should have asked more questions, different questions—that the reason he drew the hand and eye was not so she could ask about staying or going, but so she could find out more about him. *This is how you can know me,* he was saying. But within moments of receiving her answer, he was overwhelmed by tears. He put his head in his hands and choked out a horrid wail, a cry of pure misery. There was only one place for him and that was the studio, among the wreckage of boxes and her half-packed suitcase. She would be lucky to find a taxi in this part of the city, but though he was slight, she did not think she could carry him all the way home.

THE WORLD'S FAIR

THIS WAS THE MOMENT Peggy would miss the most. Soon, in a line of other girls, she would step to the edge of the pool, wait a beat, and then, with her arms raised, begin her dive. She would feel it all: the spring of her legs, her feet free of the deck, her body flashing through the air, then plunging into the pool, the shock of the water igniting every nerve. She would surface midstroke, the elaborate choreography already under way, as row after row of Aquabelles swam the perimeter of the pool, looped back in braided circuits, and formed stars and flowers with their kicking legs, their bobbing heads, their artfully turned arms.

The Aquacade was the biggest draw in the World's Fair Amusement Zone. The fair itself might lose money (and it did, by the truckload), but the Aquacade would make a richer man of Billy Rose, master showman and owner of the Diamond Horseshoe, one of the hottest clubs on Broadway. In the weeks before the fair opened, an army of workers had completed a vast grandstand cradling a 250-foot-long swimming pool that stretched from one lofty tower to another. In one of the towers, Vincent Lopez led his orchestra through a peppy mix of popular tunes, while on the other side, daredevil divers and clown acts plummeted into the water below. The headliners were celebrities long before the fair ever started: Johnny Weissmuller, the Tarzan of the silver screen; Eleanor Holm, a champion swimmer better known for getting tossed from the Olympic team for late-night carousing; and a man who never so much as dipped his toe in the water, Morton Downey, the last of the great Irish tenors.

Along with its star power, the Aquacade amazed the masses with its cast-of-hundreds water-ballet revues. The burly Aquadudes were often the first in the pool, but there were no more than twenty of them and—sorry, ladies!—they weren't the main attraction. It wasn't until the women entered the water—row upon row of lithe Aquabelles, Aquafemmes, and Aquagals—in peach-toned bathing suits that suggested no suits at all that the audience really began to cheer. Music blared from the bandstand, fountains sprayed in all directions, and the swimmers sliced through the water, shaping curlicues and sunbursts made up of nothing but arms and legs and white-capped heads. For the big finish to one number, the Aquabelles assembled at the far end of the pool and swam its length in rows of six, their heads perfectly aligned, until they disappeared below the bandstand. That always put the crowd into a frenzy, bidding farewell to that abundance of flesh, of smiles, of joy.

If Peggy had told them at the audition that she was getting married in June, they never would have picked her. Five thousand tried out and only five hundred were chosen. Even after she got the job, she kept her engagement a secret. Every day before she left home to catch the bus to the fair, she put her engagement ring in the jewelry box in her bedroom. Until she returned to her parents' house—to the room where she had grown up—she wasn't Peggy-who-was-getting-married, she was just Peggy. Some of the girls thought she was stuck-up or standoffish, and one of the Aquadudes had called her a cold fish, but she couldn't risk blurting out something about the wedding that would get her hauled in front of the bosses. It was fine for Eleanor Holm to be married. She was the biggest name on the marquee, and her mister was none other than Billy Rose himself—until recently Mr. Fanny Brice. But Aquabelles, Aquafemmes, Aquagals, and even the do-nothing Aquamaids? That wasn't a job for wives. Wives needed to be taking care of the home instead of performing four shows a day, seven days a week, for thousands of cheering, ticket-buying customers.

Peggy's final day at the Aquacade was supposed to be last week, but she had delayed and delayed and delayed. *Don't think you can climb out of the pool and into your wedding dress,* her mother kept telling her. *No groom wants a bride who stinks of chlorine.*

But what if Peggy wasn't going to be a bride? What about that?

Peggy had always hated the dreary, boring side of life—the side that her mother and Rosemary said was just life itself. But why did *that* have to be life? Rosemary lived in a shabby apartment with a landlady with cobweb hair who was always looking over her shoulder. And Rosemary was supposed to be the smart one! That's what Daddy had always said—and look where it had landed her. Mother and Daddy's house was nice enough but it was cluttery: the china cabinet was stuffed with plates painted with the Tara brooch and the end tables were crowded with pictures of spooky-eyed relatives dead since before Peggy was born. It was all so old—not just *from* the past but *about* the past—and every frame, candy dish, and scrap of Old Country lace needed to be dusted every single day. Peggy didn't want any of that. She didn't want to spend the rest of her life as a maid or a museum-keeper.

She often lingered for hours on the fairgrounds when her shift was up at the Aquacade. Everything at the fair was newer than new: it was the future. The buildings were out of a dream, in shapes that no one in the Bronx had ever imagined, and at night the fair was a magic city of fountains, neon, spotlights, and fireworks. Even Manhattan looked old-fashioned after a day of gazing at Democracity or the Futurama. In the General Motors Pavilion, she saw a city of pristine skyscrapers with landing pads on each roof for helicopters and autogiros. Out one window you had a view of the ocean; out the other, zeppelins waited to whisk you off to Timbuktu. *Sign me up!* she said. Who wouldn't want to live in the clouds, in a glass tower with a view of the future?

Tim had already picked out an apartment for them in Manhattan. *A little taste of city life,* he had said. *Just until we start a family.* But she knew they wouldn't be spending their nights dancing at the Savoy or the Roseland or even that snoozy old hotel where Martin played. Tim had chosen the apartment because it was closer to his office, where he spent all of his time anyway. And the only thing the apartment looked out to was Brooklyn, and who wanted to look at Brooklyn all day? Whenever she brought it up, Tim would say, *Swell, then we'll stay in the Bronx,* but she didn't want that either.

There were almost a hundred days until the fair closed, and that meant three or four hundred more moments when she could step to the edge, raise her arms, and dive into the water. It wasn't a bad way to spend the summer.

But summer would end, and then what?

Tim was ready to start their life together. He was past ready. He had wanted to get married right away—a two-month engagement, three months tops—but it was her family who put on the brakes. *We're doing it right this time,* Daddy had said, as if her wedding was nothing but a big do-over for Rosemary's. By waiting nine months from the engagement to the wedding, her father could prove a point to the world about the kind of girls he had raised, if anyone cared to notice.

If Peggy hadn't been forced to spend so much time with nothing to do but choose hors d'oeuvres and napkin colors for her faraway wedding, she never would have tried out for the Aquacade in the first place. It hadn't even been her idea. Two of her girlfriends were auditioning and Peggy went with them, and guess who they chose? Tim thought this Aquacade business was all fun and games, but once the fair opened and he saw her swimsuit, and how the Aquadudes gripped the girls by the heels and scissored their legs open and shut during the water ballet, and the way the crowd went bananas through it all— well, he wasn't laughing anymore. If she chose the Aquacade over being Mrs. Timothy Halloran, even if only for a few more months, she could say good-bye to any chance of being married to Tim, whom she genuinely did love.

Then what would she do?

Follow the Aquacade to Cleveland or San Francisco? Make a living doing water ballet at some circus? How awful. Peggy wasn't like the girls backstage who thought being an Aquagal was going to lead to a starring role in the next MGM picture. Those girls had stuffed themselves on dreams of a Hollywood mansion and life as the next Mrs. Johnny Weissmuller. As far as Peggy could tell, Weissmuller might be the Aquacade's number one Aquadonis, but when he wasn't high-diving into a bottle of Dewar's, he was inviting every Aquabelle in sight back to his dressing room for a private lesson in the breaststroke. Playing Jane to that Tarzan? You'd have to be crazy to want that.

But hadn't Peggy gone crazy, too? Wasn't the heat or maybe something in the pool water driving her absolutely Bellevue-style crazy? That night with Francis: that was something a madwoman did. She had honestly been out of her mind, and when she called Rosemary the next day to say *You'll never believe what happened,* the only words that came to her were *The wedding is off,* because how could she ever say what she had done?

All she wanted was to plunge. One last time, she wanted to leap and to plunge. This afternoon, when she swam into the darkness beneath the bandstand, it would be toward a future as Mrs. Timothy Halloran. She told herself that wasn't half bad, when you thought about it. And perhaps this was the best time to stop, because part of her still wanted to stick with the Aquacade. That little bit of wanting would brighten the memory of diving into the pool, and would keep it from fading too quickly.

The 4:15 show finished with the grandest finale: Morton Downey sang "Yankee Doodle's Gonna Go to Town Again," a song Billy Rose had co-written to goose the show with a harmless bit of patriotic swagger. As the horns blared and the crowd cheered, the swimmers and dancers stretched out an American flag that was bigger than a city block. From the edge of the pool to the top of the fan-shaped staircase, the fabric rippled like a waterfall of red, white, and blue. Halfway up the staircase, Peggy gripped the shimmery edge of the flag and smiled so big that her cheeks hurt, and though she would swear it was just the chlorine, her eyes burned red and the tears streamed down her face.

THE PLAZA HOTEL

MARTIN HAD BEEN UP and down the city in search of Michael. He'd spent the night canvassing every hospital and morgue north of Fifty-First Street, grabbing a few hours of fitful sleep in the waiting room of Lenox Hill Hospital before continuing his search. He returned to the Plaza in the morning, where the elevator operator—the same one who'd said he was no seafaring man—assured Martin that he hadn't seen either of his brothers since midday Wednesday. Martin implored the man to let him, the wayward MacFarquhar brother, into the suite, but he refused, in the politest way possible. "Rules are rules," he said apologetically, though Martin suspected he would have bent the rules for his big-tipping brother. Against his better judgment, he visited the nearest police precinct, but when he was handed a missing-persons form reeking of mimeograph ink and loaded with questions about names and last known addresses, he stepped outside for a breath of air and just kept walking. He tried the park and poured a fortune in dimes into pay phones calling hospitals, police stations, Rosemary, the Plaza. As the day turned toward night, he found himself again at the Plaza, hoping that Michael had returned and wondering what the hell had happened to Francis. He was preparing himself to beg the desk clerk once more for a minute inside the suite—just to see if his poor, sick younger brother was alive or dead—when he spotted Francis himself, crossing the lobby with a man who loomed like a bodyguard, or a brick wall. Martin called out his name, aliases be damned: "Francis! Goddamn it—Francis! Stop!"

All around them milled the hubbub of a big night on the town: men in sharp suits and black tie, women in sea-foam satins, their hair netted with jewels or pinned up in waves of soft curls. Francis stood in their midst, harried and stunned, his face like a cracked egg that someone had tried to reassemble. His suit was rumpled like a paper bag and his shirt had been sweat through and pasted back on him to dry. He needed a good night's sleep, a shave, and a can of pomade. He looked, in a word, un-Franciscan. The man at his side was crammed into a blue serge suit, freshly pressed or newly purchased. He wore it with all the verve of a boy at a distant aunt's funeral.

"Where is Michael?" Martin said. "And what the hell happened to you?"

"He's upstairs," Francis said. "Isn't he?" Francis had been clinging to the hope that Michael had found his way back to the hotel. He had already planned to ask the front desk to send a typewriter to the suite so that Michael could pound out pages of questions and accusations. But if Martin was here and Michael was not, then something must have gone wrong.

Martin spat out a curse. "If you're going to lock him up here, you could at least leave word with the staff that I'm coming for him instead of just having one of your pals ring us up and scare the daylights out of Rosemary."

All of this was coming too fast for Francis. His pals? And who had called Rosemary? He eyed Cronin, wondering if the man had, in fact, shown an ounce of mercy.

"And would you look at yourself?" Martin said. "Where the hell have you been?"

"I ran into some trouble today," Francis said. "And this man—he was kind enough to help me back to the hotel."

"Today?" Martin was incredulous. "I've been here since last night and haven't seen hide nor hair of you. No one has."

Two men engaged in a heated exchange on a street corner will be left alone to sort out their differences. Most passersby will cross the street or give them a wide berth if it looks like a fight is looming. But if those same men are standing in the middle of the lobby of the Plaza Hotel, and one of them is a freshly bruised and battered Scottish lord who has lavishly tipped everyone within a handshake's length, the concierge will intervene — quickly.

"Gentlemen." It was Alphonse Collier, the hotel's concierge. "May I be of some assistance?"

Francis turned, his expression oozing patience and decorum, his voiced torqued to its most peat-smoked Highlandese. "Collier, you're just the man for the moment! My older brother Fitzwilliam — you remember him from Saturday, yes? — well, Fitzwilliam is concerned that our youngest brother may not be in our suite. That he may, in fact, be missing."

Collier eyed his guest's brother. He had heard about this one from the elevator operator: a gambler and wastrel. "I was aware that he was making inquiries as to your whereabouts and those of your brother, but you must understand, we hold your privacy in the highest — "

"Can you just tell us," Martin interrupted, "if he's in the room? That's all I want to know."

Collier gave His Lordship a sympathetic look: a difficult older brother indeed. He went on to say that the housekeeping staff had informed him that at midday, the room was undisturbed. There was no sign of anyone having slept in the room on Wednesday night. Collier noted the look of anger from the older brother, and the sickened shock that registered on His Lordship's face. "You must allow me to notify the police immediately," he said.

Martin and Cronin both looked to Francis, who matched Collier tone for tone. "I would so greatly appreciate it if you did not, at the moment, involve the authorities. With the royal visit, tensions are high and I fear police involvement may spark...undue anxiety."

Collier placed a hand over his heart, as if to indicate not only comprehension but empathy with his plight. He had seen his share of scandals, and knew how easily one wayward guest could summon a gang of shouting reporters or a troop of photographers from the celebrity magazines. "But as for your..." Collier touched his cheek, mirroring the spot where a fat bruise colored His Lordship's face.

"As long as the room has whiskey and ice, I'll be grand," Francis said. He exchanged a dry laugh with Collier, and after a curt bow, the concierge returned to his desk. Francis's performance for Collier had left him spent, and though he'd barely eaten in the past twenty-four hours, he was sure that he was about to vomit whatever was roiling in his guts. He made for the front desk, leaving Martin and Cronin to wait for him by the elevator.

Through the barrage of questions and the negotiations with the concierge, Cronin had barely budged. Two of the Dempseys had converged on him, and the youngest—despite the risk he'd taken with the phone call—was missing in a city that stripped the very meat from the bones of lambs like him. Still, Cronin knew that little Michael was the only one who was truly safe. He was in the grip of fate, but free of Gavigan's grasp.

Now with a twinge he wondered if Martin would remember him. Martin must have been eleven or twelve when Cronin last set foot in the Dempseys' house in Cork. Would he recognize a man from his youth, cloaked as he was by time and age?

Standing by the elevator, under the blush of the overhead lights, Martin gave Francis's companion the once-over. He was older than Martin and hard-weathered. His face was deeply creased and his features settled into a scowl. But the face was not unfamiliar, with its blunt nose and fierce-set eyes, and the man's voice—the south of Ireland—echoed in some neglected corner of his memory. How was it that he could go years without seeing a blood relative, and then in one week it all threatened to bury him: his brothers, his father's death, his mother's stories, and now this voice from the past? "Hold on," Martin said as Francis rejoined them. "Have we met before?"

"I don't think so," the man said. And then, as if he'd given the question further thought: "We haven't. I'm sure of it."

Now Francis gave Cronin a hard look. He'd had his suspicions, hadn't he? But unspooling them here, in the lobby, with Michael missing and Martin burning mad was out of the question. There would be no way to keep from Martin the nature of his business with Cronin, and hadn't Cronin and the old man already threatened violence against Martin's entire family? His only choice was silence. The secrets of their father's past seemed to be all around them, ready to be named, but there was no time now, and with Saturday looming, that time would never come.

"You must be thinking of some other yoke," Francis said as the doors to the elevator opened. "Because I'd sure not forget a mug like this."

ONCE THE THREE of them were in the suite, Martin and Francis ransacked Michael's room for any clues to his whereabouts. The clothes he'd worn yesterday were gone. Two clean suits hung uselessly in the closet. He had no watch, no wallet, nothing, really, to tie him to this place or to indicate his comings or goings. Through their search of the room, Martin continued to fire questions at his brother: When had Francis last seen Michael? How in hell had he lost him? Where had he been all this time? And why had it taken him so long to realize that Michael was missing? Francis, exhausted and punch-drunk, could manage only half-answers, which led only to more questions.

"Rosemary wanted to call the police straightaway," Martin said. "I had to tell her not to bother. I assume your friend is aware of why that is."

"Are you boys done?" Cronin had been gazing out the window, imagining the route from the museum to the hotel. How hard could it have been to walk down Fifth Avenue? Now he spoke from the doorway of Michael's room, his face half turned, as if a glare were coming off the brothers. "You tell the police, the hospitals, anyone who needs to know, that your cousins were visiting New York to see the World's Fair. They're staying at the Plaza—they're your rich relatives—and one of them, a deaf-mute, went for a walk and didn't come back. Give them the number here and your number in the Bronx if they find him."

"Who are you to be giving orders?" Martin said. "And how do you know I live in the Bronx?"

Sloppy. Cronin was really losing his touch.

"He's good at finding people," Francis interjected.

"And you're good at losing them. What a pair." Martin looked askance at his brother. "And what are you going to do, Your Lordship?"

Now Cronin answered for him. "He's going round to the taxicabs and the bus drivers. Museum guards, street sweepers."

"Hotel staff, too," Francis added. "Every porter, maid, and clerk knows him on sight. They should be able to smell the reward that's coming to the first that finds him."

Martin's mind was racing. What were the odds of finding Michael twenty-four hours after he'd stepped off the edge of the earth? He was once again about to hit the streets in search of him while Francis went his own direction with this rough-cut stranger who was a little too comfortable giving orders and sending Martin on his way.

"For God's sake, Francis, would you tell me what the hell is going on? You say that your top job is getting Michael fixed up and then you lose him in the middle of the city? And you're so distracted by God knows what that you don't even know he's missing, and I'm only here looking for him because some mystery man told Rosemary that

Michael—excuse me, Mr. MacFarquhar—needs minding. And now here you are with some partner in crime, and you've both been tending to some piece of business that's far more important than the well-being of your own brother. Am I leaving anything out?"

Francis felt a burning behind his eyes, his throat stripped raw. *Yes, Martin, there are things I am not telling you. Like how I'm trapped in some madman's plot to put a bullet in the king. Like how this man with me is some kind of killer. Like how you and your family and Michael could all be dead in a day or two if I don't do something terrible that you'll condemn me for as long as you live—which I hope is a long time.* It occurred to Francis that once he killed the king, and was likely killed as a result, this week would begin to make sense to his brother. Martin would see a strange logic at work that could explain all of this week's oddities: the source of his brother's bankroll, the aliases and the fancy hiding place, his strange companion, his evident preoccupation even in the face of Michael's disappearance—all of it would be made to fit a pattern that frankly made more sense than the reality Francis had stumbled into. In the retelling of events, Francis would not be a hapless pornographer but an IRA assassin dispatched to America to kill a king. Michael's injury was harder to square with this new narrative—maybe it had been an accident, just as Francis described—but the wounded Michael did provide his brother with a useful alibi. Francis was an angel of mercy, an instantly sympathetic figure to all he met. The plot was foremost, though, and when Francis needed to cast off Michael, then cast him off he did.

"I'm sorry," Francis said. "I've made a mess of everything, and I'll explain it all when I can, but for now, can we just find Michael?"

The clock in the suite faintly ticked, marking time. Francis wanted to collapse onto the couch and allow sleep to erase all of this bad business for a few hours, but he held his ground, waiting for Martin to punch him or press for answers that he could not give or simply storm out into the city.

Martin let out a long sigh. The sound of a man giving in to what life has handed him, for now. "What's his name?"

"Whose?" Francis said.

"Our brother. My cousin. My rich relative in from Scotland to see the royals. What am I to call him, so the police don't catch on that you came into the country illegally?"

"Malcolm."

"And who are you again?"

"Angus."

"Angus and Malcolm MacFarquhar? Jesus Christ, Franny. Can't you even choose a proper alias?"

FRANCIS LET OUT a sigh of his own when the door closed on Martin. The past two days had left him shattered. When he had been on the run in Ireland, he'd felt maniacally alive. The pursuit, the need to find a safe place for Michael, the arrangements for the voyage, and the constant fear that around the next corner the IRA or the police were setting a snare—all of it kept him sharp. He was out on his own, with no one to rely on for aid or advice. But now he felt like a man caught between the gears of a badly built machine. All around him, springs snapped and cogs worked against cogs. The machine ground onward toward some grim conclusion, smoke billowing all the while from its poorly greased tracks. Friction threatened to tear the whole thing apart. He collapsed heavily onto the couch where only days earlier Michael had feasted on steak and baked Alaska.

Cronin stood impassively by the window again, regarding the expanse of park hemmed in on both sides by the gray faces of apartment buildings, hotels, private clubs, churches. The sky was clear and he could see all the way to the northern end of the park and to the buildings that marked the reemergence of concrete and asphalt.

Beyond that was just more of the city, as far as the eye could see. There was no point in trying to look any farther.

"Where should we start?" Francis said.

"With what?" Cronin pulled himself away from the window.

"Looking for Michael."

"That's up to your brother," Cronin said. "You have a job to do. And if you don't do it, it's not going to matter whether or not he ever finds Michael."

"How could he just disappear?" Francis said, as much to himself as to the indifferent world. He had given up trying to elicit sympathy from Cronin. To him, Michael was merely the remainder to a problem he had been tasked with solving.

Cronin looked back and forth across the room. "Where's the money?"

Francis, his thoughts still snagged on the barbed matter of his brother's whereabouts, was baffled by the question.

"The money from Ireland," Cronin said. "Where is it?"

"Your boss agreed I'd need it, for expenses. He didn't say he wanted it back yet."

Cronin didn't want it, he told Francis. He just wanted to make sure Francis hadn't put it somewhere stupid, like under his bed. "Word'll get out that you've been found, and men will come looking for it."

"Your boss can't stop them?"

"He's not my boss," Cronin said, "and he's focused on other matters, isn't he?" Cronin almost said *distracted*. He had even thought about *gone mad*.

"It's somewhere safe."

Cronin fixed him with a stare. "Safe," he said. A preposterous word. "You know what? Don't tell me. I don't want to know."

"Too tempting?" Francis said.

"You haven't caught on yet, have you? To how any of this works? If I wanted the money, I'd've put a gun to your brother's head and sent you to fetch it. And if you'd dragged your feet, maybe I'd've broken a few of his fingers, or his whole hand, just to quicken your step."

Francis ran a hand through his hair. He had fallen into a film—*Scarface, The Public Enemy*—and they expected him to play along. "Look, Mr. Cronin," he said. "I know what the old man wants of me, and I know what he said he'll do if I don't follow through. But I'm not a killer."

"That's no matter," Cronin said. "The old man is, and that's what matters. Now, we came back here so you could get yourself cleaned up. So get yourself cleaned up."

IN THE BATHROOM, Francis contemplated his face in the mirror. It was surrounded by lightbulbs, just like the mirrors in actors' dressing rooms he'd seen in the movies. Maybe that would make this whole business easier: to think of it as a play. That's all it was. He was playing the part of the assassin; some other fellow was playing the part of the king. Anisette—the shocked witness, the ingenue betrayed—would be played by an actress best known for her star turns last season as Ophelia, as Desdemona: innocents destroyed by deceit. Another actress—a real hoot, once you got to know her—would play Félicité, the sneering Cassandra who knew it all along. The other members of the repertory would divvy up the remaining parts: the widowed queen, the society matron, the dumbstruck guard.

This was the lie, Francis decided, that he would tell himself until even he believed it. *It is only a play, I am only an actor, the gun is but a prop.* And what a laugh the cast would have when the set was struck and the theater went dark and they all met around the corner for a drink.

CRONIN HAD BRISTLED at being Gavigan's errand boy, but now, fuming, he realized he was something worse. He had been tasked with finding Francis Dempsey and he had done that. He had been sent to nick him off the street in broad daylight, and he had done that. And now a new assignment—a lead role in this madman's plan cooked up by Gavigan: to keep watch over Dempsey and prepare him to kill.

How could he do that when he was crowded on all sides by ghosts? Being around Francis made him edgy enough, and now the older Dempsey brother had appeared. When Martin had called out to them, a shock ran the length of Cronin's spine, and he had to wonder if Martin felt the same. Was there some nugget buried deep in Martin's memory, alert to contact with those from his past? A man who knew his parents. Who had been in the family home. Who had blown the family to bits. Cronin had told himself for years that it was Frank who was the betrayer, Frank who had broken with his comrades and supported a bad treaty. Only later did he realize, did he admit, that he didn't plant the bomb because Frank had chosen the other side. The purpose of the bomb was to undo the man Cronin had become— the man he'd let Frank make him into. One last spilling of blood, and then no more: that was his plan. He was young enough and stupid enough to believe that Frank's death would bring him some measure of peace. When the bomb went off and it was Bernadette who died, Cronin knew he would never be able to wash off the blood. Bernadette was their saint, anyone would tell you that, and if she was their Joan of Arc, then Cronin was the man who'd lit the match and tossed it on the pyre. He was a pariah. An untouchable. Within days of the blast he was packed off on a merchant ship bound for the States, traveling under papers that blotted out his name but couldn't hide what he'd done. The only man willing to offer him refuge was Gavigan. Every other door was closed to him.

Cronin had come to understand that service to Gavigan had no end. He thought of the moment at the farm when Gavigan saw his desire to strike the old man dead. If it hadn't been for Jamie, there at the end of the lane with the long gun laid across his lap, he would have done it. Alice would have accepted it. He had told her enough.

But then he thought of the boy. What would it have done to him to see "my Tom," as he called Cronin, take the life of another man? Even a bad man like Gavigan? There would be a time for teaching the boy that the world was a dangerous place full of bad men—men like Gavigan, men like Cronin himself—but that time was not now.

Gavigan had packed Cronin and Dempsey into one of the taxis earlier that evening. He had a list of instructions for Cronin, none of which Cronin was keen to perform. He needed to round up formal attire for the boy—Francis couldn't meet the king dressed for a day in the park—and a new suit for himself. "In that country getup at the Plaza," Gavigan had said to Cronin, "you're going to stick out like a nun in a whorehouse." Gavigan wanted Dempsey back at the hotel in case his wealthy friends needed to contact him about the royal visit, and if Cronin needed any pocket money, he was free to tap into the cache Dempsey had spirited out of Ireland. It had been meant to finance a major operation, and what operation, in the whole history of the IRA, was bigger than this?

And then there was this last item on the list: to instruct Dempsey in the use of the weapon he would carry for the job. Gavigan owned an old carbarn below the meatpacking district, a place where trolleys had once been serviced and stowed. The cavernous space sat beneath the elevated tracks, swathed in a constant din that made it an ideal shooting range. That was where Dempsey would practice the quick draw, the arm extension, and the spasm of finger on trigger that could send history careening in unforeseen directions.

Gavigan's plan was pure madness, and Cronin suspected that even Gavigan knew that he was way beyond the pale. Why else did he need Cronin? Why else wouldn't he keep Dempsey at Gramercy Park himself until he was ready to unleash him? He didn't want his own fingerprints on this bomb he was preparing to toss.

This was what Cronin now realized: that Gavigan had kept his own name out of the boy's ears, but had freely thrown around Cronin's. If

Dempsey carried out his task, he would not know the name of the man who had put him up to it, but he would know Cronin's. That was a name the police could wring from him, if he survived. So now it was in Cronin's interest to make sure that Francis did what he was told and then see that he didn't leave the fairgrounds alive. Of course Gavigan saw that, and of course Gavigan knew that Cronin saw it, too.

THE BOWERY

MICHAEL FOUND HIMSELF IN bed, the same bed where he had slept the night before, and that had to be some comfort. The pale glimmer of the street lamps bled through the windows and next to him the woman—his benefactor, his caretaker—slept serenely, her back to him. He thought that if she could roll over and throw an arm around his shoulder, that might make the night a biteen more bearable.

Da was dead and there was no one to console him. Francis had been in the church, he remembered that now, and of course Martin had to know. They must have assumed that he remembered the funeral, if nothing else, and that explained the duration of the embraces he'd received from Martin and Rosemary. Here was Michael, the youngest, battered in some terrible way, and he had lost his father. The sight of him smiling like an idiot through dinner must have confirmed that he had gone simple—Michael, who had spent so many years alone with Da, the two of them ticking like the gears of a watch, barely touching but always in concord. How many hours had the two of them passed together, each with a nose in a book and rarely a word exchanged, yet each happy in his own way. Hours? It had been years. A lifetime, really.

Michael had called an end to those slow, quiet hours. After Eileen broke his heart, he looked for the surest way out of Ballyrath. He wanted to be rid of the place, and Da was part of that bargain. When he first heard that Eileen was to marry Old Doonan, he concocted wild plans of escape: they would run off to Dublin, to London, even

America, if necessary. He begged his father to speak to Mr. Casey, to propose Michael as a better match for Eileen. His father had been reading and he kept his eyes on the page—*Aeneid,* book VII—all through his son's plea that he talk some sense into Eileen's father. How could he force his daughter to hitch herself to a slatty-ribbed, toothless bachelor coming up hard on his fiftieth birthday? There had to be a reason that such a man had never found himself a wife.

Michael's father put the book in his lap and told Michael not to waste his time. His own, for thinking he could put a stop to this marriage, and his father's, for hectoring him about such a futile mission.

"Casey is a peasant farmer," his father had said, "and the only language he understands is acres and cattle. How many acres will you be gifting to your new father-in-law when the deed is done? And how many bulls?"

"He wouldn't sell his own daughter," Michael said.

"He already has, and for a price you could not match." Da lifted the book from his lap, ready to return to Aeneas, last seen trudging through the underworld in search of his own father. He stared at the page, seemingly unable to find a toehold in the text. "Michael," he said at last. "She's a fine girl but you're too young to get married anyhow."

"But Da," he said. "I love her."

His father's eyes were back on the page, scanning lines. "If only that were all it took."

Michael waited for his father to say more, to look at him again and tell him that they would take this matter in hand. Go to Mr. Casey and talk some sense into him: Couldn't he see that Michael and Eileen were meant for each other? They were young, but they could wait. Michael would someday soon go out into the world. His father had promised him a university education, and who knew where that could lead? Give him time to get established and he could do more for Eileen than Doonan ever could. A man like that was likely to leave her a widow before too long, and then where would Eileen be? But Michael already knew the answer, and he knew that Mr. Casey had made the same grim calculations. Eileen and however many babies Doonan could get from her—the thought of it made him sick—would inherit all that he had piled up in his mean existence, and Casey would add these holdings to his own meager scrap.

Was this why Eileen had been so cold to him in recent days, had refused to listen to his plans for escape, for an elopement that would prevent a union with Doonan? "For the family, Eileen." That's what her father had told her when he broke the news of her engagement. "You'll do this for your family, you selfish girl." Maybe Eileen had always known that this would be her fate. Maybe she had known for years; had known that her time with Michael—walking through fields and sitting among the stone walls, rock upon rock, and those few quick eternally burning kisses—was limited. She was snatching happiness where she could. What was the point of burdening Michael with that same foreknowledge of doom that hung over her? She knew that he'd rail against the marriage and her father and the world in a way that she no longer could. The effort had exhausted her long ago. She knew that Michael would also rail against her, for not refusing, for not running off with him toward happiness and away from the ruin of her family.

He could not live in that place any longer. He wanted to be out of Ballyrath before the wedding, which gave him little time to act. Martin was in New York, but with America closing itself to newcomers, it could take years, he now realized, to emigrate. Francis had recently landed in Mountjoy, and wouldn't be hosting visitors anytime soon. Father Hogan had been telling Michael for years that the door to the priesthood was always open. With no other means of escape that he could see, he marched away from his father and his *Aeneid* and straight to the rectory, where the old priest was reading an American detective novel. When Michael told his father that he was bound for

St. Columbanus, it was Da's turn to rail: an infantile decision, he told his son. Mooning over a country girl was no reason to make a mistake that would ruin the rest of his life.

Michael had never seen him so animated. He had certainly never had so much attention directed his way. But he was resolute. "I have a calling," Michael said.

"Bollocks," his father said.

"Am I supposed to stay in Ballyrath the rest of my life? Is that it?"

"You're giving up the whole world over a rash, stupid decision."

"The world?" Michael said. "What's that? Something I only know from my brother's letters."

"Go, then," his father said. "You're old enough to make your own mistakes."

And so he went. He said a terse farewell and made his way to the next town over, where a bus brought him to the gates of St. Columbanus. He often imagined his father sitting, a book in his lap, before the turf fire. His own chair empty. But as bad as things were at the seminary, he would not trade it for his old chair by the fire. Ballyrath was the past. Eileen was the past. At the time, he wasn't as sure about consigning his father to the long-ago—he still imagined some kind of reunion, if not a reconciliation—but now, as the séance had shown him, that decision had been made for him. That was the news he'd received that rainy morning when he was called out of the classroom. That was the reason for the desolate transit to the small church where he and Francis had sat, side by side, only an arm's length away from the box containing their father's body.

FRIDAY
JUNE 9

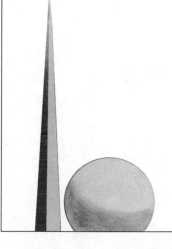

MORRISANIA

WHAT WAS THE PROPER way to dress when applying for relief? Was it better to go in rags, to create a picture of desperate poverty that would prick the sympathy of the agent processing your application? Or was it better to go in your Sunday best, dignity intact, even as you admitted to a stranger behind a desk that you could not provide for yourself? Rosemary had opted for Sunday best: a blue dress, a short white jacket, gloves, pearls. The pearls might have been overdoing it, and as she sat on the long bench, the forms in her lap, waiting to hear her name called, she stealthily tucked the strand—a graduation gift from her parents—under her collar. She didn't know if this was a busier than usual day at the relief office or if the place was always this crowded. She had waited in line for an hour just to get inside and that had been the worst part so far. The standing she could manage; what ate at her was the fear of being recognized. *Rosemary? What are* you *doing here?* She assumed that everyone in the line would feel the same way, and sure enough there were plenty who studiously avoided catching the eyes of the others. She thought about the men she'd seen in breadlines, and how they had looked stooped to half their height. She'd figured that life had broken them like matchsticks. Now she knew that it wasn't weariness but shame that caused them to hide their faces.

How then to explain the others in line—men and women both— who chatted like this was some kind of social hour? One woman

fanned herself with a copy of the *Bronx Home News* while her friend
rattled on about someone named Jimmy and how if he thought that
she was going to put up with *that kind of malarkey, well, then, he has
another think coming.* Two men smoked and talked boxing. One said
Joe Louis was washed up, a palooka, ready to call it quits. "Washed
up?" the other said. "Why you gotta admit, out here in public, in
fronta the whole world, that you don' know nothin' about boxing?" A
few years ago and Rosemary would have jumped right into that conversation. Her father had been a bantamweight in his younger days
and she had grown up with stories of the night he knocked out a
bruiser from Far Rockaway in less than a minute. As a girl, she read
the sports pages every morning, and for her tenth birthday, her father
took her to a boxing match at Madison Square Garden. She could still
remember the glare of the overhead lights punching through the haze
of sweat and cigarette smoke. The shouting surged as a scrappy fly-
weight pinned his opponent against the ropes with a flurry of jabs.
Later the Garden exploded when a heavyweight landed a sledge-
hammer right to the head. But nowadays she barely glanced at the
sports pages. Martin had little interest in sports—or *sport,* as he called
it, in his funny Irish way—and the other mothers she knew wouldn't
recognize Joe DiMaggio in a police lineup, and couldn't tell you who
the heavyweight champion was if you offered them five dollars to do it.

Once Rosemary was inside, she gave her name and was handed a
number, just as if she were at the bakery. She tried to imagine what it
would sound like if they called out her old name, Rosemary Dwyer,
and it was too terrible to contemplate. The Dwyers didn't go on relief.
They helped out the unfortunate—found them jobs with the borough, connected them to the few people hiring these days—and they
felt good about doing it. Public service, after all. But a Dwyer on the
receiving end of a handout? Never. At least she had found an office far
from Woodlawn, and far enough from her own apartment that she
was unlikely to run into any neighbors. She hadn't even told Angela

Videtti why she was going out, only that she needed her to watch the girls for an hour or two. Rosemary could hardly imagine the stories Angela would tell—dressed up nice, and twice in one week?—or the size of the favors Angela would call in as compensation.

At least the name on the forms would be Dempsey, and there were no Dempsey relatives to mortify—other than Martin. He had his pride, and he would have refused to let her come here, which was why she didn't tell him. Four years married and here she was, keeping secrets. But what was she supposed to do? He had lost his mind, quitting his job, and all he could offer her was a secret plan that would make it all better. In the meantime there were two little girls who needed to eat and have cozy beds where parents could tell them a story and tuck them in at night. That part seemed to have slipped his mind. She believed that he would come to his senses, but unless she could find a way to bring in some money, what would be left when he finally came around?

She thought again of the waitress at Driscoll's—she could do that; she could work all day without a word of complaint—and she thought again of Peggy. Everything came so easy to Peggy. Even asking for things was easy for her. She felt no guilt in stretching out her hand, perhaps because she believed that she deserved whatever came her way. Why not ask Daddy for a few dollars to bring her friends to the movies, and why not compel their mother to buy her a new pair of shoes? She wanted to go to the movies. She wanted a new pair of shoes. End of story.

Rosemary had always had trouble asking, and now asking was out of the question. How could she tell her parents that Martin had quit his job? It wasn't even their derision that bothered her—they couldn't think worse of him than they already did. It was their pity that would choke her. Poor Rosemary, who could have done so much more. Who could have *been* so much more. Now every misfortune confirmed for her parents all of the horrible things they had first said to her, and about her, when she told them she was pregnant. If she told them that Martin had quit his job and that they were on relief, the weight of their pity would obliterate her.

Of course Martin would be humiliated that she had even set foot in the relief office, but why did she always have to be the one who kept a level head and made the right decisions—the one everyone counted on, at the same time that they chided her for being too serious, for not knowing how to have fun? This was where her mother's voice chimed in: *Because the one time you thought that you could let go, give in, have fun—look what happened.* Martin said he had a plan, but she didn't want a plan. She wanted a husband who understood his responsibilities to his family. To his children. To her.

A WOMAN CALLED out, "Dempsey! Four-oh-one!" It took a moment for Rosemary to remember: yes, that was her name and that was her number. She gathered her purse and stared for a moment at her hand, which felt curiously empty. Kate's hand was always in hers when they were out of the house. The woman who had called her number waved a clipboard to indicate the office where Rosemary was to sit. In the room, a different woman was turning the crank on a desk-mounted pencil sharpener. She removed the pencil, now pointy as a knitting needle, stuck in another blunt-nosed pencil, and churned the handle: another needle.

"I just got this thingamabob and I love it," she said. "It does exactly what it's supposed to, every time."

"It's very nice," Rosemary said.

"You wouldn't believe how fast we go through these things." She held up a sharpened pencil. "We get people coming in here every day, sitting right where you are now. Wears out the pencils, then it wears out the sharpeners, then it wears out the people doing the sharpening."

Rosemary wasn't sure whether it was meant lightheartedly or as some kind of accusation. Either way, the woman stared at her without smiling. Her hair was combed into a tight bun and although perspiration dotted her forehead, over her shoulders was draped a pale blue cardigan, secured at the neck with a silver chain. In the corner of the room an electric fan spun languidly, faintly scraping its cage with each rotation. The air smelled of dust and old paper livened up only by a hint of mimeograph ink. The woman tapped a tall stack of papers on her desk with the pencil. Rosemary recognized her own handwriting, upside down, on the form at the top of the pile.

Maybe the gloves had been too much.

As if reciting a script for a role she had grown tired of playing, the woman introduced herself as Miss Costigan. She would be Rosemary's relief agent. Any question Rosemary had was to be directed to her and her only. Attempting to contact another relief agent, either in this office or in another relief office elsewhere, would only create confusion, and would be sure to delay the answer to any queries that Rosemary might have. It would also require duplication of effort, which was wasteful, and this was not an agency that looked kindly on waste. Waste would not be rewarded. Did Rosemary understand?

Rosemary understood.

Miss Costigan explained that before any assistance was made available, an investigation had to be undertaken. Not only would there be a home visit to ascertain the family's level of need, but the family's willingness to help themselves had to be ascertained as well. Did Rosemary understand?

Well, not exactly, she said.

"You would be surprised," Miss Costigan said, "or perhaps you would not, to learn that there are those who apply for relief who have no real need. Goldbrickers, we call them. And there are also people who apply for relief who are very needy but have no intention of seeking or accepting work of any kind. These people we call freeloaders. So the first question, Mrs. Dempsey, is whether you are a goldbricker or a freeloader."

413

"I can assure you," Rosemary said, "that I'm neither of those things. My husband and I are decent people who've fallen on hard times."

"I'm happy to hear that," she said through a sour smile that did not appear happy. "Then you won't have any problems with the investigation. We have your address and that's a starting point, but we'll need more information before we can really get started."

"What sort of information?"

"Next of kin, for both you and your husband. Often those closest to you are the best source of help in troubled times. Maybe you have a rich uncle who could do for you what you're asking the government to do instead?"

Rosemary's stomach sank. She tried to picture Miss Costigan sitting in her parents' parlor, on the divan, as her father poured Scotch into an ice-filled tumbler.

"And we'll need to contact your husband's most recent employer."

"My husband lost his job. That's why I'm here."

"Yes, but why did he lose it? That's one of the questions we'll want to ask. Men lose jobs for all sorts of reasons, only some of which they tell their wives. Is your husband a drinker, for instance? Does he pull his weight? Is he a goldbricker or a freeloader at work? All of these things can help us determine his prospects for finding another job."

He's an occasional drinker who mostly pulls his weight, Rosemary thought. *Except for when he quits his job.* "My husband is a very diligent man, Miss Costigan."

"And what line of work is he in?"

"He was—he is—a musician."

"That's his job? He gets paid for that?"

Rosemary had heard variations on this theme plenty of times—boy, had she ever. It was a much easier question when the answer was yes. "He's quite talented," she said.

Miss Costigan made a note on the page in front of her. "But he's open to other forms of employment?" She spoke without looking up. "Because I can tell you, we don't see many jobs for musicians."

"I thought the Federal Music Project could be a possi—"

"Budget just got cut for that one," she said.

"Or the Federal Theatre Project. He can play piano, clarinet, saxophone—"

"You don't want to go within a mile of that one," Miss Costigan said. "First off, it's full of Reds. And between you, me, and the pencil sharpener, the word is the whole project will be kaput by the end of the month."

Rosemary looked down at her hands. She'd thought this was going to turn out a bit better. "I'm sure there are many other things he could do."

"Regardless, we'll need to talk to his last employer. So I'll need names, addresses, phone numbers—all of it. And then I'll need the same for his parents—"

"My husband's parents are deceased."

Miss Costigan looked up from her note-taking. "I'm sorry to hear that," she said. "But we'll need to see death certificates for confirmation."

"He's an immigrant," Rosemary said. "His parents lived—they died—in Ireland."

"We'll need proof of his citizenship status, then. I assume that you're from here? You don't sound like you're from somewhere else."

"Yes, I'm an American."

"Then we'll need the same information for your family. Names, addresses, phone numbers, starting with your maiden name. You left that blank on the form."

"Oh, did I?" Rosemary was in a sweat. Why had she started this disaster? She wanted to keep food on the table, to keep Kate in shoes and Evie in diapers and herself from sinking under the weight of a husband who had temporarily lost his mind. She knew the relief office didn't just hand out cash to all comers, but now the calls and the visits would start and everyone from Mrs. Fichetti to the neighbors to her parents and her sister would know just how bad it had gotten.

"Mrs. Dempsey? Your maiden name?"

"Oh, I'm sorry," she said, blinking in the room's dozy haze. "It's MacFarquhar."

"Mac—you'll have to spell that for me."

Rosemary recited it, letter by letter. "It's Scottish," she said.

"And your parents? They can be found—"

"They've passed away, too."

Miss Costigan seemed annoyed. "Both of them?"

"Yes." Rosemary pressed her gloved hands together, a vaguely prayer-like gesture. Hadn't her mother taught her that there was no better way to invite tragedy than to speak it out loud? And yet it was all she could do to keep from bursting out laughing. "In a shipwreck," she said. "My father worked for the Museum of Natural History as a polar explorer. Have you ever seen the polar bears at the museum? In the glass case? Father—Captain MacFarquhar—shot them and brought their hides back to New York. It was his greatest triumph. The King of the Arctic, they called him."

Miss Costigan sat stone-faced, but Rosemary felt like her blood had been replaced by something hot and lively: the gin she smelled on Martin's breath when he came home from the clubs, or the whiskey in the decanter in her parents' parlor.

"My mother insisted on accompanying him on his last expedition, to Greenland. It was supposed to have been fairly simple—just mapping the glaciers—but their ship struck an iceberg. I was left in the care of my grandparents, but they're deceased, too. Just a few years ago."

Miss Costigan tapped the pencil, point first, into the stack of papers. Rosemary could see a Morse code of dots and scratches. "Mrs. Dempsey, this is all a bit hard to believe."

"Oh, they were quite famous, both of them, in the twenties," Rosemary said. "I have a scrapbook at home full of newspaper articles, and there's a plaque in his honor at the museum—right there in the great hall. It mentions my mother as well. She was one of the only people in all of New York who could speak the language of the Eskimos."

Outside the window of Miss Costigan's office, men and women fidgeted on the long wooden benches, waiting for their number to be called. The murmur of voices and the scraping of feet, punctuated by *"Faw-oh-ate! Num-bah faw-oh-ate,"* came through the transom window.

"That's all very interesting," Miss Costigan said. "But we'll have to start somewhere else with the investigation. Your husband's most recent employer was..."

"The Staten Island Symphony Orchestra."

"Staten Island has an orchestra?"

"They do—well, did. They've just recently gone bankrupt. A terrible scandal. Received a great deal of coverage in the *Times*."

IN THE END, Miss Costigan told her to come back at a later date, after Rosemary had gathered the information that would be needed to investigate her claim. There was so much that Rosemary had to collect: a current address and phone number for the conductor of the orchestra; her parents' death certificates, which Rosemary said she would have to retrieve from the Danish embassy—or whoever it was that now laid claim to Greenland. She could have gone on for hours, unspooling the star-crossed history of the MacFarquhars. She hadn't even mentioned how her mother came to learn Eskimo (a girlhood spent in the far northern reaches of Canada with her fur-trapper father). And she had only hinted at the tragedies that had befallen her husband's family. Long before the orchestra was forced to close its doors—only days before her husband's first symphony was to have its

417

world premiere—the Dempseys had been a family driven and derided by misfortune, from the era of the Vikings on down through the Great War.

That feeling of fire in her veins stayed with her until she rose to leave Miss Costigan's office. It was then that the weight of her mission suddenly settled on her shoulders again. Her family was in need and she had let her pride get in the way of seeking help. She'd had her fun, but when the icebox was empty and the cabinets bare, she would remember this moment.

Then it struck her: Did it have to be *when?* Couldn't it be *if?* And *if* it came to that—if Martin's plans fell to pieces and he was exposed as a fraud or a failure—couldn't she wait until then to march back into Miss Costigan's office, children in tow, paperwork in order, her hands bare and chapped, and claim what they needed to survive? For now, she was going to allow herself to believe that Martin had an absolute doozy of a plan. She was going to go home and steel herself for her sister's rehearsal dinner. She would put on her best dress, the one she had last worn before Kate was born, the one that had made Martin glow at the sight of her. She would shake the hands of the Halloran family and brag about her husband and she would stare into the future that lay ahead of them and she would not blink. After all, she was the daughter of Captain MacFarquhar, the King of the Arctic. Hadn't her family endured worse?

"Mrs. Dempsey? Mrs. Dempsey!" Apparently Miss Costigan had been calling her name, but Rosemary had been too distracted to notice.

"I'm sorry," she said, glancing around her. "It's this heat. I'll be going."

"Take this." Miss Costigan, annoyed and impatient, waved a pink square of paper at Rosemary. "Go on, take it."

On the paper was the phone number for a WPA office in Manhattan. There was a new project to produce children's books for the board of education but the first few editions had been a bust. The problem wasn't the morals of the stories, which were just what the WPA had ordered—love of country, democratic values, a sense of justice. It was that the stories themselves were, in a word, boring.

"Thank you," Rosemary said. "My husband doesn't have much experience as a writer, but I'm sure he'll take to it. He wrote a song, you see—"

"It's not for your husband," Miss Costigan said. "It's for you. Call them on Monday and tell them I sent you. And tell them I said you had a flair for...let's just call it the dramatic."

IN TRANSIT

"WHAT AM I GOING to do with you?" Lilly said aloud. "And what am I going to do with me?"

Her guest did not answer either question. He sat on the edge of the bed with that distant look in his eye. Lilly had washed his shirt in the large sink and hung it overnight by the windows. As dusty sunlight filled the studio, Lilly watched her neighbors dragging their mattresses off the fire escapes and back into their cramped, overheated apartments. The shirt, which his fit of tears had left a mess, was wrinkled but clean. Perhaps she could buy him a new suit as a going-away present—something nice, so he wouldn't be mistaken for a vagrant.

She had stayed up late into the night, labeling and packing. Beneath the bed she had found the city guidebook given to her by the Foundation when she'd first arrived in New York. The book was thicker than a cigar box, too big to carry anywhere, and even in the studio she had only glanced at it. Josef had been right about her: without the New York List, she would have spent three months wandering the city, taking pictures, never knowing where she was and overlooking the red-letter sights pictured on the postcards. But now she thumbed through the index until she found *Hospitals*. There was a Hospital for the Insane on one of the city's smaller islands, but the book said it was being "slowly evacuated." Farther uptown was the Neurological Institute, but the brief write-up described experiments conducted on children—"scientific twins" whose development was tracked by doctors—and Lilly wanted no part of that. There was a Babies' Hospital, a Doctors' Hospital, a French Hospital, and a Jewish Memorial. Finally, in the four pages devoted to Bellevue Hospital, Lilly began to believe she might have found a new caretaker for her guest. The guidebook mentioned "pleasant murals," "clean red brick," and "a program of modernization." It was almost enough to obscure the references to overcrowding, a sense of confinement, and patients drawn from the city's "alcoholics, the sexually unbalanced, and the hysterical." Her guest was none of these, but neither was he her pet, her plaything, her child, or her lover. He had to go somewhere—just as she did—but it wouldn't be today. Today would be their last together, and they would spend it as two New Yorkers with busy New York lives.

Back in April, which now seemed eons ago, Mr. Musgrove had put Lilly in touch with curators from the Museum of Modern Art. She had met with them twice, and there had been talk at the last meeting of including her work in some future exhibition, perhaps even buying some of her street photography for the permanent collection. Despite the great heavy blind that she had tried to draw over any thoughts of life beyond tomorrow, she knew she needed to think about the future. If not for herself, then for her work. A last visit to the museum would get her away from the studio and perhaps allow her to stumble into another item on the New York List. She laid the list flat on the table, its folded lines so frayed that the paper threatened to separate. Next to the list she laid the note from the séance: *George, Francis, London, the tower, Michael, no, no, nein*. Wouldn't *this* be a story for Josef? But she would get to tell him only if she ignored his letter and thrust aside the mystic visions of the medium.

FROM THE INSTANT Michael opened his eyes that morning he was smothered by the knowledge of his father's death. There was no moment of half-sleepy forgetting, no zone of questioning whether he'd been dreaming. He came into the day and there it was, just where he'd left it the night before. He lay on his side probing the wound, feeling the ache of loss and knowing that the sharp pain of missing his father would get worse before it ever began to fade. He was still in shock, he knew that. The real pain was yet to come.

He had abandoned his father, left him isolated and alone. Betrayed him, even. It didn't matter that his brothers had also left, and neither of them under pleasant circumstances either. Michael was the closest to his father and understood him better than his brothers did, and he knew that his own departure was the biggest shock of the three. Even as a boy, he knew Martin was in a fevered rush to get free of Bally-rath, and Francis had always been restless, too. Michael, by contrast, had seemed content until the blowup about Eileen. Then, at the first sign that his father had failed him, he ranted and ran off. If he was being honest with himself, he would admit that he chose the priest-hood in part because he knew the anguish it would bring his father— a man who was barely Catholic. Michael sometimes wondered if his father believed in any god who hadn't played a role in the Trojan War. To lose a son to the gold-plated promises of America or the cheap come-ons of Dublin was bad enough. But to see Michael cheerfully enlist in the ghastly corps of missionary priests was surely more than a man like Francis Dempsey Sr. could bear. But why had his father been calling out to him from the beyond? Was it to castigate him? To pull him out of the oblivion that followed Whatever Happened? To grab one last chance to say good-bye? He had wrestled with the ques-tions all morning, but he had no answers.

At no point in his deliberations did it occur to Michael that his depar-ture from Ballyrath was only the latest in a lifetime of abandonments, losses, and disappointments suffered by his father—not to mention the weight of the losses and hurt he had inflicted on others—and that every heart has more than its share of reasons to stop beating.

Michael hadn't seen Yeats all morning. Under the guidance of his host, he dressed and prepared to leave, though he didn't know where they were going. He was content to be led. The studio was sparser than it had been yesterday; even the camera whose flash had knocked him unconscious was safely stowed for travel. She seemed aware that he had been devastated in some way, and she was careful not to handle him too firmly.

They went out from her building to the street market two blocks away, and as soon as he inhaled the damp, yeasty smell of food his stomach gurgled to life. From a paper-lined bin in a pushcart, Lilly withdrew two golden pastries and handed one to Michael. It was hot against his fingers and he blew on it before taking a bite and discovering it was filled with pillowy mashed potatoes rich with salt and pepper. In other bins were braided and knotted and coiled breads, and in the next cart two tall samovars dispensed what his nose told him was tea. He tugged on Lilly's sleeve and pointed imploringly toward that cart. In a moment he had a cup of tea in one hand and the savory pastry in the other. All around him men in black caps and women toting heavy bags swayed. Children chased each other—the girls in long skirts and the boys in short pants. Michael filled his mouth with crispy pastry and spuds and sipped at his tea. Thirty minutes earlier, he would have sworn that he could taste only ashes, but he enjoyed this good food and the sugared tea even as he felt the sharp ache of loss. Until he could find his brothers and do a proper job of mourning his father, he would honor him here, among the multitudes, with a wish that the afterlife found him in better company than poor, lonely Yeats.

"HERE IS HOW we should proceed," Yeats said.

Michael had been staring out the window of the elevated train, catching glimpses of the East River and the docklands at each cross street. Now he turned to face the poet, who had taken the seat beside him. "Why didn't you tell me sooner?" he said.

"About your father?" Yeats said, seemingly surprised by the question. "Because I didn't know. And then I did." Yeats folded his hands in his lap. If he had been visible to any of the other riders, he would have seemed ungainly and out of place. He did not look like a man accustomed to mass transit.

"The next time you go … away," Michael said, "could you deliver a message to him?"

"It's not how this works," Yeats said. "There's no grand ballroom where the souls of the departed mill about in conversation." He pointed to their benefactor, who sat in the row in front of Michael. "I would, however, like to renew our efforts to communicate with our cordial host."

"Not another séance," Michael said. "I'm done with that business."

"No, not another séance. A map, but so simple in its execution that even you could draw it, and which will lead her—"

"The only people I want to communicate with are my brothers. And the only discovery that matters is that my father is dead." Michael's face was faintly mirrored on the train's window. He looked just like himself, like he had always looked to himself. Why was there no one in this city who could recognize him?

"Do you have any children, Mr. Yeats?"

Yeats seemed taken aback. "I have a daughter, Anne. And a son, called Michael."

"Michael? And you haven't thought to mention that?"

"It didn't seem relevant."

Relevant. Michael brooded over the word for a moment. With everything so topsy-turvy, who could say what was relevant? All of it was, or else none of it. "How old is he?" he said.

"About your age, I imagine."

"And that's not relevant, either?"

Yeats only shrugged.

"What sort of a fellow is your Michael?"

"Oh, he's a fine lad, I'd say. Very interested in history and politics. Last time I saw him must have been autumn. We went round and round about the Czech situation — Chamberlain and all that."

"Autumn?" Michael said. "And you passed away in winter, wasn't it? So you didn't see much of each other, then?"

"He spent — spends — most of his time in Ireland, with his mother."

"So your wife is often away as well?"

"I'm the one who's away — who was, who is...however you want to phrase it. London mostly, the English countryside. I have — I had — rather a large circle of friends and patrons, as you can imagine, and a number of...relationships, which can be complicated affairs." Yeats removed his glasses and set about polishing the lenses. "When the children were young, it wasn't possible to work when they were about. Noisy and nosy, as children tend to be." He replaced his glasses on the bridge of his nose and crossed his legs, right over left, and switched, left over right. "I'm not what you'd call a family man, if that's what you're getting at. George knew that when we married."

"I'm not getting at anything," Michael said. "Except to say that I *am* what you'd call a family man — or I'd like to be. If I could find my brothers, that would be enough. There's nothing for me in France, or London, or Ireland. My father is dead, my brothers are here — somewhere — and the girl I loved is married off to a toothless old man. The only thing I left in Ireland is my senses and I don't think I'll be able to recover those by going back. The only healing, psychical or otherwise, is going to come from a reunion with my family. So I will not draw your map, and I will not baffle this good woman with visions and voices from the great beyond. If that's not to your liking, then sod off back to the spirit realm."

THEY — THAT is, Michael and Lilly — exited the train and stood together on the elevated platform. There was no sign of Yeats. Michael's view out the west-facing windows had been blocked by the

425

standing passengers, but as the train pulled away, he saw before him the recognizable landmarks of his first days in the city: the Chrysler Building, the Empire State, and, on a straight line in front of him, the narrow-shouldered, pin-striped tower that soared above the golden man. He seized Lilly's sleeve and stretched out his arm like a man in a crow's nest sighting land.

The walk to the museum was four blocks the long way, avenue to avenue, but he stretched the distance by jogging one block south for each block west. Lilly would have tried to steer him but he moved with such purpose, and with such a sense of lightness, as if a great weight had been lifted. The tea and the potato knish had restored him somewhat, and now, having reached Fifth Avenue, with its jewelry shops, furriers, ateliers, and boutiques, he was positively rejuvenated.

Lilly's hand went to the scarf knotted at her neck as she caught sight of the shop where she'd purchased it—could it really have been only a few days since her failed interview at the Foundation? She thought again of the view from the top of the tower, looking west: the foreground with buildings, spires, and water tanks; then the rows of ocean liners jutting into the river; then the river itself set ablaze by the afternoon sun; then the high ridge of the Palisades, and beyond it nothing, she imagined, but open country.

Lilly was yanked from her reverie by her guest, who took her by the arm and pointed excitedly at the bronze-hooped globe and its burly Atlas. Across the avenue sprouted a cathedral in the Gothic style, but of a much more recent vintage. The soot of the city was only just beginning to dim the glow of its crystalline towers, but given a few centuries of smoke and pigeon shit, it could rival the dingy beauties of Europe.

He urged her forward, an impatient guide eager to show her the sights: another church fronted by sad-faced saints, a lobby entrance guarded by snake-tongued Harpies and golden-robed goddesses. None of this impressed Lilly, who steadied the boxy Rolleiflex to keep it from thumping against her chest. She typically moved at a more sedate, unobtrusive pace that allowed her to see the compositions unfolding around her. Up ahead, a thickly built woman draped in a dusky frock, her silver hair pinned against her scalp, was peering into a shop window. The display was a mock boudoir, with frothy lingerie scattered across Louis XIV chairs and spilling from the drawers of a chiffonier. If she'd been alone, Lilly would have framed a shot that captured the woman's face: Were her lips pursed and her eyes narrowed in distaste? Or did her expression suggest a long-simmering memory of some frenzied night in the previous century?

Before she could get closer, the boy jogged her arm and—*Just a little farther!*—beckoned her onward. They crossed another street, a wave of pedestrians surging around them, and then another and another. In this city there was such freedom to move, there was an excess of it, and the people flaunted their ability to walk where they wanted, when they wanted. Prague had been like that when she left it: Lilly could stroll forever, and if she ever felt boxed in by Prague, there was always Paris, just as earlier there had been Berlin and Barcelona. Why would she give up the simple thrill of walking—walking!—to return to a city where everyone would be assigned a place, and where rules, and walls, and worse would keep them from moving?

They crossed another street and now the edge of the park rose before them: a picket of trees and beyond it—or so the guidebook claimed—an urban oasis of paths, meadows, and ponds. He came to a stop in front of the grand hotel on the corner and with a flourish of his hand, as if unveiling a portrait, he directed Lilly's attention to the door. As she looked up at the white façade, its rows of windows, its steeply pitched roof, she remembered the fairy-tale castle, and of course the park was its enchanted forest. The smile on his face and his eager wish to draw her inside seemed proof that this was his home, and that her little pauper was in fact princely.

GANSEVOORT STREET

Years earlier, Gavigan had secured a deal with a city commissioner that paid him to provide storage for a fleet of trolleys, and though the streetcars had long ago been decommissioned and replaced by buses, the deal still held, buried in a single line in a back page of the city budget. The carbarn itself was a vast space, and though it was surrounded by slaughterhouses, it had been built at a time when grandeur was bestowed on even the most functional of structures. The high arches that once admitted the trolleys were flanked by Grecian pilasters. Undulant terra-cotta corbels bracketed windows that ran, frieze-like, across the barn. A pair of cupolas bookended the roofline, and in the center sat a squat dome punctured on four sides with porthole windows. This crowning touch gave the place the appearance of a failed soufflé. The building's claim to aesthetic harmony was further challenged by the construction, ten years earlier, of the elevated freight line that now ran over the back end of the barn. Inside, the barn was stripped of architectural ornament. The floor was inlaid with a web of iron rails and spattered all over with the droppings of birds and bats. The dust-fogged windows admitted only a pale glow, and the banks of Holophane pendant lights were furred with dust and bridged by spiderwebs.

It was here that Cronin brought Francis for his tutorial on assassination. Cronin knew where to find the fuse box and had been able to get a pair of the overhead lights switched on. He leaned an old wooden

428

door against one of the interior columns and with a stub of charcoal—snatched from the remains of a hobo campsite—he chalked a man-size outline on the door: head, heart, belly, legs.

"Have you fired a gun before?" he said.

"Now when would I have done that?" Francis said.

Cronin carried a brown paper bag, and from it he withdrew a stout revolver, a short-barreled .38 caliber. It was a policeman's weapon, a Detective Special. He casually handed it to Francis—"Hold this," he said—and continued to rummage through the bag.

Francis took hold of the gun, uncertain at first what to make of it. It was lighter than he'd imagined it would be, and its blue-black frame was lustrous. Cronin's back was to him, and with a shock of adrenaline—*Seize the day, Francis!*—he extended his arm.

Cronin cast a look over his shoulder and returned to the bag. "It's not loaded," he said.

Francis lowered his arm. He was trembling.

Cronin stepped forward and swiped the gun from his hand. "Did you not even check it?" he said. "Do you even know how to do that?"

"Like I said last night," Francis said, wounded and glum, "I'm not a killer."

Half of Cronin wanted to smack Dempsey in the face for being so smug, so blissfully unaware of the practice of violence. But the other half of him envied Dempsey for growing up in a time and a place where he didn't need to know how to set an ambush, how to lob a grenade, how to look a man in the eye and then end his life. Hadn't Cronin, by his actions during the war, bought that peace and stupid tranquillity for Francis and a whole generation like him? And hadn't Frank also played his part in creating for his sons a world where they didn't have to be killers? Cronin believed Francis when he said that whatever happened in Ireland had been an accident. Francis wouldn't know the first thing about organizing a raid, taking out three men—IRA men, at that—and walking off with enough loot to incite a transatlantic manhunt. But none of that mattered now. Francis was to be initiated, and it was Cronin's job to do it. Just as Francis's father had once instructed him.

Before arriving at the carbarn, they had secured formalwear that matched Francis's alleged station in life; along with a host of other Highland accessories, they had procured an elaborate seal-fur-and-silver sporran, the belted pouch favored by kilted Scots, which Cronin figured for the best place to stow the revolver. The rest of the fancy kit was zipped into a garment bag in Cronin's Packard, but now, from the paper bag, he withdrew a box of cartridges and the pouch, which resembled a small mammal on a leash. He loaded the cylinder and stood ten feet from the door where he had outlined the king.

"When the time comes," he said, setting his feet, "your heart is going to be racing, but you must remain calm. Do you hear? Keep your hand steady, but be quick about it. You need to squeeze off as many shots as you can, but you can't rush."

"*Festina lente,*" Francis said, almost under his breath.

"What was that?" Cronin said.

"It's Latin. 'Make haste slowly.' "

"I know what it means." Cronin's voice was a growl. It was one of Black Frank's sayings. He'd heard it a hundred times, at least. "The other thing you have to know: It's going to be loud. Especially if you're indoors, each shot is going to be very loud. You have to expect it."

"Let me write that down," Francis said. "Guns are loud."

"I'm telling you this so you don't flinch," Cronin said, adding silently, *you smug prick*. "It's going to be loud and the gun is going to jump in your hand. You can't flinch, or you'll miss, or you'll drop the gun, and that will be it. For you—and for the others."

They stood facing each other. The room was full of shadows.

"Would he do it?" Francis said. "Kill my brothers, if I don't go along?"

"He doesn't make empty threats."

"And would you be the one to do it?"

"He's got plenty of men who can pull a trigger. It's not hard to find them in a city like this."

"But what if you're the man he asks?"

"He doesn't ask."

A train thundered overhead, car after car hung with swaying slabs of beef. Francis waited for the worst of the noise to pass.

"Would my father have wanted me to do this?"

Cronin said nothing. Above, the train slowed, its wheels ticking against the rails.

"I know that you knew him. In Cork. Your boss said—"

"Stop calling him my boss!"

"The old man, whoever he is, said something to you about unfinished business with the Dempseys. Martin saw it, too. There's something familiar about you. You knew him."

"What did your father tell you?"

"My father never said a word about anything that mattered. He gave us plenty of Virgil and Ovid, and our fill of Homer and Sophocles. As for himself? He liked his eggs poached and his tea strong. End of list."

"Nothing about the war?"

"Loads about the Peloponnesian War. The Trojan War, too. We heard dispatches from the front practically every night. But if you're asking about a war in the last twenty centuries, the answer there is no."

Cronin set his mouth in a flat line. In the rafters of the barn, a Holophane light glowed in its cage. He and Francis stood spotlighted, like two boxers in the ring, crowded on all sides by darkness and roaring silence. Would there come a day when a man like himself stood before little Henry, grown old enough to ask questions about the past? And would that man, through malice or simple carelessness, pull down the wall Cronin had erected, silence stacked on silence, dividing what he once had been from what he endeavored to be? *Let the boy think me a brute,* he had prayed, *let him think me a dullard or a fool. But don't let him know the wickedness I have done in this world.* It was a prayer Cronin offered every Sunday on his knees in the gray stone church where he and Alice and the boy—and now the baby—drove each week for Mass. He often felt himself to be a hypocrite for asking, and in some superstitious corner of his heart he feared that the request alone—*Lord, deliver him not from his ignorance*—would bring on its opposite.

Cronin shook his head. "I'll respect your father's silence," he said.

"All we got from my father was silence! We heard barely a word from him, and all of us stuck living in the ass-end of the world."

"He left Cork to keep you safe. Whatever else he was, he was a good father—your life over his."

"What does that mean, *whatever else he was?*"

"I've said too much already."

"Too much?" Francis said. "You've not said anything."

"The old man said if you became too much trouble, I was to dump you back at the garage. Let you stew in that little room until it was time for you to be useful. Is that what you want?"

"But did you know my—"

Cronin leveled the revolver at the door and fired six shots, one after another. All six to the chest, none more than a few inches from the heart.

At the first shot, Francis leaped back, his hands going to his ears. "Jesus Christ! You could have warned me!"

Cronin lowered the gun and pointed to the sporran. "Put that thing on," he said. "And then get over here. You've a lot to learn."

Cronin insisted that Francis rehearse until the motion became like a reflex. He would reach into the sporran, withdraw the gun, and fire until the cylinder was empty. If Cronin saw the slightest hitch or stumble, he would stop Francis and make him start from the beginning. They tried it from five feet away, from ten, from fifteen, from twenty.

"Keep your eyes on the king," Cronin told him. "And for God's sake, don't hit the queen."

IT WAS EVENING when they returned to the Plaza. Francis's right hand was numb, his arm still tingled from the jolt of the revolver, and a low whine pestered his ears from all those shots echoing off the brick walls, the derelict trolleys, the vaulted ceiling. The air in the carbarn had been clammy and damp, but now he was soaked to the skin. He couldn't remember a day so warm in all his years in Ireland. His first thought had been of the bar cart in the suite—yes, he would have the front desk send up a bucket of ice as soon as he got to the room to cool his body and calm his mind—but then he remembered: Michael adrift in the city, and Martin the only one searching for him.

Cronin, with the garment bag over his shoulder, waited by the bank of elevators while Francis went to retrieve the key. But as Francis crossed the lobby, intent on the front desk, he came face to face with Félicité Bingham.

"What a treat," she said in her bored drawl. "A private audience with near royalty."

He almost answered in his Francis voice but caught himself in time to rough up the burr in his throat. "Fancy meeting you, Miss Bingham. But where did—"

"Enough of the 'Miss Bingham' talk. It's Lici"—and then she added as a joke, an afterthought—"Your Lordship."

"Please, it's Angus."

"I don't know what to call you. My mother and my sister might be taken in, but I don't buy it."

"But Lici," he said. "I'm not selling anything."

"Father says everyone is either buying or selling. Or dead."

"And where *does* your father stand? Is he sold on me, or is he not buying it either?"

"You're clever," she said. "I like that. But I don't trust you."

"Oh, but I'm very trustworthy. All Scotsmen are."

"And what if you're not really a Scotsman?"

"Would you like to see my kilt?" He pointed toward Cronin, standing awkwardly by the elevators. "It's right there, in that bag. Would that convince you?"

"Now you're making fun of me."

"I'm just having fun *with* you. That's acceptable, isn't it?"

Lici considered him again. She took a long drag on her cigarette and jetted the smoke. "Just know that I'm onto you. I didn't want you thinking you had us all fooled."

"You seem to think I'm much more interesting than I really am. Hidden agendas, secret motives, counterfeit Scotsmanship. Do you see a fair number of detective movies, Lici? Perhaps read a Dashiell Hammett novel now and then?"

"Don't be vulgar." The cigarette flared between her lips one last time, then she dropped it and crushed it under her heel. "I had my doubts that you'd ever set foot in the Plaza."

"So you came to check up on me?"

"Please," she said. "I was meeting friends for tea."

"I'm surprised," Francis said.

"That I have friends?" Lici said, robbing him of a punch line.

"No," he said. "That you drink tea. I had you figured for something stronger. But you're welcome to follow me, if it will set your mind at ease. I'll even introduce you to the staff. Collier must be around somewhere—he's the concierge—and that's Bobby at the front door, and Andy the elevator boy, for taking us to the seventh floor. He's quite the wag, that one."

"Now you're inviting me back to your hotel room. What would Anisette think? She'll be heartbroken."

At the mention of Anisette's name, a spark flared in his chest. He might have blushed. "Isn't that half the reason you'd do it?"

434

"She was engaged to be married. Did she tell you that? The wedding would have been two weeks ago—a May bride. She broke it off when it became clear to her that her fiancé was a thug. But that's not the story anyone tells. There are advantages to being a thug from a good family. A better family than ours, apparently."

Francis fumbled for a response.

"Oh, it's no secret. It was quite the scandal." She leaned in, as if sharing a confidence, but spoke in a harsh stage whisper. "Anyone on Fifth Avenue will tell you that Anisette is hysterical. That she had a nervous breakdown—walking the streets in the middle of winter, with her clothes torn and her hair like a madwoman's. That her fiancé and his family were *so lucky* to learn of her condition before it was too late."

He tried to square the image of Anisette alone and in winter with that of the girl he had escorted through the park. "Why are you telling me this?"

"Because you're going to hear it sooner or later, and I'd rather you ran off now, before my sister and my mother get any more ideas about where this is all leading. My parents treat Anisette like she's made of porcelain, and maybe she is. But I'd rather not see her shattered by the likes of you."

"I think there's more to Anisette than you realize." He pictured her with the violin, at her house by the sea, and radiant in the gallery full of Rembrandts.

"You think you know her better than I do? Really? Do you know she still plays with dolls?"

"And what do you play with?"

"Clever, indeed," she said. "But I still don't trust you." She turned toward the door, then paused and cast over her shoulder a look that was equal parts Marlene Dietrich and Edward G. Robinson. "Goodbye, Angus. Or whoever you are."

Cronin was stewing by the elevator, but before Francis could reach him, he was again intercepted—this time by the concierge.

Collier was beaming. "Your Lordship! Wonderful news! Your brother has returned!" He clamshelled Francis's hand between his and gave it a vigorous shake before remembering himself—*Don't touch the aristocracy*—and placing his hands over his heart. The details of young Malcolm's return poured out of him, but Francis took in hardly a word of it. Bodies in pastel fabrics and summer-weight suits moved through the lobby, laughter erupted as friends exchanged hellos, somewhere a piano tinkled through a tune he had heard but could not name, from the street came the whistle of the bell captain summoning taxis, Collier continued a recitation of miracles and good Samaritans, and over by the elevators Cronin slouched with a garment bag full of formal attire and the gun Francis would use to kill the king. All of it washed over him. The only thing that mattered was that Michael was back. He was safe. And tomorrow Francis would do what was necessary to keep him that way.

THE FARM

"WHEN IS TOM COMING home?" Henry looked up from his dinner, fixing his mother with those eyes, more black than brown. He asked the question innocently enough, as if it had just occurred to him that there was an empty chair at the table. But it had to be the hundredth time he had asked her in the past week—maybe even the hundred thousandth. He had wailed when they left Tom at the depot and only the ice cream brought an end to the tears. She had paid the man in the ice cream parlor with a ten-dollar bill for a ten-cent scoop, and wasn't that sure to get some folks talking—as if Alice hadn't given them plenty enough already to set their tongues wagging.

Along with the ice cream had come a white lie: Tom would be back soon. Without that lie, Henry would have bawled while the ice cream melted onto his fist, then cried some more that he had lost his treat. He quieted himself, and only when he had finished the last soggy bits of the cone did she wipe his face of tears and snot and chocolate. She told him that Tom had to go on a short trip, which meant that Henry was the man of the house, and wasn't it a good thing that he knew so much about caring for the new calf? And wouldn't Tom be proud to see how hard Henry could work?

In the days that followed, the question kept coming and Alice did her best to answer in a way that would satisfy the boy without making any promises. "Any day now," she would say. "Soon, I suppose."

But tonight at dinner, when Henry asked, Alice snapped. "Will you stop asking questions I can't answer!"

Henry didn't blink. Slowly his lip began to quiver and his eyes turned from coal to wet, limpid tar and then he was wailing again, whereupon the baby picked up the chorus. Alice sat there between them, one on each side and the smooth back of Tom's empty chair across from her, and she let her face sink into the cradle of her hands.

How had she gotten in such a state? She had been on her own plenty of times, and she had never fallen to pieces before. So Tom had been gone a week? What was one week? She had borne up against departures that had struck deeper and lasted longer.

But it was how he had left, and where he was going. He had been summoned back to the city, back into the past, and Alice knew that was dangerous terrain. Hadn't she wrapped that gun of his in an extra shirt and set it at the bottom of his valise? He'd thought he would be protecting her, leaving the gun behind, but what was Alice supposed to do with a wheel gun? She was a farmer's daughter and a farmer herself, and she had learned to handle a shotgun, a rifle even, all before she was fourteen—the world was full, after all, of foxes, feral dogs, and livestock too old or too hurt to keep on living. On the night Tom left, as soon as she put the children to bed, she took her father's shotgun down from the locked closet of his old room. She cleaned it and loaded it and laid it above the hutch where Henry could not see it. Just in case, she told herself.

But just in case of what? She knew that Tom had once worked for this man, and that the man was some sort of gangster who sold liquor and loaned money and probably did much worse. It all seemed like stories from another world, except now that world had collided with hers: an old man in a long black car, shining despite the dust of the roads, had summoned Tom back to the city, and in his place he had left an envelope full of money. Tom said to buy the boy some ice cream and before she could reply that she had left her coin purse on the chifforobe, he spread open the mouth of the envelope to reveal dollar bills stacked like a deck of cards. *Where*—she thought to say, but she knew where, and she had some idea of why. There was more she wanted to ask him, but he was already wearing the mask of a stranger, and then he turned and his body carried him toward the depot, the ticket booth, and the train that would take him to the city.

The days since Tom had left had been like any other days, which was to say full of work. An envelope stuffed with money couldn't milk the cows and pasture them, couldn't feed the chickens, couldn't toss and stack the bales in the haymow, couldn't figure out why the tractor kept stalling, or keep an eye on the baby, or walk the field at night looking for the cows that had broken through the fence. All of it fell on Alice. It was only now—as she wondered if there was a neighbor she could ask to lend a hand—that she realized how much she and Tom had built a wall around themselves; created a world where they were happy but alone. The people in town could scratch their heads and think that Alice had lost her mind and her morals and the good name her father had given her, but contrary to the their opinion, Alice didn't retreat out of shame. She just didn't want to share her happiness with anyone else.

When her father, in his mangled voice, had told her, *Marry that one,* he was speaking aloud a wish that Alice herself hadn't dared to make. Her life and Tom's meshed like the cogs of a machine, working together, coming in contact, moving apart, but always working, and always bound to circle back to each other. She had come to treasure those moments in the day when she would see him: first at breakfast, then in the milking parlor as she shoveled silage into the cows' trough, then as she crossed the yard to collect eggs, then while she hung the laundry on the line, while she weeded the vegetable garden as he led the cows in from the pasture, and at last across the dinner table. Before the end of Tom's first year on the farm, Alice knew she loved him—that she was *in love* with him—and she was sure he felt the same. But what did love and a shared appetite for labor matter when she already had a husband

and a child? Alice confined herself to believing that if she was to find happiness, it would be as a mother and nothing more. She had married unwisely, and even though she loved this man she saw every day, the only way to atone for her misjudgment—her mistake—was to deny herself, raise her son, and work.

That was one way of looking at it.

But after a year of seeing a better life right in front of her, she was worn down. Wanting had made threadbare the false satisfaction of keeping up appearances. Hadn't her own father, an honorable man who knew the pain of loss, told her that she deserved more?

If she had left it up to Tom, nothing would have happened. There would be no them, no Grace. They would have continued to circle each other, desperate and lonely and unworthy, growing older and having only their love of Henry to serve as a channel for the full weight of their feelings. Tom, schooled in self-denial, could have done it. But Alice could not bear it. One cold fall night she went to his room and—*Shush, shush, shush*—she quieted his shocked protests and climbed beneath the quilt on his bed and as she laid her head on his chest and her hands began to explore the knotty sinews of his body, she felt his resistance melt away.

If she had let the rising sun shame her the next morning, Tom would surely have fled, thinking he had despoiled her and the farm itself. Instead she greeted him, and the day, with a kiss on his wide, worried forehead and told him to get to work while she lit the stove. When he came in for his breakfast with her and the toddler Henry, he was perplexed but he knew that this was his family, if he was strong enough to accept it. Had he skulked into the house on unsteady feet or been unable to look her in the eye, she would have sent him on his way. He seemed to know it, and he washed the dust and the years from his hands and took his place at the table, giving a little nod, and they had been husband and wife ever since, as good as if it had all been settled in a church.

Sitting at that same table, with Henry sobbing and Gracie hiccup-ping through her tears, Alice pressed her fingertips into her eyelids. She could imagine her eyes popping like tomatoes left too long on the vine. She pressed, felt the shape of them, and watched the bursts of silver-black, of purple like an electric current. When she was a girl and her mother was ill, she would stare at the sun and count to ten. If she could make it to ten without closing her eyes, she believed, then Mother would get well. Her eyes would flood with inky black puddles fringed with a hot edge of red, but she would never make it to ten, and her mother never got well.

Now, watching those same pulses and shimmers, she slowly counted to ten. When she reached the last number, her eyes intact, she raised her head and began stacking the plates. She collected the spoons and the forks and scraped a crust of bread and two corncobs into the bucket for the pig Tom insisted on keeping in a sty he had built behind the barn. Henry was sniffling, his breath coming in great, wet gasps, while Gracie was red-faced and sticky with tears. Alice set the dishes in the sink and opened the pie safe, where the jelly tarts she had made that morning were piled on a plate. It had been too hot to make a pie, but a few scraps of dough and last season's blueberry preserves baked quickly enough, and when she laid one in front of Henry and wiped his face with a napkin, his sniffling gradually ebbed and was replaced with the contented sounds of chewing and mouth-breathing. She half filled Henry's glass of milk and then scooped up Gracie, holding the baby close so she could smell the top of her head. The scent always soothed her, and she made a slow whooshing sound that eventually brought an end to Gracie's tears.

"He'll be home soon," she said to Henry, and to herself. She ran a hand through the boy's hair. "I don't know when, but soon."

Henry nodded and continued to eat.

"I miss him too," she said. "But tell me, what would Tom say if he walked in and found us here, crying and squabbling?"

Henry scrunched his face, as if he were puzzling out one of Tom's quizzes. Tom knew the name of everything that grew, and he would often ask Henry, *What sort of tree is that? What's the name of that flower?*

When the answer came to Henry, he spoke in the booming voice he used when he imitated Tom: *"What's all this rumpus?"*

Alice had to admit that's exactly what he would have said. Both of them now looked at the screen door, and Alice knew that they were imagining, hoping for, the same thing. It was getting late but they were approaching the longest day of the year. The sun would be up for another hour, even here, where the low mountains cast shadows across the fields and forests. There was still time, wasn't there, for the screen door to open, for the spring to creak before snapping the door shut, and for Tom to return home. The day was long, but sooner or later, without Alice noticing the exact moment it happened, the darkness would fall.

FORDHAM HEIGHTS

BEFORE THE CALL FROM the front desk of the Plaza Hotel informing them that young Sir Malcolm had safely returned, Martin
and Rosemary were dressing for the rehearsal dinner. The babysitter
was due to arrive any minute, cocktails were to be served at the Hallorans' home in Riverdale at five thirty sharp, and yet Martin moved
like a man who'd had the marrow scraped from his bones. He was
stiff and fragile, likely to break. He had spent the past forty-eight
hours scouring Manhattan's precinct houses, hospitals, missions, and
morgues. Starting on the east side, he had worked his way down to
the Battery, then backtracked up the west side as far uptown as
Columbus Circle. Michael had simply vanished, it seemed, and it was
Francis who had lost him. All through his search, he had seen Francis
only once, escorting—or being escorted by—that phantom in the
blue serge suit. Martin was sure he would have been able to place the
man if only his rage at Francis wasn't burning so bright. Yoked to that
anger was envy; envy that Francis could turn off whatever bond of
love and filial loyalty had driven Martin to the streets.

Or maybe Martin was giving himself too much credit. Maybe it was
just the hard lump of guilt in his chest—the product of years when
he'd barely thought of Michael at all—that kept him looking for his
brother. He wanted to say to someone, *This isn't fair!* He wanted to
shout it. Why this week of all weeks? The wedding reception was going
to be his big break, he could feel it. He had put so much of himself into

the band, into the arrangements, into keeping the group together, and oh! how they could swing. Only now it was ruined. Francis had wrecked it, and he hated himself for thinking this, but Michael had wrecked it, too. But who wanted to hear that? Even the cold, selfish center of Martin's heart shrank from the raw truth of it.

Tonight Rosemary had given him a free pass—*Skip the dinner, keep up the search*—but as much as he dreaded the idea of mixing with the Dwyers and the lace-curtain Hallorans, he told himself that by going he could spare Rosemary a night of sideways glances and halfhearted inquiries into his whereabouts. It was a game she could not win—he lost his *brother?* How did *that* happen?—and it would only add another chapter in the story of Martin, the Man Who Can't Get It Right. Along with that, he had blindsided her when he quit Chester's band, and she was likely at her wits' end about his plans for the future. So he owed her one. But he also knew that going to the dinner gave him a high-minded, self-sacrificing reason not to do the thing he dreaded even more, which was roaming the grimy underside of the city to call at cop shops where midnight brawlers and jake-leg drunks were hauled in, or at the rescue missions with their reek of flop sweat and disinfectant, or at the hospitals where a hot fog of infection surrounded him, or at the morgues where the John Does lay half covered in the hallways, their bare bruised feet tagged for some other poor sod to claim. Martin didn't want to choose between the dinner and the search. He wanted some feat of magic that could give him the week he had imagined rather than the one unfolding around him.

ROSEMARY HELPED MARTIN with his tie. With Michael missing and Francis off in his own world, Martin had aged ten years in two days. He had been home only once, briefly, since he started his search and he moved like a sleepwalker. Even the news that Peggy was not, in fact, calling off the wedding hadn't cheered him, and Rosemary so badly wanted to cheer him up today. She wanted to share the feeling that had seized her when she left the relief office, and she wanted to tell him all about Miss Costigan and her crack team of investigators and her even more threatening pencil sharpener. She wanted to tell him all about Captain MacFarquhar and the iceberg and the Staten Island Symphony and the fire-in-the-blood feeling that led her to dump the relief application in a garbage can but keep the number of the Manhattan WPA office folded neatly in her purse. She wanted to tell him that all of this was a vote of confidence in him and his top secret master plan. She was anxious—that's just how she was—but they were young and in love and she wanted that to count for something. There were so many others, after all, who were so much worse off—men and women who'd been battered by time and tide and who had to endure the petty cruelties of Miss Costigan in order to get the help they needed. Yes, she wanted to tell all of this to Martin but there was no way to make it come out right. He would hear only the words *relief office* and it would be one more thing that had gone wrong this week. One brother was missing, another had lost his mind, and now he had made his wife into a beggar.

And then the telephone rang, and it was the Plaza. By the time he hung up the receiver, the added years had melted away. He had become Rosemary's Martin again, the very picture of her dashing young bridegroom.

"I'm coming with you," Rosemary said.

"And miss the dinner?"

"Of course miss the dinner! Do you really think I want to go—alone or otherwise?"

"But what about your mother, your sister?"

"We just found out that the worst thing didn't happen, and now we have a babysitter and a chance to go to the Plaza Hotel. I'll take my lumps from Peggy and my mother in the morning, and all day tomorrow I'll be the dutiful, put-upon sister. But tonight we're going out. When was the last time we painted the town red—or any color at all?"

Martin looked doubtful, or maybe he was just dazed. He'd barely had twenty winks—forget about forty—and he had to be wondering, *Who is this minxy brunette and what has she done with my wife?* Rosemary kissed him smack on the mouth and explained it as best she could—that they were adventurers, polar explorers, Thanes of Cawdor, and experts in the Eskimo tongue. "We deserve this," she said. "We're MacFarquhars, aren't we?"

FIFTH AVENUE

ANISETTE HAD SEEN FÉLICITÉ for only a minute—one minute of the whole day!—but still her sister had managed to get right under her skin. "I saw your Scotsman," she had said. "At the Plaza. He invited me up to his room, but I turned him down." And then Félicité was out the door for a rendezvous with those horrible friends of hers who treated Anisette like she was some kind of broken plaything: a mangled toy, or an easily tricked child who was too slow to understand the adult talk all around her. But she understood just fine—understood the ways that Félicité was always conspiring to rob her of her happiness. She'd been cross with Anisette for getting engaged—*Why are you doing this to yourself? You're too young! And with him?*—but that was only because it made her look like an old maid, still single while her younger sister was wed. And she hadn't shown any sympathy once it all fell apart: "What did you expect?" she heard Félicité tell Maman. "I told you about him." Félicité had plenty more to say too, but what Anisette heard was *I told you so,* and hadn't she heard that from Félicité her entire life?

It wasn't any surprise that her sister was up to her old tricks, suggesting that Angus was anything less than a complete gentleman. As if he could ever be interested in Félicité. Hadn't they had a laugh about her in the park just the other day?

She would see him for herself tomorrow and all would be well. Since they had parted at the museum, she'd barely heard a word from

447

him; nothing but a brief note delivered to the house, confirming details for tomorrow morning. They were to drive together, and that would give them some time—but of course Félicité would be there with her sour smile and her sneery eyes. And Maman, too, so perhaps she could keep Félicité on her best behavior. Not that anyone could ever do that for long.

Of course Anisette knew there was something odd about Angus, if that was even his name. Despite what her sister said and her father thought and her mother feared, she wasn't a simpleton. Yes, she admitted to herself the possibility that there was mischief in him. After all, she'd heard that delightful Scottish burr of his come and go. But he always righted himself, and he was such a gentleman—that didn't seem to be part of the act. If in the beginning it had been simply politeness or good breeding, something had changed in these past few days. Maybe the outside of him was an act, but she believed there really was something good on the inside: he cared for his brother, he cared for her, and she sensed in him a desire to be not just good, but better. Better than he had been; better than anyone believed he could be. Her sister, her mother, her father—they all worried about her. Poor Anisette. Poor simple stupid Anisette. But she wasn't stupid, and when she and Angus were together in their house by the sea, her family would understand, or they'd stop thinking about her altogether, because she would be someone else's Anisette to worry about.

MRS. BINGHAM CHECKED on Anisette, reminding her that it would be an early night. Both needed their beauty sleep, and tomorrow would be a busy day from first light: their hair was to be done, and any last-minute fixes to their dresses would need to be tended to before their departure for the fair.

She took the brush from Anisette and began working it through her daughter's hair. She talked about tomorrow, how it would be a day that Anisette would treasure for the rest of her life. She was going to meet the king and queen.

"To think," Mrs. Bingham said, "that you begin your life never expecting that such things could ever happen to you, but dreaming about them, wanting them, and by working very hard to make those dreams come true—"

"But Maman," Anisette said, "it's been so long since you've had to work." She knew that her mother had been a nurse, trained by the nuns at the convent school, but her marriage to Anisette's father had rescued her from any further toil.

Mrs. Bingham looked at her daughter's rosy, untroubled face in the vanity mirror. Anisette had been raised on her father's stories of pulling rocks from the earth, of controlling things that other men needed and making his fortune from that. He claimed land and sold it. He built mines and towns and railways. He owned houses and boats and estates that he never even visited. He bought men, or at least their opinions, their contracts, their votes. In Montana, in the years before he moved to New York, he had even bought himself a seat in the U.S. Senate, back when that sort of thing had been easier to do. All of that was work, he never failed to point out. Taken together, it formed the epic story of the labors of Emery Bingham.

But the story her daughter had never heard—not in its entirety, not in its most important parts—was the true tale of just how much work her own life had required. Anisette knew of the tender young nurse despairing over the death of the first Mrs. Bingham, and finding in the widower an answering grief—a grief that gave way to love, and a love that rejuvenated the anguished heart of Anisette's father. Told like that, it was a story governed by loyalty, sympathy, and the all-conquering power of love.

The facts of the courtship were considerably more calculated and much less sentimental. As a girl in Montreal, Delphine Loisel had been sent to the nuns, her education purchased through hours spent cooking and scrubbing in the convent kitchen. While she scoured and studied, her father drank himself half to death and her mother tended to a shop that trafficked in tobacco, penny candies, and periodicals (and, for her more worldly customers, in "preventive powders" and other abortifacients). In search of a match for her daughter, Delphine's mother kept an eye on the neighborhood's sturdy tradesmen. But the magazines in her mother's shop had filled Delphine with stories of elegant lawn parties and coastal estates, the playgrounds of Gilded Age excess, and she dreamed of more than a life spent totaling receipts for a good-natured horse butcher.

At sixteen she found another dreamer with just enough money and very little sense and convinced him to elope with her across the border. Together they traveled as far as Plattsburgh, where she separated him from his wallet and continued alone to New York City. By seventeen, with the aid of letters of reference forged in her own elegant, scripted French, she had secured a position as a nurse to Mrs. Bingham, whose health had been in decline since her husband moved the seat of the Bingham empire from Big Sky Country to this cramped and sunless city. From her first days on the job, Delphine was aware of Mr. Bingham's interest, and she embarked on a campaign of tortured resistance to his advances. Though he was thirty-five years her senior, she made it clear with lingering looks and sudden blushes that she thought about him almost as much as he thought of her, but she confessed that her Catholic upbringing and the memory of her dearly departed mother would not allow even a kiss. He made offers—of apartments, jewels, clothes, money—but always she resisted. Delphine was playing for bigger stakes.

When Mrs. Bingham at last relinquished her grip on this fallen world, Delphine in her grief went to Mr. Bingham, who offered comforting words and the greater comfort of his bed. Finally, his long pursuit would reach a sweet conclusion. But just at the moment of surrender, Delphine claimed to hear the voice of her sainted mother (still tending the till of her *tabac,* unbeknownst to Mr. Bingham), and she fled, leaving her employer inflamed and unfulfilled. Not until his promises of marriage became marriage itself did she allow him to claim his prize. Now *that* had been work.

None of that, however, was a story to tell a daughter. Instead she told Anisette that someday soon she would see just how much work it was to have one's own family: to run a household, to manage the staff and a budget, to plan for meals and entertainments, to organize and attend the never-ending galas and fetes that supported the city's cultural life, its parks, its hospitals. All of that would be Anisette's someday soon.

"But what if I don't live in New York?" Anisette said. "What if I'm not even in America?"

"Everywhere has its responsibilities," Mrs. Bingham said. "I imagine if you were in—oh, let's say London, or Edinburgh—"

"Maman!" Anisette said in poorly feigned surprise. "What are you suggesting?"

"I'm just choosing cities out of thin air, aren't I?"

In the mirror, mother and daughter exchanged a conspiratorial smile.

"Wherever you live," Mrs. Bingham said, "you will have to learn where to go, and who to know, and how to behave. Not that you'd have any trouble fitting in."

"Would you miss me, Maman?"

"Terribly," she said. "But a mother always wants what's best for her daughter." She had sometimes thought, during the past thirty years, of sending her mother a letter, just to let her know that she had not succumbed to shame and misery on the streets. But she could never find words that didn't make her life sound like a fairy tale—*I am happily married to a very wealthy man in America*—or a complete lie, and eventually a letter seemed pointless. Her own *maman* had never been a particularly sturdy woman, and Montreal was such a cold city in winter.

Anisette closed her eyes and leaned back against her mother, who continued to draw the brush through her hair.

"I'll tell you this," Mrs. Bingham said. "If you are interested in Angus—really interested—then we'll need to act soon. He has been our little secret, but after the royal visit, there will be quite a buzz. He may find that he has more than a few dinner invitations."

"He wouldn't even," Anisette said.

"Of course he would," Mrs. Bingham said. "Unless he's said something to you that might indicate his...intentions?"

Anisette had read enough Jane Austen to know that in the best of all possible worlds, you found someone who answered the call of your soul, and together you found a happiness you could never achieve with another. Now she searched her memories of the park for a moment she could point to as proof that he was being more than cordial. But there had been no promise, no proposal, no ring, no letter spelling out the secrets of his heart. Still, she knew how she felt, and she hoped—and almost believed—that he felt the same.

"He won't be in New York forever," Mrs. Bingham said when Anisette didn't answer, and she rose to turn off the lights. "And if he's going to make any decisions while he's here—well, let's just try to help him make the right ones."

THE PLAZA HOTEL

F IRST, THERE WERE TEARS. The first minutes that Francis spent in
the suite with Michael were devoted entirely to weepy hugs and
fierce backslapping and arms thrown roughly, possessively, apologetically, around his brother's shoulders. There was a woman with
Michael—Francis imagined she was a minder dispatched by the
hotel—but before he could ask her a single question, Martin and
Rosemary arrived and the waterworks began flowing anew. Martin
had last seen Michael five days ago, on Sunday night, as the two laid
hands on the wireless, and he had wondered during these past couple
of days if that would be his final memory of his brother. But now they
were together again and Martin's embrace was not just thanksgiving
but a promise to Michael, who deserved so much better from his older
brothers than he'd gotten. Rosemary wasn't the type to mist up—
honestly, Martin was more likely to cry than she was—but so much
had gone wrong this week and now here was Michael, and his life and
theirs hadn't become a tragedy. Maybe it *was* possible to live under
the threat of a disaster, bracing yourself for it, preparing for those first
peals of thunder, only to have it blow away, like a morning that had
started off gray only to have the sun burst through the clouds.

It wasn't until the end of this round-robin of hugs and tears, of
rough backslaps between Martin and Francis, of loud joy and unspoken apology, that Martin realized there were two more people in the
suite. The man from Thursday evening stood by the window, looking

453

out over the park. His arms were folded into a tight knot and his face had a squashed, sickened look. He wasn't staring at anything so much as just staring—pouring all of his energy into some faraway point, as if some magic could whisk him out of *here* and off to *there*. And then on the sofa there was a woman, rather elegantly taking in the scene before her. Though she sat at a languid angle and let a cigarette burn lazily in her hand, she did not seem unmoved by the joyful reunion.

In fact, Lilly beamed when she saw the transformation come over her guest. He had been elated to discover the hotel and from the moment they set foot in the lobby they seemed to move through a dream. The barn-then-castle he'd sketched had sprung to life and in it he was greeted as a returning hero. The doorman startled at the sight of him and escorted them personally to the front desk, where another man led them to the elevator and to this suite overlooking the park. The man in the lobby had called him "Sir Malcolm" and spoke of another sir or two who must be notified of his return. Apparently Sir Malcolm's disappearance had set off a citywide manhunt: every minor noble in New York had been deputized to find him, it seemed, though none had thought to look in the Bowery—it was, after all, not a respectable neighborhood—where he had been nursed to health on a diet of strong tea and fresh knishes.

Throughout all of this commotion, no one questioned Lilly's presence. But as cushions were fluffed in the suite and Michael stretched himself out on the sofa with a home-sweet-home look about him, the majordomo finally turned to Lilly and asked how in the world she had ever located the young and desperately missed Sir Malcolm MacFarquhar.

She answered that he had been her guest these past two days—had no one been notified? When the majordomo inquired as to her name, Lilly thought it best not to invite scandal for the young nobleman. She could not allow him to disappear into the care of a commoner, an artist, a woman of—*ahem*—questionable moral character. "Eudoxia Rothschild," she said, affecting a posture that would have impressed Madame Bloch herself. "*Countess* Eudoxia Rothschild."

Collier kept an updated copy of *Burke's Peerage* in his office to vali-
date the bona fides of the hotel's guests. While he had not found mention
of the MacFarquhars—at least not *these* MacFarquhars—Collier had
no interest in unmasking pretenders for the sport of it. His only concern
was in knowing when to extend credit and when to withhold it. More
than one brash bounder had tried to assign an unpaid bill to his titled
family's ancestral seat, but Collier had never been gulled. Whoever these
MacFarquhars really were, they paid their tabs and tipped generously. Sir
Angus was a prince in the eyes of the hotel staff, if not in the pages of
Burke's. And if this woman, who had done such a noble service for his
guests, was going to call herself a countess, who was he to object? He
issued a coo of pleasure that the hotel would play host to such a red-letter
blue blood, and prepared to leave the suite. As he offered a curt bow—
nothing fawning; he was never obsequious—he inquired whether there
was anything he could provide to make Her Ladyship more comfortable
while she awaited the arrival of Sir Malcolm's brothers.

Lilly weighed the question with a playful pucker of her lips; how
nice it was to have someone asking which of your wishes he could
grant for you! "Champagne," she said. "We have so much to celebrate, don't we?"

She could have left Michael in the care of the hotel staff and
returned guiltlessly to the studio, but she needed this story to have a
happy ending—a Hollywood ending, where all the right people get
married and the music swells as the screen fades and the words THE
END float on the screen. And she had to admit that she was curious to
meet this family, who had managed to lose one of their own but who
would now have the good fortune to see him returned. She couldn't
help but wonder if some of that luck, that magic, could rub off on her.

She was still warming up to the notion that her guest was not only
Malcolm but Sir Malcolm when the first of the brothers arrived and
loudly boomed, "Michael!" Before the confusion could be cleared up
another brother arrived and again it was "Michael!" That name

echoed faintly in her mind until the woman standing with the black-haired brother called the redheaded brother Francis—and she thought of the list from the psychic and it was all coming true. Francis. Michael. Two of the names the real Eudoxia had spoken in her trance. With a shock, she thought of Michael's headlong rush from the elevated train to the building where the Foundation was housed—the tower, another item on the list, and the very spot where she had looked west and dreamed of California. And now she found herself in this hotel, and what had she called it when Michael sketched it? A castle. The Tower and the Castle, her shorthand with Josef.

It could all be a coincidence—of course it could—but already an icy chill tingled her scalp, and the hairs on her arm stood straight even in this turgid evening heat. She couldn't say a word about it to this roomful of strangers. It would only make her appear to be the crazy woman who had taken such good care of Malcolm—no, Michael. But she knew that if the other brother or the man by the window, who had entered with the redhead, turned out to be George, then she would faint, or shriek. If Eudoxia had been right about these names pulled from the ether, then was that proof that she was also right about the only question that Lilly had actually asked and which had been answered so definitively with a string of *no*s?

Just as Michael's brothers turned their attention to Lilly, the concierge bustled into the suite with two bottles of champagne icing in chrome-plated buckets and enough glasses for the ever-growing party. Collier wrapped a cloth napkin around the neck of the first bottle and decorously uncorked it—a faint pop—and when he unwrapped the linen, a syrupy white fog flowed from the bottle's mouth. He was just as deft with introductions, presenting the Countess Eudoxia Rothschild to Sir Angus MacFarquhar with all due ceremony.

"And this is Fitzwilliam," Sir Angus said, making way for his brother.

"Oh," Lilly said. "I was expecting George."

"He arrives tomorrow," Martin said. "Angus here can tell you all about it."

Collier filled the remaining glasses and again took his leave. It wouldn't be proper to linger while the guests toasted their good fortune.

As the door soundlessly closed, Rosemary stepped forward. She had not been introduced, and God knows what name Francis might have stuck her with. "Eudoxia," she said. "What a lovely name."

"Please, it's Lilly. I only told him that so I wouldn't be the only commoner in the room. A joke of sorts. I apologize if that offends you."

Rosemary laughed. "There's not a drop of royal blood anywhere in this room. We're all putting on airs tonight."

"Before we have any more confessions," Martin said, "let's drink this bubbly before it loses its fizz." Around the room, glasses were raised and Martin prepared to offer a few words.

"Hold on, Your Lordship," Francis said. "Won't you join us, Mr. Cronin?"

The others—giddy, rosy-faced, happy as lottery winners—turned to the man at the window.

"No, thanks." His voice came out fully Corkonian: *No, tanks. Thanks* being one of those words he hadn't used often enough in America, and so it was stored in his voice box just the way he'd grown up using it. "I think I'll stretch my legs."

It was only a few steps from the window to the door, but it felt like miles. Bad enough to have all of the Dempsey brothers together, but there was the oldest one's wife, too. The one he'd seen on the sidewalk in the Bronx with her two little lambs, the baby in her arms and the little girl yammering away about who knows what, just like his Henry. Whether or not Francis was able to carry off the plan, what would this woman lose? Her brother-in-law an assassin, or would-be assassin, reviled in the papers, and herself and the husband implicated in the plot: Hadn't they hosted the brother just a week before? Or else her husband dead or disappeared under mysterious circumstances. Or would Gavigan carry through on the promise to burn down the whole family?

Yesterday at the garage, as the plan had festered and bloomed, Cronin had asked that Jamie, "Would he really do it? The missus of the older one, too?"

Jamie had fixed him with that cold eye, dead black from the pupil through the iris. He had sneered—apparently Cronin *did* have a short memory—before he spoke. "It wouldn't be the first time a wife got rubbed, now, would it?"

Cronin paused at the door and fixed Francis with a look. "I'll see you in the morning," he said. "Before." He let that word hang there, a reminder of what Francis had to do, and for whose benefit—not for Gavigan, but for the people in this room.

Cronin skipped the elevator now and took the stairs, his feet stutter-stepping all the way down. He emerged in a corridor that led him to the lobby, brightly lit and full of people enjoying a summer night. He would let the Dempseys have their fun, a last night to look back on, but he wanted no part of it: the fancy dress and the laughter of carefree people and the black cars shimmering by the curb. He pushed his way through the doors before the men in braided caps and coats could do the job for him and then he was crossing the street, looking neither right nor left but holding his hand extended, palm out, a stop sign any cabbie would be a fool to ignore. His feet propelled him into the park and it wasn't until he was beneath the trees and away from the path, his feet chuffing over the grass, that he let himself breathe.

Seven stories above his head, the Dempseys were raising their glasses in celebration, together and happy because they had cheated fate by snatching Michael from the maw of death. The boy had been saved before, by not being in his mother's arms that morning when she started the car and the wires sparked and flesh and machine were both torn apart. And if Francis was to be believed, then it had happened a second time, when the blast at the farmhouse knocked the senses out of him but did not take his life. And now he had been lost in the ravenous city and had emerged none the worse for it. You could think he was the most star-crossed of the bunch. Unlucky, that one. But you could also say he was charmed: death had tried and tried again to get its bony hands on Michael, and he had managed to give it the slip every time. Now he would have one more test of his good fortune—for his family to be pitted against Gavigan and the bastard's mad plan to set fire to the world. As for Cronin, he would have one more night in the room with the half-painted chair.

"WHO WAS THAT?" Rosemary said.

"Ah, he's no one," Francis said, raising his glass to start another round of toasts to Michael's health. "A mate of his helped me out in Mountjoy, and I promised I'd return the favor. But that's all been sorted."

Now that Michael was safe, Martin was eager to get the full story of his disappearance from Francis—the stakes were lower, the question of culpability no longer a life-or-death matter—but not tonight. He didn't want to be the one to cast a shadow over the celebration. He thought of Sunday at the apartment, how happy they had all been, and how quickly it had unraveled. Now they were being given a second chance, and just like on Sunday they toasted their good fortune with champagne. Twice in a week, and this time at the Plaza? Things were definitely looking up. Tonight they would live like Rockefellers. Tomorrow, at Peggy's reception, he would play for John Hammond, and the world would see how high Martin could rise. He would get to the bottom of this business with Francis and his shady acquaintances another day.

BY THIS TIME tomorrow, Francis knew, his life, and the entire world, would be overwhelmed by his bloody deed. He didn't want to kill anyone but that was the only fixed point in this whole mess: Someone had to die. If not the king, then himself and his brothers and Rosemary and God knows who else. In this moment, in the suite, with the drinks flowing and the fake countess and Martin and Rosemary taking in the view from the window, Francis was happy just to have Michael back. Hadn't he prayed for exactly this? His life for Michael's? God had listened to his plea and returned his brother to him—but, working in mysterious ways and all, He had left Michael's life hanging in the balance. But tomorrow, the job would be done, his debt paid, his family safe. No one would understand why, but he would know, and that would have to be enough. As for tonight, he would keep everyone blissfully ignorant. If these were to be the last happy hours they spent together, he wasn't going to be the one to call an end to the party.

Not for the first time, Francis wondered if he would leave the fairgrounds alive. The thought did not chill him. After all, that would be the easiest way to bring an end to everything. He had weighed the gun in his hand, had wondered how many bullets he would need for the king, and whether there would be any left for himself.

EVERY TIME THE door opened, Michael saw pieces of this past week falling into place. First it was Francis and the man with whom he'd left the museum. Then it was Martin and Rosemary, full of tears and smiles. He half expected to see the doctor and his chessboards or the blonde—Rosemary's friend? her sister?—whom he'd last seen leaving the hotel in the wee hours of the morning. He was still accompanied by his most generous host, the photographer, who was packing her flat for a move to some unknown location—unknown to him, though not to her. Surely, she knew where she was going.

They had all raised their glasses and Michael's head was rubbed and his arm squeezed and his back slapped and everyone smoked and laughed and his host, who was now his guest, seemed to be getting on very well with his family.

His family. It was as he'd said to Yeats: *I am a family man and I want to be with my family.* In Ireland, family had eventually meant only his father and then a constellation of mementos left by those who had departed. In place of his mother, he had one photograph and a mantel clock purchased during a trip his parents had taken to Paris long before he was born. From Martin, there were letters containing little more than the stilted well wishes of a man who had left the country when Michael was only seven. And from Francis, Michael had a different sort of letters, first reporting the high life in Dublin and then the view from his prison cell. The only fixed, living, breathing presence had been his father, and now his father was gone. Buried under the soil of Ballyrath for good, and Michael hadn't even been there to see the box lowered into the ground; hadn't thrown his handful of dirt and properly laid his father to rest.

Here in America, his family had reconstituted itself: he had Francis and Martin and Rosemary and the two girls. But for all the joys this reunion had brought, and would bring, he knew that he had left more than his senses behind in Ireland. He had left a piece of himself, and it would forever haunt the church where his father was buried, and where Eileen had said *I do.*

LILLY SHOULD HAVE spent more of her time in America with Americans, she decided, because these Americans—Francis and Martin and Rosemary and, of course, Michael—were absolutely charming. But then, they weren't Americans, were they? Not Francis or Michael, who had only just arrived from Ireland. And Martin had spent almost ten years in America, but that wasn't enough to make him into an American, was it? So Rosemary—she was an American. And Rosemary was charming.

They sat on the sofa, the two women, while the Dempsey brothers, who had moved on to Scotch and soda, drank and talked and looked out the window.

"And where is home?" Rosemary said.

"Prague." Lilly said it matter-of-factly, following up the city's name with a plume of smoke.

"Prague is dangerous since the occupation, isn't it?" Rosemary no longer read four newspapers a day, but she did read one. She hadn't given up completely on her old habits.

"Well, of course." Lilly shrugged and raised one eyebrow, an expression that was either resigned or noncommittal—even she wasn't sure. "But we hope for the best."

Rosemary was about to formulate another question—*Yes, but didn't I just read*—when she realized that Lilly was deflecting already and that additional questions would seem more like badgering than concern. That shrug, her *hope for the best,* made it clear she was bracing herself for a world Rosemary would never know.

Lilly was trying to keep the conversation light. In the past week, she hadn't spoken the word *Prague* to anyone but Mr. Crabtree and Madame Eudoxia, but here was someone who seemed reasonably informed and more than reasonably compassionate. But what could she say to Rosemary? *I'm a Jew and a maker of decadent art. My fiancé is a Jew and a communist. We make such a lovely couple. What could possibly go wrong?*

Not for the first time, she noticed Martin gazing over at Rosemary. He watched her profile as she sipped champagne, a smile playing over his lips. "Don't move when I tell you this, but your husband keeps looking at you. It's very nice."

"I think he's shocked to see me out of the apartment, without any children, dressed up for once. He's probably asking himself, *Who is this woman? She reminds me of my wife.*"

"It's nice. He's seeing you as you are."

"That's very kind," Rosemary said.

"It's true," Lilly said. "The next time he does it, I'm going to take his picture, to prove it to you."

"If he does it again."

"Oh, he will." Lilly raised the camera from her lap, cradling it near her shoulder. "How long have you been married?"

"It was four years in February."

"And do you still look at him like that?"

"When I remember to." Rosemary thought again of that kiss outside the chapel: the memory was being put to double duty this week. She and Martin needed more of those moments. "But if you're asking me if I still love my husband, then the answer is yes."

"I didn't mean to imply—"

"I'm joking," Rosemary said. "Not about loving Martin—but sometimes I try to have fun and it comes out wrong. My mother says I don't know how to talk to people."

"Your mother sounds..."

"Yes," Rosemary said. "She sounds exactly like that."

In one fluid movement, Lilly raised the camera and snapped a shot of Martin: the window behind him, gauzy with evening light, his hand cradling the glass, his eyes drawn again to Rosemary.

"What's that about?" he said from across the room.

"I'm calling that one *The Good Husband*," Lilly said for all to hear.

Rosemary made a show of smooching her hand and blowing the kiss toward Martin. "Have fun with your brothers. It's strictly girl talk over here."

Martin, who had begun to make his way toward Rosemary in a sort of mock foxtrot, performed a quick U-turn back to the window.

From the bar cart behind the sofa, Lilly took the Scotch bottle and poured a splash into her wineglass. "Can I ask you a question?" She sipped the Scotch and continued. "If you had to choose between yourself and your husband, who would you choose?"

"Pardon me?"

"I also don't know how to talk to people," Lilly said. "But if you had to choose between the man you love, on one side, and on the other was your own life and all that you had worked for—how would you do that?"

Rosemary stared at Lilly, trying to untangle the question. "I'm sorry, but I'm not sure I know what you're asking."

"Never mind it," Lilly said. "I don't even know what I'm asking."

"I know that I'd never leave Martin," she said. "I made a vow, but also I—I'd never do that."

"But what if you were already apart?" Lilly put one hand over her eyes, her head bowed. She could not look at this woman, who had made a vow, while she spoke. "What if you were on one side of a river—a dark, fast-moving river—and he was on the other, and you knew that the only way to see him was to jump in and try to swim?"

Rosemary extended her hand, placed it on Lilly's knee. She leaned in closer. "Is someone waiting for you at home?"

"Yes. Or no. Perhaps. Perhaps not." She reached for her purse, though she knew there was no handkerchief—nothing but a list of things to do, a list of one medium's nonsense. Rosemary unwound the linen from the neck of the wine bottle and handed it to Lilly, who dabbed her eyes. "These last days have—have not been easy."

"But you're leaving soon?" Rosemary said. "So you'll see him before too long?"

"If I go." It was the first time Lilly had given voice to the thought, and now it was out there. She was willing to betray love, and she had admitted it to this bright and hopeful American, who had made a vow, who would never leave her husband. "Prague is bad, and it will get worse. Everyone knows it."

"It doesn't have to be that way. The papers say—"

"It doesn't have to, but it will. It's a fact."

From the window came a burst of laughter. Martin—or Francis? It was incredible to Rosemary how much they sounded alike. She had noticed on Sunday that the Dempsey brothers all had the same walk.

"Lilly, what I said, about Martin. That was about me. You have your own life, your own—"

"You say so, and he says so, too. But what does that make me?" She took Rosemary's hand in hers. Her grip was fierce, her eyes glistened. "Who abandons love?"

Another howl of laughter from the brothers was followed by Francis loudly proclaiming that if he did not eat soon, he would be forced to roast Michael over an open fire on the roof of the hotel. He was ravenous, he said, and little Michael was looking like a pullet ready to be plucked. The truth was, his thoughts of tomorrow and what he must do to keep these people—his favorites in all the world—safe from harm made him desperate for a final send-off, a last supper. In the movies, even a condemned man got to choose his final meal.

Martin gave a hearty "Hear, hear!" to the idea of dinner out, and the Dempseys insisted, en masse, that the Countess Eudoxia accompany them. Lilly protested that she had too much to do, but Rosemary wouldn't accept it. "You can't abandon me to these hooligans," she said, and Lilly relented. Dining with ersatz aristocrats wasn't on the New York List, but she would have to pencil it in at no. 21. So Collier made calls and a table for five was procured and when Lilly saw the number painted on the lantern in front of the restaurant—21, of course—she shook her head in wonder and resignation. Coincidences had become commonplace, and all of them pointed to the veracity of the psychic's list. Shouldn't she stop claiming she was ready to brave any trial in the name of love? Wouldn't it be a relief to submit to the logic of that *no, no, nein?*

After a dinner of steak and caviar and salads soaked in lemon and anchovies, Francis insisted that the night was still young. Tommy Dorsey was at the Pennsylvania and Louis Prima had just opened at the Famous Door, but Francis said he'd heard there was a hot band at the Kensington—Chipper Kingston or some such? Rosemary put a quick end to that; the word on the street was that they didn't sound half as good since they'd lost their clarinet. As Francis paid the dinner tab, they settled at last on the Cotton Club on Broadway, only five blocks away. Martin knew what Hooper and the Minton's regulars thought of the place: nothing but white money staring at black talent. But even though he had the right face to get in the door, he'd never had the money for the cover—until now. Francis was flush with cash and Bill Robinson and Cab Calloway were leading the revue, and that was a tough ticket to turn down. Calloway always went heavy on the horns, and the whole place would shake when he went into his *hi-de-hi-de-ho*s. As for Bill Robinson, even if Michael couldn't hear his feet, he could still be amazed by what Bojangles could do.

"I saw him in *The Hot Mikado* last month," Martin said.

"Hey, buster," Rosemary said, with an elbow to his ribs. "You were going to take me to that."

He had meant to take her, and he couldn't remember what exactly had scuttled the plan, but it was easy enough to guess: another of his marathon nights in the city, with Rosemary home in the Bronx. Now he saw a chance to make good on a busted promise—and with Rosemary looking like she'd stepped out of the pages of *Photoplay,* and giving his knee a squeeze beneath the table, he had to assume that his past misdeeds were forgiven, if not forgotten.

THEY COULD HAVE stayed out all night, and what a different day Saturday might have been. Each would have slept off the hours of beefsteaks and Dover sole, crab cakes and shrimp cocktail, all of it washed down with wine and whiskey and gin in all its guises: martini, fizz, lime rickey, and gimlet. They would have awoken to the bright midday sun, taken two aspirin and a tall glass of water, and rolled toward the mercy of another hour or two of sleep. But each of them had a duty and knew it could not be ignored. Rosemary had Peggy's wedding, which included a squirming flower girl to dress and primp for a day of best behavior. Martin had the wedding, yes, but uppermost was the reception and his very special audience of one. For all of his knocked-out joy over Michael's safe return and Rosemary's loveliness in that dress, he wasn't going to bollix up his big chance with John Hammond by lugging a hangover to the show. Lilly had the studio all but packed, but no idea where she was going. Watching Rosemary and Martin had thrummed a string that ran the length of her body. They were a more Hollywood-movie version of her and Josef, but it hadn't been that long since she'd sat with him in the Café Slavia listening to a jazz combo, their feet casually mixing it up beneath the table, just as Martin and Rosemary had done tonight. Michael had begun to miss Mr. Yeats, if only for the chance to converse, but for now had sworn off striking out on his own. He would go where the others went. And then Francis. Francis had a man to kill and that required a steady hand. As the hour grew late, an acid-edged dread gouged the pit of his stomach. He had tried to smother it in rich food, drown it in a highball, but the ache and the emptiness wouldn't quit. Cronin would be waiting for him in the morning, but what was there left for Cronin to do? Francis had his gun and his orders. He had memorized the parade route and the timetable of the visit, and he had pulled the trigger so many times that he no longer flinched at the sound of the shot.

ROSEMARY, WHO HAD become fast friends with Lilly, wasn't ready to say good-bye. As they stood outside the club, waiting for Martin to hail taxis for their merry band, she invited Lilly to the wedding. Lilly demurred. Even Josef at his most impish would not have put that on the list. Their interest in the excesses of the bourgeoisie extended only so far. As the first cab scudded toward the curb, Martin told Francis to give his regards to Good King George, and it struck Lilly that *this* was the George whom they'd mentioned in the hotel. Francis, Michael, George: Madame Eudoxia hadn't wasted a single name. London still remained a mystery, but the *no, no, nein* was becoming clearer than ever. In fact, the king's name had hit Lilly with such force that she stumbled; Rosemary caught her new friend by the arm. She saw that Lilly was shaken, and wouldn't hear of her returning, at this hour, to the lonely, half-packed studio in the Bowery. Not when Lilly was tired and tipsy. Not when Rosemary knew about the choices that faced her in the days ahead. She announced that Lilly would spend the night at the Plaza. Francis and Michael could share one bed, or one of them could sleep on the sofa, but Lilly would have the other room to herself.

Lilly was more exhausted than she wanted to admit, and she accepted the plan with only mild protest. Ever since she had met this boy—her guest, Sir Malcolm, Michael—she had let herself be swept along by a series of signs she could only half read. Josef, her sweet historical materialist, would tell her she was losing her mind, but tonight she had dined on oysters as big as her hand, she was masquerading as a countess, and she had applauded like mad for a man who was perhaps the greatest dancer in the world. Now she was about to spend the night at the Plaza Hotel. It was almost worth returning to Prague and facing whatever the city had become just to tell the story of this night.

Before Francis ducked into the taxicab, Rosemary gave him a stern look: she had her suspicions about Sunday night with Peggy, and she didn't want a repeat performance. She took both of Lilly's hands in hers. Lilly leaned in, kissed her rapidly on each cheek.

"Will you write to me when you get—to wherever you go?" Rosemary said, and pressed a hastily scribbled address into Lilly's hand. "And will you promise me that you'll keep safe?"

Lilly slipped the address into her purse. "I promise I'll write," she said as she slid in next to Francis and Michael. Just before the cab pulled away from the corner, she leaned out the window, aimed the camera, and snapped a picture of Martin and Rosemary standing together, the lights of Broadway pulsing all around them.

SATURDAY
JUNE 10

THE PLAZA HOTEL

FRANCIS DRESSED, HIS HANDS steady. A starched white shirt with a black bow tie, the hose and garter flashes secured beneath the knee, the kilt, the trim black coatee. Only when he belted the sporran did he reach into the drawer for the revolver. As his fingers found the grip, he checked again on Michael, who slept against the edge of the bed, his head almost lost in the pillow.

Francis had not slept well, his mind spinning in circles, but it had been some comfort to have his brother in the bed. For years, they'd shared a room in Ballyrath, the two of them wedged onto narrow cots with blankets pulled to their chins against the chill of the cottage walls. All through this last night the faint, steady sound of Michael's breathing brought on memories of those days: Francis and the other boys out in the hills, imagining themselves knights, Vikings, cowboys, Indians; baby Michael parked on a jacket at the edge of a field where Francis proved to the fat-fisted culchies that a schoolmaster's boy could hit twice as hard as they could; or Francis spying on his father early one morning when he thought the boys were still asleep. He watched as Da removed a small box from atop a wardrobe, then sifted through stiff-backed photographs, faded envelopes bound with string, a ring too delicate for his fat fingers. He hummed a slow, sad tune to himself—this from a man who never sang—but, when he heard Mrs. Greavey approach, broke off and hastily replaced the box, returning to his usual spot at the table.

471

What had become of those mementos since his father's death? Were they lost like the memories his father had locked away? Francis had to wonder, if his father had lived another five or ten to twenty years, whether he would have revealed more of his past to his sons. He had played some part in the war, and done enough to earn the ire of the old man who now determined Francis's fate. *He left Cork to keep you safe.* Or so Cronin had said. But safe from what? Or from whom? Had the old man been stalking the Dempseys all this time? Cronin knew the answers, but he kept himself locked up just as tight as their father ever had. And really, what was the point now? The knowledge would do him no good, Michael couldn't be told, and Martin didn't seem to care.

Francis hefted the gun, feeling its weight in his palm. He checked the cylinder, confirmed that the safety was on, and placed it grip-up in the pouch. With this, he would fire the shot and the Binghams would scream, *Sir Angus! What have you done?* With barely contained glee, Félicité would direct the police to the Plaza—Cassandra vindicated at last!—and half the peelers in New York would be kicking down the door, guns drawn, only to find Michael in placid communion with a vase of flowers. To keep Michael out of harm's way—something he had done a piss-poor job of, to be sure—he would need to get him out of the hotel. Peggy's wedding made the most sense, but there was no time for that now. He should have argued for it last night, but he had been so intent on getting lost in the mountains of food, the river of champagne, and the *hi-de-hi-de-ho*s that he had forgotten all the wrong things. And then Rosemary had gotten it into her head that Miss Bloch must—absolutely must—stay in the hotel, which had only served to upgrade Miss Bloch from witness to accomplice, which would do no favors for a woman who already had about her the look of an anarchist, or a kohl-eyed spy in some film about the Great War.

He had tried last night to stay away from the eye of her camera, but she was crafty. Often he heard the shutter without any sense of whom she had caught in the frame. Now all of last night's photos would become evidence in a case file linking the notorious Francis Dempsey to this whole carousing crew. See how they toasted their plot the night before its bloody conclusion! A lavish dinner, cocktails by the gallon, and New York's hottest floor show! Cold-blooded killers, every one of them!

His world was reorganizing itself into a few broad categories. Everything he had touched since arriving in New York would be viewed as evidence, while everyone he had met would be considered a witness, an accomplice, or a co-conspirator.

The only way he could help now was to buy them all time and distance. He wondered how long it would take for the name Angus Mac-Farquhar to be peeled back to reveal the name beneath it. Would he himself be the one to give that up? Not if his final bullet found its intended target. Would Martin step forward and claim him? Not unless he wanted a stain on his name that could never be wiped away. And would the Irish state, the newly christened republic, claim him as its own: a convict who'd escaped Mountjoy, only to resurface in New York, hell-bent on dragging the whole country into war with the old empire? Not bloody likely. He would be eagerly, willfully forgotten, unless the old man was so determined to put an Irishman's finger on the trigger that he splashed the Dempsey name in the press. Striking a blow for Ireland! For the abandoned brothers of Ulster! For a history that never stopped bleeding.

If the Dempsey name did become public, then what would become of Martin? Alive, yes, but what sort of life might he have? He wondered if the sap who'd shot Franz Ferdinand had a brother, and if so, how he'd fared in the years when Europe was sending its young men first to the trenches, and then to their graves.

It was too much to figure out with only an hour before he was due to meet the Binghams. Already he was late for his appointment with Mr. Cronin, who was expecting him to turn over the bankroll that had fueled the FC Plan. That plan had come to an end and there was nothing to do but settle the tab. In his Highland regalia, Francis went to the front desk to retrieve the personal item he had placed in the safe: a small leather satchel of the type carried by doctors on house calls. Its brass clasp was all that protected the fortune in stacked currencies. As lavishly as Francis had spent in the past weeks, there was still close to four thousand dollars inside. He stuffed a thick slab of bills into the sporran, gave a fiver to the man at the front desk, and in an envelope left twenty for Collier. *To a True Gentleman,* he wrote on the outside, then added *A. MacF.* before sealing the flap.

Cronin waited in an armchair beneath a potted palm, pretending to read the morning's *Times.* He stood as Francis approached. If Francis had been expecting a smile from Cronin about his attire, none was forthcoming.

"You're set, then," Cronin said. It wasn't meant as a question, but a statement of fact.

No, Francis wanted to say. *But I'm going to do it anyway.* He shook the bag at his side. "Should I hand it over now?"

"Just don't make a show of it," Cronin said.

"So is this what they mean in the gangster films, when there's a yoke called a bagman? I guess that's you, isn't it?"

Cronin snatched the bag from him. "You should watch your mouth," he said.

"It's not going to matter much longer, is it?"

Cronin turned without so much as opening the satchel.

"Aren't you going to count it?" Francis said.

"I don't care what's in it." He gave Francis a curt nod—why was the boy drawing this out? There was a look in his eyes that Cronin couldn't place, but he was eager to get away from the hotel, from Francis, from this whole godforsaken city. "We're done, so," he said, putting an end to it.

"Wait."

"What?" The word came through gritted teeth.

"Did my father ever kill anyone?"

Cronin snapped around again. "Why are you asking me that?"

"You, the old man—you all know more about my own family than I do. I need to know."

Cronin glared at him. There was that look in Francis's eyes again: Was it fear? Was Dempsey losing his nerve? "He never pulled a trigger, if that's what you're asking."

"And my mother," Francis said. "She wasn't killed in a crash—an accident—was she?"

Cronin's lips went white. There was so much not to say. "If that's what your father told you—"

"It's what he said, but it's not the truth, is it?"

Cronin had found a spot beyond Francis's shoulder and his gaze was locked on that.

"You said he left Cork to keep us safe. But it's not as if every car in Cork was coming for us, so it must have been something else. Or someone else."

At no point had Cronin imagined confessing what had happened to Bernadette—what he had done to Bernadette. He had never told anyone, not even Alice. For years, he hadn't needed to tell it; everyone in Cork knew, and that knowledge followed him to New York. Everyone could smell the bad fortune that clung to him like a pox.

"Your mother was never a target," Cronin said. "But that was no protection. Not for her. Not for a lot of others."

"Did you know the men who did it?"

Cronin met the boy's eyes—he owed him that—and slowly nodded. "Your parents wanted a better world for you and your brothers and they knew that took work. Work that others couldn't do."

"Does that make it easier?" Francis said. "When you believe in why you're doing it?"

"It's never easy," Cronin said. "And it's not supposed to be. You do it because it's necessary. If it ever becomes easy, then you're too far gone."

"And what would my parents have thought of this?" He meant the kilt, the sporran, the gun.

"They knew that you do what you have to, for the ones that matter."

"Does the old man matter to you? Is that why you're doing this?"

Cronin absorbed the punch of it: all that it accused him of, all that it called into question. "I walked into the same trap you did," Cronin said. He wanted to leave it at that—wittingly or not, each had put himself in debt to Gavigan—but what had the boy ever done? Francis might have stumbled in his life, but any mistakes he had made were petty compared to the sins of a man like Cronin. And yet here Francis stood, with his father's grim face and his mother's brilliant shock of red hair, preparing to endure a punishment far more severe than any Cronin had ever known.

Cronin's eyes burned. He looked at the floor, took a breath, then met Dempsey's eyes again. He needed to leave, to get far from here, but his feet were rooted. "The old man," he heard himself saying, "his name is Gavigan. John Gavigan. Knowing that won't do you any good, and if you say the name out loud it's only going to bring you misery. But you need to know that a man did this to you. Not God or the devil or some force of nature. Just a man who's willing to make others suffer to get what he wants. *He* is too far gone."

Francis knew more than he ever had about his parents and the past, but there were too many pieces to be connected and still so much to ask Martin that could turn their younger years from a mad, irrational jumble into a thing, however awful, that was at least driven by cause and effect. But there was no time. There was only time to act.

"I should be going," Francis said, turning for the elevator. "I don't want to keep the king waiting."

The thing that had been eating at Cronin revealed itself. Francis had his father's face, yes, but it was the look in his eyes, the cast of his features, that Cronin had not been able to place until now. He had seen the same expression in his own eyes, in the silvered mirror in his uncle's flat, on the morning before his first operation with Frank Dempsey. Before he reached the path by the River Lee where the police informant took his Sunday stroll, before Frank whistled the tune that signaled the man's approach, before the branches that hung down in a cavern of greenery—before all of it, there was the mirror and that look: steely, excited, hollow, and frightened. When he saw himself later that night in the same mirror, he saw that something in him had broken and grown back crooked, like a bone that hadn't been set right.

WHEN HE RETURNED to the suite, Francis was surprised to find Miss Bloch pouring a cup of coffee from a cart in the middle of the room.

She was about to apologize for ordering room service, but when she took in Francis—the kilt, the Prince Charlie coatee, the sporran— she had to stifle a laugh. "You look very…Scottish," she said.

"Thank you," he said. "I think the point of the outfit is to humiliate you in the presence of your betters."

"It's very nice," she said. "But your brothers will never forgive me—my camera is in the other room."

"Must be my lucky day," Francis said.

Strangers to each other, they moved about uncomfortably: half-smiles, stutter steps, too many sips of coffee. Last night, with the room more crowded, had been easier. But now Francis's heart was full of the things he must do; he wanted no distractions. Lilly's heart was torn between being the person she wanted to be and the one she knew she was. Where Francis wanted to move, to be done with it, Lilly wanted never to move and for nothing ever to change.

"It was kind of you to let me stay," she said. "With such a day in store, you must have hoped for a good night's sleep."

"It was grand," he said. "Though Michael does kick in his sleep."

"Yes," she agreed. "He does."

Francis gave her a quizzical look, but she only poured another cup of coffee and walked to the window overlooking the park. Francis took the opportunity to steal into his bedroom, where Michael's outline was visible under the sheets. Francis closed the door and from the writing desk withdrew an envelope. He filled it with most of the cash from the sporran—close to five hundred dollars, he figured—along with the list of doctors provided by Van Hooten and the sheet from Van Hooten's typewriter. He had a fresh sheet of paper with the Plaza's crest at the top, and paused to consider what, if anything, he could write to Martin that would explain what had happened and why. He could name this Gavigan, but what good would that do for Martin? It would only invite the man's wrath, which was exactly what Francis was acting to prevent. The word *evidence* echoed. Even if Martin was smart enough to keep the money for himself, would the letter become an exhibit in the reconstruction of this crime? In the end, he wrote, *Not for myself but for all of you. I hope you can understand.* He could think of nothing else. He folded the sheet and added it to the envelope, sealed the flap, and wrote MARTIN in blue letters across the front.

YEATS STOOD NEAR the bedroom door, watching Michael sleep. He saw no reason to wake the boy. He'd had some foolish idea of saying farewell—not that it was necessary, not that the boy would even want to. Hadn't Michael told him to sod off? So he would let him sleep. The boy certainly needed it, after all that had happened and all that was to come. Yeats himself was tired, his face drawn and his clothes rumpled. On unsteady legs he approached the bed and sat on the edge, near Michael's feet. He tried to cross one leg over the other but couldn't find the proper way to arrange his limbs.

Eternity like a tide was drawing him away. He saw now that he had tried for too long to maintain a hold on the material world. He had wanted to contact George, to speak across the divide of death, but George and his writings about the *spiritus mundi* and even art itself— now all of that was just shipwrecked pieces of a life that had run aground. He could cling to the wreckage or he could release himself into the arms of the ocean. All time tended toward the eternal. All divisions—days, years, centuries—dissolved into a never-ending present. He could feel the pull. He needed only to relinquish his grip.

Michael stirred, his eyes slowly opening. "Mr. Yeats," he said, stifling a yawn. "I hoped I'd see—"

Yeats held a finger to his lips, then pointed across the room in the direction of the curtained window. Francis sat at the desk, a lapful of plaid spilling over his chair. Michael slid out from under the sheets and padded across the thick carpet toward his brother, who was consumed in the act of writing, folding, sealing. Michael peered over his shoulder and saw an envelope on the desk marked with the word MARTIN.

Francis spun in his chair. "Jaysus Christ!" he said. "Don't sneak up on a fella, will you!"

Michael's eyes were fixed on the envelope, on his brother's jagged-peaked *M* and *A,* the crooked slashes of his *T, I,* and *N.* He jabbed a finger at the envelope and tapped loudly, twice.

"What is it?" Francis bent his elbows, palms up and out: the universal sign of the interrogative.

Michael snatched the pen from the desk and bent to the task. At a deliberate pace, he wrote *Francis* beneath the first name, then *Michael* beneath the second. The letters were shaky and poorly formed, but legible.

Francis stood and pulled a fresh sheet of paper from the drawer and placed it on the blotter. He wrote, *Can you read this?* and handed the pen to Michael, who nodded vigorously. Triumphant, Francis pressed his brother to his chest. Michael recoiled; he'd been poked by one of the buckles on Francis's regalia, but stepping back for a good look at his brother, he could only laugh—a choking, snorting sort of laugh.

The clock next to the bed told Francis that he was already late but he didn't want to go, not now. A minute ago he'd been ready to commit to this awful day. But here was proof that Michael was becoming Michael again. A thought flashed—*What if we just ran for it?*—but that was impossible. Even if he and Michael could disappear, they could never get Martin and Rosemary and the girls to follow.

Who was he willing to sacrifice to save his own skin? No one.

He put his hands on Michael's shoulders to get a last look at him. The two brothers smiled at each other. Michael was giddy as a puppy, his features loose and lively. Francis knew if he dropped his smile, his whole face was likely to crumble.

I have to go, he wrote.

Where?

To meet the king.

King of what?

Long story. going w/ girl from the park.

Shouldn't she wear the skirt?

Francis boxed him playfully on the shoulder. This was the Michael who had fled with him from Ballyrath. Frank and Jesse James, on the run from the posse.

Francis picked up the pen. *I have to go. I'm sorry.*

Sorry for?

Everything.

As Michael puzzled over this, Francis put a hand on his shoulder. He tightened his grip, felt his brother's bones and the warmth of his skin, radiant from sleep and the sheets and the morning heat. Michael was real, was returned. Every day he would come closer to his old self. He thought again of his prayer, his life for Michael's.

Before he left the suite, he asked Miss Bloch for one last favor: Once

Michael was dressed, could she put him in a cab with this envelope, to be delivered to Martin and Rosemary? Their address—now where did he put their address?—but Lilly waved him off; Rosemary had given it to her the night before. She would put Michael in the cab, but was he sure that it was safe? Michael alone had not had good results.

"He can read," Francis said. "I don't know how or why, but suddenly he can read and write again. He's a new man. Or he's becoming the old one. I wish I could stay, but—" He looked at his hands, helpless. "And I'm sorry to impose, but he needs to be out of the hotel within the hour—as do you. And as a token of our thanks, for all you've done, I'd like you to have this." He handed her the rest of the money: two hundred and fifty, perhaps three hundred dollars.

She looked at the stack of bills as if he'd handed her the pieces to a jigsaw puzzle.

"It's far less than you deserve, but I hope it helps with your travels. Bon voyage."

"Forgive me," she said. Francis was acting so strange: dressed like a Highland groom, unable to stand still, speaking a hundred miles an hour, telling her Michael could read and write, and now this handful of dollars. "But I don't understand."

"It will all make sense, but right now you have an hour to get far, far from this place."

"That sounds ominous," she said lightly. After all, everything he had said last night sounded like a joke.

"It's meant to." And with that he was out the door.

MICHAEL PULLED BACK the drapes and let the morning sun stream into the bedroom. The bed linens blazed white, but Yeats remained a smudgy half-gray. He sat hunched, his elbows on his knees.

"Did you see that?" Michael said. "The letters didn't move. I could read them, simple as that."

Yeats rubbed his hands together, contemplative, then pushed himself to his feet, his back to Michael.

"Did you see, Mr. Yeats? You've no need for a medium now. If you want to write a letter to your wife—"

Yeats turned, his eyes deep and blank, framed by the black weight of his spectacles. He slowly opened his mouth.

"No, no, no!" Michael saw it before he heard it. He backpedaled toward the window and stumbled over a pair of shoes. Windmilling his arms, his balance gone, he hit the window hard enough to crack it. His head rapped against the mullion; his elbow punctured the pane.

Yeats opened his mouth and the Noise poured out of him. Michael wrenched his elbow back through the glass and pressed both hands to his ears. He was aware of the sudden pain in his arm, sharp and hot and sticky, but it was a sideshow. The main event was the machine drilling through his skull, squealing and grinding through bone and brain pulp. The floor shifted and he heaved himself forward, away from the window, as Yeats raised one hand in warning or farewell, and then the poet was gone and in his place was his host, the woman who had rescued him once before, and he had time only to register the shock on her face before the blackness came all around him and he pitched toward the blazing mass of the bed.

GRAMERCY PARK

BAGMAN. THE TRUTH OF it had stung, coming from Dempsey's mouth. Cronin was a delivery boy. He had helped to deliver Francis Dempsey to his doom and now he was toting a sack of money to Gavigan. How was that for being on the right side? How was that for being a good man? Once he was done with Gavigan he would find his way home and try to look Alice in the eye, but it wouldn't be easy. She'd say she was glad to have him back but who—what—was she getting?

All down the avenue from Midtown to Gavigan's place, the lampposts and the awnings were festooned with flags: Union Jacks on every corner, and the royals wouldn't even see them. The parade was to be up the West Side Highway and the papers said there would be hundreds of thousands lining the route. If it had been twenty years earlier, and the king's father had been fool enough to visit Ireland, and Frank Dempsey had given him the word? And if Bernadette had told him it would advance the cause, that it would put England on the back foot? Of course Cronin would have done it, and with no more animus than when he shot a police inspector. But it wasn't twenty years ago, it wasn't Ireland, and Gavigan's reasons were a poor substitute for the Dempseys'. The Americans had had their war with another King George—hadn't they called him a tyrant, too?—but that was history and now they waved flags and roses for the king. Some histories you washed off quickly. Others you wallowed in like a sty.

Cronin found a place for the car on the far side of Gramercy Park, where the low iron gate separated him from a riot of rhododendron and azalea, flocks of bearded iris. He caught the wet smell of the earth, of mulched bark: a reminder that a better world existed somewhere. He should have used the back entrance to the brownstone, but Gavigan had gone out of his way to expose Cronin, so why shouldn't he return the favor? The small, petty defiance of a man who has been beaten and knows it. With the bag at his side, Cronin rang the bell and Helen, the Jane-of-all-trades, opened the door.

"Well, if it isn't our bad penny," she said. "You keep turning up."

"This'll be the last time," he said. "I need to see him and then I'm off."

She beckoned for Cronin to follow her down the carpeted hall. She was a stout woman, built like a coffeepot. "The two of them have been in the study all morning listening to the radio." She stopped when she came to the door. "You don't suppose they're waiting for the opera, do you?"

Gavigan was behind the desk. Jamie leaned, arms folded, against the bookcase, like he had all the time in the world.

"Come to join our party, Tommy?" Gavigan said. "I've got a nice bottle set aside for a toast, but not until we have a reason to celebrate. It could be a few hours still, and I know how you get thirsty. Think you can wait?"

Cronin ignored the question and set the bag on the desk. "Here's your money, or what's left of it. Dempsey wasn't exactly pinching pennies."

"A small price to pay," Gavigan said. "They'll be writing songs about him soon."

"Well, then," Cronin said. "I'll be on my way."

"What? So soon? We couldn't have done this without you, Tommy. For all his charm, I don't think Jamie would have had the patience to see Dempsey through all this. He was all for dumping him off a bridge days ago."

"I'm not the babysitting type," Jamie said. "But I'm glad that some-one is."

Gavigan barked a laugh that tripped into a manky, wet cough. He was practically giddy. His plan was coming together, bigger than any heist or hit in the old days. By nightfall, the world would be in an uproar. He would make clear to the Army Council just who had masterminded this operation—and wouldn't that give them a shock! Of course they wouldn't breathe a word of it. It was too easy to con-nect the dots and link Gavigan back to them, and who would believe that Gavigan alone had freelanced this entire operation, without the knowledge or consent of the IRA? No, they would be gobsmacked. Maybe now he would get the respect he deserved.

"That's right," Gavigan said. "Tommy wants to get back to his farmer's wife and his baby. You be sure to give them a kiss from their old uncle John."

Cronin had heard enough. He turned for the door.

"I'll tell you what, Tommy." Gavigan reached for the satchel and came out with a wedge of banknotes. He peeled off bills like he was skinning a potato. "Here's a little something extra for your troubles. Why don't you buy that woman of yours something nice?" His laugh was croupy, malicious. He was the king of all jokes today. "Maybe a wedding ring? Make an honest woman of her, why don'tcha?"

Cronin stopped, his hand on the doorknob. On the desk, Gavigan had laid out five hundred dollars in tens and twenties.

"Oh, don't be so sour. I'm just having a bit of fun." He stacked the bills into a neat pile and then proffered it to Cronin. "Take it," he said. "If you don't want any gifts, then you can consider it a down payment for the next time."

Cronin's left hand balled into a fist, the way it had in front of the farmhouse. "This is the end of it," he said, as much to himself as to Gavigan.

"It's the end for now," Gavigan said. "I know where to find you when I need you."

CRONIN WHEELED ON Gavigan with the revolver and fired, catching the old man in the neck. The wound was messy and Gavigan lingered only long enough to know that it was Cronin who had done it.

Even as he was squeezing the trigger, Cronin knew that he should have shot Jamie first. That would have been the smart thing to do: take out the muscle. But he had let his temper get the better of him— Frank Dempsey would have had stern words for a lapse like that— and some small part of him must have thought that Jamie wanted to be free of Gavigan too.

The bullet that struck Cronin's shoulder announced that Jamie did not want to be free of all this. And the fact that the shot hit him in the shoulder rather than the head or the gut told him that Jamie, for all his vigilance, had been caught off guard. Before Jamie could fire a second time, Cronin pivoted and fired, practically point-blank, and sent him spinning face-first to the carpet. The Webley was a battle-field weapon. It rarely required a second shot.

The pain came in hot, electric pulses down Cronin's arm and into his chest, as if he were wrapped in burning barbed wire. In two strides he reached Jamie and kicked free his gun and then, with the same foot, he rolled him onto his back. The blood was already spreading across Jamie's shirt, around a shredded spot in the fabric where the bullet had torn into his chest. Cronin knew that something similar was happening to him. He could feel the ooze of it on his arm.

"You stupid goddamn langer," Cronin said to Jamie. "He's dead. You could've walked away."

Jamie's eyes were rolling in his head. Whatever Cronin was feeling,

Jamie was feeling it worse. He spoke in short breaths, between gritted teeth: "Fucking hell. If I'd'a wanted him dead, I coulda done it any time."

Cronin tried to lift his left hand, but the pain wouldn't allow it. He sat on the arm of the wingback, and with the Webley still in his hand, he poked at the lapel of his jacket with the gun barrel to peek at the damage.

Jamie's eyes were canted to the side and fixed on Cronin. His breathing came fast and shallow. "You gonna finish the job?"

"I'm done," he said. "I wasn't planning on shooting you—you made that happen. It's not up to me whether you live or die."

JAMIE CLOSED HIS eyes. The crisp white shirt that Helen had starched and ironed for him was soaked and sticky with his own blood. He had taken more time than usual that morning to decide on a necktie; ridiculous as it seemed to him now, he had actually pondered whether to wear the green one to recognize Gavigan's grand scheme for Ireland, or just go with the blue, because it favored his eyes. Only an hour ago, the decision had seemed to matter.

How had he let Cronin get a shot off? He had seen the man boiling in the moments before the gun flashed out from under his jacket but Jamie felt like he was watching it happen in a movie. All week long, Cronin had taken whatever abuse Gavigan had heaped on him, and like Gavigan, Jamie came to believe that Cronin was a broken man, easily bullied. Well, cheers to Cronin, then. He had proven them both wrong.

Jamie wanted to get off the floor but nothing in his body responded to the thought. Helen must be somewhere in the house, but if she had any brains she was hiding until the ruckus came to an end. Perhaps she would call the police. There were still a few men on the force sympathetic to Gavigan and the largesse he could dispense. And perhaps there would be an ambulance, though it was sure to arrive too late to matter. It wouldn't be long now.

* * *

THE CORPSE THAT had recently been Gavigan was slumped in the big chair behind the desk. The portrait of his mother glared out into the room, as if she could not bear the sight of her dead son. She must have loved her boy as he loved her: fiercely and despite the opinions of the world.

The fire that Cronin had felt when the bullet hit was already starting to ebb, replaced now with a different sort of ache. It felt like someone had taken a rusty saw to his left arm and detached the limb, then hastily stuck it back in place. His fingers still moved and that was a good sign, but the blood had reached down to his shirt cuff and that seemed to bode ill. Cronin had been in plenty of scrapes that had left him bruised and in need of stitches, but this was the first time he'd been shot. Surprising, really, considering the ways he'd spent the past twenty years. It was almost funny now that it had finally happened, but he knew that if he started laughing about it—if he really did find it funny—it was a sure sign that he was losing too much blood, or perhaps just losing his mind. Jamie lay on the floor, clearly not long for this world. His staccato breathing had become an occasional hiccup and his face was going slack. It struck Cronin that their places could have easily been reversed: Jamie only winged, while Cronin breathed his last. Jamie would have cleaned it all up, and if Alice ever received any word of his fate, it would only have been to brand him a murderer, and to lay bare every misdeed of his past. A great sob heaved out of Cronin's chest, followed by another and another. His legs shook and for a moment he thought that he might fall from the arm of the chair to his knees. But he had not come this far—on this godforsaken errand or in this life—to die alone and be counted among these men.

Cronin hauled himself to his feet. The pile of money was still on the desk, the top bill spattered with Gavigan's blood. Cronin peeled it from the stack, left the lone bill on the desk, and put the rest of the money, along with the Webley, back in the satchel. He might have his principles, but he also had his responsibilities.

He looked again at Jamie. If Cronin had never stepped off that train, then Jamie would not have taken his place at Gavigan's side. He could tell himself that Jamie's life might not have turned out any differently—that the years might, in fact, have treated him far worse—but he could not erase the fact that it was he who had put an end to it all, both for Jamie and for Gavigan. He was not a new man, not a different man since he'd found Alice and the boy at the farm. But a different sort of man could not have walked out of this room alive. Cronin knew who he was, and he knew that he could not be saved, but there were others who were not yet lost, and they were the ones he would serve.

He reached for the fat black telephone and turned it so the dial faced him. The phone number was still in his jacket pocket, and with great effort his fished it out. The paper was now half soaked in his blood. He stabbed his fingers one by one into the dial, which buzzed with each rotation like a nest of bees. It rang twice, and then the oldest Dempsey's voice said, "Hello?"

"Listen to me," Cronin said. "Your brother is about to do something terrible, and you have to stop him."

Martin started to ask, "Who is—" but Cronin cut him off.

"You know my voice and you know my face," Cronin said. "And you know your brother is mixed up in something."

"Just what are you and Francis up to? And don't give me the runaround this—"

"Your brother is going to kill the king today." Cronin growled through gritted teeth. He took a deep breath, trying to steady himself. "I knew your parents in Cork, and on their graves I swear it's true."

"Look, I'm on the way out the door to a wedding." He said it as if it mattered, as if it could put a stop to anything Cronin had said.

"Your father and mother had a home on O'Donovan Rossa Street, close to the university. There was a piano in the parlor and a marble fireplace. There was a clock on the mantel—shiny, brass or bronze—with a man on one side of the clock's face, and a lady on the other."

"How do you know this?"

"Because I was there. I served with your father in the war."

"My father was a professor."

"And I was a gardener. But that didn't stop me from pulling the trigger when the professor told me to shoot."

Martin's breathing came through the receiver like bursts of static.

"Francis has a gun," Cronin said, "and he's been told that if he doesn't do it, then you and your brother and your wife are all dead."

"Hold on now, what? My"—his voice dropped to a whisper—"*my wife?*"

"You need to stop him."

"You just said if he doesn't do it, then we're all—"

"I took care of that," Cronin said. "You're not in danger anymore. But if your brother pulls that trigger, God only knows what hell he'll unleash."

"There must be a million people at the fair today."

"Find the king and you'll find your brother. Tell him it's off. Tell him the old man is dead. Tell him that."

"What old man?"

"Tell him," Cronin said.

Cronin's left arm hung limp and blood pooled in the palm of his hand. He could feel himself slipping into that pool. Going under. But if he thought about it hard enough, he could get his fingers to move. Every small motion sent a jolt up his arm. The jolts were enough to keep him from sliding under, but not for long. The Dempsey boy's voice was coming through the receiver but it wasn't making any sense. Cronin wadded up the paper he had torn from the phone book, all the M. Dempseys in New York, and put it in his mouth. He chewed it slowly, the pulpy mass spiked with the salt iron of his blood.

"One more thing," Cronin said into the receiver, every word a stone he could barely lift. "After you stop your brother, you find Alice, and you tell her I tried to do right."

"Alice?" said a voice from far away. "Who's Alice?"

Who's Alice? There was no way to answer that question. Alice was Alice. "On the farm," he said. "With Henry and Gracie."

"Hello?" said the voice, but the voice was so far away. The receiver lay on the desk, and Cronin found himself on the floor, and though the voice continued to say, "Hello? Hello?" Cronin thought only of Alice, and the boy, and the baby, and the farm.

FORDHAM HEIGHTS

As soon as Martin hung up the telephone, he called the Plaza. There was no answer in the suite, but what did that mean? Only that Francis had left for the fair as planned, that Michael couldn't hear Big Ben, let alone a telephone, and that Miss Bloch must have gone about her day. Hadn't Rosemary said she was bound for Prague, or was it Budapest?

Still, there was no way around it. He had to go. He wanted to believe that the man on the phone was spouting nonsense, but he knew it was the truth, even before the man began to describe Martin's boyhood home. He tried for the third time to knot his tie, but his hands were trembling so badly that he couldn't make it work.

Explaining it all to Rosemary would be another matter. Missing the rehearsal was one thing—a lark. It had been a wonderful night, one that they would never forget. But the wedding? He couldn't miss the wedding. And what about the reception? His band? If he left on this mad errand to stop Francis and save the king and prevent the next Great War, then by the time he got to Woodlawn the bride and groom would already be on their honeymoon. Rosemary, Peggy, the Dwyers, and John Hammond himself—they would all agree that they had been let down by Martin. *Get used to it,* Mr. Dwyer would say to Hammond. *This kid is a walking, talking disappointment.* Only Hammond wouldn't stick around long enough to get used to it. The world was full of bandleaders, horn players, and lady singers who needed only one chance to impress. Hammond couldn't waste time with time wasters.

Everything he had done this week and the weeks that led up to it was predicated on his faith in the band he had assembled. Hoop would blow that horn, Exley and Gaines would keep the rhythm swinging, and Martin would sit down at the piano—right where he had always belonged!—and take the whole outfit for a drive. He had quit his job for this, quit it and set the bridge burning! He had wanted Rosemary to see this thing he'd built, which would justify all the faith she put in him, all the times she'd deflected, ignored, or outright argued with her parents when they made their nasty comments, their tinker talk and *What a shame* and their disappointment so thick you could put it in a pot and call it soup. All of her forbearance—and, truth be told, she had put up with a fair bit of malarkey from Martin— would be recognized and paid back when she heard what this band could do.

But now. Christ, now.

Rosemary was in the children's room, preparing Kate to be a flower girl. The dress had been ironed one last time, and Rosemary was slowly unwinding the curlers from Kate's hair. She looked like a min- iature Shirley Temple, and when Martin entered the room, she twirled in a circle to show off how well her dress could spin. Martin told her she was lovely—just lovely—but inside he was reeling with the news that she could have been orphaned, or worse.

He hadn't known it, but there had been a black cloud hanging over his family, and if the man on the phone was to be believed, then that cloud had lifted. It was all because of Francis, and now Francis was going to unleash another kind of storm, one that would devastate the family in a whole different way. Kill the king? Martin was certain that it all went back to the farmhouse where Michael was nearly killed and Francis came away with the pile of money that had fueled their time in New York. What had Francis said? *Fellas run off all the time?*

Only Francis had been found, and somehow the stupid bastard had wound up with a gun in his hand.

Martin couldn't unspool the entire story for Rosemary—Francis, the gun, the call, the man who knew his parents—so he stuck to the parts that would most directly affect her: There was a problem, a big one, and he needed to go. He said he was likely to miss the wedding, but he would be back in time for the reception. It was a complete lie, but easier, in that moment, than the truth. Rosemary pressed him for details—was it Michael again? Francis? What was happening?—but Martin would only say that he'd explain it all at the reception. That he wouldn't be leaving her at this moment if it weren't important. That, if nothing else, she knew how badly he wanted to play with his band.

"And Rosemary," he said. "About the reception. If"—he lied—"if I'm late, I need you to tell Hooper to start without me. To play bandleader till I get there."

"Hooper? The one you told me about from Minton's?" she said. "But isn't he—"

"The best trumpet your father's money could buy?" Martin avoided her eyes and checked his pockets: wallet, keys, cigarettes, lighter. He needed to get moving. "Just tell Hoop to keep things running. He knows the set list."

"Wait just a minute," she said. "The wedding starts in an hour, and you're telling me now that you're not going, and oh, by the way, you've got a colored musician—"

"Hoop doesn't say colored." Martin looped his tie around his neck and tried again with the knot. "I think he says Negro."

Rosemary slapped him—a full-handed, Bette Davis slap, just like in the pictures. Kate, who had been sashaying around the room, warbling a tune, stopped, wide-eyed, and stared at her parents.

Martin put his hand to his jaw. He deserved at least that much, putting Rosemary through the wringer like this. But he was also wasting time, and needed to get moving.

"Why didn't you tell me?" Tears were coming up in Rosemary's eyes but she shook her head to fight them back. "Why don't you tell me anything—about quitting your job, or your secret plan for what's next, or why you're suddenly skipping the wedding, or how your band is going to throw my parents into an absolute—"

"Because you would've worried!" he interjected. "And you would've tried to talk me out of it!"

They stood facing each other, unsure of what to say next. He had spoken the truth, as he saw it, but he'd also admitted that he didn't trust her. Not completely. He muttered something, the makings of an apology, and ducked out of the girls' room. His jacket—where had he left his jacket?

In the silence, Rosemary's hand throbbed. She had never slapped anyone, not like that. She wondered if that was what her father felt, those times when he hit her mother, or had his hands gotten too callused to feel the buzz and the heat?

Martin reappeared in the doorway. "I'm sorry," he said, "but I have to do this." He had his jacket in his hands, the collar of it bunched in one fist. "And I should have left already. Jesus, the time."

"Just tell me what's happening."

"I'll explain it all at the reception." He tried for a smile—composed, apologetic—but it came off as a grimace. "You can even slap me again, if it makes you feel any better."

THE FIRST CABBIE he saw spelled it out for him: because of the royal parade and the millions gawking along the route, half the roads leading to Flushing were closed and the other half were twice as crowded. "You can get in," he said, "but the meter's gonna run for hours. How about it, Mr. Rockefeller?" No, the train was the only way, and that meant two, maybe three transfers, and that meant an hour or more, on a good day. This was not a good day. He bought a paper at the newsstand and gutted it for the special supplement on the royal visit. Photos of the king and queen filled each page: walking among a crowd in Canada, their path picketed with soldiers; riding in an open-topped carriage at the coronation; posing on a Scottish hillside with their two girls when the littlest was no more than Kate's age. An inside page listed the itinerary for the day, from the moment they arrived by boat at the Battery to the long trek up the West Side Highway and then on to Queens. A close-up of the fairgrounds marked points of interest with numbered dots: the Trylon and Perisphere, Perylon Hall, the Federal Building, the British Pavilion, the Lagoon of Nations. The royals would see it all in a motorized cart at a touring speed of three miles an hour—faster, Martin believed, than the subway train that was slowly, slowly approaching the tunnel that would take it from the Bronx, to Manhattan, to Queens, and, if the stars aligned, would deliver Martin to the fair before Francis could blow the Court of Peace to pieces.

All that had been pent up during this mad week came at Martin in a rush: the funeral, the questions about their father, the men with their map to the bomb factory, and this hanger-on, this stormcock— what was his name?—who sent Martin on a cross-city chase and then ran off as the family gathered last night, only to call again with news that Francis, with his party of millionaires' daughters and wives, was going to kill the king of England. Martin wouldn't have believed a word of it if not for that voice; the man was right, Martin had known it before, in Cork, in the house where he was a boy. The man knew the house, the piano, the mantel, the clock. His mother had carried that clock home from a trip she and Da had taken to France, much to Da's consternation. Ares on one side, Aphrodite on the other, both slouched against the mother-of-pearl face. *Is that supposed to be me?* Da had said, pointing to the bearded Ares leaning shirtless on his shield. *Of course not,* she said. *That's me. You're the pretty one on the other side.* Mam always got a laugh from that story. For his part, Da would play the peacock, pretending offense while he primped his necktie. After the flight from Cork, Martin never again saw that side of Da — playful, rising above his resentments. The clock was one of the few items Da took with them to Ballyrath, where it marked the minutes and hours of their shared confinement.

As the train lurched and scraped its way beneath the city, Martin thought back on those early, happier days. Tossing paper boats in the river near the university gates and racing to see which were first to reach the weir. Sitting with his mother in the opera house, her eyes full of tears, and learning from her how deeply music could cut, and that it was good to open yourself up to that ache. Walking with his father through the smoldering ruins the morning after the Brits had put the city to the torch. December, was it? He couldn't have been more than ten. The air was wet and the smell of charred wood and the fog of crushed brick clung close to the ground. A man who had seen it burn said the clock on the city hall had chimed all the way until it collapsed into the rubble. Martin secretly hoped that the statue of Father Mathew might have burned — he'd always been afraid of the way the Apostle of Temperance glowered at the river — but the bronze priest had stood his ground. When Martin and his father returned home, their faces were streaked in soot and their clothes reeked of smoke. His father crouched in front of him, his thick hands on Martin's shoulders. *Who's going to build it back, Martin?* Da said, and then answered his own question, like a catechism. *You are, that's who.*

Martin remembered this, too: Walking the twisty uphill lanes to the candy factory near Shandon, Francis in tow and a few shillings in his pocket. Most of what they bought, they gobbled on the spot, but Martin had learned to save a few sweets to bribe the rough boys who controlled safe passage from the Butter Exchange to the river. In those days, he would watch the ships at the port and in a notebook sketch their flags and list their countries of origin. He walked the bridge over Patrick Street, marking the low tide that exposed the barnacled walls of the quays and the high tides that lapped the underside of the other bridges. He listened to the gulls careening for bits of bread and river trash, the echo of the newsmen on George's Street, the clop of dray horses toting jugs of milk, each tolling its own bass timbre. All of this was music to him. He heard every note and stitched them into unwritten compositions. By the time he was ten, he spent more than an hour a day at the piano and when Francis pestered him to kick a ball or line up a column of lead soldiers, he would practice for twice as long. He also played the tin whistle, the clarinet, the French horn. In the months after their last Christmas party, he had begged to be taught the violin. His mother had just arranged for him to take lessons, and then Mam was gone.

He was in the parlor playing Scott Joplin—his mother had been mad for Joplin since her days at the conservatory in Boston—when a boom from the street rattled the windows and shook the china plates on their stands. He paused his playing for only a moment, waiting to see if the sound would repeat, and then he resumed, his fingers bouncing over the keys, right hand chattering with the left. Then came the thunder of his father on the stairs, not even like feet on the treads but like a whole body tumbling end over end, and then the wrenching of the front door and the clack of the knocker against the brass plate, then a shout. None of it stopped Martin from playing. He played faster and louder, an endless loop, just the way that Joplin wrote it, until his father burst in, smoke-stained and wild-eyed, with a look Martin had never seen but would come to know well in the years ahead. *Leave it!* he said. *For God's sake! Leave it, will you!* Martin pulled his hands away like the piano had been electrified. It was six months, at least, until his father arranged for him to use the piano in the pub in Ballyrath, and only in the mornings when the pub was closed, and only if he didn't play too loud, and for God's sake, he was never to play any ragtime.

THE WORLD'S FAIR

FRANCIS THOUGHT HE HAD already seen the Binghams' best car, but he was mistaken. The car that had conveyed him to the Plaza on Monday was apparently used for short excursions and the ferrying of minor nobles traveling without retinue. The Pierce-Arrow that delivered Francis, Mrs. Bingham, Anisette, and Félicité from Fifth Avenue to Flushing was a men's grill on wheels, a mobile Union League Club. The interior was done in burled walnut and red leather and fitted in lustrous brass. A hinged cabinet concealed crystal tumblers and a decanter of bourbon beside an ice bucket that had apparently been filled just before departure. The Bingham women fell into familiar roles: gracious, glowing, glowering. Félicité had arched one eyebrow when Francis arrived that morning, no doubt surprised that he had kept the commitment. To her, his appearance would mean that he was either a faithful suitor or twice the con man she'd figured him for, someone willing to stomach a little scandal if it meant a life of luxury.

Crossing the East River, Mrs. Bingham asked after Sir Malcolm, and whether Sir Angus had yet conveyed news of his brother's progress to his parents. "A mother worries," she said. "Especially when her babies are so far from home."

Francis assured her that his brother had spent the week in splendid leisure—if anything, he said, young Malcolm was growing bored at the Plaza—but he hadn't the energy to concoct for her any stories about their dear, sweet mother, Lady MacFarquhar. For her part, Anisette seemed positively serene, and communicated with him mostly through smiles and glances.

As they neared the fairgrounds, Félicité peered out the window and commented on the dreariness of Queens: "Bad enough we have to drive through it," she said. "But can you imagine living here?"

Francis aimed for the easy bonhomie that had carried him through dinner on the *Britannic* and at Bingham Castle, but he felt the effort showing through the frayed spots in his Angus MacFarquhar costume. The fear and dread boiling in him couldn't possibly be contained by the calm, clubby charm that Angus affected. He expected that, if he failed, men with guns would be roaming the city by nightfall to make good on Gavigan's promises. If there was a lesson that Cronin was trying to impart by telling him the name of the man who had outfoxed him, Francis wouldn't live long enough to learn it. For now, it only gave him someone to curse.

THE GUESTS WERE asked to arrive by noon, and by eleven o'clock an armada of Rolls-Royces, Duesenbergs, Regents, and Cadillacs jostled for berths along the curb. Automobile parking near the fair was limited, and the chauffeurs engaged in a more decorous version of a Midtown taxi bullfight, their engines purring and surging, their black flanks shining in the midday sun. The guest list had swollen, a cattle call of the city's elite, but each was aware of who had made the cut and who had opted for exile in Westchester, or Greenwich, or Newport on this sun-blasted Saturday.

Just as they were to exit the limousine, he caught Anisette's eye and gave her a wistful half-smile, an empty gesture that could not carry the weight of what he would take from her when he fired the shot. Of course she would be standing next to him. She would see it all. He thought for a moment that if she preceded him to the dais, he could use her to shield himself from view as he reached for the—and he realized with shame just how quickly he had turned her into not merely a pawn but a prop.

Once outside the car, the party passed through a cluster of boxy white pavilions celebrating advances in pharmacy, electric shavers, and wristwatches. These buildings lined the Street of Wings, which gave way to the Court of Power, the Plaza of Light, and Commerce Circle. The Bingham party was led to Perylon Hall, which resembled a midmarket beach resort during the off-season: two white slabs stacked one on the other, with curved balconies supported by slender pipes that called to mind rain gutters.

The interior of the hall, however, had been reimagined as a fantasy of Merrie Olde England. Every room and corridor had been gauded up in carpets and tapestries, altar screens and bishop's chairs and portraits of minor nobles. Honestly, the place looked like a jumble sale at a bankrupt monastery. One entire wall of the banquet room where the guests were asked to wait was decorated with a tapestry depicting a medieval pilgrimage. Its weavers may have begun with a vague notion of *The Canterbury Tales,* but there were too few nuns and priests and too many rose-petal-lipped youths sporting beneath a canopy of ivy. Women in conical fairy-princess hats demurely eyed curly-headed squires in muscle-packed tights. Banners decked in chevrons, rampant lions, and stout towers suggested allegiances that divided this happy pack into factions indistinguishable to outside observers.

Against the opposite wall, a broad window overlooked a spiral garden and offered a picture-postcard view of the fair's signature pieces: the Trylon and Perisphere. A long line of fairgoers stretched up a sinuous ramp that cut through the tower and into the belly of the giant white orb.

"Now what do you suppose is in there?" Francis said.

"It's Democracity," Anisette said. "The city of the future. I read about it in *Life* magazine."

"How ridiculous," Félicité sniffed.

Anisette exchanged a knowing look with Sir Angus—hadn't they shared a laugh about her sister's foul temperament during their walk? It was just the sort of inside joke that would set Félicité's teeth on edge.

TWO LONG TABLES in the banquet room were lined with cards, one for each party in attendance, with numbers on the cards indicating the order of entry for each group of twenty. The procedure was explained by a man whose golden Trylon and Perisphere lapel pin conferred on him an instant legitimacy—as if they were visitors to a strange land, and he the ambassador. He was quick to say that the numbers had been assigned entirely at random, using a computing machine created expressly for the purpose of random-number generation. The Binghams found themselves in group 17.

The man with the lapel pin invited the first group to assemble at the door. Each party would be led down a broad corridor by a woman in a straw hat topped by a replica of the Trylon and Perisphere. In a chamber arrayed in antiques—not just Louis XIV, but Louis XVI, too— they would be presented to Their Royal Highnesses, each of whom would offer a beneficent nod as the Americans' names found purchase in the royal ears. Many in the hall wondered if anything more than an answering nod would be appropriate. "Charmed to make your acquaintance" seemed awfully familiar, and wasn't there a rule against Americans bowing to foreign kings? Wasn't that why everyone was so suspicious of the Catholics, with their Italian popes and their bowing and ring-kissing? Perhaps the king himself would offer some arcane salute used since the days of Richard the Lionheart to acknowledge the fealty of loyal vassals? That would be a sight to see.

As soon as the groups began to form, a film of sweat rose on Francis's forehead. These were the final moments. The doors would open and the procession would begin. The groups were led into a long corridor and lined up, groups 1 through 20, but no one was allowed past the final door and into the royal chamber. There was a great buzz and chatter; the royals were ten minutes late, then twenty, then thirty. The well-wishers had queued along the corridor like the world's most lavish breadline when, with a gasp from groups 1 through 5, the double doors parted and the ones on whom the computing machine had smiled disappeared from view. Francis steeled himself. If he had tried for charm and wit in the banquet room, he now wanted silence and an end to small talk. The line was moving, group 2 was through the doors, and he knew that he would not have much time to act.

A ripple of shocked whispers raced to the back of the line: The Italian ambassador—who invited him?—had saluted the king with the raised fist of the Fascists. Definitely a breach of etiquette. The line moved again, and Francis figured that he had ten minutes, perhaps fifteen, before he reached into the sporran for the gun. A tremor twisted his guts. He closed his eyes and took a deep breath, picturing how he would slide the gun from its pouch, raise it, and fire. Just like Cronin had shown him.

"Sir Angus, could I have a moment of your time?" Mrs. Bingham was at close quarters, speaking in a near whisper. Anisette had drifted from his side, feigning interest in a pair of wimple-and-ruff portraits in order to open a channel for her mother. Félicité stood stern and alone by the edge of the group.

"You'll have to forgive me," he said. "You caught me daydreaming."

"I do apologize, but I wanted to take *une petite minute* to address a delicate issue, but one it is my duty, as a mother, to perform."

In imagining the sequence of events in the royal chamber, Francis had not yet reached the part about what he would do after the king had fallen: Would he wait for the guards to return fire? Or immediately place the gun to his own head?

"As I'm sure you're aware," Mrs. Bingham went on, "Anisette is quite fond of you. But before I encourage this fondness to grow into something more, I need to know whether these feelings of hers are shared by you. Forgive my bluntness, but do you have any…intentions regarding Anisette? And I know this is an inopportune time—"

"It is, I confess, not the best moment—"

"—but a mother must always protect the heart of a child as dear as Anisette, and if your feelings are not aligned with hers, then I need to prepare her as best I can for the—well, for the blow that will cause."

"I assure you, I am quite fond of Anisette," he said. "But now isn't the right time for me to make any…declarations."

"Of course," she said, with a grim set to her eyes. "I think I take your meaning."

Why was he being coy? He could vow to make Anisette the queen of Scotland or the queen of the moon. In a few minutes, all his promises would be null and void.

"You're not pledged to another, are you?"

"Oh no, nothing like that," he said. "But with so much on the agenda for today—"

"No one said it had to be today!" Mrs. Bingham tittered with obvious relief. "But is it safe to say that we are in accord regarding the future of your acquaintance with Anisette?"

"Quite safe," he said, and when Mrs. Bingham winked at him, he winked back. If he could speak in a voice that wasn't his, and kill for a cause he didn't believe in, then why couldn't he make promises he could never keep? It was easier to let everyone bask in the warm glow of dashing Sir Angus right up until the moment it all collapsed, like this city of the future built to impress but not to endure.

The line shivered with a spasm of whispers like the night sounds of crickets—had the German ambassador made an appearance, too?—and then Anisette poked her doll's face through the crowd and said, "Maman! The king!" and sure enough the king was striding past them, politely waving, and then the queen as well, and then they were gone, moving quickly and apologetically past the line and out another set of doors. The crowd was stunned into silence. Written on their faces: elation turned to dejection; a welter of voices, half-formed questions and expressions of pique and gall. The man with the lapel pin reappeared before the doors of the banquet hall and raised his hand to call for quiet. "On behalf of Their Majesties and the commissioner of the World's Fair, Grover Whalen," he began, and the rest came in bursts barely audible through the thicket of disappointed American gentry: *delayed, regrets, unprecedented, regrets, overwhelmed, regrets, outpouring, regrets.* Someone in the throng demanded to speak to Whalen, another to the mayor, and a third to the governor. Still another called for an investigation of this so-called random-number generator.

Francis had lost his chance. He felt, oddly, disappointed. More disappointed than anyone in the building. He'd been prepared. He knew he could have done it. He also knew that he must still do it. He must find another, more difficult way, but still it must be done. Already Gavigan could be dispatching his killers into the city. Francis hoped Miss Bloch had heeded him; he couldn't have been more clear without giving it away. The wedding would offer some cover, but if Francis failed, it would end for all of them at Martin and Rosemary's home.

As he calculated his next steps, the man with the lapel pin announced that refreshments were served. Trays of triangle-cut sandwiches—watercress, cucumber, sliced ham—were placed on the long tables. Piles of melon balls and bowls of Waldorf salad appeared. Champagne was poured. The mood of the room shifted from self-sorrow to resignation to an almost festive air: the crowd, elegantly attired, were guests at perhaps the most exclusive party of the summer. For the sake of Anglo-American relations, they vowed not to raise a fuss about the tardiness and the tactless departure of the royal couple and the inconvenience it had caused their American hosts. They chose instead to celebrate, to show—what was the English phrase?—a stiff upper lip. When one of the men raised his glass and loudly proclaimed, "God

save the king!" the others raised their glasses and repeated the proclamation with all the lustiness of tavern-goers in an opera.

Francis sought out the man with the lapel pin and asked in his best
Angus-ese if he knew where the king was going next: Had they recon-
figured his entire agenda or was he still expected to luncheon at the
Federal Building and then to receive guests at the British Pavilion?
The man looked Francis up and down; something about the tartan
and the brogue passed muster. "Now, let me see," he said as he withdrew from his jacket a typed timetable of the day's royal comings and
goings, down to the minute.

"You're a lifesaver," Francis said, sliding the sheet from his hands
while giving him a hearty clap on the shoulder. Ignoring the man's
squeak of protest, Francis darted back through the crowd and its
What a wasted Saturday, its *God save the king,* its *Blame it on FDR.*
He thought he might simply disappear—Anisette had been spared
the sight of him gunning down the king, and that might be all he
could offer by way of a farewell—but in the center of the bustle, he
ran directly into the Bingham women awaiting their Scotsman.

IN SIR ANGUS'S absence, Anisette's mother had told her of the conversation in the corridor, and Anisette felt like a balloon about to burst.
He had confessed his feelings, her mother said, and some next step
was imminent—not today, but soon. Anisette was excited, of course,
and nervous for what was to come, but mostly she wondered how one
person could contain all this happiness. She looked around the roomful of bald heads and powdered faces and she was certain that no one,
not at this moment, felt a joy like hers. And just then, Angus emerged
from the pack of tuxedos and chiffon with a slip of paper in his hand.

"I am so sorry about this turn of events," he said. "I know how you
all looked forward to this day."

"On the contrary," Mrs. Bingham said. "I think we will remember

506

this day most joyfully for years and years to come." Her face was pure triumph. The only topper would have been if Sir Angus, on one knee, had presented a ring to Anisette in front of the assembled throng.

"I'm so glad you feel that way," he said, darting a look over his shoulder, "but I regret that I must take my leave, for now. There is an urgent matter that I must attend to."

Mrs. Bingham looked baffled. Anisette registered a shock, but recovered quickly. "I saw you talking to that man," she said, her voice bright and playful, as if she'd caught him in a fib. "The note he gave you—was it from her? Forgive me, from Her Majesty?"

All around the Binghams, heads began to turn. The sight of the kilt, the timbre of the empire in his voice, the mention of Her Majesty. He had seen it before on the *Britannic,* like a gravitational pull.

"You've found me out, clever Anisette." He tried to keep his voice down, but still a circle had begun to form around them, taking in the spectacle. "I've been informed that it would be Her Majesty's great pleasure to renew our acquaintance, but I am afraid it's strictly tête-à-tête. Protocol and security and what have you. But Her Majesty did ask me to extend her personal gratitude to the Bingham family— and to you, ma'am, especially—for the warmth of your hospitality to two so closely linked, in blood and sympathy, to Her Majesty's ancestral home."

By the close of his brief oration, the Binghams had become a magnet for the curious, the softhearted, the envious, and the ambitious. Mrs. Bingham beamed magnanimously and Anisette, abashed, studied the lotus pattern of the carpet. Angus's speech was worthy of, if not Darcy, then certainly Bingley, and hadn't she always thought herself more Jane than Lizzie anyway?

Félicité, for her part, edged away from this sudden effusion of adoration. She wasn't buying it, not for one minute. Tomorrow she would begin packing for a summer at the Connecticut farm, and if that became as terminally dreadful as she expected, she would tell Father to have the Wyoming ranch readied for her. This city, with its inane people, was suffocating her. If her own family couldn't see when they were being deceived, then she could try only so hard to save them. Horses were never dishonest; a piano never lied. Each responded to your touch and each could punish you for your mistakes, but at least the touch and the mistakes were yours and yours alone.

Francis used this upsurge in interest in the Binghams to make his exit. He had meant his speech to be a parting gift for the family, but by day's end they would no longer be the particular favorites of the queen's cousin; they would be the dupes who had provided cover for an assassin. The Binghams would be tainted by a scandal that would make the slights against Anisette look like schoolyard taunts. But hadn't it been like this since the moment he fled his father's funeral? He left a trail of wreckage behind him, and always it was the ones closest to him who bore the brunt. His turn would come—the day of reckoning was at hand—but first he had to find the king, and add one more bit of wreckage to the pile.

He was already sweating, feeling the panic rise in him, but halfway through the door, he turned for one last glimpse of Anisette. She was still in the center of the crowd. The crush of the curious obviously unnerved her. As she caught sight of Francis, she started to raise one hand, as if to wave, but something about the gesture must have seemed too extravagant, too public. Instead, she rested her hand lightly against her cheek, and her face lit up into a smile that was just for him. Francis could almost imagine his own hand brushing a strand of hair from her face. He gazed at her a moment longer, wishing this was not the end, and then he was out the door, an ache chewing at his false heart and his traitor's stomach.

GRAMERCY PARK

A FIERCE PAIN JOLTED Cronin, like a hot poker thrust against his skin.

"I thought that might get your attention."

Cronin, bleary-eyed, looked up into the face of the woman—Helen, it was—who brought Gavigan his tea. He was on his back and when he tried to move he found one arm, his good arm, bound at the wrist with his belt, the other end of which was tied around a leg of the desk.

"For your own good," Helen said. "And for mine."

She had sliced his jacket from cuff to shoulder, then scissored off the bloody sleeve. Now she squeezed a cloth into a basin of water and dabbed at the wound, then knelt with one knee on the palm of his hand.

"Hold still," she said. "I think this time will do the trick."

Almost as an afterthought, she placed a rolled bit of cloth between Cronin's teeth, then leaned in close. She probed the wound with what looked like a pair of tongs, the sort used to remove a sugar cube from a bowl. If he had felt a jolt before, this was the whole power station wired through his shoulder. He tried to turn toward the pain, like a bird with a broken wing, but the leather strap held and her weight kept his hand and the rest of the arm immobile.

"Steady, you big baby," she said, and then, "Aha!" She withdrew the tongs and waved in front of his eyes the slug she had harvested from his flesh. "Nasty piece of damage that was, but it could have

509

been worse. For you, I mean. I don't think there was much more you could have done to them."

She took her knee off his hand and sat back on the floor, rearranging the folds of her long skirt. He flexed, and while there was a crackle, it was nothing like the raw pulse he had felt when the bullet was still lodged in his arm. She wiped her forehead, where a streak of his blood colored her hairline.

"I'm not going to ask who shot first," she said, "but I have my suspicions. Now hold still. I have some sewing to do."

She first swabbed his shoulder with iodine, then deftly threaded a curved needle and set to work. Again and again, the needle went in and the needle came out.

The needle was nothing compared to those tongs, but to keep himself steady Cronin stared at the ceiling. He'd sat beneath it for years but had never paid it any mind. It was pressed tin with some sort of scrolling, filigreed pattern repeated in each panel. Lying there, trying not to think about his shoulder and Helen's efforts to repair it and the possibility that he might actually walk out of here—to the farm? into a police car?—he stared hard at that ceiling, and as the pain faded and his eyes regained focus, he saw finally that the curlicues were shamrocks, thousands of them.

What was it about the American-born Irish that made them embrace so fiercely the slogans and symbols of the Old Country? This room, with its shamrocks, its death mask, its tricolor, its Easter Proclamation and all its medals and badges: these were the trinkets of revolution, all purchased with the blood of people Cronin had once considered brothers, sisters, comrades. He would bet that none of them—none who survived—had so many trophies in their homes, but here, far from the action, was a triumphant museum constructed by a man who had never risked the reprisals that came with every ambush: towns put to the torch, men killed in their beds, women and children

turned out of their homes by the army, the Black and Tans, the Auxiliaries. Irish Americans sang their songs and drank their beer and wept
for Mother Ireland. They lined up for the Body and the Blood and
they marched on St. Patrick's Day. All of them believed they were
descended from Irish kings, and that gave them the right to insist that
the actual Irish had to keep up the struggle, forever and ever, amen.
Struggle kept the men strong and brave, the women pure and chaste,
and everyone poor and scared and fretful for the future.

"I heard him say you had a family." Helen had nearly finished her
stitching. "Tell me: Are you good to them?"

Cronin looked right at her. He couldn't find the words to fit her
question.

"Do you knock 'em around? Your wife, the children? There's plenty
of men who don't see a thing wrong with it."

He shook his head. Their faces flared before him, and again he felt
that sob welling in his chest. "I've never raised a hand."

"And what about when you've been drinking? You could put away
your share and then some, if I remember right."

"I gave it up. After I left this place."

"You see that it stays that way. I'm not fixing you up so you can add
to someone else's misery."

"You have my word," he said.

"Words are liars, Mr. Cronin." She twice looped the needle through
the thread, tying off the knot. "Now tell me," she said, "how old are
your wee ones?"

"The boy is five. Five and a half, is what he'd say. And the baby's
not yet a year."

"Five and a half? Then he's not yours, is he? Unless you were keeping secrets from us."

"His own father left him," Cronin said. "But he's a fine boy. The
best there is."

On hands and knees she scuttled across the floor to the desk, where she untied one end of the belt. Cronin shook his wrist free of the other end, and with her help was able to sit, then to stand.

"It's good to see that your time here didn't ruin you," she said. "Not completely. God knows it's done that and worse to plenty of others."

Both of them looked at Jamie, then at Gavigan. Jamie's face was a mask, a waxwork version of the living man. Gavigan's neck was torn apart, his shirt was soaked in black blood, and his mouth hung open in an empty roar. The room was hot, and for the first time the smell of it hit Cronin full in the face.

"Wait in the hallway," Helen said. "I'm going to fetch you a clean shirt, though I can't guarantee a good fit. And you might be out of luck for a jacket."

"It's no bother." He looked at the desk, where the telephone receiver lay. "You're not calling the police, then?"

"I am," she said. "As soon as I have you packed up and out the door."

"You didn't happen to hear any news on the radio, did you? Anything from the fair?"

"Now, where would I find time for that?" she said. "Don't I have my hands full cleaning up after you?"

THE WORLD'S FAIR

ONCE MARTIN WAS AT last off the train, he faced a queue to enter the fair that seemed to stretch for miles. It could take an hour, he reckoned, to get inside. His whole head felt like a cracked tooth, raw and exposed, and he bounced on the balls of his feet like a desperate sprinter preparing for a race he knows he can't win.

To the left of the main gate was an entrance marked OFFICIAL BUSINESS ONLY, and Martin knew he had to risk it. He was Fitzwilliam MacFarquhar, wasn't he? Surely there was some official business — saving the life of the king and such — that required his immediate attention. He strode toward the gate, the picture of nonchalance, looking neither right nor left. Just as he reached the opening, a man in a uniform emblazoned with a Trylon and Perisphere patch put out a hand to bar his way. Martin grabbed the hand and gave it a hearty shake.

"Smashing day, isn't it?" he said. "The king himself couldn't have ordered better weather." Martin had aimed his accent toward British lord but he probably sounded more like a cockney bootblack. It was no matter. The man, somewhat perplexed, returned the greeting and Martin breezed into the fair.

He immediately found himself in a crush of people streaming between the House of Jewels and the Hall of Fashion, blocky white structures that looked as if they had been stamped out of industrial molds. Down one lane towered a two-story mural of a faceless giant celebrating ASBESTOS: THE MIRACLE MINERAL. The aesthetic seemed to be two parts Mount Olympus to one part comic-book hero: the statues and murals all sported hulking chests or ice cream–scoop breasts. And with the skies clear and the brutal temperatures of yesterday having faded to a milder form of heat wave, everyone seemed jubilant. Children waved miniature British flags, and a smiling woman walked past wearing a hat topped with a miniature Trylon and Perisphere. Martin took it as a good sign that the fair didn't feel like a place that had just witnessed a regicide.

Indeed, the World's Fair, in that summer of 1939, was a place full of promise. It promised a world of frozen food and hot jazz, a world that would be better supplied and better organized in power, communications, transport, and amusement. Ribbons of highways would connect skyscraper cities where every citizen had a home in the clouds and a car on the road. Food grew in abundance under glass-domed orchards, or came flash-frozen, or Wonder-baked, or in strips of bacon fanned like playing cards and ready for frying. Not to be outdone by the likes of General Motors, the nations of the world offered their own visions of organization, abundance, and peaceful coexistence. At the Italian Pavilion, a waterfall cascaded from the feet of the goddess Roma to a bust of the famed inventor Marconi, while inside visitors read of the return of a new Roman empire. At the Soviet Pavilion, larger than all the rest, a golden worker hoisted a red star into the godless heavens, while the British Pavilion embraced the whole of its empire, from its northern corner of Ireland to Australia and New Zealand, then on to India and Southern Rhodesia—all connected along a grand Colonial Hall.

Martin considered the possibility that Francis had lost his nerve—the best outcome, really—or had already tried and failed and was right now dead or in custody. Without a better plan, he had to follow Cronin's diktat: find the king and you'll find your brother. Working his way down the glutted Avenue of Patriots, he passed pavilions dedicated to science, religion, and the WPA. In the plaza that surrounded the Trylon and Perisphere, he asked a woman in an extravagantly floral hat if the king had passed by already. "Yeah, mister!" she said. "He went thataway!" and pointed up the long central axis of the fairgrounds, with its gargantuan George Washington, assorted demigods, reflecting pools, and fountains. From far off wafted the unmistakably aggressive brass of a high-school marching band, all trumpets, trombones, and tubas, and he edged his way in that direction. He still carried the morning paper's special section marking in minute detail the route of the royal visit through the fair's themed zones — up Constitution Avenue, right on Rainbow Avenue, left at the Pennsylvania Building — and naming every national pavilion that the royal entourage would pass, from Belgium and Japan to Czechoslovakia and Romania. But nowhere did it mention whether Francis was alive or dead, captured or lurking between the Court of Peace and the Town of Tomorrow.

ONCE HE'D EXITED Perylon Hall, Francis found himself in some sort of circular garden. He was sweating, feeling the panic rise in him, but as he picked his way through the garden, he began to think that perhaps chasing the monarch would actually be easier, in the end, than the tension of standing in line. It would be a game of hide-and-seek played in a dreamworld of gleaming white towers and titanic statues. He had seen the king with his own eyes as he strode past the unlucky members of group 17. He was just a man, like Gavigan had said, as if that was supposed to make it easier. Nothing about this day was easy, and it would have to get so much harder before it was over.

According to the schedule, the royals would soon begin a slow-motion tour of the fairgrounds. Cronin had told Francis that if the original plan broke down, he should look for the hinges, transitional moments where opportunity lurked: the royal party getting into or out of a car; the protocol-driven hesitation that followed the opening of a door. Franz Ferdinand had been shot when his car took a wrong turn and tried to right itself in a narrow lane. Cronin had told him that the archduke's assassin had pissed himself before he took the fatal shots. *Try to hold your water, will you?* he had said. If it was an effort to lighten the mood, then it was Cronin's one and only attempt at humor.

On a tourist map of the fairgrounds, Cronin had traced the king's route with a thick line of ink. Xs marked the hinges where Cronin saw the best chance to act, and now Francis could cross-reference the map with the timetable: 1:00 to 1:50, lunch at the Federal Building; 2:19, Canadian Pavilion; 2:40, Australian Pavilion. It was easy enough on paper to find the king, but in the flesh-and-blood world, Francis faced a crowd unlike anything he had seen before, not to mention the legions of police in their blue tunics and Coldstream Guards in their shaggy black bonnets. Pressing his way toward the fair's main boulevard, he found himself surrounded by a girls' pipe and drum corps that had just emerged from the Perisphere, which Anisette said contained the city of the future. So the future would have bagpipes; what a shame for the future. Now merely one among the kilted masses, Francis again checked the map. The best thing to do was get in front of the king, and be ready when the moment came. He put his finger on the last X Cronin had drawn: the British Pavilion.

He checked his wristwatch. Off in the Bron-ix, Peggy was now a married woman. In another hour, Martin would start warming up his band. And if Miss Bloch had played her part, Michael would be there too, no longer Sir Malcolm but simply Michael Dempsey again.

As MARTIN DODGED through the crowd, looking in every direction for his ginger-haired brother, he had to ask himself: Wouldn't they all have been better off if Francis were still in jail? If Francis were locked up in Mountjoy, Michael would be in the seminary, still in full posses-sion of his senses, and he himself would be setting up at the Croke Park Club for the break that would bring a new and better life. But instead, look at how much Francis had cost them. All around was damage and disarray: first Michael had been hurt, then all of them were put in danger, and now Martin was here—surrounded by some fantasy of the future—trying to stop his brother from killing a king instead of at the reception, where his real future was waiting. His brother's recklessness knew no limits. Even Peggy had almost called off her wedding after only a few hours with Francis.

But if not for Francis and his wild schemes, Michael would still be stuck in the seminary and miserable. Francis himself would be rotting away in jail for another year or more, and who could prefer that to the chance of freedom? And without Francis, Martin would have learned of his father's death through the mail, and likely would have boxed up and set aside whatever pang of guilt or sadness the news provoked.

There was something to it—the business of having a family that extended beyond the walls of your own home. He had felt it during the dinner on Sunday and again at the bar with Francis and then all last night as they painted the town. Without Francis and Michael, he would have gone about his life in America without admitting that some side of himself was missing, silenced. If having his brothers around forced upon him a knowledge of his own shortcomings, his own selfishness, then so be it. So much of his and his brothers' past had been hidden under years of silence and separation. He hoped there could still be time to fit the pieces together—of his past, of his family—and all he had to do to make that possible was stop Francis from one more reckless act.

Pressing closer to the Court of Peace, where the crowds were a dozen deep, he caught the sound of a band playing loose and fast. He stepped onto a bench for a better view: Clusters of police and a mili-tary color guard occupied the near end of the massive plaza, backed by a sea of five thousand teenage Boy and Girl Scouts. At the far end of the court, the monarchs and the mayor dined inside on capons and corn fritters, but the police-and-fire-department band had grown restless with waiting and launched into a Benny Goodman number. Hundreds of the Scouts, always prepared, began to jitterbug. All around Martin, people cheered, and a roar went up when the mayor himself appeared at the window. At least Martin wasn't the only one at the fair who was supposed to be at Peggy's wedding.

Moments later, the dancing stopped and the band launched into "God Save the King." Fountains spouted water the color of syrupy shaved ice, fireworks popped against a background of cloudless sky, the king reviewed the troops, and then his party mounted a blue-and-orange tractor train, of the type used at a children's amusement park. If this was the future of royal transport, then the future was sure to arrive slowly. Through the festivities, Martin scanned the masses, his eyes searching for his brother's face. Police and soldiers seemed almost to outnumber civilians around the court. He could not imagine how Francis could get close, but then Francis was clever, and reckless. If he saw a chance, he would take the shot. Martin was sure of it.

EVERYTHING INSIDE FRANCIS strained to move, to have this done, to wipe the slate clean. No more king, no more debt, no more Angus, no more Francis. But this mob with their sunburned faces checked him at every step. *Watch it, will you? What's the rush? Nice skirt, buddy!* He tried to move with purpose, knifing between couples, surging when he could. Cronin's map had been drawn like a cartoon, without regard to scale. On the map, the buildings were enormous, the gaps between them small, but in reality the distances were broad and pockmarked with obstacles: pushcarts selling lemon ice, souvenir vendors, and angular statues ready to hurl lightning bolts at the unsuspecting. Again he saw soldiers, and everywhere, again, police. They formed a wall against the crowds, they milled about on the lookout for trouble. Francis had to remind himself that for all they knew, he was just another Scotsman bound for the reception in the English garden. The sweat that glazed his skin could be blamed on the heat and his formal attire and not on the clock that ticked in his head and told him that time was running short. At 3:40 there would be a twenty-one-gun salute marking the king's departure, and if it sounded before Francis could fire his own gun, it would also mark the end of the Dempseys.

As he neared the British Pavilion, a band was finishing "God Save the King," and with the closing bars, the fountain in the Lagoon of Nations erupted in colored lights and flames. A cheer went up and fireworks crackled overhead. Tiny flags—British and American—rained from the sky and the people whooped and scrambled for the souvenirs. Francis paused to take it in. He wished for a moment that Michael could be here to see it; in some other world, it would have been nice to spend a day at the fair surrounding themselves in the wonders of the future.

But now the king, on some sort of motorized cart, was approaching the British Pavilion. In the paved courtyard fronting the entrance, men in cutaway coats and top hats, and women in floral-print dresses with their own flowery toppers, waited for a royal handshake. Two massive lions perched at the doors of the pavilion, claws raised and teeth bared. Francis couldn't get in the courtyard and he didn't trust his aim from the fringes—his hours in the warehouse with Cronin had proven that he was useless outside of ten feet—but if he could get to the point where the king would disembark from his cart, then he might have a chance, and it was likely to be his last. The king would be indoors for an hour inspecting the handicrafts and artifacts from his far-flung empire and then, if the papers were to be believed, he would be bustled into a car whose running boards were lined with bodyguards. Twenty-one guns would fire and that would be the end of it.

Onlookers leaned forward, five deep, six deep, then ten. The police shifted their line as the king's motor train neared, and a gap opened in the crowd, just ahead of the advancing monarch. Francis checked the clasp on the sporran to make sure it was unhitched. In a moment, he would grasp the gun, raise his arm, and fire. He saw the face of the king now, the queen next to him. The king waved to the assembled throng, leaving his heart a target. Francis's hands were shaking. *Festina lente,* he said to himself. He yanked the gun from its pouch and prepared to punch his hand through the line of police.

MARTIN WAS SWEPT along in a surge of well-wishers eager for a closer look at the king. He stood on tiptoes as the train made its slow advance toward the British Pavilion, but there were so many heads and such a thicket of bodies that it was hopeless to think he could ever find his brother, if he was even here. The cart swept in a wide arc, and the cordon of policemen linked arms and pushed back against the mob, opening a lane to the pavilion's entrance. As the crowd before Martin parted, he saw Francis not twenty feet away, and with a clear path to the king. Martin tried to push closer, but he faced a hedge, all shoulders and elbows, and it would not budge. The gun was in his brother's hand, and Francis's face was white, stricken, empty. This was his brother, reckless and selfish, but also generous and large-hearted. He was going to kill a man to save his brothers from death and misery.

"Francis!" he shouted, and again: "Franny!"

FRANCIS TURNED TOWARD the sound of his name, a reflex, a flinch. Every face was to the king except for one: Martin? His brother was raising both hands, imploring him to—what? And then came a crunching blow and he was on the ground with another man atop him. The thud of his head against the pavement, the rough fabric of a police uniform, the scrape of buttons against his face. As Francis went sprawling, the crowd surged away, and a second policeman joined the first. He scooped the gun off the ground and together he and his partner hauled Francis unsteadily to his feet, each of them grabbing an arm, and dragged him away from the pavilion.

Martin had saved the king, but he had failed his brother. And now Francis and all who knew him were done for. Already the cops were double-timing Francis to some Jail of the Future where he would be cuffed, searched, interrogated, imprisoned. Martin could only fade into the pack of fairgoers and brace for the blow that was sure to come.

Or, like Francis and Michael had done, he could run.

He ran. In the direction of his brother and the two men hustling him away, he ran. He dodged, lurched, and came up in front of them. In full voice, his eyes sparkling with rage, Martin bellowed, "What in God's name have you done to Sir Angus?"

The policemen stopped, both looking as dazed as Francis himself. A gash branded the cheek of the one who had tackled Francis. The other, no older than Martin, was trembling from the chain of events: the gun, the tackle, the collar of a would-be assassin.

"Outta the way!" the first cop said. "He had a gun!"

Martin tried once again to ape the accent of a British lord. "Of course he had a gun! He's one of the king's own bodyguards! Just look at him!"

One of the men had Francis by the back of the neck, forcing his head down. Now they pulled him upright and gave him the once-over: red hair, kilt, sporran, high socks.

"If he had his gun out," Martin continued, "it was for a good reason!" He couldn't stop himself from shouting. He could hear his pulse thudding in his ears.

"I saw him headin' for the king—"

"Do you have any idea of the threats His Majesty is facing?" Martin said, still shouting. "This city is crawling with IRA men!"

The second cop threw back his shoulders. "We haven't heard a word about—"

"Ninety percent of the police in this city are Irish," Martin said. "Half of you would probably help them put a bullet in the king, given a chance."

"And who the hell are you to tell us what's what?"

"Inspector Fitzwilliam MacFarquhar," he said. "Scotland Yard." Martin glowered at the policemen. An insolent bunch, these Americans. "And what are your names? I'll see that the mayor himself strips you of your badges."

He looked from one to the other. If he so much as blinked, he knew, the whole enterprise would collapse.

"Look, we don't want any—we just thought—"

"You were doing your jobs. You saw a gun and you reacted—but you reacted against the wrong man. Now leave him be and get back to work." Martin took his brother by the arm and turned him toward the British Pavilion, then stopped and faced the policemen again. "Aren't you forgetting something?" he said.

The two policemen looked at each other uncertainly.

"Take the cuffs off him. And give me his bloody gun." Martin stretched out his hand. While the first policeman fit the key into the cuffs, the second one put the revolver in Martin's hand. It was heavier than he had imagined, but without giving it another look he slipped it into his jacket pocket and stormed off. "This way, Your Lordship," he said.

Francis matched him stride for stride, wondering how much of this was real and how much was the result of the blow to his head. "Martin!" he said through gritted teeth. "Martin!"

"Shush!" Martin chugged on purposefully, aiming for the back of the pavilion. He felt as if his heart might give out or his bowels give way. Without raising his voice, he said, "As soon as we round this corner, I want you to run like hell."

They rounded the corner, out of sight of the police, and they ran like hell. Behind the pavilion, across a bridge, and through the Town of Tomorrow with its model homes and picket fences, they ran like they had as boys from the rough lads who patrolled the banks of the river Lee, and like they had in Ballyrath from the farmers' sons who delighted in pounding the jackeens who had blown into town (*Feckin' eejits,* young Francis had once said. *Don't they know jackeens come from Dublin?*). Martin laughed as he ran, and Francis started laughing too, as the hem of his kilt whipped about his legs and the sweat poured off the both of them. The speed and the effort burned off whatever had fueled Martin's flight of fancy with the two policemen, and by the time they neared the gate to the fairgrounds, both were out of breath.

"Jesus, Martin!" Francis gave his brother a shove. "The balls on you! And then asking for the gun!"

Martin was doubled over, his lungs working like a bellows. He handed his pocket square to Francis and pointed at the blood on the side of his brother's face.

Francis looked from one direction to another, getting his bearings: the House of Jewels, Petticoat Lane, and, farther down, the Administration Building. The king would pass this way soon, but moving fast in an automobile instead of that toy train. "I don't know what you're doing here," he said. "But I have to finish what I came for."

Martin shook his head and stood. He scanned the lanes and pavilion lawns for signs of pursuit. "Your man called. The old man's dead. He said it's off. He said you're safe."

Francis slumped against the wall. His legs could no longer support him and he slid down to the gray-stone pavers.

"I tried to get to you sooner," Martin said, "but you're a hard man to find."

Francis held his trembling hands before him. He gulped for air as he spoke. "I almost—"

"I know," Martin said, "but you didn't." He extended a hand, waited for Francis to see that it was there. Francis squinted up at him, took the hand, and his brother pulled him to his feet.

"Now let's get out of here," Martin said. "And can we steer clear of those MacFarquhars from now on? It's a fucking job of work to have them around."

FORDHAM HEIGHTS

MICHAEL SAT ON THE front steps of Martin and Rosemary's apartment, waiting for their return. His left arm, bandaged, hung in a sling, and his head still had that rattling, boxful-of-bees feeling that came after every encounter with the Noise. He had hoped that was all in the past, but the past, this week was showing him, had a way of reasserting itself. If that was how Yeats said good-bye, then the old ghost knew how to make an exit.

Lilly had shared the cab with him for the ride up from the Plaza. After his fall in the hotel room, she could not think of leaving him alone. Even as the cab reached the Grand Concourse, her nerves were still frayed. She had heard the crash when he hit the window, and when she wrenched open the door she was certain he was about to topple backward through the glass. Instead, he staggered a few steps and flopped unconscious onto the bed. She'd seen him like this after the flashbulb knocked him from the stool, only now there was blood streaming from a gash that ran from his elbow to his wrist. She ran into the bathroom and retrieved a towel, which she wrapped tightly around his arm, and then called the front desk. Then she waited, taking his head into her lap and smoothing his sweat-slicked hair.

The man who had last night delivered the champagne bustled into the room, a model of cool efficiency. That the countess and young Sir Malcolm were in bed together, and had apparently had some sort of altercation, did not shock him, nor did it slow his response. Collier

525

peeled back the towel, viscous with blood, and with his own belt made a tourniquet for Michael's arm. By the time he had wrapped the arm in a fresh towel, the hotel's doctor on duty had arrived, and Lilly began to explain what she knew of his condition: deaf and mute, he was prone to fits, and this latest had almost pitched him out the hotel window. If Collier was skeptical of her narrative, he did not show it.

Lilly asked if they shouldn't take Michael to a hospital, but Collier assured her that the medical staff at the hotel was top-notch for such injuries — certainly better than what His Lordship would find in the emergency room of one of the city hospitals. As the doctor checked Michael's breathing and began his first look at the cut, a nurse entered the room with a lamp and a room-service cart bright with stoppered glass bottles and surgical instruments. The light was switched on, the doctor probed Michael's arm for shards of glass, and Lilly excused herself to the parlor, where she poured herself a Scotch and sipped it while gazing at the park.

She would not leave today. How could she? And she did not think she could leave tomorrow. She had fallen too far behind in labeling her prints and her negatives, and in packing her clothes and cameras. The men from the shipping agent's office would find her door locked. With no number to call, they would move on to the next job and forget all about her. Lilly would not forget — not about Josef or Prague or the year they had together — but neither would she go back. Earlier that morning, while drinking her coffee, she had read in Friday's newspaper that a German police officer had been killed near Prague. The response had been swift: "measures amounting to martial law." The speed of the new dictates was proof that they had been readied long before, just as Josef's friend in the Castle had said. Prague's new masters had merely been waiting for the right excuse to implement them. Some of Lilly's coffee had spilled on the page, and she watched as the dark spots spread across the blocks of black type and white paper.

She could tell herself that this latest news had made her decision for her, but she no longer needed signs from the world of spirits or dispatches from the world of the living. She knew where she would not go. The only open question was where she would: New York? California? Or Paris, her halfway home?

AFTER THE DOCTOR had stitched his arm—a fat, ropy line that would heal into a thick scar—Michael lay sleeping, as he had after his collapse in Lilly's studio. Francis's warning was still fresh in Lilly's ears—an hour, no more!—but what was she to do? It had already been twice that long and the sky had not fallen. She maintained a vigil in the room, a breeze coming through the broken window. The day's paper had been delivered to the suite and she avoided the international news of the first section. Instead she read of the World's Fair and the royal visit, and wondered why the paper's photographers opted for such stiff, formally posed shots.

When Michael woke, early in the afternoon, he was famished. His arm throbbed and itched. He was momentarily puzzled by the bandage, but then the chain of events came back to him: Yeats, the Noise, the window, and now here. Lilly smiled to see him awake and Michael put a hand to his stomach: *So hungry!* As there were no carts in the hotel selling knishes, she handed him the room-service menu and he almost cried for the joy of being able to read: *Rib Veal Chop Casserole with Hearts of Artichoke, Breast of Guinea Hen, Jellied Consommé.* He was connected again to the world of words. With the pen Lilly had handed him he circled *Steak Frites,* then wrote, *Your name is_____?* She filled in the blank: *Lilly.*

His face bloomed into a grin: *How gorgeous.*

A short while later, they ate, and then she helped him dress, rolling the sleeves of his shirt. It was another hot day, and freed from being a Scottish lord, Michael could dress like an American teenager—or a Czech-Irish approximation of one. Lilly collected the envelope that

Francis had given to her, took Michael by the arm, and together they left the suite.

"Let's get you home," she said.

Mrs. Fichetti had come outside to shoo these strangers off her steps, but Lilly would not be moved. In calm tones, she explained their situation—Michael was another Dempsey brother and she was a close friend of Rosemary's. Though Mrs. Fichetti eyed them skeptically, she relented. She would have a word with Martin and Rosemary about the number of strangers who came to the apartment. It made her nervous, didn't they know, to have so many strangers in her home. Before she went back inside, Mrs. Fichetti insisted, though they hadn't even asked, that she wasn't going to let them into the apartment, if that's what they wanted. You couldn't be too careful, not these days, she said. But with the sunshine filtering through the scraggy trees, Lilly and Michael were happy to sit on the steps.

A car came to a stop in front of Mrs. Fichetti's house. The stilled engine ticked in the heat and the man at the wheel eyed Michael and Lilly before opening his door. He was a big man in a crisp white shirt and, like Michael, he had one arm in a sling. In his good hand he held a small brown leather bag, too small for a valise, but too nice for tools. It took a moment for Lilly to recognize him as the man from the hotel suite, the one who'd left in such haste just as the champagne was being poured. Michael, too, remembered the man and waited as he made his slow progress around the car and onto the sidewalk. The Rolleiflex sat next to Lilly and as the man considered how to lift the latch on the front gate, she casually angled the twin lenses in his direction and shot.

"Hello again," she said once he was through the gate. She was reclining against the steps, taking in the sun, and had to shade her eyes as she spoke.

"Any of his brothers about?" Cronin said.

"No, I'm afraid it's just the two of us." She extended her hand. "I'm Lilly."

Cronin looked at her hand, then down at the bag. This wasn't meant to be a social call. "Are you the one who found him when he was missing?" he said.

"I am," she said. "Though I'm finding it very difficult to say good-bye."

"What happened there?" He nodded toward Michael's arm.

"Oh, just a little slip at the hotel. And you?"

"Something like that, I suppose," he said.

Michael followed the movements of their mouths and tried to guess at the course of the conversation. He could be doing a lot of this, he imagined, in the years to come.

"I came to drop this." He set the bag next to Michael. "It belongs to him and his brothers."

"You're welcome to wait with us," Lilly said.

Cronin shook his head. "I'll be on my way," he said, but he did not move. Michael's nose and eyes were so like his mother's, and his hair was as thick and black as his father's had been.

Michael squinted up at him, this big man with the sun behind his head.

"So," Cronin said. The word had a finality to it, as if he were bringing an end to one thing, and whatever came next would be something new. He wanted to be home by nightfall. He had decided to keep the car, so when the family drove to church tomorrow and all the Sundays that followed, they could do so in the Packard and not in the truck. He also kept the five hundred that Gavigan had stacked up on his desk, all but the one bloodstained bill that he'd left behind. The Webley would go back into its box among Alice's hats at the top of the closet. Cronin hoped that he would never again feel its grip.

Michael and Lilly watched as the car rolled away, turned left, and made for the Grand Concourse. Michael had brought a pad of paper emblazoned with the Plaza's crest, but he wouldn't need it for these questions. He pointed to the bag and shrugged. *What's this about?* Lilly raised an eyebrow and waved one hand: *Why don't we open it?* Michael, in his sling, could not manage the clasp, so Lilly set the bag between them, released the catch, and opened the hinged top. She let out a shriek at the stacks of dollars and bundles of pound notes and slammed the bag shut. She and Michael exchanged a goggle-eyed look, like two children who had stumbled on a pirate's treasure. Lilly opened the bag again and shut it just as quickly. It was barely pin money for Countess Eudoxia Rothschild and Sir Malcolm MacFarquhar, but to Lilly Bloch and Michael Dempsey, it looked like a fortune.

WOODLAWN

WHENEVER HE TOLD THE story of his big break, Elston Hooper—Fess to generations of jazz aficionados—would say it all started at an Irish wedding in the Bronx. It was a onetime gig, cooked up by a cat he'd met at a late-night jam session, a white fellow from one of the Midtown bands who was always hanging around the Harlem hot spots: Minton's, Monroe's Uptown House, Tillie's, Club Hot-Cha. How he'd talked Hooper and Teddy Gaines into playing in a wedding band was a mystery for the ages. He must have been one of those gift-of-gab Irishmen who could argue a leprechaun out of his pot of gold—or convince two black musicians that they'd be welcomed with open arms at a social club in the whitest neighborhood in the Bronx. The way Hooper told it, things looked ugly at the get-go: the bride's father was a local bigwig who carried on like they'd stepped in the wedding cake; the club's manager said they didn't have a *policy* against integrated bands, they'd just never done it before; and to top it all off, the fellow who'd put the whole job together—the bandleader and, if you can believe it, the brother-in-law of the bride—was a no-show. Apparently, he'd cut out to see the king of England at the World's Fair and hadn't even told his wife. It was that kind of gig.

What could they do but play? They started off slow, some nice and easy numbers, though with a change here and there on account of losing their piano player, who also happened to be the bandleader, the brother-in-law, the husband at the fair, et cetera. But Hooper hadn't signed up for a snoozy set of light-and-sweet. After the happy couple's first dance, "Begin the Beguine," they turned up the heat song by song until the joint was ready to boil. That room might have been chocka-block with old folks expecting to shed a tear or two to "Danny Boy"—there was even a table full of nuns!—but the bride wanted to dance and she had a dozen friends who were ready to help her cut loose. After the floor had filled and the young folks realized there was a party in the works, Hooper leaned into the microphone and, in his best radio-announcer voice, said, "I know we're in Woodlawn, but how about we try 'Jumpin' at the Woodside'?"

This was the part of the story where Hooper had a tendency to play the professor. His wife of fifty-plus years, the incomparable Lorena Briggs, would say that he had always been that way, that even straight off the train from Baltimore, with his feet having been on the sidewalks of Lenox Avenue for only a day, he was already telling everyone in Har-lem how it was done. Maybe it *was* bred in the bone, and maybe it was his late-in-life turn as a visiting professor and artist-in-residence at Rut-gers, but Hooper couldn't resist explaining the difficulties of launching into "Jumpin' at the Woodside" with an eight-piece outfit and no piano. People had to understand just what sort of on-the-fly improvisation it required to pull off a stunt like that—improvisation, he would remind students and listeners alike, that was grounded in years of practice and a reverence for the possibilities of one's instrument.

By the time the band took its first break, the room was really hop-ping. The bride was a blur of blond hair, white veil, and klieg-light smile. The groom, a string bean who had to be coaxed out for the hot-jazz burners, had undone his bow tie and loosened his collar and was dancing like a man still trying hard to get the girl.

Hooper wasn't about to mistake this good feeling for what it wasn't. During the break, he didn't set foot in the dining room, didn't even cast a look at the bar, where the white fellows in the band were order-ing club sodas with—when the bride's father wasn't looking—a shot of something extra. While Teddy Gaines took five outside, Hooper waited in a back hall close to the kitchen, wiping his head, his neck, his face with a cold towel. A lanky white man in a Park Avenue suit approached him with a tall glass of ice water and asked if he had a minute. After the man handed over the glass, Hooper said sure, he'd give him two, maybe even three. And when the man introduced himself as John Hammond, Hooper told him he could take all the time in the world.

AS THE BAND returned for its second set, Rosemary gave up on Martin making an appearance. All of the hard work had been done without him, anyway. She told her parents that there was a family emergency: "Since when does he have a family?" her father said. She had intervened when the club's manager refused to let Hooper and Gaines change in the men's locker room: "This is my father's favorite band," she said. "Are you going to tell him they're not welcome?" And when the music started, she'd seen that Martin was right about the band—they were brilliant—but she was also right about her father. "What kinda crap is he trying to pull?" was the kindest of the assaults unleashed on her husband.

It was a wedding where the guests could truthfully say they had never seen a more beautiful bride, and where the toasts about the bright future that lay ahead of the happy couple—the daughter of Dennis Dwyer wed to a scion of the Hallorans, another family of Bronx-Irish royalty—had, if anything, underestimated just how fortunate these two could be. And yet Dwyer himself spent most of the reception grinding ice between his teeth, as if he needed to crush the bones of every Scotch on the rocks that touched his lips. As he scanned the tables, no longer paper doilies but the real deal, life-size and occupied by the Boston aunts, he counted the ones who weren't there: La Guardia and Flynn, sure, but also dozens of others who thought the smarter play was bootlicking the big shots invited to see the royals, rather than hoofing along to some half-colored band at Dwyer's daughter's wedding. If he had known that Martin was also at the fair, and that he had been not ten feet from the king, and that he had stopped his brother from pulling the trigger? *Well,* he'd have said, *thanks for nothing. If you actually gave a rat's ass about this family, you'd've let him kill the guy who tried to make a monkey out of me.*

THAT DAY IN Woodlawn was the start for Hooper, and for Lorena, too. Basie needed a new trumpet and Hammond had heard enough to know that Hooper was his man. On Monday he would be on a train bound for Chicago—good-bye, World's Fair!—and in the fall he would tour the West Coast as the newest horn player in the Count Basie Orchestra. He tried to convince Lorena to follow him to Chicago but she wasn't having it. Set up home in the Windy City while Hooper was all the way out west? Had he looked at a map lately? There was a reason why they called it the *Middle* West.

No, she wasn't going to follow him to a place where she was unknown and knew no one, but she would happily take a nicer apartment in Harlem, one that wasn't so cold in the winter, so stifling hot in the summer, and so noisy all the time. Maybe in one of those newer buildings on the edge of Sugar Hill? She would keep on making a place for herself in New York, and once Hooper had professored Basie into realizing that the Big Apple was the one and only place to be, he would find his wife and his home waiting for him. So she said, and so she did, but though her pride would never let her admit it, she missed him terribly during the months they were apart. All through the fall, as the nights grew longer and the knife-edged winds swept in from the Hudson, she sang like she was back in Reverend Hooper's choir when Hooper was off at Howard and Lorena was sure he was gone for good. Then one night in November, after months of Hooper saying that his wife could sing like one of God's own angels, Hammond caught her late-night set at the Lenox Lounge. Early the next morning, he sent a telegram to Count Basie—FOUND YOUR NEW GIRL SINGER—and by the end of the day, Lorena was in a sleeper car racing west. Years later, when remastered copies of her early recordings were issued, a critic for the *Village Voice* would write that no lovers could say they'd been heartbroken until Lorena's voice told them how it really felt.

HOME

MICHAEL AND LILLY HAD walked to the corner store, Lilly in charge of the satchel, and returned with six cans of beer and a church-key opener. Sooner or later, they figured, they would have company, and sure enough, while the cans were still sweating, the older Dempsey brothers arrived and claimed places on the steps. While they drank and smoked, Lilly related the drama that had occurred in the hotel room—the window, the blood, the doctor—and almost as an afterthought, Michael nudged Francis and showed him the bag. *Where in the world?* Francis thought, but he realized that he knew, and a greater sense of how Cronin must have spent his day settled over him. They had both walked into the trap, but it was Cronin who found a way to spring them. When Lilly asked Martin how the wedding was, he nodded toward the cab slowing to a stop in front of the house and said, "You'll have to ask Rosemary."

With the baby in her arms and Kate by her side, Rosemary opened the gate and took in the scene: Lilly, the red scarf around her neck, elegant and relaxed, laughing at something Martin had just said; Michael, his arm heavily bandaged and in a sling, but his eyes lively and alert; Francis bedecked in a tartan kilt, his shirt scuffed and torn, and blood caked in his hair; and Martin, rumpled and exhausted, his tie askew, his shirtsleeves rolled up, his jacket thrown over the steps.

"Daddy, you missed the party!" Kate said, and Martin put his hand on her head, her curls thick in the humid air.

Rosemary sat between Martin and Lilly and opened the last can of beer for herself. She took a long drink and looked at her husband. "Do I even want to ask?" she said.

"Oh," he said, "you're not going to believe what the MacFarquhars got up to today."

Before they went inside, Lilly snapped a picture of the family: Martin and Rosemary and their girls across the top step, Francis and Michael just below. With their bandages and bruises, their torn clothes, the plaid kilt, the matron-of-honor and flower-girl dresses, they looked as if they had survived a fight in a costume shop and come out smiling. Visible just behind Martin's back was the satchel containing the family fortune, and over his shoulder the shadowy outline of Mrs. Fichetti, peering through her curtains at the ruckus on her steps.

After they had cleaned up Francis and changed out of their battered finery, they walked around the corner to an Italian restaurant, where they tried their best to make sense of the day and all that had led up to it—more than one night's work, they knew, but a start. Then, over glasses of fiery grappa, they decided how to divide the contents of the satchel. Lilly was granted a full share for saving Michael not once but twice, and when Francis suggested naming her an honorary Dempsey, Rosemary put a consoling hand on her arm: "Careful," she said. "It's really not all it's cracked up to be."

FOUR MONTHS LATER, a print of the family photograph arrived in a stiff cardboard envelope with a Los Angeles postmark. The next letter from Lilly would come the following March, postmarked London, and then another from Paris in May, a month before the Germans took the city. Then the letters ceased, and Rosemary did not know that Lilly fled Paris, or that she was arrested on the train to Marseille and sent with other foreign-born Jews to a camp near the Spanish border. Nor could Lilly write to her American friend about the night that she and two of her fellow inmates escaped in the bin of a truck used to transport rubbish. She could not write about how she fell in with the Resistance, and used her camera for reconnaissance and her abilities in the darkroom to create identification documents. She could not write of the countless times she was stopped by Vichy policemen demanding to see her papers, and how she would raise that great Gallic-seeming nose of hers and heave a sigh as only a long-suffering Frenchwoman could—a sigh she had learned from her mother as she cast aside the first price offered by the Parisian gallery owners.

Rosemary knew only that Lilly had disappeared. Then, shortly after V-E Day, five years after Lilly's last letter, Rosemary flipped through *Life* magazine and came upon a picture of a Frenchwoman, her head shaved, being paraded through town for having had an affair with a German soldier. The picture shocked her: the stoic set of the woman's face, the sneering rage of the crowd. She studied the photograph, poring over every detail, and when at last she glanced at the credit line and saw LILLY BLOCH, she was overcome with tears. So many had been lost during those years, but here was proof that Lilly, her fast friend of two days' acquaintance, had survived. Rosemary wrote a letter to Lilly in care of the magazine and three months later she received a reply posted from the American zone in Germany. Lilly was returning to Paris, she wrote, after having seen for herself the death camps that had consumed Josef and so much of the world she had once known. Her correspondence with Rosemary would continue for the rest of their lives.

EVEN AS THEY posed for the photograph, Francis knew that he must leave. Gavigan was gone but he was not the only one who could connect Francis to what had happened at the house outside Cork.

Someone had passed his name to Gavigan in the first place and could pass it to someone else just as easily. As long as he stayed, he put all those around him in jeopardy. It was not a lesson he needed to learn twice. He told Martin that same night that he would go, and Martin, despite his anguish, agreed it was for the best.

"What about your heiress?" he said, but Francis had accepted that he could not take the risk, for her sake or for his. There was no way to ensure Anisette's safety, and sooner or later he would have to produce an actual castle and a family of kilt-wearing lairds. Francis considered writing a letter to explain his disappearance—some secret mission on behalf of the king—but he couldn't bring himself to lie again to Anisette. As for the truth, he could never find the right words to explain himself, and how he felt.

In the end, Félicité saw his disappearance from the fair and from their lives as proof that her run-in with Angus—or whoever he was—in the lobby of the Plaza had served its purpose. He had been gallant enough to accompany Anisette to the fair, yes, but not so gallant that he was ready to make a match with such a delicate, notorious girl. Mrs. Bingham let it be known around town that the dashing young Scotsman who had made such a splash at the fair had been summoned home on urgent business, and with the outbreak of the war she scripted a rotating series of suitably noble endings for him: on the road to Dunkirk, in the skies above the Channel, in the sands at Tobruk. He always died so valiantly. Anisette did not abandon his memory so easily. She pressed her parents to hire private investigators, Pinkertons, anyone who could locate Sir Angus, but his trail had gone cold almost from the moment he left Perylon Hall. In the years that followed, she often retraced their walk from the carousel to the museum, wondering what he hadn't told her, and what he really wanted from life. Her walks always ended in the same gallery, with the dour, shadowy faces of the old masters the only witness to her grief.

* * *

THE MONEY FROM the satchel allowed Martin and Rosemary to rent a small house with a piano and room enough for Uncle Michael. While Martin had missed his chance with Hammond, there were others who had listened: Artie Gold had grown tired of the in-and-out bookings at the Dime and reached out to Martin to form a house band. A bandleader at the Dime made little more than a clarinet player for Chester Kingsley but more than an out-of-work musician or an entry-level clerk at the Department of Sanitation, and Martin said yes before Artie could even finish making his pitch. For the next two and a half years, the gig let him sharpen his chops as an arranger and add an occasional original into the band's repertoire, and while the Dime never drew the hordes that flocked to the Famous Door or the Hickory House, Martin's eye for talent made his band a proving ground for young musicians new to the city and on the rise. His run at the Dime ended in early 1942, when he was drafted into the navy and posted to New Jersey, then Corpus Christi, and finally to a naval base in San Diego, rigging parachutes for carrier pilots. In his letters home, he ached to see his "Rose of my heart"; he wrote of wading in the Pacific surf and promised a trip to California when the trains were no longer full of soldiers. When the war ended, he worked out a deal to buy the Dime from Artie. Big-band music was on the wane, but in the decades after the war, the Dime became one of the spots where a new generation of musicians took part in the remaking of jazz. Fess Hooper's contribution to the Live at the Dime series, recorded in 1959, long remained one of the era's most coveted live albums—not least for Lorena's rendition of "Darn That Dream."

During the war years, Rosemary wrote almost two dozen books for the New York City Board of Education, so many that Martin took to calling her Rosie the Writer-er. Her tales of polar bears, baseball players, Scottish terriers, and leepercons each imparted an important civic virtue: decency, loyalty, citizenship, hand-washing. She continued writing children's books after the war, and in her correspondence with Lilly Bloch they often spoke of collaborating, though it never came to be. Schedules were difficult to manage, and truthfully Lilly's photos never really lent themselves to stories for children. Rosemary once joked that it would be the saddest children's book ever written, a guarantee of bad dreams or long, sleepless nights.

Michael lived with Rosemary and the girls throughout the war. He walked Kate home from school every day, and the two of them played cards and drew pictures while Rosemary tended to Evie or worked on her latest book. Michael had a special fondness for Peggy's son, Jack, a redheaded bruiser born almost nine months to the day after her wedding. They all had their suspicions, but no one spoke them aloud, not with Peggy and Tim just starting out as husband and wife, and certainly not once Tim was deployed to Europe as an aide-de-camp to a brigadier general, and definitely not after Tim was killed in action in Italy. Jack would be Peggy's only child, even after her second marriage, to a man whose family owned the biggest department store on the Grand Concourse. Jack would grow up surrounded by cousins—Martin and Rosemary's girls, then the boy born to them after the war, and later Michael's children—who regarded him as a brother, albeit one lucky enough to have his own bedroom and a houseful of his own toys.

It was during the war that Michael began frequenting the library at Fordham and then, later, at Columbia, where he was eventually offered a fellowship in the classics department. While receiving his doctorate for his translations of Virgil's *Eclogues,* he taught himself Italian, and began work on the edition of the *Divine Comedy* that became a standard college text after its publication in 1964.

As for Francis, his path was never easy to trace. After he left New York, he posted letters from Boston, Chicago, San Francisco, and points in between. He reported that he was engaged in the import-export business, which raised fears in his brothers that he would soon find himself behind bars again. He itched to return to Ireland, but both the government and the IRA had a claim on his body, and he didn't want to end his days in a prison cell or earn himself a boggy grave. He had long fancied himself a man of the world, but often, as he felt the creeping suspicion that he needed to move on, he caught himself thinking of Anisette's house by the sea and wondering if he could ever find for himself a place of such peace and security.

On a rain-spattered fall day in 1943, he made a brief, unexpected appearance in New York to have dinner with Michael and Rosemary. He had done well for himself and as the wine was poured, he announced that he was going all the way back home, to Cork, though under a new name: "Call me O'Donovan," he said. "There's loads of them in Cork, and even they can't tell one from the other." His plan was to patch things up with the IRA and then to buy one of the fine Georgian homes that overlooked the city. He would get himself an office on the South Mall, conduct business in the lounge of the Imperial Hotel, marry a feisty Cork girl, and raise a rowdy brood of his own.

This was his new plan, his FC Plan Mark 2, but he never had the chance to put it into action. Two days out of Boston, his neutral, Irish-flagged freighter was sent to the ocean floor by a German U-boat prowling the North Atlantic. When Rosemary wired Martin in San Diego, telling him that Francis was dead, he wanted to believe that it was another of his brother's schemes: a death certificate would wipe clean his accounts. Francis would be free to resume his life as Angus MacFarquhar, find his heiress, and spend his days in luxury. But Martin knew the truth. He felt it like a lump in his chest, choking the breath out of him. After ten long years apart, that week in New York was all the time that he would ever have with his brother. Francis would never appear at his door, decked out in a costume and with a story to tell. He was gone.

* * *

MORE THAN FOUR decades later, an exhibit at the Jewish Museum in New York City collected Lilly's photos of life in Vichy France. At the opening reception, Lilly and Rosemary were reunited for the first time since they'd said good-bye in 1939. Lilly had brought with her a packet of photos from her first visit to New York, the negatives of which had survived through the years at the home of a friend outside London. Martin had died two summers earlier, but in the pictures from the suite at the Plaza he and Francis were young and full of life. Kate and Evie, now in middle age, couldn't get over how beautiful their mother looked and how dashing their father had been as they held hands beneath a glittering marquee. Their younger brother, Francis, named for the uncle he had never known, was keen to see a photo of his namesake raising a glass in a toast at the 21 Club. Michael's wife signed to her husband that he was so small back then she could have knocked him over with a single breath, but Michael could only stare at the pictures of his lost brothers. His hands, which were always so lively on the subjects of love and loss and poetry, were stilled.

On that Saturday evening when Lilly took their picture, they could not have known that it would be the last night they would all spend together. Nor could they have known that the story of the months and years ahead would be broadcast in boldface headlines and urgent radio bulletins. It would be told in V-Mail and telegrams from the War Department and in prayers offered in church. More than they could know, it would be written in silences, absences, and empty spaces. But the story of those years would also be told in love letters saved and bundled in ribbon, and in songs dreamed up during nights in the barracks, and in the warmth of the spotlight before the first note was sung, and in sunlit hours when it was possible to believe that everyone you had lost was only late, and would be home soon enough.

* * *

ON THE NIGHT he left the Dempseys for good, Cronin was reaching the end of a long journey. The Bronx was now a hundred miles behind him. Even so, as city became town became country, he grew anxious. In the city, the Packard was practically invisible, a dime-a-dozen car that witnesses would have trouble identifying. But as he drove north, past the neatly organized towns of Westchester and out among the farms, the car made him feel conspicuous. Against the tasseled grass and the sprays of forsythia, it was a boxy black slab, a storm cloud on the move. He wanted to believe that the only men who knew where to find him were dead, but he would need to be vigilant. After all, the dead had their stories to tell, too. They could be restless in pursuit of the living.

But his anxiety was about more than that. He was returning to Alice with his arm in a sling, stitches in his shoulder, and the blue suit that Dempsey had purchased for him: his Plaza Hotel outfit. Alice would have a laugh at the idea of him, her Tom, squirming in that suit among the millionaires and the socialites. But how could he tell her any of the story without telling her all of it? Or would she already know, just from the look of him?

The terrain was becoming familiar. The hills, bursting with green, were illuminated by the low-angled sun. Fat white clouds billowed upward, pinking at their edges. He wanted to reach the farm before dark. He didn't want to creep into the house like a thief, nor did he want the dark to provide any cover. He wanted Alice to see him—all of him, who he once was and who he was now—so he could tell by her eyes if he was still her Tom.

He knew this road now. He had driven this way when he took Henry to the county fair last summer. Alice had been pregnant with the baby—a surprise, though it shouldn't have been; a blessing, and one he could never do enough to deserve. She needed her rest and could never get it with Henry about, so she'd sent them both out for the day. They had all been to the fair already, just like a family, but Alice had kept them from the livestock sheds. Didn't she get enough of that at home? Without her, Cronin and the boy spent hours surveying the Holsteins and the new milking machines. They considered the sheep and gaped at the hogs, all the while sweltering happily among the loamy scent of hay and manure. Henry, only four, stayed with Cronin step for step, shaping his folded arms to match Tom's, cocking his head the way Tom did when he listened to one of the 4-H'ers extol the virtues of Jersey milk. Riding home in the truck afterward, Henry slept across the bench seat, his little belly full of lemonade and cotton candy. There were worse things you could do than spoil a boy at the county fair. When Cronin carried Henry into the house, Alice was sitting on the sofa knitting something soft and pink. She looked at him and at the sleeping boy, so slight in his arms, and Cronin could have sworn that tears welled in her eyes. He had never in his life seen anyone so beautiful.

At last he turned, and the road leading to the farm was like a cave through the forest. On each side, the trees bent toward the center of the road. The leaves, backlit by the fading sun, glowed like stained glass. He pressed the gas pedal and felt the Packard respond. Down this road and then to the right. He was almost there.

Alice had been waiting on dinner, later each night, pretending to herself that Tom had lingered in the fields looking for the calf that never seemed to return with the rest of the herd. But she could make a five-year-old wait for his food only so long, and then they sat in silence. Tonight, Henry had looked at her once, about to speak, but he had swallowed his words and returned to the mess of chicken and dumplings, his favorite meal, which he'd been pushing around his plate. He was learning that there were questions it was best not to ask.

Alice was in the kitchen now, a plate in each hand, as a pair of headlights swept the front of the house. A car she did not recognize drew up between the barn and the milking parlor, out of sight of the road. She set the plates down unsteadily. The sun had nearly set, and in the onrushing twilight, with the cicadas rattling their last song, she heard a car door shut, heard footsteps on the gravel, and for a moment her eyes went to the hutch, where the loaded gun was sheltered. But then she saw his silhouette over the lilac hedge he had planted last year. Before Tom could reach the front door she was running to him. Her arms were open and she called out his name and then she had him, and Henry was at the screen door, his little boy's voice singing, *He's home! He's home! He's home!*

ACKNOWLEDGMENTS

This book began as a single handwritten page in the summer of 2009. Most of the pages that followed were written in coffee shops, libraries, or at the kitchen table. I'd like to thank the coffee shops of Berkshire County for space and caffeine—especially Lenox Coffee, Haven, Dottie's, Fuel, Rubi's, and Six Depot—and the Lenox and Stockbridge libraries for their tables and stacks. Thanks, too, to the Mount for allowing me to write in the haunted sewing room, just down the hall from Edith Wharton's bedroom.

This book needed space and time, but it also needed the support of true believers. And so I offer a thousand thanks to my editor, Ben George, a comrade in the cause who saw from the first pages where this long journey could lead. And a thousand more to my unflappable agent, Gail Hochman, for her patience and wise counsel.

For their generous support, I would also like to thank the University of Virginia, the Massachusetts Cultural Council, the Martha Boschen Porter Fund of the Berkshire Taconic Community Foundation, the Sustainable Arts Foundation, the Simon's Rock Faculty Development Fund, the Fulbright Scholar Program, and the Fulbright Commission of Ireland.

Crucial to the shaping of this book was a semester my family spent in Ireland. For making that time possible, I owe a great debt of gratitude to Claire Connolly and everyone at the School of English at University College Cork. And for making six wayward Yanks feel right at home, cheers to Claire, Paul O'Donovan, Linda Connolly, Andy Bielenberg, Kieran and Sheila Hannon, Nuala Fenton, Mick O'Connell, Tony McGrath, the members of the Sidney Park Men's Debating Society, and the staff and families at St. Luke's National School. Thanks as well to Paige Reynolds, who put it all in motion.

Thanks to my colleagues and students at Bard College at Simon's Rock, and to my friends in the Berkshires and beyond who cared enough to ask, *How's the novel going?*—and actually wanted to know. Thanks also to Mary Beth Keane for reading a much rougher version of this book, George Valli and Mel Goldberg for their memories of the Bronx, and Beverly Kellar for always being here when we need her.

Special thanks to my grandparents, Eileen and Thomas McKiernan, who left the Bronx for Dutchess County, and Helen and Peter Mathews, who united Queens with County Meath. And of course to my own band of brothers, Colin, Devin, and Kiernan, who breathed life into the Dempseys, and to my mother, Susan McKiernan Mathews, and my father, Robert Emmet Mathews, who raised us in families with plenty of stories to tell.

Finally to Nora, Fiona, Cormac, and Greta, who cheered me on from first page to final draft, and who often asked at dinner, *Did you finish your book today?* And to Margaret: my first reader, toughest critic, and fiercest champion, who always believed and whose love has sustained me all these years.

ABOUT THE AUTHOR

BRENDAN MATHEWS was a Fulbright Scholar to Ireland and a Henry Hoyns Fellow at the University of Virginia, where he received his MFA. His stories have twice appeared in *The Best American Short Stories* and in the *Virginia Quarterly Review, Salon,* and the *Cincinnati Review,* among other publications. He lives with his wife and their four children in Lenox, Massachusetts, and teaches at Bard College at Simon's Rock.

MAP OF THE
NEW YORK WORLD'S FAIR
AND APPROACHES

Published by C.S. Hammond & Co. New York.

Approved by
New York World's Fair 1939, Inc.